to
dare

JEMMA WAYNE

Legend Press Ltd, 51 Gower Street, London, WC1E 6HJ
info@legend-paperbooks.co.uk | www.legendpress.co.uk

Print ISBN 978-1-78955-9-835
Ebook ISBN 978-1-78955-9-828
Set in Times.
Artwork by Sarah Whittaker | www.whittakerbookdesign.com

Jemma Wayne is the author of two previous novels: *After Before* and *Chains of Sand*. She has been longlisted for the Women's Prize for Fiction, and shortlisted for both *The Guardian's* Not the Booker Prize and the Waverton Good Read Award.

Jemma's journalism has appeared in *The Spectator, National Geographic, The Huffington Post, The Evening Standard, The Independent on Sunday, Red Magazine, The Jewish Chronicle* and *The Jewish News*, among others.

Born to an American musician father and English mother, Jemma grew up in Hertfordshire and lives in North London.

For my parents Jeff and Geraldine, who taught me to dare.

Simone

They are so quiet.

Others might not notice that.

Others might see his flash BMW, and her perfect, unscratched arms struggling under the weight of boxes, nails cut sensibly, not plastered with gelled glamour. They might see the easy way they touch each other around the waist, the sharp contours of his rugby-chiselled frame, and the way that her eyes look outwards as though she intrinsically knows she is allowed to do this, entitled to see everything. Except, of course, they are both blind. They haven't even noticed Simone, standing, watching, from the other side of the tree-lined street. If she wanted, she could already have swiped one or two of the smaller boxes without anybody blinking. The ones right at the opening of the removal van would be easy, or a couple from the pile balanced by the front door. But she doesn't want their boxes. It is their quiet she is absorbing.

Simone stubs out her cigarette and starts another. It's not that she minds noise. When she was a teenager, lack of noise was one of the things she despised – the silences over dinner, the closed door to her father's small study behind which there came only the scratching of pencil on paper, the muted moments when she let herself in after school and there was no music, no laughter, nothing to pull her back. But

Terry's noise is so robustly noisy. It swirls around him like a cyclone, sweeping away everything not chained to the ground. He won't be pleased that she's got herself a job. It's only part-time, just a little bit-work on reception at the gym down Camden High Street. She's opening barriers and arranging leaflets on counters. There's no glitz to it. But it's money. It's legal. And it's doing. Doing something.

Terry will tell her she's a mug. What's the point of slaving away for less than she gets on social, he'll say, less than he can give her for pocket money, another hamster on the big wheel. Why belittle herself? Or, he'll think she's trying to be like them: the quiet people moving in next door. Or not them specifically, but the girl two doors down who leaves for work every morning at five-thirty in Manolo Blahnik heels, and a taxi. Or any one of their other neighbours who are out all day, doing, and from their well-kept houses look at them, her and Terry – not doing – as if they're scum to be picked off their polished railings.

Attached to the new neighbours' balustrade, there is already a beautiful pale blue bicycle. It has one of those old-fashioned baskets into which you need to balance things like French baguettes or fresh flowers. The slim woman and her rugby husband stand behind it on their new doorstep and wave goodbye to the removal van driver. The woman is white blonde, her hair long and loose, dancing around her elbows. She has that sharp, petite nose you see on the BBC, and the kind of skin tone that suggests it's regularly deepened by trips to sunny mountaintops and sprawling beaches. Simone sees her visibly breathe in, as if inhaling an imagined future. And the man breathes out, as though unburdened of his charge to provide it. Then together they turn and go inside where Simone can still see them in the front room, standing close together, encircled by boxes, and, she imagines, brightly coloured dreams.

Terry is not dreaming. He's not sleeping much at all. He'd

had no idea how difficult the move from the estate was going to be, and Simone wasn't going to be the one to tell him.

Looking up, there is a movement of curtain from the bedroom window of their flat. It's possible that Terry has seen her standing there across the street. It's possible that he has been watching her for a while. Watching her watching.

She'll go in in a minute.

She'll just finish her cig.

By then the new neighbours might be done with their boxes and their quiet.

Simone takes one final inhalation of smoke. The nicotine should steady her, but as soon as she throws the stub to the ground her hands feel empty. Looking up at the flat, her stomach tightens. She crosses over slowly. The road is devoid of further distraction. On the corner, there's a gastro pub where at lunchtime there are trendy mums with stylish buggies, or artsy professionals, not in suits; but it is now too late for lunch and too early for the school kids and not even a floaty-skirted cyclist to delay her passage home. As she reaches her doorstep, however, searching inside her bag for the key, the door to the new neighbours' house flies open, and the woman she has been watching appears – blondeness and shininess and a gentle scent of coconut. Up close, an audaciousness Simone hadn't noticed before dances across the woman's lips, like the edges of laughter. She's holding a wrapped box. Remaining on her doorstep, the woman lifts a hand in greeting, then leans boldly over the dividing iron boundary.

"Hello." Her tone is cheery and confident, her skin smooth and perfect, her smile alluring. Simone doesn't answer. "Sorry, I'm your new neighbour," the woman clarifies, laughing and withdrawing her body slightly. "We're finally in. So sorry about all the building work, it must have been absolutely irritating. I hope it wasn't too awful." The woman has a plummy, boarding school, house-in-the-country voice.

"That's alright," says Simone. She speaks flatly, but in more clipped tones than she would normally employ. The fact that she has done this is immediately irritating to her and she winces internally. Terry never does that, never puts on a pretence. Why should she? She doesn't care what this woman thinks of her. But there is an unfamiliar scrabbling inside her, an uncalled-for desire to make a good impression. Finding her key, she forces that feeling away and turns without further comment towards the door.

"Oh, they're for you!" the woman declares, laughing again and thrusting the box forwards. "Just some chocs. A little thank you for your patience. But we're in now." She glances up at her house and inhales again. "I'm Veronica." She puts the chocolates into Simone's hands.

"That's alright, you keep them," says Simone.

"Don't be silly. Please."

Silly? Who does this woman think she is? Simone glances up at Veronica who is still smiling, sillily. She could put this condescending woman in her place in a second if she wanted to. She could wipe that smile right off her face. But, something she can't quite discern holds her back. She finds herself noticing Veronica's assured, easy poise. She finds herself admiring it. An image flashes through her mind and all at once she sees herself, or a different version of herself, in a different life, leaning with Veronica against the railing, both laughing with equal ease. Then on the other side of the door, Simone hears movement on the stairs.

Terry is waiting for her. He isn't a large man. There was a time when he used to box, flyweight, and then there was a certain width to him, but too much coke has sucked the muscle away. Both of them are rakes these days, Dominic too. Only Jasmine is rounded with flesh. She is growing taller finally, but her legs still fold into dimpled layers. Simone hears her daughter cry out from upstairs.

"Hi, Tel," she says breezily, smiling at him as she climbs

a few steps of the stairwell to where he stands, and touching him gently on the arm. "Everything alright?"

"Where the fuck have you been?"

He isn't a large man. But he has a way of dominating space. "Shall we go in?"

Terry allows Simone to pass him and together they enter the flat where the quiet of the street dissolves into the blaring of the TV, and the bawls of their daughter, Jasmine, sat screaming in her high chair. Jasmine's hair is matted together with something sticky and there are remnants of the cheesy puff crisps she loves dried onto her skin. Her nappy is full and smelling.

"Jesus, Terry, how long's she been sat there?" Simone asks, lifting Jasmine into her arms and having a go at the dried crisps with a wet wipe.

"Well you wouldn't know, would you? You've been off fannying around, haven't you?" Decisively, Terry takes Jasmine back from her. "Your mum just left you all day, didn't she Jas? What's that?"

Terry has spotted the box sticking out of Simone's bag.

"I dunno. Chocolates apparently. That new woman next door gave them to us."

"What for?"

"To say sorry for the builders' noise, she reckons."

Terry takes the box out of Simone's bag and opens it, Jasmine tugging at the wrapping. "Truffles!" he exclaims, dumping them on the floor, and Jasmine next to them. Jasmine promptly opens the box and helps herself. "Well la-di-da."

Simone says nothing. She lets Jasmine take a handful of the chocolates and then scoops up the rest from the floor. There's a bowl on the table and she fills this with what's left of the sweets to save for Dominic.

"You've taken a bit of a shine to them, haven't you?" Terry asks. "That couple? I saw you watching them."

"I was just having a cig," Simone answers.

"Yeah I saw. Having a cig while I'm up here with this." He points at Jasmine. "What do you think I am? A mug?"

Simone says nothing. She knows he doesn't mean it. Terry's not perfect, but he's wonderful with Jasmine, with both the kids. She notices other parents smiling admiringly when he's kicking a ball with Dominic, or carrying Jasmine on his shoulders. If he's not going anywhere, he doesn't normally mind an hour or two at home with Jas. It's the street that has rattled him.

"I see the way you look at all these rich idiots," Terry continues. "Are you in love with them?"

"Course not," Simone says.

It's the street. With the move, he'd done something at last that she'd never seen before – he'd stepped outside. Not only of the estate, but of his comfort zone, his world that though minimal, was reliable. Predictable. *You can make that kind of thing work for you if you have to.* This was one of the first things Terry had impressed upon her when he was sorting her out. There's a certain vibe you need, he'd explained, a don't-mess-with-me aura. You have to live in a state of readiness. But once you've learned that, a kind of security emerges, because yes you're living on the edge, but you know you are, and so you navigate it with that knowledge, like a goat on a cliff top, or a fish in shark-infested water. He'd used these metaphors. He's been poetic and enchanting. What you don't do though, he'd told her, what you mustn't do, is attempt to shift course, or change things. You could fail that way, slip, fall, be knocked down by something you were unprepared for. You don't risk that. You don't try to make things different. You don't try to be or do anything.

Except now they had.

From the floor, Simone picks up Jasmine who has a mouthful of chocolate. "Come on. Let's sort that nappy."

Terry stays in the kitchen looking with partial interest at a documentary on TV he has saved, while Simone takes Jasmine off to the bedroom. Unlike their flat on the estate, there are three bedrooms here, so Jasmine has a room of her own. She hasn't gotten used to it yet. She screams like hell at bedtime, but at least they can shut the door, and at least Terry's paraphernalia is no longer scattered about a few inches from the cot. Even to herself, Simone calls these items Terry's, but she'll still have a hit sometimes. Jasmine laughs as Simone undoes her nappy. It should have been changed ages ago.

"You need to start going potty," Simone tells Jasmine, poking her gently in the stomach.

Jasmine laughs again, but doesn't say anything. Simone's sure Dominic was talking more by age two. Jasmine used to babble a lot as a baby, but these days she's usually either crying, or quiet.

"When are you gonna start answering Mummy?" Simone says, poking her again.

Jasmine still says nothing. Nappy changed, Simone lets her play with the box of plastic princesses in her room. The carpet's old and worn, a dark beige colour that she can't imagine was ever fashionable but hides the dirt. Simone sits on the edge of the windowsill. The room is small, but the whole house is festooned with sweeping great windows and high ceilings, so it feels airy. Luxurious even. The style is very much akin to the flat in Kentish Town where she grew up, and she finds herself spending time looking at it, although she is not so stupid as to entertain illusions of grandeur. She's aware that the flat isn't even theirs. They've only been in it a couple of months, and the lease still names Milly – one of Terry's ex-girlfriends who moved down South with a new man. Simone has all sorts of questions as to why Milly felt so indebted to Terry as to gift him the key – not strictly allowed, but who was going to tell – but she has resisted asking. Because Milly's flat is not in a tower block or a sprawling concrete rabbit warren. Instead, it occupies the top two floors of a white-fronted Victorian terrace a short walk from Regent's Park and slap bang in the middle of exclusive Primrose Hill. It is one of a spattering of council properties on the street – easily discernible in their lack of fancy doorstep tiles – so the flat isn't even Milly's, really. And Simone knows that the geography she happens to find herself in doesn't manifest itself under her skin. But it almost feels as though it does. Almost. Like the walls in the estate. For the first time in years, instead of feeling trapped in, she's looking out.

An abrupt noise of something smashing suspends Simone's brooding. It has come from the kitchen, and, "Clever place to put a bowl!" Terry shouts.

Simone stays where she is. She shakes her head at Jasmine as if to say 'Silly Daddy', and takes out a cigarette.

Dominic hates her smoking. He's eleven now and says less about it, but she can picture him aged seven or eight, eyes frightened like a rabbit, pleading with her to stop, thrusting a flyer he'd found in the doctor's office into her yellowed hands. Back then she'd thought that his panic was hilarious. Terry did too. They'd both been high on something and had laughed on that for hours.

Simone flaps her hand now as though this might drive the memory away, but all it does is make her drop ash over herself. With the cigarette she is still smoking. Despite her son.

It wasn't for Dominic that Terry gave in to the idea of moving. It wasn't even for her. In the end it seemed only that he was trying to spite something. But Simone took it running.

"What's the point of my giving you a proper kitchen?" his voice comes again. "Can't cook, and now you can't even find the intellect to put a bowl away right. You are a dense one, Simone, aren't you? Jesus. Look at this."

Again, Simone shakes her head at her daughter, and notices that Jasmine has stopped playing with her princesses. Not as in she has put them away or moved onto something else, but as in she has frozen, one doll still grasped by the hair in her left hand. She did this a few days ago too when she cracked her head on the kitchen table. Simone noticed it then because it was eerie to look at. The child had entirely stopped moving, stopped blinking even – from shock, she'd reasoned.

But this time there is no head injury. Simone looks at her daughter intently. "What's up Jassy?" she says. The girl still doesn't move. Balancing her cigarette on an ashtray, Simone kneels right next to her and clicks her fingers in front of her face. Jasmine barely blinks. A little roughly, Simone takes the princess out of Jasmine's hand, but there is still no movement. She is about to pick Jasmine up when Terry appears at the bedroom door.

"Well? You coming to clean this up then?"

"Can't you see to it, Tel?" Simone protests, still watching her unmoving child, but she gets up.

"Brainless place to put a bowl."

Simone follows Terry down the corridor and enters the kitchen. She sees the bowl that has smashed, and instinctually, she laughs. "That wasn't me, Tel. Must be one of your ex's. I haven't touched that shelf."

As soon as she utters the words, she realises that Terry is looking at her with a foreboding intensity. This alone wouldn't be unsettling – Terry's always been intense, it was one of the things that first drew her to him and it shoots often through his eyes: that penetrating blueness, dotted unpredictably with mischief and passion. She'd felt so special at the start – she the only one to see the softness in the blue. But today Terry's eyes have a hue of red about them. The skin underneath is dark and puffy. His sometimes soft, wispy hair is thin and flat against his head. He hasn't showered. A few days ago he went on a binge and hasn't scored since. She should have noticed all this sooner.

Softly, Terry takes her wrists, one in each hand, and pulls them slightly downwards. It is not hard, yet her body feels weighted. Leaning forward he sticks his face an inch before her own. She can smell beer and something stale on his breath. He is waiting for her to look at him. Slowly, she meets his eye. For a second, he holds her gaze. Two seconds. Three.

Until suddenly, he snickers. "Well, Milly's a dense cow also!"

Now there is an explosion of laughter, first from Terry, then from Jasmine who has finally unfrozen and followed them into the kitchen, and eventually from Simone who smiles and tentatively joins in. Terry thinks he has been hilarious. He releases Simone's wrists with a flourish and lifts Jasmine high into the air. She seems fine now, Simone notices. Unbothered by the tension that has preceded this moment and perhaps was only ever in Simone's head. As her father starts throwing her up and down, she giggles profusely, louder with every flight.

"Jassy," Terry shouts as he launches her. "Jassy!"

Simone feels her own chest relax. Everything's fine. She was being paranoid again, typically, seeing problems that aren't there. Terry's always telling her she's doing that. And he's always had a dark sense of humour. Given his childhood, he does well really to be as balanced as he is. She should be more understanding of that, more mindful. Especially when he's on a comedown. Especially with the move. Jasmine shrieks again and now Simone laughs a little louder, with careful pleasure. Noticing her mother, Jasmine giggles even more generously, gesticulating for her to join in. But as Simone moves closer, reaching for her daughter's outstretched hands, Terry stops still. Face instantly devoid of lightness, he spins around and stares at her again, as though her presence is a rude, unwelcome intrusion, and they haven't moments ago been laughing together. She feels she should back away or disappear into the floorboards.

"Go on then," he says.

This time, the curtness to his tone is unmistakeable, not imagined, and the relief of the previous moment is replaced with a shooting panic. What does 'go on then' mean? What does he want her to do? Back away? Could he hear her thinking? The TV is still blaring, politicians arguing about something irrelevant, and the room feels unbearably loud. Confusion creeps. They were just playing, weren't they? Laughing? *Go on then*. She's worried she hasn't heard him properly, or that she's missed something, and if she asks for clarification he'll think she wasn't listening, that she's making him look like a mug. She hesitates for a second. Two seconds. Three. But her anxiety is still misplaced. Again, she's read things wrong.

"Go on then," he repeats, and this time he says it in a coaxing, sing-song voice, as if it's a great joke, or as though he's talking to Jasmine, as though Simone is a child herself. She is still unsure of the instruction, but he helps her now with a wave of his hand. Tentatively she picks up the dustpan and brush to which he is indicating. "Stupid Mummy," Terry tells Jasmine, shaking his head as he hurls her into the air again.

It is not the right time to tell Terry about the job. Maybe later, once he's had a line or two. Or when their friends are round. Or once Dominic is home from school and has eaten the chocolates from the silly blonde woman next door.

Veronica

Veronica had managed to unpack all of the boxes, with the exception of the ones labelled for George's study. Those were sitting neatly piled in the third bedroom atop the olive green carpet she had finally managed to convince him was coming back into fashion, and anyway a good colour for channelling the fields and calm-inducing pastures of their childhoods, which they did not see in the city. Despite being a stone's throw from Regent's Park, landscaped gardens fanned the mind with precise, ordered beauty; they didn't drench the soul with wild terrain. She and George both agreed that during their teen years, they would have been lost without such wilderness. Their boarding schools, it turned out, were less than five miles apart in the Kent countryside and they have often spoken of how while she was performing in her school's open-air drama festival, he may have been shooting down a frosted pitch, legs muddied and hands bloodied in worship of the fast-clasped rugby ball. Over a decade since his last match, George retained a steel pin in his left shoulder, a knee that was in constant need of physiotherapy and a nose that would never be quite as straight as God may have intended. But like her love of American rock music, and a series of dalliances with unsuitably young male English teachers, her husband wore these badges like the proofs they were: attestation to the years of privilege and opportunity and community and neglect.

He had promised to tackle the boxes at the weekend, but for the time being Veronica had shut the bedroom door to hide them. It may have taken her until almost midnight, but tomorrow they would wake up in the house they had been visiting at various stages of demolition and resurrection every week for the past six months, and it would be just as they had dreamed it. Even the wedding china, which while they were in the flat languished in storage, had now been meticulously removed from bubble wrap and placed on the exact shelf of the exact cupboard that she had been planning. For his part, George had fitted the feet of every chair and table and moveable piece of furniture with thin felted cushions, so as to protect the dark oak floor. He had read all of the instructions for the gas and electricity metres, for the boiler, for the alarm system. And he had phoned the council to find out which days each of the different bins were collected. He had not, yet, touched her.

Their bed had a high romantic headboard, waffled in cream, and the wardrobes and bedside tables were painted a slightly peeling white in the shabby chic style of Louis XIV. These were pieces they had garnered over a series of months, visiting showrooms and antique fairs, each fastidiously chosen to complement the sweeping floor to ceiling windows and luxurious cream shag rug at the end of the bed. The effect was a success. Despite the dust, which even a professional post-build cleaning crew and three attempts by herself had failed to dispel, the room exuded airiness, tranquillity, and, of course, amour. This last was an added pressure she had not accounted for. Since the miscarriage, everything was a pressure. Yet without discussing it, Veronica felt that both she and George had been viewing the house as a new start, building it up in their minds as the fresh slate upon which their dreams, their family, would materialise. The only problem was that now the house was complete, there was a call for action. Now they had to do something. Not something, one specific thing. And now, all they could do was lie on opposite sides of their soft, vast bed, petrified by the prospect of continued catastrophe, continued ways in which they had failed and would fail each other.

She was not the woman he fell for. A long time ago, at their wedding, he had described her as indomitable.

But she had never before desired and failed. Not openly. She had desired and pretended otherwise. She had feigned contentment with things fleeting, and steered her course away from the solidity she could not have. Only now they had said it to each other, out loud: they wanted a baby. And in voicing it, as though to mock her flat stomach, the longing inside her had swollen. It had made her yearn with a deepness that churned her chest to pieces and ruffled her exterior. She felt anxious where she was once fearless. She felt weak where she should be bold. She felt needy where she had been so independent. Because for a baby, she needed George. And in needing him, she had become repulsive.

George was not asleep. They had put down their Kindles and switched off the lights, delighting in the feat of the integrated lighting system working exactly as they had planned it, and now they were lying in darkness. Both were aware that this moment was an overt First that ought to be marked with a christening – their first night in their new bed in their new home. But he was facing the wall away from her. And she was doing likewise. Besides, it was still at least four days until she would be ovulating. Veronica allowed the darkness to sink through her, heavy and enveloping. There was a sliver of light creeping through the very edges of the curtain from the lampposts outside, and every now and then there was a clip-clopping of heels, or a slow car pulling respectfully to park, but otherwise the carefully crafted tranquillity of the room was undisturbed.

Despite the acres of fields that had surrounded her boarding house, it was never as quiet as this. Aged twelve, she'd arrived late – during the autumn term of the second year when everybody else had begun a full three terms earlier.

The decision had not been hers. Due to the demands of her father's job, her parents were relocating to Oman, and her options, if they could be described as such, were to attend the international school there, which itself was weekly boarding, or to board full-time in the UK. She chose the latter, though even as she was doing so she was aware that it was not really from want. Mainly, it was because of her parents' indifference to the outcome, an indifference that drove her to the much further afield, screw-you-if-that's-how-little-you-care option, and passed unnoticed.

At night, four to a dorm, she would listen to the sounds of pattering footsteps transgressing between rooms, the bell from the great clock three floors below them, the clattering about in the kitchens an hour before they had to rise, the owls, the crickets, the rumbling of distant trains, and the constant flushing of toilets. Compared to this, rowdy university halls had been nothing. City living had been a doddle. And now, the gentle noises of their new abode were positively serene.

They had looked for a long time to find exactly this blend of urban interest and suburban calm. A plethora of estate agents had held their hands through Chelsea, Mayfair, Islington, Marylebone, but the moment they crested the eponymous hill, they were sold on Primrose. A tiny collection of roads and crescents and pretty squares, the area was like a country village supplanted into the city, except that every café and shop had shed its parochialism and was absolutely chic. Each house was painted a different shade of pastel, and blue plaques dotted the frontages in abundance, denoting which world famous writer, poet, diplomat or explorer once occupied the honoured abode. People greeted each other in the streets, shopkeepers knew their customers by name, and as she and George had strolled smug through the sweet squares that converged onto beautifully kept communal spaces, they had both agreed that their discovery of this place was nothing short of fate. Because together, they got it. They were Primrose Hillbillies already.

George sighed deeply. Veronica turned over and tentatively

stroked his shoulder with the tips of her fingers. He smelled clean, freshly showered. He didn't move. Perhaps he was already asleep after all, immersed in the soft folds of tranquillity. Moving closer to him, Veronica dared to wrap her body around his. As usual he was many degrees hotter than she was and she tucked her feet between his legs, noticing as she did so that the tops of her thighs had begun to itch again. Two different doctors were yet to diagnose why, but over the past few months she had developed this low-level creeping beneath her skin. Sometimes she barely noticed it, but other times it irritated like a mosquito bite stretched wide across her thighs, and then it took all of her will power to stop herself from scratching her skin to shreds. Veronica attempted to endure the itch now, so as not to bother George, but after many minutes she couldn't resist one quick rub. Still George remained motionless, his breath steady. Until all at once, they both stiffened.

From next door had come the abrupt sound of something thumping. Or rather, of someone being thumped. There was a distinct yelp, almost like a dog crying, but clearly not a dog, a woman, and then something unintelligible in a deeper tone. Another thud hit their adjoining wall, and instinctively, Veronica froze. Despite the extra soundproofing, it seemed as though the people were right inside hers and George's bedroom, and as the woman next door moaned again, Veronica found herself physically recoiling. There began a series of moans, and a rhythmic pounding against the wall, then a shrill, penetrating wail, as though somebody, the woman, was gasping for breath, or pleading for something, and then that wailing sound was muffled. For at least five minutes this went on, while Veronica and George lay intertwined, unmoving. At last it stopped, but then, almost immediately, it was replaced by the blaring of 90s dance music and the unpalatable tones of a man singing along. It was another full three minutes before finally, Veronica whispered to George in the dark.

"Are you asleep?"

George sat up. "Of course not. What the hell was that?"

Untangling herself from George's legs, Veronica moved a little away from him, allowing them to avoid the confirmation that he had been faking sleep. The music was still blaring and the man continued to shout in accompaniment. Veronica turned on her bedside light and glanced at the clock: 3am. "I guess, that was the neighbours."

"The neighbours doing what? Jesus, that sounded... I mean—"

"I know."

George got out of bed and strode over to the adjoining wall, as if he would find evidence there of what had just occurred. "Do we call somebody? Is she hurt? Or is that just, I don't know, is that what rough sex sounds like?"

For a moment, Veronica wondered if this was a dig at the current infrequency of their own sexual relations, or about the clinical, baby-optimising nature of them, but this wasn't the moment for that argument. "I met her today."

"Oh yeah?"

"She seemed quiet if anything. Not the type you'd expect to be, well, enjoying that."

"What did she look like?"

"Very thin. Quite pretty but, I don't know... bit... you know."

George shook his head. "Of all the houses to be next to." He nodded his head towards the wall. "Did you meet him?"

"No. But I heard a baby crying earlier."

"A baby? Living with that?"

Next door, the song ended and another one swiftly began. The man continued to shout the words at the top of his voice. It sounded as though he was jumping too, or dancing, or using a bat to bang at the floorboards. George sat back down on the bed and put his head in his hands.

"A year looking for a place, three months planning, six months of work, all that money, and we're next to this."

Listening to him, Veronica felt a sudden wave of concern for her husband. It was rare to see George so defeated. He was the kind of man who controlled a room. If he had moments of despair or fear, even after all these years Veronica wasn't immediately party to them. She tried not to reproach him for this, understanding well the importance of self-sufficiency. She may have been sent to boarding school at twelve, but he went at eight, the instructions of his father on parting – *be a man* – set hard and fast in his head. In any case, self-sufficiency was her hallmark too. She managed, despite change. She achieved, despite unreliability. If there was a problem, she fixed it. They were both fixers. Both good at ushering the world before them. Doubly powerful when their forces were combined. Until the doctor had told them that there was no heartbeat, and neither one of them could fix a thing.

"Do you think she's okay?" said Veronica.

George looked up. "Maybe I should go round."

"No, don't."

"She might be hurt."

"What are you going to do? Demand to see her? Tell him we've just heard him pummelling his wife? You can't do that, and I don't want you squaring up to him."

"I think I'd be okay," George prickled.

Veronica sighed. "I know, I know you would, but he sounds crazy. Besides, do we really want to start a confrontation with our new neighbours our first night in? We have to live next to these people. I think either we do nothing, or we call the police."

"So maybe we should call the police," said George.

Veronica nodded. "Maybe. But, what if we're wrong? Maybe it sounded worse than it was. We don't really know what happened. Maybe that *was* just them having sex."

George strode back around the bed to his side of it and unplugged his phone from the charger. He started searching on the screen. "Perhaps there's a noise pollution unit or something. Maybe we can get them to check it out without actually getting the police involved."

"Good idea," agreed Veronica. It had been a while since she and George had been drawn together by something that wasn't related to their own 'situation', and it felt good to be so united. "Although, do you think they'd tell them it was us who complained?"

"You really don't need to worry about them," assured George, puzzled, she supposed, by her anxiety, her new weakness. "I'm here. Besides, men who batter their wives are usually cowards."

"I just don't want to feel awkward every time I leave the house," Veronica attempted to rationalise.

George nodded. He had found a number to call. "I'll ask them to keep it anonymous."

Veronica moved nearer to him and rested her hand on his shoulder as he called. She listened to him explain the situation to what turned out to be an answering machine, and then call another number and repeat the same thing to a respondent. She listened too to the still blaring music and wondered if the slip of a woman she had met earlier was lying on the floor somewhere, unconscious of its beat. Veronica felt herself shaking a little. She wondered what she would say when she saw the woman again. What was her name? Christ, she hadn't even asked it. If the woman was dead and the police questioned her, she wouldn't know what to tell them. They had talked about building work. She had given her chocolates. She should, surely, have noticed that something was wrong.

"They're going to drive by," said George.

"Pardon?"

"The noise unit. They're going to drive by, and if they can hear the noise from the street, they'll knock on the door."

"Oh okay, that's good," breathed Veronica. "Well done."

George had always been tirelessly practical. He always got things done. In the low gleam of the bedside lights, they lay back in bed. The music continued to blare and there was no longer any pretence that either of them were asleep. Nevertheless, they remained on their far sides of the mattress. George's chest rose and fell in a strained, artificial attempt at breathing deep. Veronica's legs itched. She was starting a new teaching position the following morning and would surely now be a mess for it. At least she had already narrowed down her outfit – either a long red dress, or a shorter blue. But she'd wanted to be bright, sparky. Every now and then the man next door would explode into a short bout of shrieks, and Veronica's breath would stick in her chest, and she would sense George tensing. Occasionally there was a lull in the music, and he would gradually relax, but then like a stab to the gut the music and the man would return with their abrasive beat.

"If it was Sinatra or Fitzgerald, it wouldn't be so awful," Veronica mused at one point, and George laughed gratefully at her attempt at humour, reaching his hand in a rare gesture of affection across the bed. As their fingers intertwined, Veronica felt a sudden surge of tears rushing to her eyes, but she resisted the heaving in her chest, and in the dimness, George didn't seem to notice.

Nor did he notice Veronica slipping into recollection of another night, many years ago, when she had steadied her breath and gripped the edge of another bed in much the same way. She had been sixteen, at her parents' house in Oman. There was a party to mark their imminent departure for Nairobi and a friend of her father's had been gallantly swinging her from room to room. He was much younger than her father, perhaps thirty or thirty-five, and she'd had a crush on him for years. That night he talked on and on about how mature she was, how beautiful she'd become. When he led her to her bedroom, it had seemed inevitable almost, natural...

Cutting into her own musings, Veronica wondered why she was suddenly remembering this now.

Brushing the thought aside, she laid a hand on top of her empty stomach. George didn't notice this either, and it no longer surprised her to catch herself this way, but familiarity didn't stop the sadness. With her other hand, gently, she squeezed George's still intertwined fingers, and he squeezed back, but she didn't feel bolstered. The intimacy of skin seemed only to illuminate its more usual absence, and without intention, tears threatened again – hot, burning, laced this time with a feint fury directed squarely at the man next to her. Because it was him, after all, who had made her feel this way. It was his doing – he with his cool, constant composure, his pulling away from vulnerability, his pulling away from her. It was his fault that she had become so pathetically grateful for the fleeting touch of skin, for these scraps he threw to her.

Veronica glanced at the clock. It was 4.13am. "I can't believe he's still going," she said. "It's getting light out."

"I can't do anything else."

A slight curtness had appeared in George's tone and he withdrew his hand from hers. She moved her head to study him. They hadn't spoken in many minutes now and she wondered what he had been thinking about to shift his mood. Had he somehow sensed her tear-tipped anger? Something in his mind had quite plainly hardened, like clay left too long unattended. It was a pattern that seemed to be growing increasingly frequent between them. What had once been malleable and soft and waiting for the tender imprint of the other, was all at once brittle and breakable and cold to touch. Often now, they found themselves this way, slipping without warning between alliance and combat, unspoken thoughts erecting themselves between them, and once begun, neither of them could stop the hardening in the air.

"Do you think they've been yet?" Veronica attempted to sidestep, ignoring George's edginess. "The noise unit?"

"No idea."

"Well," she started carefully, "will you call them?"

George exhaled loudly and turned towards the wall.

"George, don't be like that. I'm only asking if you'll call them." Veronica's own voice was edged now, fringed with frustration.

"They told me before they only work till four."

"So what are we meant to do?"

He sat up. "Why are you having a go at me?"

"I'm not. I'm just... exhausted. Can you please just try them again?"

"Why don't you call them?" George demanded, flapping his hand toward her.

"Because you spoke to them before."

He didn't move.

"Why is it so hard to make a phone call?"

Theatrically, George picked up his phone and dialled the number, then with a great show of action, dialled the number again. "Answerphone," he declared eventually.

She rolled her eyes, and huffed, and found herself wondering in a way that was also new but also increasingly frequent, how she hadn't seen this aggressive, petulant side of her husband before. He wasn't loving – he was insensitive, and stubborn, and emotionally stunted. Within the space of the following minute, she shortcut the more and more familiar spiral of internal rumination, and she was on to divorce, and how that might work, and how she would declare it to George, imagining herself empowered and liberated and bold again. Secure in the reliability of impermanence. But then, as always happened, her mind caught a glimpse of it, and the thought of waking up without him flooded from mind to gut, choking her with the dark, suffocating, unbearable notion of his absence.

Lying back in bed this time, George switched off the bedside lights and turned again towards the wall. Veronica did the same. The space between them felt cold and barbed, uncrossed by outstretched palms, not even softened by the smooth cream waffle.

In the darkness, the music continued. And the coarse singing continued. It seeped through the wall onto the clean slate of their bedroom. And then, at 4.48am, from the other side of the wall, a baby started crying, a baby just like the one they longed for, and its wails carried on way past five, and long after the music was finally turned off, and far beyond the time when, Veronica imagined, everybody in Primrose Hill, except for her, and George, and this poor, unheeded baby, were asleep.

Simone

The remnants of Jasmine's crisps are squashed between the floor and her cheek, though Simone is not sure if the stickiness is from them. She imagines hot, cleansing water rushing over her, washing her clean. But the dirt is caked thick. The grime. It was always the grime that struck her most, at the beginning, seeping into her, clinging to her clothes, as though it knew that this time she was there for good, conjoined, no longer a thing to be brushed off at the end of the day.

She had been to the estate often. She'd been staying at Noah's, preferring his warmer smaller rooms, and his richer poorer parents. The estate was where they played, hanging off the wall outside the bet shop with a cig and a beer, waiting to score something better. She'd swished her arms with the pride of the enlightened as she walked the familiar route to his family flat, hauling her suitcase behind her. There was a garden on the east side, where she often paused to admire the carefully dotted colour of the bedding, and she stopped then. She chatted to the old woman pruning. The woman asked about school, about her friends, about her romance with Noah, as though they were not separated by walls, or five decades. Three floors above them, the confident smells of home cooking wafted out of the rooms of an Iranian family bustling in sing-song tones, and Simone glanced up, breathing it in. A little further along, there was a wall plastered with posters – for a church meeting, a bingo night, a local art exhibit. Simone had not yet attended any of these events, but they wrapped themselves around her, plumping the imaginary nest she was building.

Until that first evening in their real, own flat (blagged by way of her expanding belly), unpacking a suitcase of stuff she'd pulled from neat cupboards and squashing them into a single broken drawer, she saw everything differently, as if for the first time: the dirt and the darkness; the way the stairs smelled of piss; how rubbish littered doorways; how pairs of random, dishevelled people were always loitering.

After a while, months or maybe years, these were quirks she stopped noticing, or else she began to blend in with them, became like them too, even if some people still called her a posho.

Until Noah died, and she started giving out hand jobs in exchange for a hit, and then nobody thought her posh at all.

There were whole days, afterwards, when she sat on the wall in the Concourse and stared at the families unlike her own. The ones wrapped up tight in determination. Sometimes they were English, but as often Romanian, Syrian, Afghani, Somali, indiscernible from each other in the way they kept to themselves, focussed, and then moved on. She could not focus. She could not move on. She wasn't sure she wanted to.

She clasped her cig and her beer, and something better.

Time blurred.

There were others. Some old granny banged with her shopping trolley up the stairwell every day at exactly 11am. Her hair was always immaculate, her shoes polished, and she would stop to tell loitering kids not to litter the corridors. They waited respectfully till she had reached her flat, till she had closed her door, then chucked their crisp wrappers on the floor.

Sometimes Simone was approached by the estate's

do-gooders, people intent on rallying, improving, starting up resident groups, handing out petitions, talking about the 'community'. They made pains to notice her sitting there. They said hello, they asked how she was, they cooed at Dominic crying in his pram, or perhaps it was Jasmine. They invited her to things. And into their flats, only a floor up, or down, or across from her own. Often these people were local councillors, or teachers, or NHS workers, or churchgoers, professions of care, pretending they cared, pretending like they wanted to know. But they didn't know her. Because in the daytime they went to work, and in the evenings they made dinner for their kids, and okay, maybe their salaries didn't stretch to the end of the month, same as Simone's benefits, and maybe the rubbish in their hallway wasn't cleared either, and maybe their kids had been mugged too; but still they lived a world apart. They weren't like the people Simone knew, the people she had come to know, since Noah. Since Terry. They didn't even see them.

No, she and Dominic, and Jasmine, lived separately, in the shadows, in invisible cracks. Though there were enough others who occupied those dark spaces with them. Equally unseen.

Like the family where the mum was always in jail for shoplifting. Or another family, two doors down, where the step dad fiddled with the three daughters, and nobody blinked when one of the girls got pregnant. Then there were Terry's brothers, two of them anyway, who everybody said for sure had a hand in things when their mum OD'd. And there was Dominic's little friend Lacey, whose mum threw herself off a bridge.

These were the people that Simone knew, that Simone saw. More and more she saw them. Illuminated in Dominic's gaze. Because these were the people he was growing up with – united not by money, or lack of it, not by ethnicity or religion, not by the estate, but by just one thing: the way they hurt each other, generation after generation, round and around. They kept each other bound by that, like an inescapable magnet. Hurt people hurt people, don't they?

Veronica

George had already left for work when from the window of their new kitchen-come-living room, Veronica spotted a boy emerging from the house next door. It had been exactly two hours and six minutes since the music had finally stopped. She had been listening intently ever since, hoping for reassuring kitchen clatters or other proofs of life; but she had not yet heard the voice of the woman, nor the sound of a baby. Still, here was a boy. A scrawny thing like his mother, she would have guessed he was eight or nine from the height of him, but his gait suggested otherwise, all self-consciousness and measure, far more befitting of a pre-teen. Most adults blundered at attempts to estimate the age of children, forgetting, in the stretch between now and their own childhoods, the minute, invisible, colossal developments that separate a Reception child from a Year 1, and an eight-year-old from a boy knocking on eleven. But at her last school, Veronica had taught ten- and eleven-year-olds, so she was familiar with the gradual creep of adolescence into the frame. At her new school, the youngest in the class would still be six.

Veronica watched as, on the other side of the road now, the boy pulled a packet of crisps from his bag and ate the first few while staring up at the top floors of his house. Veronica wondered what he was looking for. A wave from his mother perhaps. A sign of something. She followed his line of sight, but didn't have the angle, and after a moment, the boy turned and scurried along the road, a peculiar mixture of anxiety and machismo. Veronica wondered where he was going. Glancing at her watch, she saw that it was only seven-thirty – too early for school, and besides, no reason to make him so shifty – yet every few steps he glanced around. Nobody crossed his path, however, and soon, he was round the corner and gone. Veronica stopped munching her toast and listened again. The downstairs neighbour next door had left even earlier than George. He seemed to run some sort of roofing company and had loaded up his van a full thirteen minutes before their alarm was set to wake them. She had been watching the street, first from the bedroom and now from here, ever since. If the woman had left, it was improbable that she would have missed seeing her. But why then was the house next door so quiet? Even if the adults were asleep, surely the baby would have stirred. While pressing her head against the window for a better view, it occurred to Veronica that she need not be so invested. The neighbours had most likely existed at their abode long before she and George had arrived on the street, and for all she knew, the noises they had made were normal, or consensual at least. Perhaps then she should be less concerned with their internal dynamic and more with the impact of their noise upon them – her and George.

Neither had yet dared to voice it, but the horrific noise of the previous night had been a devastating disappointment: the idyllic home far from idyllic, George's hard-earned savings invested foolishly, the new start tainted already. Yes, this is what should be occupying Veronica's mind. But as she sipped her coffee and picked again at her toast, she couldn't stop picturing the visuals that might have accompanied the sounds – the woman against their adjoining wall, the baby unattended. Why was the child not crying now? Where was its mother? Veronica looked at her watch again and tapped her fingers impatiently against the window, subconsciously scratching her thigh. She would have to leave for her new job soon. It might not be possible for her to determine what had happened after the sounds had ceased.

Moving her plate and mug to the sink, Veronica gave them a quick rinse before loading them into the new Miele dishwasher. There was something acutely satisfying about these tiny gestures of homeliness. She and George had lived together for almost four years now in various rented flats, and before that she had house-shared in a lovely maisonette in Chelsea. All were sufficiently homely, but all were launch pads rather than bases, and she'd rarely stayed inside any of them long enough to make a meal, let alone do the washing up. She couldn't remember ever seeing her own mother do the dishes. This isn't to say that she didn't do them – her father would never have found himself in the kitchen and they didn't have a maid in every country they lived in, so her mother must have washed up sometimes. But Veronica didn't have a visual memory of this. She couldn't picture her at the sink. She couldn't conjure images of a roast cooking in the oven, or potato peelings littering the counter, or her mother letting her taste the bubbling Bolognese straight from the pan on a metal spoon that burned her tongue. Those were experiences she'd collected from other mothers, the mothers of friends who invited her sometimes for a bank holiday weekend, or Easter lunch, or for a three-week stint the last summer before everything altered.

Glancing again at her watch, Veronica flipped the dishwasher closed with her foot, and sprinted up the stairs to the bedroom where she planted herself in front of her newly filled wardrobe. There hung the red and the blue, but now she couldn't seem to make a decision. Neither could she decide whether to tie her blonde hair into a proficient bun, or let it hang soft and loose. Or whether to invite the new parents she would be meeting into the classroom at the end of the day so that she could say a few words to the group, or stick to individual hellos and handshakes at the classroom door. The itching of her legs was incessant.

Veronica closed her eyes and pushed her hand towards the competing materials. Red. She switched to blue.

Veronica had chosen to cycle to her new job. Boarding in Kent, she had biked into the nearby village upright, without holding onto the handlebars, and pretended to her friends that this skill came naturally, but really it was from two formative years during primary school spent in Holland. Today's cycle was an easy two miles away in St John's Wood. She knew the route already, though not as well as her mother supposed. Veronica still wrote, and received, a weekly letter from her mother. In the last one, her mother had mused that now Veronica was living back in North London, she would of course remember the old house in Hampstead Garden Suburb, and the walks on the Heath, and did she know that the school she was teaching at was just a road away from the music academy they'd driven to every Saturday for violin lessons? Veronica didn't remember any of this. They'd lived in the Hampstead house for little over a year. But she'd been to the school three times now – two interviews, and one lengthy induction day at which she'd been thoroughly introduced to the campus. It was not hyperbole to call it a campus. Despite being a stone's throw from Central London, the school boasted its own playing field, a swimming pool, and grand old buildings that reminded Veronica of the similarly grand institutions of her own childhood, filling her with the immediate sense of greeting a long lost relative. Familiarity, however, did not provide her with the easy confidence she might have presumed.

As she pushed away the unsteadiness in her stomach and unlocked her bike, Veronica considered this. There was a time when she would have swept into a new position, charming the men, captivating the women. She should, now, have been sweeping through the pretty Primrose streets. But at the first traffic light she stopped too abruptly and almost came off over the handlebars, and she physically felt her legs wobbling.

As she arrived, she saw already a small group of elbows-out parents huddled together many minutes before the ringing of the bell. One of them spotted her, and pointed.

Her nerves were, however, unnecessary, as far as the children went at least, turning out to be a delightful balance between respectful and precocious.

"Mrs Reddington?" one girl interrupted at least three times during the first lesson. "Mrs Reddington, my mummy says I should ask you lots of questions so you remember me. Can I ask you a question please?"

"Mrs Reddington, you're so pretty," blushed another, a dark-haired, caramel-skinned boy already possessing a cheeky charm.

"Mrs *Green*ington," dared a third, easily coerced into apology by the slightest lift of Veronica's left eyebrow.

There was only one child who unsettled her. Sheathed in a halo of wilful, auburn curls, and freckled in glorious splashes across her cheeks, Amelia Beckham stood well under four foot, quiet unless spoken to, at which point a smile would spread infectiously into her speech so that even the most exacting of her peers would listen. From the first minute, Veronica could not take her eyes off her. The girl was seated near the front of the class and paid keen attention, raising her hand every time a question was asked, or wrinkling her brow earnestly if she didn't have an answer. She was lovely, exactly the kind of child Veronica could imagine having herself. But she didn't know why she felt such a magnetic pull towards her.

At break time, Veronica skimmed through some of the children's books and noted that Amelia was neither at the top nor the bottom of the class. She was not one of the children that the PE teacher had told her was especially athletic, nor one that the singing teacher had said would soon enough be on the radio. Peeking through the classroom window, she saw that she was not the best or worst at cartwheels in the playground, nor the funniest, nor naughtiest, nor the most or least popular. But there was something about her. She was one of only three children in Year 2 to have already moved on to Year 3 reading books, but Veronica didn't think that was it. And it was only at the end of the day when the parents lined up at the door – she had decided on hellos and handshakes – that Veronica finally put two and two together and realised why Amelia had affected her so strangely.

"Sarah?"

Sarah Beckham, née Johnson, stood, clearly stunned, just outside the classroom door. Aside from the elegantly cut suit, and the hair that was a few shades lighter and far more manicured than when they'd last met, Veronica could have been looking at the exact same girl she'd known twenty-two years earlier. Her jaw was a little sharper than it had been, she was, as age dictated, significantly taller, a few faint lines dotted her complexion, and she had finally got the hang of make-up, but her essence was unchanged. There was no mistaking it.

"Sarah Johnson?"

"Beckham, now," Sarah replied, finding her voice through the surprise. "Veronica."

"I can't believe you're here." Despite first-day protocol, Veronica pulled Sarah into a fierce hug, ignoring the slight awkwardness in Sarah's returning arms, and the curious eyes of the onlooking parents. "We were best friends when we were twelve," Veronica told them. Then to Sarah, "It's been what, more than twenty years?"

Sarah nodded. "I can't believe you're Amelia's teacher. You teach now?"

"I do."

"Wow." Sarah shook her head as she took this in, her blonde-brown bob flapping endearingly against her chin.

"And you?" probed Veronica. "You have a child."

"Two actually. My son's at home."

"Typical."

"Typical?"

"Leaving the boy at home. You always were a feminist."

"He's eighteen months," said Sarah quickly. But already one of the other parents in the queue had laughed. Another smiled, impatiently, and at least three more strained their necks forward in an effort to hear the conversation and not be left out of any potential judging of, or bonding with, the new teacher.

Veronica wanted to bond. Talking to Sarah was all at once like rediscovering a forgotten but favourite taste, teasing her tongue with familiar and delectable flavour. And the confident girl Veronica had once been, oblivious to things like life and miscarriages, the child who had once basked in Sarah's friendship, was bubbling gleefully to the surface. Veronica heard her in the slightly impudent words tripping out of her mouth. She felt her resurgence, just out of grasp. Within her grasp, she placed her hand on Sarah's, and leaned out of the classroom to the queue of parents. "Apologies, everyone." Then keeping hold of her friend's hand, she called Amelia to come to her mother. "I guess I'll see you tomorrow," she said. "It's so lovely to find you here."

"Actually, my husband will be picking up tomorrow," Sarah replied as she enveloped Amelia in a comfortable hug. "David usually does the pick-up, but Mondays are my day."

"Oh? What do you do then?" Veronica queried, feeling herself inexplicably prickling, her unease returning, as though Sarah's failure to show up on the school run was somehow a rejection of her.

"I'm a lawyer."

"Oh. Right. Unsurprising."

"Really? Why?"

"Well you always liked rules, didn't you?"

The same mother who had laughed earlier, laughed again, and Veronica smiled at her, enjoying the fleeting sense of command, wondering where the slight barbs in her speech were coming from. Sarah furrowed her brow. She did this the same way Amelia did, the same way, Veronica now remembered, she always used to. Sarah began to usher Amelia away from the door to make room for the next parent, but Veronica touched her arm again. "Dinner then. This week. I'll get your number from the office."

Sarah smiled and nodded agreeably, though, Veronica noticed, it was with not quite total enthusiasm, as she shepherded her daughter away.

Veronica didn't leave the school campus until well after five o'clock. Ordinarily, she supposed, she could be gone by four, but she'd had a short meeting with the headmaster to debrief about her first day, and besides, wanted some time to explore the classroom alone. On the wall hung photographs of each of her new Year 2s, and she tried to put names to faces. Managing sixteen out of twenty, she lingered for a moment on Amelia's, and then spent a few minutes memorising the four that had eluded her. Names learned, she walked slowly around the room, looking at each of the pieces of work on the wall, noting which children had exceptionally neat handwriting, and which seemed in need of development. She stood for an especially long time in front of the collage of self-portraits, attempting to see past the precision of paint, or lack of it, and through to the more important clues of self-perception. On the cycle home she pondered further the enigma of one very pale-skinned boy painting himself a deep brown, the oddity of one face that had been fashioned as almost entirely mouth, and Amelia's creation, which included every freckle, every red curl, and a meticulously accurate depiction of both shape and colour of the eyes and mouth, revealing that the girl saw herself almost exactly as she was, and suggested she was just as straight-shooting as her mother.

Veronica was still thinking about this when she saw him – the boy from next door. She was mid locking up her bike, carefully threading the cord through both railing and wheel, when something in her periphery caught her attention and she looked up to see him standing on the other side of the street, looking at her. He had not yet crossed over, and she watched as he pretended to notice something of interest on the pavement. Veronica lingered. Even in the day's flurry of new pupils, and new parents, and then the surprise of Sarah, the noises of the previous night had not stopped echoing in her mind, scratching just below the surface, like the itch beneath her skin. More than once that day she had thought about the uneasiness of this boy. More than once she had thought about the baby crying. More than once she had wondered whether the woman was okay. Just once, her father's friend in Oman had intruded again into her mind...

She'd wanted to kiss him that night, she had. Only when he had pushed her backwards onto the bed and tugged at her dress, it was more abrupt and with greater force than seemed necessary. And never before had a man pressed his hand over her mouth as he reached greedily into her knickers. When he entered her, he had knelt hard with one knee onto her thigh, and kept her face pinned fast against the pillow, and even if she had wanted to scream out, she would have been unable. So she'd pretended that she had not wanted to scream, and that yes, she'd enjoyed it, and even allowed him to kiss her goodbye, then left herself the following day with her parents without telling anyone.

Veronica shook her head. She had barely thought about that night since, other than to laud her affair with an older man over her teenage schoolmates. Of course, with hindsight, it was easy to see why. If she had allowed herself to think about it, then she would have had to acknowledge that she had not actually intended to sleep with the older, influential friend of her father's. And if she'd admitted how powerless she had in that moment been, then she would have had to acknowledge all the other areas in her life where she felt powerless too, and it was much better to feel strong and brazen, and to be in charge of herself and everything and everybody. Besides, she'd told herself then, and again now, she wasn't underage, she hadn't resisted, he hadn't even been her first.

Yet the night was pushing its way back into her head, and there was a new thought too: had she been the first girl he'd taken that way? Had others followed after she said nothing?

Slowly, Veronica pulled a plastic bag from her blazer pocket and, in case of rain, tied it around the saddle of her bike. Then she spent a long time gathering her various bags and rummaging through them for her house key. At last, the boy crossed over.

Up close, his face didn't look anything like his mother's. Though hers had been pale and a little gaunt, the complexion disturbed by patches of red, her eyes had been strikingly large and blue, her lips full. The boy's upper lip barely existed. His eyes were beady and too close together. His skin was darker than his mother's, but instead of the luxurious olive or velvet tones she often admired, his had come out a dull fawn that gave a sense of poor health. He was the kind of child to whom, if he'd turned up in her class, she would probably have taken an early and irrational dislike. Though she would of course have tried not to.

"Hello," she smiled genially as he reached his doorstep. "I'm your new neighbour, Veronica."

The boy didn't look at her. "Hi," he muttered in a show of haste, but despite having key in hand, he waited a moment in front of his door.

Veronica took this as a sign to continue. "I met your mother yesterday," she said, glancing up to his flat. "Is she in now?"

"I dunno," said the boy. "Sometimes she's not."

"Oh, does she work?"

The boy shrugged his shoulders. Still he didn't make to go inside.

"Is your dad home? I haven't met him yet."

"He's not my dad," the boy declared, quickly, before, as though correcting his openness, shrugging again.

"What's your name?" Veronica asked. She was watching him closely, the frail hunch of his skinny shoulders, the sharp darting of his eyes. He gave the impression of one of those meerkats you see in zoos – small and furry, but deeply alert, likely to bite.

"Dom. Dominic, but Dom." The boy was finally looking at her, and now that he was, there was an unnerving focus to his stare. Though she was used to talking to children, Veronica felt an odd wariness.

"And how old are you, Dom?"

"Eleven. It's my last year in primaries."

"I teach in a primary school," said Veronica. "What subject do you like?"

At this, Dominic returned his eyes to his door. Again, he shrugged. "Dunno."

"Well I like English," Veronica continued hastily. "I love books. Don't tell my students, but I'm awful at maths."

Dominic looked at her again, the focus still intense. "I won't tell," he assured her.

She smiled at him with exaggerated gratitude.

He didn't move. His eyes held hers.

"Well, it's lovely to meet you, Dom." Veronica said this with forced breeziness. Part of her wanted to keep talking, to keep the boy outside with her, to find out what was going on in that flat, to make sure the boy's mum was alright, and the baby; but another part of her was suddenly compelled to get away. "I'll see you later," she said. "Please send your mum my best."

She trod the single step up to her own door, and he nodded. Simultaneously, they turned their keys. From inside Dominic's house came the sound of a TV blaring. From inside Veronica's, the beeping of the alarm.

By the time George arrived home, Veronica had already made her signature Thai green curry – one of a handful of dishes that she had learned the recipe to, didn't require too much cooking nous, and she produced in rotation; she had enjoyed a first bath in their new freestanding tub, the water thankfully dulling the leg itch; and she had texted Sarah. It was a carefully crafted text, offering three dates over the next two weeks for dinner, and alluding gently to their friendship of old. It had only lasted a short time, during their first year at secondary school, before the move to Oman and the start of her boarding, but it had been an intense affair, all endless love and drama, and Veronica often thought of that year as one of her happiest. Perhaps it was because she'd been living at home with her parents, or because she'd liked her school, or any number of other factors, but in her mind it had always been because of Sarah. Veronica conjured her as somebody who made her feel strong, stronger than she was, and over the years there had been more than one occasion when Sarah had sprung into Veronica's mind: her sincerity and gravity; or the ease with which she'd argued with and adored her sister and parents; or the taste of her mother's Bolognese. So it was a genuine joy for Veronica to see her again. There was something about it that lifted her. Strengthened her. It seemed serendipitous that she had reappeared at this particular juncture.

George seemed largely unfazed by the coincidence. "I suppose it's not that surprising. Most people tend to stick around the areas they grow up in."

Veronica took a sip of her wine – still three days clear of ovulation. "Yes, but out of all the people I could have seen – her, my absolute best friend."

They were sitting in the living room, drinking wine while they indulged in a Netflix box set. It was almost midnight and George would be up again in less than six hours, she in seven, but on nights when he came home as late as this, if they didn't stretch the hours of evening, they would barely see each other. Wine helped to mask the cracks in this joint gesture of sacrifice. There was a time when their legs would have been intertwined on the sofa, a time when their hands and lips would have been light with small caresses, a time when the depth of their conversation had felt endless.

"Your best friend for a year."

"A year is a long time in the life of an eleven-year-old."

"When I was eleven, I was best boys with Richard Darfus. Do you know what he does now? He's a brain surgeon. An actual brain surgeon."

"Did you just say, 'best boys'?" Veronica smiled at him teasingly.

"Best boys. Sure."

Veronica laughed. "Cute."

"Not cute. Very, very manly."

George grinned, with an old warmth. The open balcony door adjoining the living room let in a soft summer breeze. Through the speakers, the gentle music accompanying the programme credits sounded softly. The cracks seemed almost invisible. Bolstered by her encounter with Sarah, Veronica felt a rare, whispering hopefulness. Even the noise from next door had subsided. Perhaps the neighbours were not going to be as bad as they'd feared. Not that either she or George had so much as mentioned this fear. George had rushed out of the house that morning without a word, and Veronica had understood from this that the potential disaster of the new home they'd ploughed their savings into was too much for him to acknowledge in the daylight. She wanted to talk about it, about whether they should have called the police, or still should, she wanted to dissect her encounter with Dom, but all evening she had tucked this conversation away. Without consultation, both of them had decided to play at paradise.

"Five episodes down, five to go," George declared, switching off the TV and draining the last of his wine. "Bed?"

She nodded, carrying their glasses to the sink while he repaired the remote control to its charger and plumped their dented pillows. They still moved in effortless congruence. She had hoped many times over the preceding months, that these ingrained habits would be enough to buoy them, and in a way they were. While their bodies failed them, and words faltered, they clung to the fluency of their routines. In the bathroom, they brushed their teeth in unison and, playfully, George made a face at her in the mirror. She laughed, and aped his expression, hopefulness giving way to exuberance. She barely dared to believe it, but something felt different between them that evening – lighter, easy, like they used to be. Perhaps, now that it was quiet, the house, with its freshness, was working its magic after all. In the flat, by the end, all she had been able to see were proofs of disaster. When she walked into the kitchen – there lay the morning she'd pounced on George at the counter, thrusting the pregnancy test beneath his nose. In the spare room – there lived the Sunday they'd spent plotting out where to put the cot. And their bedroom was never safe, always the site of her collapse. Briefly, Veronica wondered whether the woman next door also cried into her husband's chest as she had done that night, soaking sodden the cotton of his shirt. Or if instead, she cried away from him, because of him. There was, however, still no noise, and she pushed this thought from her mind.

Together they spat. George reached for his moisturiser, she for hers, branded in the same packaging. In the cupboard on her side of the double sink were the ovulation sticks, but she managed to ignore the sight of them on the shelf. Instead, Veronica dared a purposeful, lingering smile at George in the mirror. He grinned back at her, and as he manoeuvred around her out of the bathroom, again hopefulness flickered inside her chest. Until she realised that as he passed her, he hadn't attempted to squeeze her bottom, or slip his hand around her waist, or kiss her cheek. And as she watched him climb into bed, she saw that he turned immediately towards the wall.

Veronica felt a bitterness surge inside her. George was relaxed that evening not because of a nascent restoration between them, not because he missed her as much as she missed him, but because of the lateness of the night, the demands of sleep that afforded him, the protection from intimacy, from failure, from her. When, testing him, she snuggled up to him in bed, though it was barely perceptible, she felt his back brace against her.

"Is it time?" he whispered dutifully into the darkness.

"No," she whispered back.

And then she felt his muscles ease.

Three minutes later, music blared through the bedroom wall.

"Absolutely no fucking way." George exploded from bed and over to the wall that adjoined the offending neighbours' flat. He banged with a fist on the brick, but the music was so loud that even with twice the force, nobody would have heard him.

"George," Veronica soothed. "George, stop, don't bang."

"Oh, okay, I won't bang, I'll just let this idiot destroy our sleep, again."

"I'm not saying that," said Veronica. "Just don't bang. What's the point? All it does is make things louder, and annoy me."

"*I* annoy you? Not him? He doesn't?"

"Of course he annoys me." Apparently they were on different sides again, this time of an argument she hadn't even realised they were having. "Maybe we should call the noise people? Or the police? After last night…"

George rolled his eyes and banged the wall. His anger was engulfing. It was as though the reoccurrence of noise, the proof of it, gave proof too to all his other unspoken suspicions: proof of abysmal neighbours, proof of dashed hopes; proof of the state between themselves.

"Or what then?" demanded Veronica.

"I'm going round."

Already George was pulling on his tracksuit bottoms and t-shirt, and stuffing his phone into his pocket, and despite Veronica's irritation with him, a flash of fear flew suddenly through her throat.

"Don't," she choked. "What are you going to say?"

"I'm going to be nice."

"Really?"

"I'm just going to ask him to turn it down."

By this point, George was already out of the room and halfway down the stairs, but even if he'd been within grasping distance, Veronica knew there was no way she would have been able to dissuade her husband. He, like she, was a determined, unflinching animal. She, like he, could never have chosen anybody otherwise.

"Be careful!" she called after him, before moving to the window where she peeked out from behind the thick, double-lined curtain onto the street below.

Veronica's heart pounded in her throat. It was unusual for her to feel so acutely on the cusp of danger, and despite the immediacy of it, she noticed her own distress with a strange, detached observation. There was a sepia sensation to it, as though she was in a movie-style bar brawl, or a thriller, the music low and suspenseful. Not that she really expected George to start anything physical. He was a strong, well-built man, gifted with both height and muscle, the kind of chaperone you might wish to walk you home on a dark night; but he wasn't a fighter. George was far too sensible and pragmatic to either land himself in trouble with the law, or to endanger his, or her, safety. Still, they were yet to meet the man next door, and the irritation she'd felt with George minutes earlier dissolved into an urgent, consuming concern.

Veronica opened the window in an effort to hear the exchange below, and held her breath. The thought of George getting hurt seemed to constrict her lungs, and the longer she waited, the more she realised that it wasn't actually like a bar brawl at all, because this fight was not in a beer-stained building somewhere, it was here, on their doorstep, where adversaries could not simply be thrown out and sent packing. Whatever the outcome, they would all have to live with it, each day, staring at each other as they left the house in the morning and as they came home at night. Why had George been so reckless? Down at the street, he had already rung the bell and somebody had come to the door. She prayed it was the woman. She could see George gesticulating up to their bedroom. She couldn't make out his words with clarity, but thank goodness there was a conciliatory tone to his voice, and the exchange lasted only a minute. Before he turned away, George offered his hand, and somebody shook it. A few minutes later, he was back in the bedroom.

"Well?" she asked as soon as he entered, stifling a desire to throw her arms around him and squeeze him tight.

"He's a pipsqueak," he smiled, triumph on his tongue, the rage evaporated. "You could take him."

Veronica smiled, lungs releasing. "What did he say? What did you say?"

"I just introduced myself, nicely, explained that the music was very loud, and asked if he could turn it down a little, and he said no problem, they'd just gotten used to living next to an empty house. Then we shook hands."

"Wow. Okay," said Veronica. "What a relief. Well done."

It was a relief. A victory. A reason again for hope. Perhaps the man wasn't as aggressive as he'd sounded. Perhaps the woman was fine. Perhaps their own clean slate wasn't already dirty and tainted; though Veronica would not test this theory with further attempts at intimacy. George removed his tracksuit and t-shirt and climbed back into bed. He plugged his phone back in and rested it on his bedside table. Veronica switched off the lights. She pulled the covers over them. In unison, they lay down.

Minutes passed.

Slowly, George's breathing returned to a resting state. Slowly, so did her own. Slowly, she counted more ticking seconds.

663 seconds later, she reached across the bed and put her hand tentatively to George's shoulder. "George," she spoke softly. "George."

"What?"

"The music's exactly the same."

He didn't answer. Even after a long time, he didn't answer.

Veronica didn't speak again. Her legs were itching unbearably and she allowed herself to scratch, savouring the respite, overlooking the soreness she knew would follow. George didn't notice. In the darkness, she could see that he was restless too, his chest moving rapidly up and down, his breathing more shallow than normal, his face buried as far as he could press it into his pillow. She paused her scratching. Was he crying? She had never seen George cry. Veronica listened, but suddenly, as though sensing George's desolation, from the other side of the wall, the baby they had heard the previous night began to cry again. Not a whimper, not a moan, but a loud, inconsolable wail that continued for the next thirty minutes, unheeded, unattended, as though, like George and Veronica's own child, it wasn't there at all.

Simone

On the street below, summer is bursting forth in grand displays of colour. It drips extravagantly from window boxes and swishes with bohemian confidence around corners. Flyers appear on lampposts to announce a local street fair, a farmer's market, a concert in the park. Children whizz past on balance bikes and scooters and two-wheelers, graduating with age, decorated with bells and spokes and streamers. Parents saunter behind with unbranded cups of ethically sourced coffee. The air smells of cut grass.

It is the shame that keeps Simone inside. She sits for a long time at the window, smoking a series of cigs, watching Veronica dismount from her bike and glance upwards. There is a part of her that longs, irrationally, to dart out onto the street and somehow befriend this woman, to find a way to create that imagined casual conversation against railings. But the shame throbs. There is a spongy, purple-redness to it.

They would never have been friends anyway. It was a stupid fantasy. Somebody like Veronica would never have been fooled; sooner or later the grime and ugliness would have seeped out of her. What was the difference then if it crashed through walls? The foolishness was only in her caring.

She can't go to work. The bruise by her mouth is too visible for standing on reception, but at least she hasn't lost the gym job altogether. She told her manager that she was ill with a vomiting bug and he allowed, nay encouraged, her to delay her start.

Dominic didn't say a word. She can't help feeling hurt by this, let down, though she realises that her son has neither the power nor the imagination nor the motivation to do anything. And much of that is her fault.

Jasmine can survive for a few days without going outside.

Back on the estate, Simone wouldn't have cared. She would have covered the bruise with make-up and got on with life and nobody would have said anything. But here, people were bound to spot the darkened patch of skin and concoct a conclusion about how it must have been formed, what sort of person she therefore is, and he is, and they are. They would look at Dominic then. And they would look at her. And they would judge. The idea of this makes Simone's stomach turn – pity and condescension as sickening as each other. She can't bear to picture her neighbours thinking those things. She can't stand the idea of them looking at her that way. So maybe Terry's right. Maybe she does care too much about the poshos. Maybe she has got carried away in this street, imagining she's something she isn't, or isn't any longer. Maybe she is forgetting what's important, forgetting him. Why does she need a job anyway?

It's funny now to think that when they first met, she believed Terry liked her 'poshness'. Of course, by then it had felt ridiculous to her that anyone would imagine she possessed even the faintest scrap of gentility. When she thought back to the clean flat she'd grown up in, and the grammar school she'd attended, and the academic parents who'd raised her, her overriding sensation was of an untouchable cleanliness, wholesome and unsoiled. And there was little left to suggest she could be either. But it was a mistaken notion in any case. She'd never felt wholesome really. She'd seen first-hand how toxic and tainted the lives of even the most 'upright' could be. She knew how false the lines of division were. Still, after all the passed years, she felt an unbridgeable separation from even that sullied existence. If an 'us' and 'them' did exist, she stood on the estate, walled in.

Still, Terry had told his friends: *Know where she grew up? Posh flat on Croftdown Road.* (It wasn't posh, it just wasn't an estate – a distinction her parents had always made clear too. They had both grown up in council housing, but had 'worked hard' and 'had ambition' and made the leap. There was a big difference, they said, between the aspirational working class – them – and those living off others.) Or he'd ask, with what she'd mistaken then for pride: *How many GCSEs d'you think she's got then? Eleven. And what d'you think – Ds, Cs? Bloody As and Bs mate, this one.* He'd gently taken the piss out of the way she spoke and the clothes she wore, and she'd confused that with admiration. It was only later that she began to understand that Terry's obsession with her grades was less to do with appreciation, and more because when she was stupid or needy or weak, it made him feel doubly strong. He, the one with no grades to speak of, better after all.

He was the fourth son, the only one not to at least get a few GCSEs. His eldest brother had gone the whole hog through university, and the others went straight to the trading floor – not in a bank like their father, but on the street where the money grew faster and, they said, was only equally dirty. They all dangled these achievements over him. But even when they were younger, there was a pecking order, and he was right at the bottom of it, a fact exacerbated because of what Simone suspects is a severe, undiagnosed dyslexia, preventing his academic achievements from ever matching what to her is clear cleverness, and because he never grew bigger than anyone, not even his mother whose expanding width made up for what she was lacking in height. Simone would never use a word like 'exacerbated' to Terry. He took complicated vocabulary as a jab, a book word, another way in which people tried to keep him there at the bottom. Like when his mother had locked him in his room when he asked for help with homework, throwing the book at his head, her patience gone, her fancy friends too, drained away with her gin. Or like the time he wet his bed and so the following night was strapped naked to a toilet. Or the way his father, before he left, had never called him 'Terry, but Runt, accompanied often by an unpredictable blow from the back of his hand that would send him across the room, to prove it. Or the way that later, with his dad gone, his mother had been too intoxicated to get up and notice when older, bigger brothers working out their own demons, pushed him around with that same ease and amusement as their father had done, frequently holding his face for too long against a pillow and, once, forcing him to eat on his knees out of the dog's bowl. As adults, they still punch him too hard on the arm when they see him, though his years boxing have set the limit there, and they tell these stories about their childhood, with a jocular hilarity that disgusts Simone, and that Terry takes as a joke, because it is the only way not to sink even lower. Still, his brothers think they are hard done by too. Many years earlier their father had flashed his cash at their young, once-beautiful mother, lifting her off her estate and into a Marylebone apartment where he adorned her with designer clothes, and jewels, and fake friends, and alcohol, and impregnated her four times in seven years, and got the boys believing they would live that life and be like him; but in the end took off with his cash just as fast as he had flashed it. Terry was six then. There was an article in the paper, and rumours of dodgy dealings. And their dad was long gone out of the country before anybody realised he'd left them all with nothing. Whose fault is that, the brothers often demanded, two out of the three of them back on the estate in the flat their mother had been forced to return to, the third stuck at an entry level marketing job, none of them, including Terry, mentioning the wads of money that turn up occasionally, unpredictably, in their accounts from somewhere offshore. The big lawyers and the big bankers and the big politicians making the decisions, that's whose fault. The Eton boys, like their father, in their ivory towers. The neighbours Simone spent too long watching as they unloaded boxes into the house next door.

Terry had told her that to be honest, he couldn't really remember it, the life his brothers described, but it was true – he'd been middle class once, upper-middle class even, way richer than her, with a father who liked and bought the best of everything. Terry's mum had even held on to one sparkling ring as proof, proof of what she'd been tricked by. But Terry didn't feel tricked. As a teen, he'd wished only that she'd stop talking about it, stop trying to make out that they were different from everyone else around them. He felt embarrassed by the way she tried to be 'better'. Was 'better' a father who abused and left them? He didn't want to be like that. He didn't want to be rich. He didn't want a job. A job to join the great turning wheel, the foolish race, the structure that feeds the fat cats, like his father? The disgusting symbol against which he measured everything? She could understand that.

It's why he lost it with her. She can understand that too.

What Simone cannot understand, is exactly what she did to make things go so spectacularly wrong. It's the worst fight they've had in months and for the past three days she has been thinking about it. Clearly, she hit a nerve when she told him about the job, and she feels so stupid because she'd been aware of that probability. Yet for all her preparations she'd still chosen the wrong words, or the wrong tone, or maybe it was the timing. You'd think that by now she'd be better attuned to his sensitivities, but she always seems to make him flip eventually, she always does something.

The problem is, she wants the job. She does. Even though it's small. Even though it's barely anything. And no matter how sympathetic she tries to be to Terry, she can't see anything so terrible about it. So she had to tell him. Plus, there is an unfamiliar new emotion brewing in the bruised aftermath of this time. There is still remorse, guilt, and a knowledge of her own idiocy. There is still fear of further reprisal. But there is also, this time, a rage of her own. Not large enough to match Terry's, but there is nonetheless. A slow, festering rage carved from that deep, disturbing shame.

Because all she could think about, this time, was that Veronica was hearing it. Prim, perfect Veronica, and the rugby husband she hasn't yet met. They were hearing her head thudding against the wall. They were hearing the blow of her shoulder against brick as Terry flipped her around and pressed her forward. They were hearing her inexorable wail as he ploughed into her. Beneath their clean, new sheets they were hearing everything. And most likely clasping to each other in grateful response, caressing one another tenderly, whispering congratulations that they themselves were not as animalistic as him or as stupid and slutty as her, and consoling each other on the pity of having such neighbours.

At least they would not have been able to hear his hand pressing down on her face, or the force of his teeth on her breast. And they would not have seen her lying there afterwards, her nose bleeding, her pyjamas still around her ankles.

Dominic saw.

In the years before Terry, it was Dominic who would have picked her up from such collapse. If she was throwing up, he brought her a towel and some water, helped her into bed, and whenever she didn't have a boyfriend, he slept there with her, pretending not to be disturbed by her retching into the night. She liked to feel the warmth of his skin nearby, the sound of his breathing, and on the hazy mornings that followed, she would fondle his hair for a while, trying not to notice how needy and grateful his face was, before propping herself up in bed for a spliff, remembering halfway through that it was a school day. In the realisation of that she would throw on some tracksuit bottoms and a coat, and she would tear with him across the Concourse, fingers interlinked, laughing together at their flying frames. Then later he'd tell her what dress to wear for her date, and hold her cig while she tried it on, and when she got home, if she was still standing, he would stay up late with her watching TV.

That's what they were doing the evening that Noah smashed the window. Dominic must only have been about four, but by then Noah wasn't living with them. The locks had been changed and he was banging at the door, kicking and thumping. At first Simone had simply turned up the volume of the TV, but suddenly there was a clattering of glass from the window. She'd left Dominic on the sofa while she went to sort him, and in the end, all that had happened was she'd called Noah a fool, among other things, and let him come in, wrapping his bleeding hand in a bandage before pushing him back into the night. But after she closed the door, she'd spotted Dominic hiding behind it, trembling, standing guard with a steel saucepan he'd somehow dragged from the kitchen drawer. "I would have hit him for you, Mum," he'd told her with a fierce, frantic sincerity. And it had been all she could do not to laugh at her little knight, who she pulled playfully towards her and carried back to the sofa. "I wish he was dead," he'd said then. To which Simone hadn't known what to say, so had only looked at her brooding, intense son, who until then she'd imagined only adored his father, and wondered what else about him she didn't know.

This time, lying on the floor, there was no Dominic to pick her up. Jasmine had started to cry and for a moment she'd heard Dom's footsteps moving towards his sister's room, pausing at the door to the lounge where she was crumpled, but then, abruptly doubling back.

She knows that endeavour – the dodging of disaster. Though when she was a child her fight was to be seen more rather than less, her parents somehow blind and deaf, despite their esteemed qualifications to the contrary. Was she blind now to Dominic? She tried not to be. In fact, that's how the afternoon had first got out of hand, her trying to see him more clearly. He'd come home from school and thrown his bag on the floor and plonked himself straight in front of the television.

"Don't you have homework?" she'd asked.

Terry was already sat watching some kind of fringe-movements documentary that he'd saved and urged her to watch too. He'd relaxed into an easy unwinding since the bowl-smashing tension of the morning, and now with a beer in hand, he'd welcomed Dominic by passing it to him for a swig. They did this sometimes. Terry only ever allowed Dom a little, and only when he was in good humour, but sometimes this sharing of manliness led to a game of football, or a pleasant hour spent together in front of the TV, and so Simone didn't ordinarily mind it. Since the move to the new flat, however, she'd been mulling the possibility of restructuring things for Dominic, reinstating just a few of the rules that her own youth had been assembled upon, and she'd cast aside. It was after all her fault and not Dominic's that his youngest years had been so chaotic. So much was her fault. And still is. She knows this, and in case she forgets, Terry reminds her. But there was still time to put things right.

"Yeh," Dominic answered. "So?"

At this, Terry sniggered, and protected by his approval, Dominic kicked off his trainers and settled further into the sofa.

Simone stood in front of him. "Homework first," she insisted.

"Fuck off," said Dominic. He said this with blithe nonchalance, not aggression. It wasn't an unusual way for them to talk to each other, mother and son. They often cursed in jest, and she'd considered more than once over the years how inane the idea of sanitising language for children, when life itself was so dirty, especially for children. But now, in the face of her newly grown parenting ambitions, Dominic's words felt deflating.

"Don't you swear at me," she countered.

At this, Terry looked up from the television. Dominic did too, his face painted into confusion. Terry was less confused.

"What are you on?" he asked her. "He'll do it later if he wants."

"It's not optional," said Simone. "It's homework. He's gotta stop thinking it's a question of 'if he wants'."

"And where have all your fancy grades got you?" laughed Terry. "Jog on," he told her.

Perhaps, if she'd left it there, that would have been the end of it. She could have taken Jasmine off for a walk, or put the chips in the oven, or gone to the bedroom on her own for a smoke. But instead, she answered him.

"You're right," she said. "They should have got me a lot further. That's why I've got a job."

"Fuck off," Terry laughed again. But now Dominic was looking at her with a new expression. Was that perplexity she saw still around the edges, or admiration?

"I'm not joking, Tel. I've got a job at a gym down Camden. Just reception work for now, but you know, it's a start."

For a moment, Terry said nothing. He just sat and looked at her as though she was talking a foreign language, or had come home with a new haircut and he didn't recognise her for it. The pause was unsettling. Still, Simone stepped with an attempt at boldness into it.

"So, homework," she told Dominic.

Dominic looked first to Terry, and then back to her. Compared to Jasmine, Dominic always seemed so grown up to Simone; but in that brief moment, navigating the intensity of Terry's disdain and the determination of his mother, he looked painfully small.

"Fuck off," Terry exploded suddenly, with forced, loud laughter, slapping Dominic on the shoulder in an effort to make him join in. Dominic smiled awkwardly. Then to her, in quieter tones: "Are you undermining me? Are you trying to say something? Speak, woman."

"He's my son," she muttered.

Simultaneously, they both looked at Dominic, but it was too dangerous now for the child to move in either direction, and Simone knew it. She wished desperately that she could take it all back. Why on earth had she picked a fight? She really was a dense one, just like Terry told her. But it was too late to unravel. And just this one time, she didn't want Dominic to see her back down. Tension threaded itself around them and knotted tight. For what seemed like an unfathomably long time, nobody moved, nobody spoke, nobody did anything. Until, like an angel from heaven, Jasmine burst into tears, and Dominic leaped to pick her up. The two of them bustled away.

Terry continued to stare, almost as though he was daring Simone now, now they were alone, to keep looking back at him; but she didn't dare. She lowered her eyes and turned away, walking hurriedly to the kitchen area where she got out the chips and took a pizza from the fridge, and twenty minutes later served it up in front of the TV.

For the next three hours, Terry didn't say another word. He only looked at her, and looked at her. And then went out with a fistful of his father's money without saying or doing anything.

It was much later, when he was back from wherever he'd been to get a fix, and she was lying in bed in foolish sleep, that he woke her with a blow to her jaw, and then pulled her by the hair into the living room where he first berated her with all the words he hadn't come to earlier, then chose, with what she was sure was calculation, the sole wall that adjoined the new neighbours' house, to throw her against, again and again.

Veronica

When Sarah's husband arrived that Friday to collect Amelia, Veronica signalled for a word. She'd been watching him all week, an increasingly absorbing pastime, distracting her from competing thoughts of next door, and her ever empty stomach. Days earlier, she'd already mentioned that she was an old friend of his wife's. He'd smiled amiably at that, acknowledging that Sarah had indeed told him as much; but so far Sarah herself had replied to Veronica's dinner invitation only with apologies, and not yet provided an alternative date. Veronica had restrained herself from texting again, pretending not to feel the thump of rejection or the seed of resentment that planted, but when she glanced now at Sarah's hovering husband, and their perfect daughter, she felt a dark tension creep through her chest.

Now that she knew what she was looking for, Amelia Beckham was so very much like her mother. Veronica saw it in the way she double-wrapped her skinny legs around each other when sitting, and tucked her wild hair determinedly behind her ears. She saw it in the earnest way Amelia approached the reward chart on the wall at the front of the class, carefully making sure that each of the oval-shaped stickers next to her name were coloured gold. And she had seen it very specifically that afternoon, when Amelia flouted the playground code of not telling, and to the chagrin of her own best friends reported to Veronica that the small, unfortunately round boy who also had the lamentable habit of being a nose-picker, had been excluded from a game of chase and was crying behind the scooter shed. Amelia led Veronica to the spot and quite seriously gave an account of what had happened, before taking the boy by the hand and striding bravely back to the playground where she started her own game with him herself, handing Veronica the perfect excuse to corner her father.

It was a protracted procedure. Before they could talk, Veronica had to see all the other children out of the classroom. Parents arrived with scooters and snacks, and warnings of just a short visit to the school's adventure playground since a seeming array of ballet/piano/tennis/Mandarin teachers would be waiting. On behalf of the less advantaged children she'd years ago taught in Kenya, Veronica sometimes rolled her eyes at this; but then she remembered how unlucky she had often felt as a child, in the throes of such overt, material fortune, and she looked harder at the children who leaped onto, or unfolded themselves into, or reluctantly conceded to depart with their arriving carers. Veronica reproached the parents who sent nannies in their stead. Silently of course, and in spite of identifying herself as a career woman, but Lack had a way of hardening judgment. Without intention, every day, she spent countless minutes imagining how, if she had a child of her own, like these, like Amelia, she would cling to every moment possible, and stuff the Mandarin, she would play with them and create with them and tell them a million times a day how very wanted they were. Sometimes, into these ponderings would seep a toxic feeling of injustice: how unfair it was that parents like some of these, like her own, were gifted with children they rarely seemed to desire; how unfair that the dreadful man who lived next door was able to spawn a baby whose cries he wilfully ignored and she had to listen to each night, in mockery; how unfair that her childhood friend, the same age as herself, had been granted not one but two children already.

Amelia and her father, David, greeted each other every day with the same not-so-secret secret exchange: a thumbs up, followed by a wink of the left eye, and then when they were within touching distance, a hug that lifted Amelia's feet clear off the ground. David was not arrestingly handsome in the way that George was. He was of average height, not skinny but certainly not fashioned from an athletic mould. His dark hair was just beginning to grey, but it flopped across his brow in a pleasing, comfortable fashion, and beneath a pair of tortoiseshell glasses, his eyes were soft and warm, if not striking. He wore jeans and t-shirts, either unconcerned or oblivious to both the other fathers in their city suits, and the mothers who regarded him with territorial friendliness. Usually he had the little boy, Amelia's brother, strapped into a sling on his chest.

"Mr Beckham, thank you for waiting. Just a very quick chat."

David leaned over to deliver another kiss to Amelia's forehead before she ran off to the playground, then he entered the classroom, perching easily on one of the tables and with another kiss, this time to the cheek of his son, let the little boy down from the sling. "So how's the first week?" he asked Veronica warmly. "You've survived I see."

"Just," she laughed, distracted by the tenderness of the man's interaction with his children, and remembering abruptly how Sarah's parents had smothered Sarah in similar affection, declaring their love every time one of them left the room: "Love you" "Love you". She recalled how alien that had felt to her back then, and how she'd wondered if it was a Jewish thing, and thought about converting. She shook herself. "Actually, with the help of your daughter."

"Oh?"

David looked to her expectantly, but instead of offering an explanation, suddenly, with ridiculous belatedness, it dawned on Veronica that this was a totally unnecessary conversation. She had already held an extra Carpet Time with the children to talk about inclusion. The boy at the centre of the incident seemed unscathed. And obviously, it was his parents, if anybody's, that she should have spoken with. Why had she wanted this meeting with David?

David smiled patiently.

"So, actually it's not urgent," she laughed quickly. "Only I wanted to let you know that during lunch break today, Amelia stood up for another child who was being excluded. Amelia came to tell me about it, we sorted it out together, and what was so striking is that she really showed such maturity and empathy."

"Oh. Good. Well, that's nice to hear." David waited for a moment.

She should speak. What had she imagined she would say? Awkwardness spilled into the silence. David looked back to her.

"Was there... Sorry... is there something you'd like me to reinforce with Amelia at home?"

Veronica's arms felt awkward as she stood in front of him. Her legs too, itching horrendously. It was as though she'd forgotten how to stand normally, and now gangly, misshapen limbs made best attempts but fooled nobody. The idiocy of it maddened her. The unnecessary meeting. The weak unsteadiness. This wasn't her. The Veronica of old would have effortlessly manoeuvred this conversation into easy repartee, she would have had him eating out of her hand. The Veronica that Sarah had known would, at the very least, have faked confidence. Now, all she seemed able to do, was nothing. She listed her failings. So far that week she had: failed to get her own husband to desire her, failed to knock on the door of a woman who was possibly in danger or alert any authority to it, failed to talk comfortably to an eleven-year-old boy, and now she couldn't even speak to a parent with elegance. "I was just touched by it," she hurried. "And I've been trying to find a moment to chat to each parent this week, and I thought it something that you, and Sarah of course, would like to know.

How is Sarah?" Veronica listened to her stream of seemingly rambling inquiries as though it wasn't her speaking them, as though she was only just now, impartially, observing the direction the conversation was about to take. But as she listened it dawned on her: of course there had been a reason for the meeting, of course, and of course it had never been about Amelia.

"Oh," said David. "Okay. Well thank you, yes, it's always nice to hear good things." His little boy toddled back over to him and David bounced him on his foot. "Sarah's, fine. Busy as ever."

"We're trying to arrange a dinner; did she tell you?" Veronica pressed with a little more ease. "For some non-school-oriented conversation. It's been such a long time. I think she just needed to check your schedule actually. Do you have your diary on you?"

David lifted his son into his arms, planting another kiss onto his squidgy cheek, and took his phone out of his pocket. "Oh, she didn't mention. But sure."

Veronica went to her handbag for her own phone. "Sorry, I hope it's not inappropriate to do this at school. It's just that I know Sarah's always at work so it's easier when we're both right here, isn't it? How's next Tuesday? Or Friday? Come to ours."

"Thursday's good," said David, naively, typing the arrangement into his phone.

As he typed, Veronica felt her spine straightening. "Lovely," she smiled. And inhaled deeply. Breath came tinged with June humidity, warmth lapping with giggles from the playground. Balmy air tickled her nostrils. Suddenly, however, all Veronica could smell, was February.

One February in particular. It cleaved like fresh wallpaper, giving off that new room aroma, cleaning the space where it sat in her memory with immaculate, unsullied lines. She was nine. Veronica's father was between postings – after Holland, before Belgium. She was 'between' too; transferring after half term to the alternative primary school in Brussels. In the meantime, they had taken a chalet with another family in the Swiss Alps. There were two children: one, a boy a year younger than herself, and his sister four years older. Having never had but always longed for siblings, Veronica responded to the admiration of the younger and the sophistication of the older with equal pleasure, and she spent the next weeks locked in the fantasy of an extended family who lived in a cabin on a snow-coated mountainside, and whose parents never worked but guided them off-piste and made them hot chocolate, and were still there in the evening when the lights were out and their wine-tipped voices reverberated pleasantly through the wooden rooms, and lulled her to sleep.

In the intervening twenty-odd years, there had been only two other periods in which she'd felt the same illusive contentment of that February. Not to say that she hadn't felt joy; there had been plenty of moments that had thrilled and pleased and satisfied. But those emotions bounced around unchained and unreliable, drifting off at their whim, and very often they were accompanied by other feelings: desire, hollowness, longing, envy. What Veronica identified aged nine that February was different: a sense of everything being just, perfectly, enough.

The longest and most significant of the two other occasions, was during her first few years with George. They had met in Nairobi where for almost a year she had been teaching in a neighbourhood school. George was there for just a few days as part of a more expansive Kenyan safari, but one evening they'd found themselves entangled in wine and debate at a party thrown by a mutual expat friend named Hugo. Hugo was not only a colleague at the school where Veronica taught, but he was the reason she taught there, or taught at all. Like George, she had begun her own journey in Kenya on a holiday – a one-month break from her job in celebrity PR, a role at which she was exceedingly good, and most days left her with the same conviction she had harboured throughout her childhood – that something was stubbornly, relentlessly, missing. Hugo was joking really when he suggested she try teaching. But when Veronica visited the school in one of Nairobi's slums, when she met the children, and saw the look on Hugo's face when he interacted with them, she knew immediately that that was it, that candid joy – she wanted that delight for herself. And so she began to teach.

If it hadn't been for meeting George, she probably would never have left Kenya. She thought about that sometimes, more lately, and wondered if she'd made the right choice. But when George had looked at her that first night, he seemed to see her, to know her. And after he extended his trip and they spent almost two weeks together under the sticky Kenyan sun, she found that she still both wanted him and felt wanted by him, yet, astonishingly, was not in control of him, nor controlled by him, and thus, in possession of such rare, mythical grounding and balance, agreed to follow him home.

There ensued the search for a flat they could share; the greedy immersion into each other's circles of friends; and they spent long hours dissecting their childhoods with an honesty that startled and thrilled them, measuring their own experiences against the other, both finding providence in moments of symmetry. Throughout this sustained flurry of early exploration, then later commitment, engagement, marriage, Veronica knew that things with George were different from any relationship she'd had previously. She felt not so much his presence, but, simply, an unaccustomed lack of lack. As though he was the illusive piece that had always been missing.

It lasted a long time really, those years of contentment. Three, almost four years. Until slowly, gradually, the old sense of absence crept in again, and George felt it too, and they realised that what they lacked now, was a baby.

The only other occasion in which Veronica could remember

feeling this way was the summer before Oman, before Kent, when she spent three weeks living in Sarah's house, enjoying Sarah's family, and forgetting that she wasn't, in fact, Sarah.

"Lovely," she smiled again to David.

Sarah

The text from David arrived just as Sarah reached her parents' house: *Dinner with Veronica next Thu. 8pm. See you after your session x*

And just like that, all the calmness and clarity that she had spent the last hour assembling with her counsellor, dissolved into a dry mouth, shortness of breath, and heaving nausea. Telling her mother that she needed some air, Sarah threw open the back door, and without intention, found herself here, at the bottom of the garden.

The pool house that had existed twenty-two years earlier was now a dilapidated shed, but in truth, 'pool house' had always been a flattering fancy. Even back then, 'in its heyday', as her mother would say, the wooden slats of roof were regularly commandeered by nesting birds, the banister that enclosed a token deck dripped some kind of sticky substance which nobody could identify, and the three tiny rooms inside were never decorated with anything beyond a fridge. There were a few summers when Sarah's mother 'rolled up her sleeves' and 'got in gear' and spent a day cleaning and clearing and fighting with cobwebs. Then she would bang the lounger cushions until most of the gunk from the previous summer had landed in the bushes, and fill the fridge with Cherry Coke and white chocolate Magnums, and stock the changing room with spare towels, declaring the pool house open. But then inevitably, being England and being June, it would rain for three weeks solid, and by the time they actually spent an afternoon swimming, the cushions would be sodden, and persistent spiders would have re-spun their webs, and the towels would somehow have developed a stale, slightly rotten odour. In the end, they dashed with dripping costumes inside the main area to grab ice creams from the fridge, and sometimes remembered to put their wet goggles and floats into the changing room, and didn't even enter the third space at the back. None of them could quite say what that room was for anyway. It had the idea of bunk beds, except that the 'beds' were hard slats of painted wood, and there was no ladder to the top one, and there was only one miniscule window, not even big enough to climb through, and an inadequate single light bulb, and the door that led from the changing room sometimes got stuck.

It was Veronica who decided that this would be their chatting place. The Chatting Room. TCR, she called it. Whispered to Sarah, depending on her mood, either as a question or a command.

Sarah had been part dreading and part looking forward to Veronica's visit. It had been 'in the diary' for months, requested by the girls but arranged painstakingly by their parents. Veronica's father worked for the UN and that summer he was needed – so they were needed – for six weeks in Oman. Veronica had pleaded with her mother to stay, but the most her mother would agree to was a week with Veronica's grandmother, and two weeks at camp. That left three long weeks unaccounted for. So they had concocted this scheme. "It's really a lot of hassle you know," Sarah's mother had said to her after one logistics phone call with Veronica's mother. "And Veronica is used, I think, to a fair bit more… space, and… stuff. Are you sure you're not going to get fed up with each other after a day?"

"She's my best friend," Sarah had answered, in the superior tone specifically endowed to twelve-year-old girls.

Eliza, sitting in the corner of the lounge engrossed in a Sweet Valley High *book, rolled her eyes. She did this frequently of late. She'd 'started' four weeks before her thirteenth birthday and since then seemed to think she was above everything, or at least everything to do with her younger sister. As though a knowledge of sanitary pads demarcated adulthood.*

"And Eliza's tedious these days," Sarah added for good measure. "Veronica will actually do something with her life more adventurous than reading books we could have managed when we were six."

Eliza rolled her eyes again.

"Oh, no comeback?" Sarah goaded.

Eliza didn't even look up from her page.

It was true: as desperately as Sarah longed for her sister to delight in the games they'd once conspired in, she would these days have more fun with Veronica. But all this was before they'd broken up.

It was terrible timing, two days before the holidays. They'd been 'in a two' all term. The previous term there'd been talk about joining up with Jenny and Nicole to form a four, but Veronica didn't like Nicole since she'd stolen her box of ink cartridges, so in the end they'd stayed as they were. Until Lisa Markozy's sleepover.

There was always a danger with sleepovers that if you didn't attend, everyone else would bitch about you, and come Monday you'd find that the whole social order of life had been rearranged. This is exactly what happened to Sarah, who had been at Grandma Sadie's seventy-fifth birthday in Dorset, and not the sleepover, when Veronica had started sucking up to Beth.

Usually, they both considered Beth to be just a little too close to slaggy. All of the girls talked about what they had done with boys – snogging and laying on top of them and such; but nobody had really done any of that. Beth, on the other hand, had a real boyfriend she had not only 'got off with', but had let 'touch her up'. She'd already 'started', the first one in their class, and had pert apple-sized boobs that needed a real bra where the rest of them still had uneven chicken nuggets. So that was why Beth's boyfriend had wanted to touch her; but Sarah and Veronica had agreed that Beth should not have said yes.

It was Lisa Markozy herself who told Sarah about Beth and Veronica. Apparently, it started while they were still eating pizza and playing truth or dare. Beth had spun the Coke bottle and it had landed on Veronica, who had chosen Truth. Beth's question had been the following (Lisa recounted it word for word): "Do you sometimes wish that Sarah wasn't a bit sad? And do you think she holds you back?" 'Sad' did not mean unhappy; it was their lingo for somebody who was a loser, not necessarily geeky but definitely socially stunted, too childish, not cool. On the cusp of puberty and teenage-dom, it was the biggest insult they could throw at each other. Of course, Veronica was caught. She could hardly say that Sarah wasn't holding her back, because that would make her sad too, and Beth had cleverly elevated her as something different and better. But, "She should have told Beth to stop being a bitch," Lisa declared. Instead, Veronica had confirmed Beth's suspicions that Sarah was indeed the reason for her own curtailed coolness, and later they'd pulled their sleeping bags next to each other and whispered into the early hours. The next day, everybody somehow knew that Sarah's uncle had tried once to kill himself – which was something she had told only Veronica – and also that Sarah wished she had bigger boobs.

In English on Monday, Sarah had sent Veronica a note to say that she should consider their friendship terminated, but Veronica had already been sitting next to Beth by then and showed her the note, and laughed. So it was definitely over, and that lunch break they gathered their friends by the lockers and announced together that they were broken up. There was general shock. Sarah and Veronica had been a two since, well, forever. It had been almost an entire year since they'd joined the school and their names ran into each other when people spoke. Saranveronica. Saranveronica. It had always slightly gratified Sarah and irritated Veronica that Sarah's name came first.

But no longer. And unless she wanted to 'swallow her pride' and confess to her mother that worse than growing fed up with each other after a day, they were already not speaking – in other words, that Sarah was wrong and her mother had been right – there was no way she could tell anyone at home what had happened. Had Eliza not been entirely obsessed by her own life, then it was possible that even without being told, her sister may have guessed that something was up, and fixed it; but she didn't. So Sarah awaited the arrival of her ex-best friend seven days into the summer holidays, freezing every time the phone rang, trepidatious both that it was and wasn't Veronica's mother calling to cancel. The call, however, never came and Veronica arrived, as planned, in time for lunch that Friday.

While the mothers were having tea in the kitchen, the girls, unspeaking, heaved Veronica's suitcase up the stairs to Sarah's room. A second bed had been pulled out of the spare room and Veronica sat on it, staring at her feet. Sarah sat opposite her, waiting. There was no reason that she should be the one to cave and speak first, she was on home ground. She folded her arms and crossed her skinny legs twice around themselves.

At least three minutes slowly ticked by before Veronica started to giggle. "You idiot, you look like a pretzel," she laughed, slapping Sarah's leg playfully. "You're such a doofus."

"Too sad for you?" Sarah prickled. She lifted her legs away from Veronica up onto her bed.

"Oh Sawah, you know I didn't mean it," Veronica soothed *in a sing-song baby voice. "I'm so-wee. You know I don't think you're sad."*

"Stop doing the voice," Sarah admonished, *though she knew Veronica was aware that she found it hilarious, especially when she did it to teachers. "If you don't think I'm sad, then why did you—"*

But Veronica had now leapt onto Sarah's bed and was nuzzling her face into her shoulder. "Sa-wah, don't be cwoss Sa-wah…"

And it was difficult and not entirely practical to keep the argument going.

She supposed she could 'forgive but don't forget'. (There were a number of phrases like this that Sarah's mother had doctored, unintentionally, and passed on in their distorted state to her daughter.)

"I'm so-wee Sa-wah. You're my BFF Sawah. Sawah—"

"Oh fine," said Sarah, *pushing Veronica away, though struggling to remain aloof amidst the infectiousness of her affection. "Fine."*

Veronica grinned then, kissing her smack on the cheek. And Sarah could not help but bask in her enthusiasm, and feel glad that Veronica was here for three whole weeks.

And so their days at the swimming pool began. Punctuated by games of swing-ball in the garden, and trips to the tennis club, and occasional dinners out. One night, after a dinner at TGI Fridays, Veronica arrived back home bursting with excitement, and even after an hour making up a dance routine to Bon Jovi's 'Always', and after an 'extension' downstairs so they could watch a 15 rated video, she was incapable of calming down. Even an hour later, after Sarah's mother had been in twice to tell them to go to sleep, and Eliza had screamed at them from across the corridor, Veronica still kept leaping out of bed to tickle Sarah's feet or chuck something across the room at her, and in the end Sarah herself went past sleepy, and they sat together on her bed, listing in reverse order first the prettiest girls in their year, then the cleverest, then the ones most likely to get off with somebody first, until they ran out of ideas for lists and Veronica suggested a midnight swim.

Sarah's parents' home sat in its semi-detached plot of suburban greenery, with open windows and unbolted doors. A gleaming 'top-of-the-range' alarm system had been fitted a year or two earlier, but since the dog was likely to set it off in the middle of the night, it remained gleaming and unset.

Saranveronica slipped quietly out of the lounge door and padded gleefully across scorched, crunchy grass, down the steps to the sunken pool area. It was still warm, with just the faint chill of night-time. They were already in their costumes – Sarah's a multicoloured two-piece with a frill around the knickers; Veronica's a matching neon pink version. They hadn't dared open the linen cupboard in case of a squeak, so carried damp towels that they'd used earlier, and made a great show of stuffing them over their mouths to stifle their laughter. If anybody was looking, the far right corner of the pool could be seen clearly from Sarah's parents' bedroom, but the rest of it was shielded from sight and together they darted through the dark, down the steps, and to the pool house. As suspected, the key had been left in the lock, and Sarah swiftly turned it, allowing them to fall into the changing room and right through to the room at the back before releasing their guffaws against the closed door and wooden walls and tiny window. The single light bulb illuminated a moth that seemed to flutter on the rise and fall of their sniggers.

"Come on then," Veronica said eventually, when their laughter had at last died down, and she opened the door to

the changing room where she unlatched the cupboard that housed the switch for the pool cover.

"You know, my parents will go mad if they catch us," Sarah warned, a grain of sense for a moment interrupting the adventure. She was blighted by this always, unable to resist the great family sentiments of responsibility and right. "We're not allowed down here without them knowing. Even in the day."

"It's not dangerous," Veronica sighed, hand on hip.

"I know. But they don't like it. And they might see the cover moving when it gets to the deep end."

"It's dark."

"Yeah but the movement and stuff…"

"So let's only open it halfway."

To this Sarah had no response, so stood aside, tension curling her bare toes, while Veronica carefully held down the switch until the cover had retreated halfway up the shadowy water.

The swim was short-lived. Although the water was heated, in the night air their teeth quickly chattered. And though it was thrilling to dive down, lost in the darkness of liquid abyss, they found themselves to be suddenly alert to every rustle of leaf and squawk of bird and floating piece of garden debris. The adventure, however, was not a failure, Veronica made sure of that, despite their premature return to the pool house. Instead of swimming, she coined The Chatting Room and made such a production of it that quickly this seemed the real objective of their night-time sojourn, and not the fleeting frolic in the water.

"This room will be for serious chatting only," she stated, wrapped in her damp towel, the two of them shivering and huddled with bent knees on the bottom bunk. "Things we wouldn't usually talk about. Or that we don't want other people to hear."

"Okay," said Sarah. "Like what?"

"Like, what we really think about people. Or, about each

other. Or things about our families, or just things we think, but stuff we wouldn't tell other people."

"O-kayyy," Sarah repeated. "Like what?"

"Like... I don't know."

"It's your idea."

"Forget it," Veronica decided with a nonchalant flap of her hand. She stood up and with the towel still draped over her, wriggled out of her wet costume. With her foot, she flicked it up to her hand and hung it on the top bunk, the drips splashing on the floor between them. Veronica clicked her toes against the floor. "Okay, I've got a different idea."

"Okay."

"Okay, so we'll come down here every night. And each of us has to think of one really hard, really embarrassing question, something we wouldn't usually ask, and the other one either has to answer it, or do a dare. But it has to be a really hard dare, harder than the question."

"Okay."

"Okay, you start," said Veronica, pulling her scrunchie out of her fair hair and tugging knots between her fingers.

"I haven't had time to think of anything good," Sarah answered, untying her own ponytail and sucking on the chlorinated end.

"Fine, well then tonight let's just do dares," Veronica grinned. "You go first." She abandoned her knots and pulled her towel closer around herself, looking at Sarah with an air of excited defiance. "But it has to be hard."

"Okay," said Sarah. "Okay..."

More clicking of Veronica's toes punctuated ticking seconds. "Come on," she sighed.

"Okay. Okay, I dare you... to go outside on your own, and stand on the deck for thirty seconds—"

"Hard, Sarah," Veronica admonished.

"Naked," finished Sarah. "And you have to leave your towel inside." She giggled. "And you have to do thirty seconds of our Bon Jovi dance."

Now Veronica giggled too. "Aw, really?"

"Yep. That's the dare," Sarah nodded. "Off you go."

Veronica held her towel tight to her chest, but stood up. Together they opened the TCR door and trod carefully through the changing room. Veronica opened the door to outside and put one foot on the deck.

"You have to leave the towel inside," Sarah reminded her.

Veronica sighed dramatically, but nodded assent. "Leave the door open," she ordered. And in an instant, she had thrown her towel at Sarah's feet, leapt into the darkness and begun shimmying across the deck to the silent Bon Jovi beat.

Sarah bent double with laughter. Flashes of white limbs darted past the doorframe. In and out of shadows Veronica's bareness moved. From the darkness, Sarah heard Veronica stub her toe. She looked at her waterproof watch. "Ten more seconds!" she called between giggles. She saw Veronica crouch down in the move she knew preceded the cartwheel into the chorus. Legs flailed. And, all of a sudden, Sarah felt a strange guilt, and pleasure, in watching. The next moment, Veronica was in the doorway, hands dramatically covering her privates, grabbing her towel from the floor. "Your turn," she grinned.

The tightening in Sarah's stomach caught her by surprise, but she didn't show it to Veronica. "Go on then," she challenged. "What do I have to do?"

Veronica turned towards the pool, mulling slowly. "You have to go back in," she declared after a while. "And you have to go under the cover, all the way to the end—"

"It's pitch-black," Sarah interrupted.

"I'm not finished. We're going to put the underwater light on—"

"Someone will see."

"They won't. You have to touch the end, then swim back and do a handstand in the water. And you have to be naked and leave your towel here."

"That's so much worse than yours," Sarah complained.

"Not my fault. You could have said anything."

Sarah shook her head disapprovingly, but there was a knot of excitement in her chest and she already knew that she was going to do it. "Put the light on then," she said.

Sarah's phone beeped again, snapping her out of her reverie. David: *Hope session good. Love you x*

Sarah smiled, but she didn't reply, the nausea persisting.

It had been years since she had thought about Veronica. When she'd seen her at Amelia's school that Monday, despite over a decade cultivating the kind of composure that saw her dubbed one of the UK's fastest rising barristers, she was wholly unprepared for the jolt, and for the entire drive home, she hadn't heard a thing that Amelia had said to her. Every day since, she had found her mind going back to that moment – seeing Veronica – and thinking about how David was having lots of such moments, seeing Veronica, and engaging in private conversations with her. And now, agreeing to dinner.

If it had been possible, Sarah would have called Eliza when she received that piece of news – she the only person Sarah had made privy to that summer's escapades. As it was, she was here.

She would go in soon and spend a bit of time with her parents before the dreaded train journey back into town. Her mother had barely had a chance to tell her how pale and tired and too thin she appeared, and thus far she'd only waved at her father. He was, as usual, in his vegetable patch on the front lawn. He'd only come to this in his latter years, but approached the agronomy of garlic, peppers and other spiced fare, with a childish gusto and equally ingenuous awe in discovery. Sarah suspected that occasionally their green-fingered next-door neighbour re-did some of his planting, but she didn't mention this to her father, because of course the harvest and not the process was the point of the thing for him, the successful creation and resurrection of life from stillness. They all mourned Eliza differently.

Her mother's strategy was busyness, embracing this with the kind of inexorable energy that made others tired from watching. She doubled her client list, concocting all the homeopathic remedies she had professed throughout her career, but now brought her none of the relief she had avowed, except in the time it took to create them and thus not spend thinking about her eldest daughter.

Sarah could not even begin to pretend that she herself was coping. She had at first combined both of her parents' strategies: she instructed her clerks to approve more and more requests for representation; and she threw herself into the nurture of newness in the form of Amelia and Harry. But nothing was able to fill or distract her from the half of herself that had once contained her sister. Everything felt empty now. The past as well as the future. It was as though every memory was suddenly spliced in half, the parts that remained with her throbbing for those missing. How could she teach Amelia to skip rope without Eliza's voice chanting the rhymes with her? How could she speak at a university alumnae event without remembering the way Eliza had leapt squealing from her bed the morning that Sarah had received her offer letter from Cambridge? How could she do anything without her greatest confidante, cheerleader, exemplar? Eliza had been there for everything. She had known everything. She had known Sarah. And in Eliza's knowing, Sarah had known herself.

In the end, the only strategy that made a dent in Sarah's devastation was collection. From the Latin *colligere* – not necessarily accumulation, but gathering together. In the twenty months that had passed since the accident, Sarah had spent hour after hour at their childhood home, collecting. David worried. He viewed it as a kind of atonement, a self-imposed penitence – it had after all been Sarah's train that Eliza had been driving out of her way to meet, because Sarah was too petrified of the just-around-the-corner tube. Too nauseous to face it. Sarah's mother suggested this hypothesis too and told her not to blame herself. Her father agreed. It was for them that she had finally conceded to a counsellor. But it made no difference. Methodically, Sarah collected pieces of her sister: the kitchen table, where Eliza had sat in pigtails, then with strands of blonde bleached into darkness; the shared bathroom where they had compared suntans and the evolving size of their breasts; the old TV on which they had watched *Dirty Dancing* on repeat; the tennis rackets that had once been bright and shiny and instrumental for their doubles triumphs; the closet that housed the coats they 'borrowed' from each other without asking; the swing-seat out front where they'd resolved a thousand tiny quarrels; the bedroom Eliza had presided over and where Sarah had sat, listening to tales of playground foes, and revision notes, and first kisses, and boyfriends, and ambitions, and plans. After the accident, people had remarked that the saving grace of the tragedy was that Eliza had not yet married, she had not left young children behind. But children may have borne Eliza's blue eyes, or her infectious smile, or at least her blood and her genes, and even in glimpses and flashes Sarah may have had a way then to see her sister again. As it was, there was nothing but inanimate objects for her to collect. And memories. Like the summer at the pool house, when Eliza had buried herself in books and hormones and thoughts that Sarah wasn't yet privy to, and Sarah had swum naked with Veronica.

Sarah ran her fingers over the flaking wood of the pool house door and considered how, despite the intangible sense of foreboding that the sight of Veronica incited, perhaps her reappearance was fateful. Perhaps it was significant that after all these years, now was when she materialised. Perhaps she was part of Eliza's story too. Perhaps she was supposed to be a part of Sarah's collection.

Veronica

At the top of the high street, between an expensive children's boutique and a café that served tea in floral pots with hand-knitted cosies, stood Veronica's most recent Primrose discovery: a convenience store that stocked everything from American graham crackers, to Chinese ready-meals, to proper deli-standard chunks of brie. The place had a bohemian quirkiness, and she always managed to find something there that she hadn't even thought of needing. Besides, it padded the time between finishing school, and going home.

She should of course have been rushing there. After her conversation with David, she'd made it out of school well before 4pm, and she could have been dashing in glorious pleasure to the new house with the perfectly designed kitchen, and the duck feather-filled sofa; their city haven. But at this time of day George wasn't yet home, and the neighbours were.

The noise hadn't abated. Not in five days. Music and television blared through the walls, the man's voice often accompanying it in obnoxious, yobbish tenor, and after George's appeal to them, the fact of this felt like a deliberate two fingers up. When she was on her own, there was an intimidating flavour to this, even behind brick, and often Veronica found herself thinking about how very much worse it might be on the other side of the wall. Veronica hadn't mentioned her unease to George. She didn't want to burden him with another thing he would be unable to fix. But she couldn't fix it either, not the neighbours and not the way she felt. More than anything, she dreaded the sound of the baby.

Veronica was standing in the snacks aisle contemplating this, as well as what she would prepare for the dinner party with Sarah, when the boy, Dominic, walked in. He didn't see her. Hands in his pockets, he paced purposefully towards the counter where the lady serving was busily talking to a French customer about a spate of bicycle thefts. As he joined the queue, Dominic's narrow eyes darted around the shop. Veronica wondered if he had been home from school yet, or if he, like she, was avoiding the inevitable. She wondered too, for the millionth time, why since the night of the thuds, she had still not seen, or heard, his mother. Every morning that week, she'd asked herself if she should be doing something, telling someone. Over the years, it was a question she'd asked more than once before. But she still hadn't managed an answer. Her week had been consumed: by her new job, by the surprise of her encounter with Sarah, by George, by Amelia, and by the usual, empty-belly longing. Besides, it wasn't her business, she'd told herself.

Veronica took a step forward. Joining the queue behind Dominic, she tapped him lightly on the shoulder. "Hello there."

The boy looked up jumpily, and at the sight of her he sunk his hands further into his pockets, shifting his weight from foot to foot. Just like the first time they'd met, Veronica couldn't help picturing a meerkat, or a squirrel, something feral and angst-ridden – ready at a moment's notice to leap in any direction, at once timid and threatening. "Hi," he muttered.

"What are you after then?"

"Nothing," he shrugged. "Just something for my mum."

Veronica noticed the boy's lack of basket. "That's nice of you." The queue moved forward a little and Veronica and Dominic shuffled their feet accordingly. "Is she okay, your mum? I haven't seen her for a few days."

Squirrel-eyed, Dominic glanced up warily. "Yeah, she's fine."

82

"Really?"

There followed a split second in which understanding suggested itself. The boy's expression changed, staring at her quizzically (gratefully?), and Veronica wondered if 'fine' might be about to be qualified, if her concerns might be confirmed. She held her breath. But the next second Dominic turned away with a muttered, "Yeah, 'course". And, surprising herself, Veronica audibly exhaled.

The relief was unexpected but it came with a surge of validation. They'd been right not to do more. The woman was fine, her son had said so. And here he was, picking something up for her, looking after her. They must be close. Veronica instantly romanticised an idea about an unbreakable bond between them – in the face of adversity, mother and son, always having each other. Once authorities get involved in domestics, who knows what could happen to that. Yes, she and George had been right not to interfere.

"And your dad?" Veronica continued, much more breezily.

"He's not my dad."

"Sorry, yes, you did tell me that. Where is your dad?"

It was an entirely inappropriate question. Veronica hardly knew this boy, only what she had heard through the wall, only what she had judged from the doorstep; but on the gentle gust of relief, she felt suddenly an irresistible compulsion to probe further, to help him.

This feeling was not unique to Dominic. It had been a pattern of Veronica's throughout her life, a conscious strategy even: digging, embroiling, analysing, fixing. Her first 'project' had been a girl at school who suffered night terrors. Then at university there was a devout Christian girl who needed help coming out to her parents. Dominic was merely another. It wasn't altruism. Veronica knew this. The reason was far more self-serving: it was simply easier to fix others than to acknowledge fractures of her own. But the motive was irrelevant. The result was good, helpful. Besides, it worked. It distracted her from herself. It gave her that crucial sense of control and confidence, just enough to stop her, untethered in her own life, from spinning out of reach.

She was untethered now. Each morning that week, she had felt the seeds of resentment taking firmer root, and she was barely able to look at Amelia – the manifestation of everything she didn't have. She longed to tear something down. Longed for it. She could feel that longing rising, self-sabotaging and untameable. But, here was Dominic. Offering her a chance at distraction.

"My dad's not around," answered Dominic, looking at Veronica now with something between curiosity and suspicion. "He died when I was four."

"Oh, I'm sorry."

"S'okay. I did it."

"What?"

Dominic had now reached the front of the queue and he didn't answer. Instead she noticed him lower his voice a little as he asked the lady at the counter for Rizla papers. The lady lifted an eyebrow. "Are you eighteen?" she asked him loudly, looking downwards at his scrawny frame.

"It's only the papers, not tobacco," he answered with surprising boldness. "Where I usually go, they never care. You don't have to be eighteen for the papers."

"What are you going to do with the papers?" pressed the lady. "Wallpaper your room?" A woman further back in the queue supressed a chuckle, but Veronica felt a stab of sympathy for the boy.

"They're for my mum," said Dominic. The back of his neck had flushed red.

"Then better for her to buy them herself," replied the lady. "Sorry, but I have a duty of care."

Veronica noticed Dominic floundering, his feet moving, his fists clenching, and she was about to offer to purchase the papers for him, when, "Fucking stupid," he declared, loud enough this time for everybody to hear.

The lady didn't know what to say. She opened her mouth to

respond, then closed it again, and by the time she'd formulated a rebuttal, Dominic was long gone, slamming the door as he stormed out of the shop.

In the company of reliable Primrose Hill sympathisers, the lady now put away her reproach and smiled with incredulity at Veronica. "As if it's really for his mum," she said. Her head shook gently in a tilted, slow movement, as though to convey her sadness about the state of the world, or at least its youth. "What mother would actually send her child to buy cigarette papers?"

Veronica agreed, adding the woman next door to her list of mothers who, despite their own suffering, did not deserve the gift of a child.

Simone

Terry is all smiles. Simone watches from the window as, in the summer sun, he returns from an afternoon at the pub and stumbles pleasantly into the flat. Dominic is already home with her papers and is actually doing his homework on the living room table. Terry slaps his head in jovial greeting before throwing Jasmine into the air and settling onto the sofa with her on his lap. He turns the TV up to high volume. It has been gently playing *Peppa Pig* for Jasmine but now erupts with the vicious arguments of a panel show – something about trade unions that Simone can't follow but the people on the TV, and Terry, seem impassioned by. The noise is deafening. Simone leans back against the window. She is smoking a joint. Ordinarily she'll only have one a day, usually in the evening, but this is already her second. Through the roar of the TV, Dominic pushes his homework angrily into a pile and looks over to her, waiting for her to say something, to do something. With what she hopes is sympathy, she returns his stare, but remains in her pleasant fog.

There's a sheet of 20th Century poems on the top of Dominic's pile. He used to make up poems, trying to set them to self-taught chords on the guitar that was once his father's. The instrument smelled of wood and smoke and something else indiscernible that still conjured him, and Simone used to watch Dominic breathing that in, savouring the man he surely couldn't remember, caressing the strings he couldn't really play. Until Terry sold it one day for a tenner.

Dominic's exams are in a few weeks. It doesn't matter. He'll go to the local school, which is not a grammar, but no worse than the rest of them. Anyway, Terry was right – where did all her A grades get her? Dominic stands from the table with clear contempt – for her, for him – but shuts the door to his bedroom quietly. Even in temper he will not slam it.

There never used to be punishments. Most of the time, when she was lucid, she and Dominic were mates. She never wanted to be the kind of aloof, lofty parent that thinks they know best, when life had proved so completely that they didn't. Occasionally, if Dominic happened to pick a moment when her head was pounding, and said something cheeky about one of her boyfriends, or joked about her making them late again, she would feel her mood hardening, and without meaning to she would round on him, and tell him he was a rude little brat with no respect. But still there were no punishments. Terry was the one who started on those. It was for Dominic's own good, he explained at the beginning. She'd been too soft, she'd let him do whatever he wanted, children didn't need that. And since by then it was clear she'd been doing everything wrong, she thought he was probably right. At first it was chores – doing the washing up, cleaning the bathroom. But later there were slaps around the head. Not hard at first, just enough to shock, they didn't leave a mark, a lasting indictment. Until once, Dominic fell sideways against a door and lost a tooth, and Simone found herself persuading Dominic that Terry didn't mean it, he didn't mean it, and concocting a story for his teacher. After that, frequently, there was a belt. Or a fist. And then occasionally, without warning, there were weird penalties that she could never understand, like the time Dominic had been painting a poster for a school project, and used the kitchen table without asking, and so Terry made him drink the muddy paint water. She remembers Dominic looking at her in bewilderment when

Terry had ordered him to do that, his face as clouded as the water; but she had only shrugged – helplessly, uselessly. She didn't get it either. And she said nothing.

Things have been better lately between Terry and Dominic – a fact that she can see makes her son's shoulders almost rigid with anticipation, because calm sometimes means that something is brewing. Increasingly over the past weeks, Terry has been talking, or preaching, sitting them all down for lectures: about the devious Tory government, or the history of class exploitation, the way the working classes are mollified, the way that bankers are still getting away with everything. He spends hours talking about the idiot poshos who live on their street, rubbing privilege in their faces. He quotes documentaries he's watched, and YouTube commentators, pulling together disparate ideas like a manic professor. And as Dominic listens, Simone watches him preparing, steeling himself, like the saucepan he once lifted. But the harder the steel, the harder it is for her to read him. Dominic is scared, she can see that. But there's something else too – anger, madness? Sometimes she wonders what her son is capable of.

Now, she wonders, if the TV was quieter, whether behind Dominic's closed door she might hear the sound of paper scratched by pen.

She will not knock. Her father taught her early on that knocking was not allowed, certainly not when he was working, his tiny study a place of reverence; but she would know he was there by the unceasing caress of that scratching sound. Lost in a haze of smoke and thought, she listens harder now for Dominic, until a few moments later, Terry's voice cuts in.

"Oy oy Dom," he shouts. "Fancy a kick around?"

Within seconds, the bedroom door flies open, homework and scratching pens abandoned, and Dominic returns to the living room with a ball under his arm. It is a prized possession, a match ball from a Chelsea game, won in a raffle. "Is Mum coming?" he asks.

Nobody has said anything, but Simone has still not left

the flat. The bruise by her mouth is fading but its placement atop her lip, and its particular shade of green-black, now renders it as unfortunate facial hair. She looks like her father. Dominic casts his eyes anxiously towards her. He feels guilty she thinks – for his pre-teen moods, for not looking after her, for not protecting her this time with a saucepan. She knows that she should tell him it wasn't his fault, that it's not his job to look after her. But it feels so good to be looked after by somebody.

"I'll come," she nods, and now a new expression flashes across Dominic's face – pleasure, relief, indifference? He is a strange one, her son; so hard to read.

Terry carries Jasmine on his shoulders and holds Simone's hand. Dominic dribbles the ball just ahead of them, looking back every now and then to smile, or maybe to check that she is smiling. If it wasn't for their clothes – which are neither chic nor authentically vintage enough – they could very nearly blend in with other Primrose families. There, descending the steps from a pink-fronted house is a pre-schooler and her father, holding a frisbee. On the other side of the road skips a nine or ten-year-old bedecked in full ballet regalia, the mother laden with bags behind her. Passing them in the other direction, holding the hands of twin sons, is a comedian Simone recognises from TV. Terry nudges her as he notices this too, and she nods with just the right amount of excitement and derision. Just before the park, they stop at the convenience store and Terry goes in for a pack of beers.

"For my lady," he pronounces as they settle onto a patch of green on the far slope of the hill.

She sits on the grass, hiking up her cargo trousers to reveal skinny white calves. Jasmine is in a summer dress and her skin shines luminous in the sunlight, a culmination of her parents' pasty complexions. It occurs to Simone that she has neglected sunscreen, but it's almost four-thirty and the walk back to the house is too long to return for it. Dominic's alright in a t-shirt and shorts, and his deeper complexion.

"Flashing the flesh," Terry says, raising his eyebrows teasingly at Simone's exposed legs, then nodding approvingly at the low cut of her vest top.

Simone grins responsively back at him, shaking her bare shoulders.

Terry flickers his eyebrows at her again and a knot of pleasure pulses through her, then he jogs a little way off with Dominic. "Nice one mate," he calls as Dominic kicks the ball in a solid straight line. "Now try this." He shows off some fancy footwork, then pats the ball back to Dominic who attempts to copy. Simone watches. Terry is handy at sports and his confidence stretches here – playing, displaying, inhabiting territory he knows well. As the ball travels back and forth between them, there is a broadening in Dominic's frame too, an almost touchable expansion of self. Simone sips on her beer. If only the whole world could be a football pitch, or a boxing ring. If only Dominic could live fenced safely within the edges. If only Terry could always know how capable he is, and not feel the need to prove it.

He slept on her couch for almost three weeks before they got together. Terry was twenty-four, fresh out of a relationship that had ended with the kind of drama that saw his clothes cut to shreds and his flat burnt to nothing, but he must have done worse to his ex since he never did anything about it, besides calling her a crazy bitch. Although Simone didn't know him properly, he was a friend of a friend, and somebody who, right from when she was first with Noah, she had noticed. They weren't in the same crowd back then and Noah didn't like him – Terry was part of a group where everybody was on drugs, hard ones, properly, and they were in and out of jail, and lacking in the aspirations that Noah and his cohort held up like the bible. But he was at parties sometimes. It wasn't so much his looks that took her, it was the intensity of the eyes, the lean boxing bravado, the tightly coiled energy, the attitude that told her and everybody else, that he knew the score, he had things sorted. Often, she had heard him talking about politics: the appropriation of power by the capitalists; the criminality of tax dodgers; the way that immigration was alright for Them with their Polish builders and Romanian cleaners, but they weren't the ones who ran out of school places and waited for months on the NHS. He'd been passionate and articulate, she'd noticed. Fiercely intelligent. Most of the time, she'd been too drunk or monged to follow the argument properly, but just hearing him talk lifted her eyes enough to see him. And the sheer fact of her noticing said a great deal, since with Noah's arm around her, it was rare for her to notice anyone.

When, years later, she heard that Terry needed a room, she without hesitation offered her sofa.

When he said he needed an alibi, she agreed to provide one.

When he turned on her in the street on the way to the courthouse, throwing her against the wall and pressing hard on her throat while he demanded she promise again that she would testify, she understood that he was scared, and vulnerable. And needed her.

After that, it seemed granted that he would see away boyfriends who weren't good enough, and instruct her on how to better keep charge of her six-year-old son, and take over the benefit money, and sort things. It was repayment. Thanks. When he moved himself into her bed one evening, it seemed inevitable. And she was glad. Glad not to have to think for a bit, not to have to decide, glad somebody else was so sure. Glad that this man who was passionate and athletic and political, and also damaged and in need, had chosen her.

As they walk home, hot, sweaty, drunk, Terry slips his hand into the back of her trousers. His fingers play at the top of her bum. She loops her own arm around his waist. Dominic holds Jasmine's shoulders. Every now and then he steers her away from the road, letting his sister carry his prized ball in front of her. Behind them, she and Terry sing. They are loud and people on the street look at them, an old lady even sticking her head out of her kitchen window to see. But Simone throws her head back. Let them look. None of them have this kind of passion. They prance around in their fancy yoga gear and drink their organic almond milk cappuccinos, but this is what they're all reaching for really – this, what she has: a family, and freedom, and a man erotic and besotted enough to need to feel her bum on the street.

Simone sings louder.

People judge, but they don't know.

Terry is intelligent. He sees their weaknesses.

He sees her. And he needs her.

Using a stick, he drums against neighbours' railings. He does this the entire length of their street. Until, as they reach their door, Veronica cycles towards them.

Her hair is shiny and perfect, despite the heat and the bike. As she dismounts, she waves to Simone, and Simone sees her visibly looking, taking in Terry, waiting for an introduction perhaps, but Terry averts his eyes. He has turned towards the door and is hastily finding his key. Not caring? Not daring? Simone follows suit. She doesn't look back, and the next instant, Dominic has Jasmine in his arms, and they are all inside, and Veronica is left, Simone supposes, still looking, while Simone and Terry begin again to sing.

Sarah

Sarah did not tell her counsellor about Veronica. It was only their third session. Besides, what would she tell? A feeling? A sense of trepidation? Perhaps if she could have predicted the way the summer would end, she'd have spilled out everything, but instead she spent that Thursday's session talking about pressures at work, and concerns for her parents, and only when gently, and then not so gently, pushed, Eliza. She stopped in after that at her parents', where she talked about the children, and their upcoming summer holiday, and then slipped off into Eliza's old room. It wasn't therefore until the over-ground journey back to West Hampstead, that she allowed herself to think about the dinner she'd been dreading, and was now only hours away. And how she would entice Veronica to add to her collection.

A warm summer rain splattered against the train's windows, regulating her shallow breaths. She concentrated on it hard. Drip, drip, drip.

It was already spitting when they woke up the morning after the midnight swim – late at ten o'clock. Sarah's mother had been 'up and at 'em' for hours, and Eliza, wrapped theatrically in a blanket at the breakfast table, had long finished her cereal, the remnants clinging like shrivelled leaves to the side of the bowl.

She lifted her eyes from her book when the two of them slunk sleepily in and begrudgingly said 'morning' when Veronica greeted her.

"What are you going to do today, Eliza?" Veronica asked, but at this extended interruption, Eliza rolled her eyes.

"Not go swimming," she answered.

"Not do anything probably," Sarah goaded.

"Get me a drink," Eliza said, as Sarah opened the door to the fridge.

"Get it yourself."

Eliza rolled her eyes again. "You're right there. You're such a little brat."

"You're such a bitch."

"Ugh," Eliza sighed with exaggerated condescension.

"Oh, that's an excellent use of the vernacular."

Eliza stood up, flicking her beautiful dark hair over her shoulder and picking up her book. "I'm having an 'evening-in' on Saturday," she announced. "There's gonna be ten of us, including the boys. So can you make plans to not be here, brat?"

"Like I really want to spend time with you anyway," Sarah called as Eliza swept out of the room. But her throat was gripped by a tight, constricting sensation, somewhere between rage and heartbreak. She and Eliza had always shared parties. Secrets. Lives. "She's such a bitch," Sarah said to Veronica.

"I know. She thinks she's amazing. She's not even that stunning. What a bitch."

Suddenly, Sarah rounded on her friend, her pulse loud in her throat. "Don't say that about my sister."

Heavily, Veronica put down her juice, but she didn't respond.

Aware of her hypocrisy, Sarah too said nothing more.

Quietly, they poured their cereal and sat staring out at the rain, the steady rhythm of water on pane ticking minutes away. Veronica moved the letter-shaped cereal flakes around her bowl.

Finally, after enough minutes had passed for the tension to ease, Sarah casually asked, "What shall we do today? Shall we try to get my mum to take us bowling or something?"

But they both already knew where they would spend their day. They had known it even before the rain had excluded outdoor things. And before Eliza had quashed the morning's sense of triumph and conspiracy. Veronica tapped her spoon meaningfully on her bowl. On the side of it she had collected three letters: T C R.

At first, they made a gesture towards asking questions. Sarah had thought some up while she was brushing her teeth and Veronica too seemed to have stockpiled some good ones. They went back and forth: "If you had to kiss one of the male teachers at school, who would it be?" "What do you think is better, your legs, your bum or your boobs? And which is the worst?" "Who do you like best out of your parents?" "Do you wish your family was as rich as mine?" "Have you ever cheated on a test?" "Have you ever masturbated?" For a while they got stuck on 'To save your family's life…' questions: "To save your family's life, would you… chop off the tip of your finger, or all of your hair? Would you smear your whole body in honey for a day, or for five minutes go in a cage full of spiders? Would you go to school naked, or lay on the floor in the middle of assembly and let everyone in the year wee on you?" They squealed and winced at their own disgustingness, at the grossness of what their imaginations could conjure, and they pretended to weigh each fantasy carefully. But the game was not in truth a test of their loyalty – it quickly became clear that Sarah would do absolutely anything for her family, even for Eliza, and whether Veronica felt this way or not (Sarah suspected she didn't), it was the line she stuck by, too. No, the test was not of their answers but of the questions, of their stomach for depravity, their repertoire of it, their boldness in speaking it aloud.

Before lunch, however, they ran out of questions, and so

returned to dares. They did this as though by accident, but of course it was what they had been building to all along. TCR dictated talk, and so they had humoured each other in a kind of childish foreplay. But the excitement of the dare...

Veronica

George had actually managed to make it home from the office a full hour before Sarah and David were due to arrive and was now upstairs showering. Veronica could hear the slight gurgling of pipes and the creak of bathroom tiles, but otherwise, there was near serenity. In relative terms, the neighbours had been barely audible all week. Typical, Veronica thought, just as she had determined to make Dominic her project. Still, there was a relief to it. Veronica had finally seen the woman on the street, looking nowhere near as oppressed as she had been imagining, and though there remained the daily yobbish sing-along at unsociable hours, and the wrenching taunt of a crying child, there had not been a repeat of those first frightening sounds of aggression. Veronica still felt an irritating stab of anxiety every time she approached the house, but having now seen the man for herself – not exactly a pipsqueak, but certainly no match for George   and having noticed the way he averted his eyes from her own, she found that she was far less nervous than she had been. Veronica felt almost solid in her dinner preparations.

She sat at the table, carefully lain with the newly unpacked wedding china, and surveyed her efforts. In the oven was the most elegant of her signature dishes – a sticky teriyaki salmon – to which she would add an assortment of salads and a vast platter of rosemary-roasted vegetables. In the fridge were nestling two different desserts that she had purchased from the bakery on the high street, but would claim as her own. A white wine was chilling, a red opened on the counter to breathe, a whiskey ready on the sideboard. And following a Sunday spent welcoming a group of friends to their new abode, she and George were well practised in their spiel as tour guides; only when they'd presented the two spare bedrooms and somebody had joked about the need to fill them, had either of their facades faltered.

Veronica's hands started now towards her belly, but she redirected them to the arrangement of candles on the table. It had never been clear to her why they had decided to keep the miscarriage secret. At eleven weeks, they had not yet told anybody about the pregnancy, so she supposed nobody would miss something that never was. Except that it was, to Veronica, or at least it had been. Sometimes she suspected that not even George understood this fully. But perhaps he was right in what he'd said that day, the only time they'd ever talked about it: it was simply not meant to be. Still, she had seen her belly thickening – no bump but a tender shifting of shape. She had felt her breasts enlarging, and nausea threatening. She had eliminated her intake of alcohol and sushi and undercooked eggs. She had followed the pregnancy app on her phone to see when the baby was the size of a poppy seed, or a pea or a fig. She had prematurely glanced through a book of names. She had in fact thought every minute of every one of those seventy-seven days about that not-meant-to-be being. So by the time the bleeding began – unstoppable, despite George's practicality; unstoppable, despite her resolve; unstoppable, gushing between her legs – it wasn't only the ill-formed foetus that they were losing, it was the dream of what that foetus would have become, the imagined future of what they would have become together. All of it bled away from them, and in its wake followed their relationship, as they knew it anyway – their openness, their trust, condemned the moment they stumbled into failure.

The first week after the loss, Veronica had burst into tears in her yoga class, right in the middle of Upward-Facing Dog. The instructor had moved quietly over to her, a healing hand on her back.

A week after that, she had silently streamed tears for the full hour of her facial. The beauty therapist had said nothing, but continued to stroke her skin.

Often still, she will have to hurry out of a shop when she is unexpectedly confronted by a buggy, or a pregnant woman, or a child, like Amelia, or the others she has to see every day at school, and it feels as though she'll never breathe again.

She has not burdened George with these moments. She has not written them into her letters home. She has not told anyone. Because of course, that's why the miscarriage was a secret: pain was far too unattractive an emotion to share.

Veronica stopped tormenting the candles and moved to the window seat in the front room. It was still a good twenty minutes until Sarah was due, but she glanced up and down the street anyway.

George had performed commendably over the past four nights during which sex was required. The haloed week of ovulation had crept doggedly towards them, thin white sticks decreeing when the moment had arrived, and as always they accepted the declaration like a deserved punishment. Veronica hated that this is what their sex life had been reduced to. She hated more that George didn't do a better job of pretending otherwise. Even on the nights when she attempted to set the mood, wearing a silky piece of something small, he waited for her to spell out what was needed, never seeking her out, never desiring her. Even once she made it clear, he seemed to approach the bed with a heavy sense of duty. The worst nights were when they'd been quarrelling, over nothing usually – a disagreement about weekend plans, a misunderstood word, an excuse for being late – but in a way that manifested all of their unsaid frustrations. In the old days, if she was annoyed at George, there was no way she would then have had sex with him. Perhaps at the end of an argument, in the throes of apology or rekindling, but not while still charged with anger and venom and blame. Fertility, however, only peaked for a few days – the sticks told her so – so there was no time to wait for an organic resolution to their quarrel, she couldn't afford to abide her emotions or exert any choice; sex was necessary. She hated this. It stirred something dormant inside her. She hated submitting her body when her mind screamed otherwise. She lay there, but she hated it, and sensed him hating it, and for those moments hated him too. She prayed nevertheless, for a baby, half his.

Veronica heard the bathroom door upstairs close and George's feet travelling back and forth across the bedroom. Now that the prime period of fertility had passed, the dynamic between them had shifted slightly, easing into a brief interlude of respite. It would intensify again in a couple of weeks as the time to test for pregnancy approached, mired always in the weight of their combined hope, but neither of them would mention the harried anticipation they carried. Neither of them would speak it. After all, anxiety was as unattractive as grief. Not jolly or good company. Far better to get on with things, not minding about trivial matters such as changing schools or moving house or living without one's parents.

It had taken them twenty months to conceive the first time. It had been almost a year since the miscarriage.

George appeared at the door to the front room. Fresh. Smart. Smiling.

They blustered in.

"So sorry," breathed Sarah, removing her coat. "The children's bedtime ran on, and the babysitter was late, and there was traffic on the Finchley Road."

"But we're here at last," smiled David, placing a hand softly on Sarah's arm.

Smiling back at him, George reached out for David's other

hand and shook it with practised confidence, a brand of which, Veronica had noticed, often made other men shrink a little. Not David. He accepted his palm with quieter conviction, but manifest warmth, and on the back of a comment she couldn't quite hear, both he and George set about giggling like old chums. Without Amelia and the boy littered around his legs, David gathered about him a charisma Veronica hadn't noticed before. Sarah remained close to him, her legs wrapped in pale, loose trousers, a silk top tucked in at the waist, a single necklace adorning her freckled décolletage. She was the kind of pretty that didn't jump at you across a room – not stunning, her hair neither blonde nor brown, too hawkish a nose, and a little short; but when you looked closely, she was nevertheless lovely. They hugged in an awkward embrace, the men watching.

The more Veronica thought about it, she realised that it had been such a fleeting year of friendship, and she wondered if this was why Sarah had seemed reluctant about reconnecting. Perhaps it had simply not mattered to her. Veronica herself could barely remember the names of any of the other girls from that year, with whom she was sure she had equally shared maths and science and PE; but the solidity of Sarah had rooted. The solidity of that summer. She loved the way that in Sarah's ordinary house, amongst her ordinary family, there never seemed to be a concern about saying the wrong thing, or being rude, or not being interesting enough to deserve attention. Veronica had been fascinated by that, noticing how it gave Sarah an inner, easy confidence, which although she exuded blindly, exploded out of her – a deep, inalienable sense of self-worth directing her effortlessly through the pitfalls of Year 7. Externally, Veronica mirrored this confidence with exaggerated vim. She had the money, and the looks, and she knew this. People thought her bold and assured, more so than Sarah; but next to her friend, she always knew she was lacking.

Veronica took the coats and found herself covertly

mimicking Sarah's grateful smile as she put them away. Why had she done that?

"Can I help you with anything?" Sarah called from behind her, and Veronica swivelled back around.

"Not in the slightest." She smiled broadly as she noticed David's arm around Sarah's waist, but behind Sarah's back she made yet another face, and it began to occur to Veronica how incredibly jealous she had been of Sarah back then – of her proper family unit, proper love. Everything she longed for. Veronica wondered why, in the light of that, she was so keen on reviving the friendship, tormenting herself. But she knew why. It was for the flicker of remembered contentment. It was for the younger, bolder girl itching gently beneath her skin.

The tour went as planned, the wine was poured, sticky salmon accompanied long, digressing accounts of which universities they had attended, how they'd fallen into their various careers, and when they'd met their partners. It occurred to Veronica that in fact her very first partner, her very first kiss, had been procured at Sarah's house. That summer. Sarah had not then been ready for such things, and had they been guessing all those years ago, they would surely have bet on Veronica marrying first, Veronica being the one to spawn a family. Had they bet on those things? As they reminisced across the table, memories crawled out of sealed wood.

For Veronica, it was a peculiar, scrambling resurfacing. She had so long held Sarah and the wholesome summer at her house in nostalgic regard, that she had somehow forgotten all about the less virtuous pastimes they'd together created: the obsessions they'd had with lists and people, and choices, and hierarchies, and the future. As conversation floated around her, Veronica struggled to remember the details, but slowly, the hum of Sarah's voice seemed to rub away at rose-tint, and Veronica shook her head in sudden comprehension. Because of course. Of course! It was never Sarah's happy home that had made her feel such contentment. That would only have grated on her. No, it was the constant battle between them. It was because she'd proven that summer, that despite her own lack of the family life she longed for, she could gain the upper hand, even in Sarah's home.

It wouldn't have been as contrived as that. At the time, aged twelve, Veronica had probably felt only an inexorable yearning. But she realised now that like fixing, before fixing, this too had been a pattern for her, the precise point from which her confidence stemmed: the triumph of not only being fine without the things she secretly lacked, but better, better than fine, better than anyone else, better than everyone else. Only that meant that others had to be worse, feel worse.

No wonder Sarah had been reluctant to reignite things.

Though now, the loser was not Sarah, but her, Veronica – weak, timid, without power. No longer better, but visibly, emptily, lesser. Exposed.

Looking at Sarah across the table, it occurred to Veronica that she'd never actually been the winner, not even when they were children. The difference was only that she'd had armour then. Armour that she'd foolishly shed.

It had happened gradually. As she'd grown into herself – discovering teaching, meeting the children in Kenya, and then George – the taking off of metal was imperceptible really, inching in its progression. But one day, instead of pretending to be enough, she somehow had become, truly, authentically, enough.

Until once again, she wasn't. Not even for George.

Veronica took a sip of water and tried again to recall the years before that. How she had done it. How she'd convinced herself, and Sarah, and others, that she was better. What her armour had been made from. And then it hit her. Even without remembering the blurred details of that summer, it was clear. Before she'd become a fixer, a builder-upper, the easiest route to triumph, to being 'better', her old trick, had been to pilfer from others.

"So the museum is officially all about the RAF," David was saying as Veronica tuned back in to the conversation. "Life-size models, flight simulators, the works. But what I'm in charge of is the fine art, which you might not expect to find there but actually we have Rothenstein, we have Kennington. It's a fabulous way to track the evolution of thought and perception during times of war, especially when you set that against conventional narratives of those eras."

"David knows everything about art," Sarah chipped in, glancing, Veronica noticed, at her. "I am an artistic ignoramus unfortunately."

Veronica nodded, and smiled. It was not the first time that evening that Sarah had negated her own achievements in favour of her husband's, and a thought tickled inside her. If she wanted to pilfer, how easy it would be. "And you work there, part-time?" asked Veronica innocently.

"Three mornings a week and till three o'clock on a Friday. Of course, when Harry was a baby it wasn't possible, but I've been back over six months now. He goes to Sarah's parents' two mornings and my mum helps out with the third, so it's wonderful really. He's so close with all the grandparents, Amelia was the same, and the rest of the time he's got me, and Sarah as much as possible. What will you two do? Are you planning a few rug rats?"

George flashed Veronica a concerned look, but she didn't meet his eye, concentrating instead on heaping thick slices of the shop-bought pastries onto plates. When she'd fetched them from the kitchen earlier, she'd substituted her wine with a carefully colour-matched non-alcoholic elderflower. "How much is as much as possible?" she said.

"The mornings," replied Sarah, accepting the deflection, perhaps more sensitive than her husband to possible reasons for childlessness. Primed with pity. "We all wake early so I have an hour or two with them before I head off. Then some evenings I make it back before bed. And there're the weekends. These look delicious."

Veronica put down the serving spoon and looked Sarah in the eye. "Oh, poor things," she said.

Slowly, Sarah raised a wary eyebrow and took an even slower sip of her wine. Without looking at him, Veronica could feel George's eyes on her again, this time not anxious but questioning. Again, she didn't meet his stare. Something in her veins had quickened.

"I think Veronica just means that it's an unconventional set-up," rescued George. And then, to David, "I hear raising kids is the hardest job."

"Most rewarding," David smiled, putting his arm protectively around Sarah. "But we can't all be so lucky. Sarah took the first three months off with each of them, but she's always been the more ambitious of the two of us, and the higher earner, so it was a good solution. My idea as it happens. Actually, we planned it years ago, sort of. We got together first year of uni – Sarah was crushing law, I was pretending to do History of Art; she was always going to be the professional and I the struggling artist."

"Except you weren't so keen in the end on the struggling," smiled Sarah.

"I had a few exhibitions early on."

Veronica watched as Sarah placed her hand on his shoulder. "Really, you should see his stuff."

"But I lost the juice for it. In the end I was happier exploring other people's art than creating my own. I do like painting with the kids though. Do you have any hobbies, George?"

"Golf. Had to throw in the rugger after the last surgery but—"

"And that's enough for you now?" Veronica interrupted. She put her own hand over George's and smiled at David endearingly. "What a sacrifice."

"But it's more than a hobby still, your painting, really, isn't it David?" rushed Sarah. "Hobby suggests it's only for leisure, that it couldn't be your profession. But of course, it was your profession so now it's just more of a freelance, private thing, right? He's hugely talented. And so valued at the museum. Really, David's far cleverer than I am."

David frowned, at both of the women. "I've never been much of a golfer."

An uncomfortable pause followed, during which Sarah smiled at David, and David avoided the smile, nodding amiably at George, who in turn looked bemusedly to Veronica. Now it was Veronica who took a slow, deliberate sip of elderflower-wine. But her mind raced. What on earth was she doing? George must have thought she'd gone mad; she, usually so adept at putting people at ease, suddenly a saboteur? It was childish. Undignified. And unplanned. Yet it was irresistible. And now that she'd begun, she remembered the rhythm as though she'd never stopped swaying to it; the careful dance of concealed slurs, the compliment turned insult, the craft of condescension. For the first time in many months, she felt in control, and powerful. Besides, they were tiny, tiny manipulations. Trifling. She was only experimenting, not doing harm.

"Well," laughed Veronica warmly, pulling herself back. "Amelia seems very well adjusted on it, so you must be doing something right."

Yes, good. She mustn't go too far. She was no longer an insecure child; she didn't have the excuse of that. Besides, despite the jealousies that were clearly re-emerging, she liked Sarah, genuinely, she always had. It had been an actual joy to see her so unexpectedly, nostalgia wrapped neatly in a power suit and bob. Even now, in the discomfort of awkward pause, titbits of tenderness crept to the fore – secrets they'd told, the summer smell of Sarah's house, a nonsense language they'd invented. Warm, comforting memories, the flavour of Bolognese. Having said that, other memories were resurfacing too, like how intoxicating it felt when the power was tipping her way.

"Didn't your parents do something similar, Sarah?" spoke Veronica carefully. "That wonderful summer I spent at yours, I seem to remember your father being there constantly."

"Dad was a barrister, same as me, so unlikely," Sarah replied, buoyed it seemed by safer territory. "Though he brought his work home a lot. And there were lulls between cases, so maybe that summer–"

"And your mum had that crazy clinic with all the hippy dippies coming in and out of her sweet little office. Is she still into all that homeopathic mumbo jumbo? Oh, and how's Eliza?"

Sarah flinched, visibly. Both men stopped eating. Had Veronica gone too far? What with? Hippy dippies? Hadn't they both used to joke about that? Yes, all summer long they'd giggled at the pashmina-draped women and bead-adorned men who parked outside the suburban house in cars that almost always brandished a rainbow-clad bumper sticker. Veronica noticed David flash Sarah a meaningful look, and Sarah subtly shake her head to subdue it.

"Mum's busier than ever," she smiled with exaggerated cheer. "It's Dad who's retired. That was a strange old summer though, wasn't it? And then you left for that school in Kent. We thought we'd see each other in a few weeks, and then, never again. Until now of course."

"Until now," agreed Veronica, raising her elderflower carefully to toast the reconnection.

But Sarah continued. "We didn't spend much time with Eliza though, really, did we? We were so intent on, swimming. I'm surprised you remember her. Do you remember her?"

There was something about the way Sarah intoned 'swimming'. The slight pause. And all at once Veronica did remember the swimming pool, sunken at the far end of the garden, and the pool house next to it. Her stomach lurched abruptly. "Gosh, the swimming!" Veronica exclaimed. Sarah shook her head very slightly, but now that Veronica had remembered, there was so much to say. "We swam naked in Sarah's pool," she mock whispered to George.

David glanced up at Sarah inquiringly, mirth dancing at the tip of his mouth.

"But Eliza hardly swam, did she?" Sarah flailed on. "Eliza read all summer."

"Probably because you hated her. She treated Sarah like an infant," Veronica explained to the men before turning back to Sarah. "You hated her. Do you remember her party? That was my first kiss, you know. I just remembered that this evening. It's funny, I just remembered a lot of things this evening."

"I didn't hate Eliza," said Sarah softly.

Veronica noticed David reaching for Sarah's hand under the table, their fingers locking in familiar intimacy. George had his own clasped around a glass of wine.

"No, of course. But you did detest her a little. You were jealous I think. She was older, and very beautiful." Veronica said this again to the men, not quite meaning to sway to the beat, but feeling the pulse of it. "And you were still much more a child. You definitely didn't like me getting friendly with her."

"Eliza was beautiful," agreed Sarah. "But I wasn't jealous."

"I think you told me one evening that Eliza had... Oh wow—" Veronica stopped. "Do you remember that game – 'What would you do'?"

"Eliza had what?" prompted Sarah. "What about Eliza?"

But Veronica only smiled. The tempo had touched her. She was doing this now.

Veronica reached over to David and intercepted the hand he was using to reach for his wife. "We played this game where we would concoct all sorts of awful choices, and then have to decide which horror we would pick."

"It was typical childish stuff," Sarah shrugged, shaking her head ever so slightly at David, but finally conceding to the direction of the conversation.

"Like what?" asked George.

"Like, to save your family's life, what would you do: go to school naked, or kiss the ugly science teacher."

"Well that's a good one for you now," joked George.

"Didn't you tell me there's an ugly science teacher? What would you do?"

"Oh, we absolutely have to play this now," grinned Veronica. "I'd kiss the teacher of course. You wouldn't mind would you, darling?" She kissed George quickly on the lips, and he looked at her, puzzled. It was, she realised, the first time in months, even when in the throes of ovulation, that they had kissed.

"I might mind a little," grinned George, looking at her questioningly.

She kissed him again.

"Okay, your turn," Veronica declared, turning to Sarah.

"Uh oh," laughed George, a more open laugh than she'd heard in many months.

"Sarah, what would you do... never be able to sleep with your hubby again..." She mimed a breaking heart to David. "Or, be able to sleep with him, but first have to make out with another man in front of him."

"What?" Now Sarah laughed, uncomfortably.

David intercepted. "Make out?" He shook his head in exaggerated bemusement. "There's been a time warp, surely. I'm fifteen again."

George chuckled, but Veronica grinned boldly. "Yep, make out. Smooch, French, snog, kiss, whatever you kids want to call it. With another man, let's say a man who you both know, let's say, well how about George?"

George gamely raised his eyebrows at Sarah in mock seduction. Sarah laughed again. She shifted on her seat.

"I'm not sure if—" David began, but this time it was Sarah who interrupted. Raising her gaze to Veronica, she looked at her defiantly. Daringly.

"Well I'd kiss George of course," she decided.

Now George laughed loudly and David was forced to smile along with him, even adding a 'lucky man' or two. But the women only stared at each other.

"Wow," said Veronica eventually.

"What?"

"I just mean, wow, that's my husband. And yours is right there."

"Veronica! Seriously?"

Veronica allowed a long, cumbersome pause, watching as it almost visibly stretched across the table. But finally, she laughed. "Of course not seriously, Sarah! Gosh!"

Now they all laughed, uneasily, except for Veronica who felt uncommonly in command. She hadn't quite decided to pilfer from Sarah's confidence, not consciously, not wholly, but it was working. It was working.

"Your turn," she said, pointing dangerously at David. "Would you..."

But he held up his hand. "I can answer already," he told them.

"Oh? Interesting..."

"My answer is... I would... thank you so much for a wonderful evening, but regretfully mention that we have to relieve the babysitter."

"Cop out," shouted George. "Total cop out," but he got up to get the coats, leaving Veronica to stifle a sudden, sinking sense of deflation.

There followed the usual exchanges of thanks and declarations of how lovely the evening had been and promises to do it again, and soon they found themselves in the hallway where Veronica drew Sarah into an embrace, as she did so inhaling the summer scent of Sarah's old family home. "Have you been to your parents' today?" she inquired. "You smell of it."

"I smell?" said Sarah. "Lovely. Thanks." She gave another forced laugh, but Veronica continued with renewed earnestness, fondness, the scent grabbing her lungs.

"I've always remembered that smell – mango and coconut. Your mum had those candles everywhere."

"Oh," said Sarah more carefully. "Yes. She still does. Good memory."

"There you go!"

Sarah looked at Veronica then in a way that she couldn't quite decipher, before shrugging off the strangely extended pause as though it was nothing. "Goodbye, George, lovely to have met you." She air-kissed him on the cheek. "Bye again, Veronica."

"See you soon Mrs Beckham." Veronica said this cheerily, innocently, then leant forward to kiss David. "And you too, Mr Beckham. Don't be late for school. Oh wait, wow, I've just heard it."

"What?" asked Sarah.

"David, Beckham. Like David Beckham, the footballer."

"Oh that's brilliant!" exclaimed George, clapping David on the back. "I can tell my mates I know Beckham."

"Except," continued Veronica. "Sorry, David, but you strike me as more of a chess player. And you were so sporty, Sarah, I might have expected the real thing."

David laughed. "Unfortunately you're right, I'm no footballer," he said.

His smile was as warm as ever, but it was with notable decision that he placed his hand on Sarah's back and guided her towards the door.

Sarah

David T Beckham was in fact born Tennyson David Beckham, a gesture of reverence to his mother's favourite poet. The more commonplace middle name was a concession to his father's desire to bind just a hint of Jewishness to the son they had already agreed would be raised secular. But the two doting parents hadn't accounted for the singular love of tradition, nor the determinedly unassuming nature of their artistically brilliant boy. By the time he moved into secondary school, Tennyson had been discarded in favour of the just-a-hint David, and David had reintroduced Shabbat prayers and kosher food into the Beckham household. When, just a year later, the eponymous footballer shot to stardom and David became subject to continual school-yard jibes – generally centred around the irony of such an un-athletic boy sharing a name with such a specimen of athleticism – David merely laughed at the incongruity, and continued on in his own passions, which were piano, drama, and of course his beloved art. He never told his growing group of faithful friends the history of the T initial, and stuck fast to a course of quiet self-possession that as he grew older disarmed men and women alike. After their first date, Sarah described him to Eliza as the most generous, kind and emotionally intelligent man she had ever met, not to mention handsome. To which Eliza obligingly mock-puked.

But David really was all of those things, and Sarah knew that he remained entirely comfortable in their decision for him to be the children's primary carer, their means to let her fly. Besides, he loved his part-time position at the museum. And he had never once regretted the choice not to pursue a path of artistic illustriousness, despite the talent for it.

He would, however, she knew, have noticed her over-compensation. Her own need to explain and justify.

"Sorry," she said, the second they were in the car.

"She riled you," he shrugged. "How come?" He started the engine of their Toyota Prius and quietly pulled out of the street.

"Old power games."

"You shouldn't play them."

Sarah threw her hands into the air with exaggerated drama. "I know. Tell that to the twelve-year-old inside me!"

David pulled to a stop at a traffic light and looked at her. "Why didn't you tell her about Eliza?"

"Ugh, I don't know." Sarah lowered her hands and placed one comfortably on his, slipping her fingers into a familiar tangle. "I guess I just feel wary of her."

"I can see why," said David. "Was she always like that?"

"Yeah. Master of manipulation. But a lot of other things, too."

He nodded.

And Sarah nodded. And squeezed his fingers in full stop, pushing deeper inside her the nagging sounds of resentment and blame, the secrets of the TCR sealed still in wood. "Sorry," she offered again, and this time David bestowed his forgiveness with a counter-squeeze.

Then he grinned. "Now, about this naked swim…"

Simone

Terry traces her spine with the tips of his fingers. She's drunk too much, with him, but he is still standing and she is curled up, vodka and beer prying frozen memories out of their icy vaults.

"Don't waste your tears on them," Terry is saying, without having to ask. "They ignored you, they didn't deserve you."

She sniffs.

"They made you hurt yourself."

She sniffs again.

"I won't ever ignore you, you know. I see you. I always have."

Simone sits up and arranges herself across Terry's chest. The bruise by her mouth doesn't hurt anymore and she presses her face into his shirt. His fingers still stroke her, but gently, not pushing for more. He never means to push.

"We're two peas in a pod really, aren't we? We're the ones who see things how they are. We found each other. We protect each other. You've always got me now. I'll see you right."

She smiles at him. He's right. He's always right. His chest is sturdy. His breath steady. His arms around her, strong.

Veronica

The cotton of her dress stuck to her thighs, which were itching with an unprecedented fury. It was one of those rare English days when it is hotter in London than even Lake Como or Cannes or the blue-topped cliffs of Santorini. She had been awake all night, tossing in the heat, listening for the neighbours whose too-loud music had continued undiminished, and feeling her breasts. Even in the light of day, her nipples were tender and she was sure they were marginally enlarged. There had been a gentle throbbing in her abdomen all morning, and she had felt distinctly light-headed. She could barely breathe with the hope of it. She had said nothing to George.

Since the dinner party, there had been a tentative bridging of the distance between them, a cautious probing of possibility. It was as though they'd glimpsed different, older versions of themselves, and were bathing now in that sliver of nostalgic light. They'd been snapping less, returning to a state of presuming good intentions, instead of the opposite. But if she was wrong, if she wasn't pregnant, if this wasn't it, the disappointment would smash everything.

They talked around harmless things. George had wanted to know all about Veronica's friendship with Sarah. He had listened with mirth to her stories from that year, as much as she could remember in any case, and at the end of it all he had declared Sarah good for her.

"I like David, too," he told her one evening when they were grabbing a small glass of wine at The Lansdowne pub, basking in the energy of the creatives around them, pretending the passion was theirs. "He's a salt of the earth type, isn't he? Refreshing."

"Yes. Sarah's like that too. Always was."

"Not very ambitious though." George ran a hand through his hair and looked up at her with unusual attention. He was still in his suit, though his tie was removed, and he had selected the Piaget with the white face and simple numerals. On his wrist were the cufflinks from their wedding. There was something about a well-dressed man that was endearing to Veronica – not the price tags, but the care with which it suggested he shaped himself. Some people saw such dressing as an expression of money, or power, but to Veronica it revealed the reverse – a thoughtfulness about oneself, a concern about the opinions of others, a susceptibility.

"Sarah is. Ambitious."

"Oh I don't mean it derogatively," George clarified. "It must be nice to be content with your lot, not feel a need to achieve."

Despite the clues of clothing, this was as close as George had come in the past year to actually articulating a vulnerability. "Like you do?" she asked.

"Like *we* do," he corrected.

"Do you *like* to achieve though, or need to?" Veronica probed carefully, her tone shifting a little towards the soft searching of their early days. This, however, was too much for George. He sidestepped her earnestness and laughed jauntily.

"It's just like a game of rugby, isn't it? Glory goes to the man who makes the try."

"No stickers for participation?"

"Definitely not."

Veronica laughed, reluctantly accepting George's

blitheness. Her legs itched and a frustration crept with it through her skin. She could feel herself growing impatient. But it was better to be talking about something than nothing. "Oh the stickers!" she declared cooperatively.

They were in safe territory now. Veronica, George knew, despised the relentless supply of stickers she was required to distribute to already sheltered children. How would they ever learn that the world wasn't like that, she'd demanded once of George. Not everybody won, not everybody could have all that they wanted. "What if you don't play rugby?" she asked him breezily.

"Football then. If you're playing footie, you want to be up front, scoring the goals."

"Like Beckham," smiled Veronica.

"That was brilliant," George laughed. "He's so not a Beckham. I like him though."

As it happened, both Beckhams had, in Veronica's estimation, been avoiding her. Sarah had not even done her Monday school collection, sending David in her stead, and although David had conversed with apparent warmth at the classroom door, there wasn't the familiarity Veronica had thought might have flourished over the sharing of secrets and wine. The resulting feeling of rejection stirred a dormant rage in Veronica. It wasn't that Sarah had been nasty. It wasn't that David was impolite. There was nothing specific she could accuse either of them of doing. But there was a lack of something, again a lack.

It burned most in regard to Sarah. Of course you can't force somebody to like you, you can't force a person to care. And perhaps, to be fair, Sarah had simply recognised the oh-so-subtle dinner-party conversation for exactly what it was: a game of manipulation. In the aftermath, washing wine glasses at the kitchen sink, Veronica had regretted those childish digs. Despite the fleeting restoration of confidence they had imbued, despite the seductiveness of that, it wasn't necessary, she'd told herself. She had plenty of friends now with whom there was a healthier dynamic, friends she had made in the years of enough-ness. That bitchy pre-teen wasn't who she, now, wanted to be. Yet, for some reason, she couldn't let Sarah go. And she couldn't stop trying to taunt her, either into friendship or defeat. She'd 'lost' a homework that Amelia had clearly spent much time upon and requested she do it again. She'd chosen not to select Amelia, plainly one of the best, for that term's chess team. She'd written all sorts of comments on Amelia's work, hoping to provoke Sarah into coming in. All week she'd done everything she could think of to see her again, to reel her back, to make her want her, to prove, just as she had proven once before, that she, Veronica, wasn't the one lacking and in need. The thought accompanied her as cotton flapped against itchy thighs. It accompanied her as she felt again nausea rising in her mouth. It was there as she breathed deeply in, and more deeply out, and held the air in her lungs in alternative waves of hope and envy.

The heat, however, that Friday, seemed to smother everything. At speed on her bike, Veronica weaved past the mosque on Regent's Park Road and veered right. Pulling over in St John's Wood High Street, she tried not to dwell on the pregnancy test she was buying from the pharmacy. She slipped it into her bag as though it was a pack of gum, as though all it might do was freshen her breath, and then jumped breezily back onto her bike, trying to ignore the poppy-seed-sized hope in her belly. But throughout the remainder of the journey to work, thoughts slipped through whirring spokes. She couldn't stop them: images of herself taking the test into the staff toilets, wrapping the validating stick in tissue, trying to hide her elation until she could present it at the end of the day to George. She thought over and again about how delighted that would make him. She calculated how many weeks it would be until they could reveal that delight to the world. She envisaged which room they would use as a nursery and wondered how they might further soundproof it from the neighbours' raves. She allowed herself to explore the imagined future in which two became three, lacking nothing.

In the furthest-most cubicle, her stomach churned. It was silly really, she had done this so many times before – waited for a few seconds of pee to pronounce her future. But on all those other occasions, she had already felt the answer somewhere inside of her, and thus prepared herself for disappointment. This time was different. This time she knew, knew it to be the opposite, and in readiness she unboxed the test and removed the stick from its plastic casing and held it at the ready.

The blood was not heavy.

A thin, barely-there streak on her knickers.

But barely-there was still there, masked during her journey, she supposed, by the sweatiness of the day.

She stared at it staining cotton. The redness choked her, darkness around her throat. Tightening. Suffocating.

Yet, also, deep inside the thumping of her veins, there was a pushing back. It couldn't be true. Not this time. She'd been so sure. Perhaps this blood was implantation bleeding. She'd read about that – women thought they had their period, but it wasn't, it was this, and they didn't realise they were pregnant until months later. She touched her breasts. Her nipples were still sore, and her stomach throbbed, and there'd been that dizziness. It had to be. Veronica thrust the stick hopefully beneath her, forcing herself to relax enough to pee, then wrapped the test in tissue while she waited for the result. One minute. Two. Three to be certain. It was long ago that she'd given up on the tests where you had to squint your eyes to determine the presence, or not, of a blue line – anything could be wished into visibility. Now she bought the digital ones that were firm and forthright; either she was Pregnant or Not Pregnant. She was right or she was wrong. She was a mother, or she wasn't. Success or failure. The answer would not be ambiguous. Still, she waited a fourth minute more.

Not Pregnant stared insolently out at her.

Not.

Not.

The blood had not lied.

It was, as always, only herself that was lacking.

Veronica did not re-wrap the test to save for George in her bag.

She paused, for a moment. She gave herself just a moment, hunched, eyes closed in front of the bathroom mirror. She allowed one, long, deep breath. Then she tossed the test into the bin, forcing the same flippancy she had employed on purchase. She stuck a sanitary pad into her knickers. She checked her make-up. And she went to class.

All day the children were riled by the heat. They loped about the classroom, groaning every time they were asked to fetch a book or put a note into their bags or listen to the ways in which it was possible to spell the 'ay' sound. Though she tried, she had no patience for it and her inability to rally them made her feel even more incapable than usual. Her stomach was throbbing now, a constant reminder of its pronouncement, her legs itched, and all she wanted to do was to take a chilled Chardonnay from the fridge and lay on the sofa letting TV waft her mind into happy oblivion. "Is anybody awake today?" she prodded them, but even Amelia lacked concentration, taunting her with her presence, existing for Sarah, where nothing existed for Veronica. Sarah, who didn't even spend time with her daughter. Sarah who had been given everything. Veronica found herself glaring at Amelia, though existing was not her fault.

She shook herself. Despite the propped open door, and the fan now on her desk, the hot room seemed to stoke everything. When somebody hit their head against the door handle and had to be sent to the nurse for an icepack, Veronica felt herself suddenly on the brink of tears, as though it was she who had been knocked to the floor. Her own head was pounding.

By the time they'd had lunch, Veronica had decided to abandon the day's lesson plans and in an attempt at decisiveness, she instructed sun hats and water bottles, and then lead the whole class into the playground where they found a shaded tree at just the right angle to the gate to allow the tiniest breeze. She had brought *Matilda* with her, which she had occasionally been reading them snippets of, and she hoped to encourage an un-taxing discussion of their other favourite Dahl books. But Amelia was so far the only one to raise her hand. Brazenly, overtly there, blatantly being.

"*The BFG*," she volunteered. "Mummy read it to me in the Christmas holidays."

Mummy. Sarah. Veronica had a vision of the two of them cuddled up in bed, Sarah's arm enveloping the child into her chest, laughing together at the giant's muddled English. Laughing at her. Veronica had read her own copy of *The BFG* when she was living in Holland. She remembered because there had been a window in her bedroom that she'd imagined was like Sophie's in the book, and so that's where she chose to read it, nestled on a bean bag beneath the sill, every afternoon one half term when her parents were at work. She'd loved that book. She'd loved the idea that a child could be purposeful and important, and listened to, even by somebody so big.

"Anybody else?"

None of the other children answered and Veronica felt exasperation rising. One boy called Ryan flicked the ear of his neighbour, who immediately broke into whiny complaint. Amelia raised her hand again.

"Ryan, we don't touch other children unless they allow us to, and we certainly don't flick people's ears," Veronica sighed. "Over there please."

Grudgingly, Ryan shifted himself half an inch in the direction that Veronica was pointing. Amelia reached higher into the air. "Mrs Reddington?"

"Ryan, further away please."

He moved another half inch. Amelia began bouncing her arm up and down above her head. Sarah used to do the same. Veronica's stomach throbbed harder. Her bra felt too tight, and sweaty beneath her top. She looked away from Amelia and cast her eye across the group.

"I asked, what are your favourite Roald Dahl books. Has nobody read any Dahl?"

There were nineteen vacant pairs of eyes staring back at her. Two pairs had even closed. Amelia's danced eagerly.

"Nobody?"

Ryan was to the left of Veronica's view. He kept his eyes obediently on her, but when he thought she wasn't watching, shot out his leg to kick his neighbour.

"Ryan."

He didn't answer. In her periphery, Amelia was still bouncing her hand. The bouncing made Veronica feel sick. More nauseous than before. She wished the girl would sit still.

"Ryan, do you think you are invisible?

Silence.

"Mrs Reddington," begged Amelia, still bouncing.

"Ryan, I am asking you a question. Do you think I didn't see you kick Ishaan?"

"It was an accident," he whined. "My foot just moved by mistake."

Veronica stared at him hard. The itching in her own legs had become unbearable in the dry grass and she wished she could kick out as he had. Her stomach continued to throb. A pool of sweat gathered on her upper lip. Ryan held her stare.

"Mrs Reddington, Mrs Reddington, I have another favourite," enthused Amelia. "It was Mummy's favourite too and—"

And that was the moment that, despite her intentions to the contrary, despite her desire not to pilfer, despite the years in which she had grown and evolved and become, Veronica Reddington rounded on Amelia Beckham, calling her a 'relentless irritation', and docked three of the golden oval stickers that she, and her 'mummy', so treasured.

At the museum, the air conditioning pumped freshness onto grateful visitors. It was two o'clock, a couple of school groups beginning their retreat onto coaches, heat-weary mothers just surfacing with sweaty, post-nap toddlers, a few lone men, nodding earnestly at military displays. Standing beneath an air vent, Veronica regarded David Beckham's surrounds. Under the guise of 'not feeling herself', she had asked the headmistress to cover her class, and she had come straight here. It wasn't a lie, she wasn't herself; the deceit was only that she hadn't been herself for a long while.

Now that she stood in the great lobby, aeroplanes lining the space with a feeling of flight grounded, she didn't know why she had come. She had exited the school gates, and taken a taxi, and here she had arrived, as if there was no agency in it, seemingly remembering only as she walked through the doors that on Fridays, David worked until three. Where would he be? Veronica consulted the lady at the information desk and headed as instructed to the Battle of Britain Hall where David was readying a display. She called to him from the doorway and he hurried over at once, understandably anxious as to why Amelia's teacher was appearing at his place of work in the midst of a school day. Why *was* she appearing?

"Is Amelia okay?" he rushed, before hello.

"Yes, she's fine," calmed Veronica, shaking her head slightly as though he was the crazed one, rather than she. "The headmistress has my class this afternoon."

"Oh. Okay. Thank goodness, I was worried for a moment."

"Nothing to worry about."

Now that he had been assured, David's expression altered. Still holding a stack of papers from the display, he looked down at them, and then carefully up at Veronica. "Are you, were you just visiting the museum?"

"Not exactly. I did want to see you."

"Oh?"

Veronica smiled. She reached out and put her hand over his, still clasping papers. "Don't worry, Amelia's fine. It was a fun evening the other night, wasn't it?" She paused, but David said nothing. "Delicious to see Sarah again. And getting to know you a little was, unexpected. We should do it another time soon."

Awkwardly, David moved his hand. "I don't mean to be rude, Veronica, it was a lovely evening, but actually, I'm not sure you're the best person to be around Sarah right now."

"Oh?" Veronica flinched. She'd been sensing this reluctance all week, but people usually had the manners to pretend otherwise. She wondered if the hostility was Sarah's, or David's, or both. Surely it wasn't David. She'd always been able to magnetise men. "Did she not like my question about kissing George?" she recovered, winking with, she thought, just the right amount of sass. "Sarah always was a bit strait-laced you know, I shouldn't have teased her. You can tell her I'd have kissed you too though, in that situation of course." She smiled irreverently now, with a daring openness she hadn't employed in years. David took a step back.

"I think it's best just to give her some space." He shuffled his papers, then half-turned towards the vast room behind him. "I'd better get back. Not long till pick-up, as you know."

"Of course." Veronica smiled, but inside her, rejection raged. And mingled there with something else. Suddenly, her stomach throbbed more acutely than ever, her head pounded, her legs itched. She scratched at them and wondered if through the thin cotton she had drawn blood. She wanted to sit down. Desperately. And, she wished George was there – old George, the George who had loved her irreverence and learned her heart and was the only person to whom she had ever been able to unfold everything. And had not yet told about the pregnancy. Or lack of it.

In George's stead, David hovered. "Are you alright?" he asked her.

Veronica flapped her hand dismissively, but she felt her face draining of colour. David would think it was his effect on her. Or her failure to affect him.

Perhaps it came with infertility, this inability to enchant men, perhaps they could sense it. Perhaps Sarah could sense it too, the waning of her power. Clearly the woman no longer felt compelled to court her friendship. That was, if she had even courted it when they were children. Maybe it had been Veronica all along. Contrived from the very start.

Veronica's stomach throbbed harder.

David began to back away.

You can't force somebody to want you, Veronica reasoned. You can't force love into existence, or something to love, or something to love you.

But, you can force some things. Words spilled.

"Sorry, David," Veronica began, regaining her composure and raising her hand to halt his departure. "Before you get back, there is something wrong actually. I was trying to downplay it before, I didn't want to make it a thing, knowing you and Sarah of course. But actually, there was a reason I came. Amelia is not quite fine. She was rather badly behaved today. I had to take away some of her Golden Time."

"Oh," David frowned, looking at her suspiciously. "Okay. Isn't this something you could have told me at school?"

"Yes, of course, and I will, I'll be in touch more formally to set up a parents' meeting, I just wanted to give you a personal heads-up, being friends."

Small manipulations.

"Okay…"

Trifling.

"We'll do it when Sarah's available too, of course." At this, David raised his eyebrow, and Veronica smiled. He knew what she was doing, and she felt an energy pulse through her. Life. Where all day there'd been a lack of it. Still smiling, she began to move towards the door. "I'll let you get back to your work now. Sorry to have disturbed."

"Sarah might not be able to make it," David said suddenly, with what Veronica could see was an attempt at firmness. "But of course, let *me* know when to come."

Veronica gritted her teeth and smiled. "The thing is, David, I've been noticing rather a lot of things about Amelia lately. You know, some behavioural issues that are, well, unusual, and worth exploring. Today for instance, a lack of awareness of social norms. I'm sure you'll have observed. And I'll have to be writing my report soon for the move up to the Junior school next year, so, well I think best if we try to tackle this together first."

She spoke softly, smoothly, only the glint in her eye betraying anything less than compassion. Eyebrow still raised, David listened to her in silence, watching carefully. She felt sparks ricocheting from his eyes all around the grand room, pulsating inside her, like a secretly bidden strength. Stuff her previous moralising, the manipulations were only small. Trifling. Worth it for this.

She turned. Swept away. As she reached the door, however, David spoke.

"When you see Sarah..." he started abruptly. "At the meeting... Look, she didn't want to say. But all this talk about when you were kids together, and Eliza, it's not—"

"It's not appropriate for school," Veronica interrupted. "Of course it isn't. But the meeting's not about us, is it? I'm thinking only of Amelia."

Sarah

"What's 'material prejudice'?" called Sarah's leader, a distinguished QC twenty years her elder, spotting her as she strode past his open door towards the stairwell.

Sarah retraced a few steps and stuck her head into his room. Andrew Shonubi was one of the most senior barristers in the chambers and one of the few who still led Sarah on cases. Mostly, these days, she ran her own. "Anything, I suppose, above *de minimis* prejudice. There must be a tangible effect."

"But it can never be tested. It's a hypothetical."

Sarah entered the room and sat down. Andrew's office was a high ceilinged, book-lined haven with vast bay windows overlooking the garden in the middle of Lincoln's Inn Fields. Just outside of Lincoln's Inn itself (one of the four Inns of Court), it remained a stone's-throw from The Temple, and embedded enough to retain the feel of an Oxbridge college. All stone walls and sweeping arches, for Sarah, this had felt a natural progression, but there was a junior barrister new to their chambers who'd joined them from Birmingham University and before that a comprehensive in South London, and he'd remarked many times on the oddness of it all, as though he'd walked through the Narnia wardrobe and found himself in an unrecognisable realm. Was there prejudice in that, in the void between backgrounds? Was it material?

"Is this for the Dewer case?"

"Yes. It's a hostile takeover, but the effect is hypothetical since it hasn't happened yet, so the material effect can't be proved. Material being the opposite of hypothetical."

Sarah nodded thoughtfully. She liked Andrew. Born in Uganda, he retained a gentle shape-shifting of certain vowels, and she liked to listen to the sonorous hum of his voice. She liked his sureness. She especially liked this unpicking of words he often invited her to join, and the speed at which her mind leapt gratefully into action, forgoing the distractions otherwise tugging. It was easier here. Eliza had never existed in chambers, so there was no absence to wrestle with, no collection to be made. Not that her latest foray into collection had been the slightest bit successful. It had been foolish to entrust Veronica with it, to trust her with anything. Prejudice, when it came to Veronica, was material and clear.

Or was it? She still wasn't sure if it was possible for one person, one moment, to really make such an impact. More likely, Sarah was fixating, as she'd always done. Sometimes it was on the Latin roots of words, sometimes it was on ethics and principle, for a long time, and still, it was on Eliza. That's what her counsellor had suggested anyway. And now Veronica had seeped into her consciousness. A new subject to scrutinise.

What were the facts? They'd only been girls. And there was just one dinner party.

Sarah had never told David how the summer with Veronica ended. It seemed so trivial now, unworthy of the posited impact. David knew only about the distance that Sarah had recalled between herself and Eliza that year, sisters momentarily bound to different sides of adolescence: one, contemptuous of a childish abandon that had slipped suddenly away; the other envious of ungraspable, un-gettable teenage-dom. Even without knowledge of Veronica, this was enough for David to insist she not make too much of that summer in her mind. Willingly, he would talk about Eliza. He would recall the first time he'd met her – when Sarah brought him back from university for the weekend and Eliza had flown in from Milan, failing to tell them anything about her past month singing gigs in Italy but insisting on knowing everything about 'Sarah's beau'. Just as willingly, David would retell for Sarah the number of times – thirty-eight – that Eliza had called to be updated on Sarah's progress during Amelia's birth. He even took a photograph from Eliza's last birthday – Sarah and Eliza in candid, uncontainable laughter – and in a rare yielding to suppressed talent, he painted it for her on canvas. But he would not humour relics. No staring at rusted tennis rackets. No worship of cast-out necklaces found in her parents' attic. Those things did not possess Eliza, he said. Active memories were one thing – she was alive in them, real – but there was no point in collecting things inanimate, or distorted. A necklace cast out meant that Eliza no longer saw herself in it. People evolved. It was not fair to tie their memory to something that was just a meandering, just an experiment, unrepresentative of the whole. The summer with Veronica for example, he said, was exactly that. So what was the point in collecting it?

Sarah had already explained to David her theory of collection. Not atonement, she insisted. She had explained too why that drew her to Veronica: the lure of relearning any part of her sister. And David had sympathised. He knew that Sarah had a void inside her; but, he said, Veronica was not the one to fill it.

Sarah's phone rang. David. With another quick word on prejudice, she excused herself from Andrew's office and ran past the chambers lift, down the three flights of stairs to the street.

"Don't get worried, we know Amelia, so I'm sure it's all a mistake," David began through the phone line, immediately sending Sarah into panic. "Apparently Amelia's been acting out at school, and we're required to attend a parents' meeting."

Sarah stopped at the pillar outside her chambers and placed one hand on cool stone. "The school called to tell you that?"

"No." There was a hesitation to David's voice. "Veronica turned up at the museum."

"What?" Instantly, Sarah couldn't breathe. "Veronica came to see you?"

"I think she wants to see *you*."

Sarah crossed the road, sitting on the bench just inside the gated park. "That's a bit odd, isn't it? Coming to your work?"

"She said she wanted to give us a heads-up. Nice of her, I suppose. But I don't actually believe Amelia would have done anything terrible, so yes, probably excessive. It was strange, Sarah. Veronica seemed to be suggesting that Amelia has some sort of behavioural issue, or learning difficulty, or, something. She mentioned having to write a report."

"What? That's ridiculous! How dare she suggest something like that!"

"Wait. Sarah, really, I don't know why, but I think she's just looking for a reason to see you again."

"That's crazy," said Sarah. But even as she said it, her mind flew back to that summer long ago, to the anticipation she had felt then for Veronica's arrival, to the way her friend's powerful tentacles had wrapped themselves around her family, to all that happened afterwards. Sarah had been so infatuated with Veronica then. Was it normal for girls of that age? Had Veronica felt the same way about her? Did she feel it still?

"I don't like her being in charge of Amelia," Sarah said, surprising herself.

"What?" There was a beeping on David's end of the line.

"Nothing, you're driving. I've got to go anyway. See you at home. We'll talk about it then."

The tube would have been far quicker, Chancery Lane was round the corner, but every bit of her resolve was going into staying calm for what lay ahead. The MRI scans were a yearly challenge – an annual check on a benign brain tumour they'd found when she was sixteen. Of course, open scanners were shiny new and available, but not covered by her health insurance, nor by the NHS, so once a year, every year, Sarah had to steel herself for the tunnel. She had at least developed a few tricks to get her through. Although generally opposed to drugs – refusing when others at university dabbled in cocaine, or ecstasy, or other names she lost track of – now, a sedative was a necessity; she always brought somebody with her to wait outside; and there was a mantra that she repeated to herself over and over: the fear wasn't real, the fear wasn't real, the fear wasn't real. Nor, she attempted to convince herself, was the dizziness, the dry mouth, the gripping of her chest, the constriction in her throat, the feeling that she was trapped and trapped and going to die that way.

Her father greeted her with a hug as she stepped out of the cab in front of the hospital and promised earnestly to break down the door of the scanning room if she did not emerge within one minute of the scheduled half hour slot. He promised the same thing every year. She loved him for this. In chambers, she had not told anybody about her claustrophobia (despite a number of humiliating episodes which she had explained away as a stomach bug, a hangover, a result of skipping lunch), but her family knew all about it. More specifically, they knew that she had it, and what it entailed for her, they didn't know its cause. Even Sarah couldn't be certain – perhaps it had always been there, sleeping, dormant, waiting for the trigger. Perhaps she couldn't blame one incident, one person. Then again, she remembered in vivid detail the first time she felt this way – drenched in the wet smell of chlorine, and the coolness of slatted wood.

Veronica went first. "I dare you," she said slowly as she picked at peeling nail varnish. "I dare you to be my slave for ten minutes."

"No. That's not one dare, that's as many dares as you can fit into ten minutes." Sarah had procured a Cherry Coke from the pool house fridge and rested her bottom lip against the cold glass, blowing gently to make music.

Veronica laughed. "No, I won't ask you to do anything

stupid. *Just things like, well like being a servant in olden times. But you're only allowed to answer 'Yes' to me, and you have to do whatever I say."*

Sarah furrowed her brow, placing the glass bottle on the floor next to the slatted wood of the bunk. She crossed her legs around themselves. Loud thumping occupied her chest and her stomach clenched. Servitude? It was degrading and both she and Veronica knew this, seeing it exactly for what it was – an absolute concession of power, a hundred miles away from the self-respect that Sarah's parents had always instilled in her. 'Be true to yourself'. 'Stand up for what's right'. 'Be the leader'. These were practically family mantras – the imperative to be the shepherd and not the sheep, to be aware of the choices one made, to not blindly do as one's told. They talked about such things over the dinner table. Sometimes in relation to trivial issues, like not succumbing to fads; other times, in recollection of the Holocaust, and family members lost there. Even as a young child, Sarah had absorbed her parents' outsider mindset, their integrity too, and by twelve, this had evolved into a tangential fixation: a need to always be in control – of the moral code, of the situation, of herself. But, there was something enticing about the opposite: the challenge of letting go. There was something freeing about it. "Fine," she agreed, as though it was nothing. "What shall I do for you, Queen Veronica?"

"You say only 'Yes'," Veronica reminded her. "And we're not starting now. We start when I say 'go'."

"I'm not going to wait around all day for you to think of things," Sarah complained. "Dare me something else, this is boring."

"No, it's when I say 'go'," Veronica insisted.

And there was no more time to argue about it because that's when Sarah's mother called them up to lunch.

"Wouldn't you two have more fun up here than in that cramped pool house?" Sarah's mother asked lightly after they'd all dashed in from the rain and set upon ever-large slices of quiche. "Then Eliza could join you."

Eliza looked up from her lunch and shot an accusatory glance at her mother.

"We don't want Eliza to join us," Sarah responded. "And she doesn't want to anyway. She doesn't even want us to go to her oh-so-fabulous party."

"Don't you?" Sarah's mother asked, squinting at Eliza.

"It's an evening in," Eliza corrected.

"We were hoping we could go," Veronica piped up suddenly. "Weren't we Sarah? Didn't you say you wanted to go? Didn't you say you really hoped that we could 'go'?"

Mid bite of quiche, Sarah froze. Veronica was winking furiously behind a carton of juice. A public dare! Enduring for ten whole minutes! It was so demeaning, so carefully cruel. But excitement tightened Sarah's stomach.

"Yes," she answered slowly.

"Then that's fine, Sarah and Veronica can come," Sarah's mother declared, nodding pointedly at Eliza.

"I don't even care," Eliza shrugged.

"Thanks," smiled Veronica ungelically.

"Okay, I have two more patients," Sarah's mother said, getting up from the table. "How about we give it till four then go to the cinema? This rain's horrendous."

"Fine," answered Eliza on behalf of them all. Then, when their mother had returned to her office: "I couldn't really care less if you come to my party or not, brat, just stay away from me, okay?"

Sarah opened her mouth to respond, but from the other side of the table Veronica shook her head. She looked at her watch and held up eight fingers, before speaking carefully: "Sarah, will you get me another glass, this one's dirty?"

Sarah hesitated. She looked at her sister, but Eliza seemed barely to be listening.

"Sarah?"

Another glance at Eliza. She was fiddling with the buttons

on her new Discman and appeared totally disinterested in the exchange of the two younger girls.

"Yes," Sarah said as casually as she could, getting up to retrieve the vessel and quickly plonking it down in front of Veronica.

"Do you want anything, Eliza?" Veronica asked. "While Sarah's up?"

Now Eliza raised her eyebrows and studied the two of them, Veronica seated, Sarah hovering just behind her. "I'll have a Coke if there is one."

Sarah didn't move.

"Sarah, get Eliza a Coke," Veronica prompted.

"Yes," said Sarah, her face flushing red.

It was four long, embarrassing steps to the fridge. She sensed Eliza's gaze searing into her as she fished around inside it. And Veronica's triumphant eyes. At some point she would have to turn around and face them both, but the coldness felt like a sanctuary. The Cokes were right in front of her but she lifted cartons and packets and opened drawers, every movement feeling awkward and acutely observed. Eventually there was nothing left to do but turn. She set the Coke roughly in front of Eliza.

"That was a bit rude, wasn't it Sarah?" said Veronica.

"Yes," growled Sarah, shaking her head and sitting back down, not daring another glance at her sister.

"Get me a Coke now," Veronica instructed.

Obediently, Sarah stood up again. Eliza watched her. This time she fetched the drink as quickly as she could.

"Pour it for me," Veronica demanded.

Eliza watched.

Sarah poured.

Veronica picked up the glass pointedly with six fingers. Sarah stood uncomfortably, unable to look at Eliza. Suddenly, however, her sister spoke.

"You two are weird."

Veronica opened her mouth to answer but Eliza held up her hand.

"Grow up," she said, perhaps only to Veronica, or perhaps to both of them. And with her Coke and quiche and Discman, she left the room.

Sarah burst into hysterics. "That was so embarrassing—" she began, but before she could say anything more, Veronica interrupted her with a held up hand, raised in the same haughty fashion that Eliza had done.

"Only 'yes', remember?" she asked patronisingly.

Sarah blinked. Now that they were alone, she had assumed the dare was over, but Veronica tapped her watch.

"Five minutes," she grinned. "Can you count to five?"

Sarah could have refused to answer. She could have stuffed the dare, recaptured her integrity. Or just laughingly done it — without spectators, it shouldn't have been embarrassing. Yet, somehow, this private exchange between them felt even more humiliating than before. Sarah knew that Veronica's family had maids. She wondered if this was how she spoke to them. Veronica stared at her boldly. Testingly.

"Yes," replied Sarah, with equal boldness. She jutted out her hip and placed her hand upon it.

"Stand up properly," said Veronica. "Take your hand off your hip."

Sarah obeyed.

"Lower your eyes."

Sarah obeyed.

"Whoops," said Veronica, and tipped her coke slowly onto her bare feet. "Get that cloth," she instructed. "Clean my feet."

Over the following days, the dares spiralled. Sarah's next for Veronica was to invoke not only the notorious baby voice, but baby crawling and bawling in front of Sarah's father who had no idea what was going on and pretended not to notice. At some point, one of them had to make three prank calls in a row to Lisa Markozy, confessing love for her. And *somebody had to go up to the aging postman and ask him, quite seriously, if he wanted fries with that shake. There was nothing dangerous, or criminal, or even particularly daring, but all sorts of boundaries were tested and pulled at, and the thrill was the not knowing how far they would go. By their fourth night-time meeting in TCR they had all but forgotten who was daring who, and now they concocted challenges they were both equally repulsed by, or pretended to be. Sarah had to pose naked while Veronica drew her. Then Veronica had to open her legs while Sarah stared at the knickerless area between them – without blinking Sarah, you're not allowed to close your eyes. And then they both had to skinny dip, illuminated by the underwater pool light, with extra points for breaststroke. Giggles punctuated giggles. They couldn't stop even as they returned to the house and snuck back upstairs to their beds. Dry and pyjama clad, they lay and somehow found conversation to fill another whole hour, or two, or three. It was easy, and delicious, and they stopped only when Sarah's mother opened the bedroom door at two in the morning and properly told them off because it was ridiculous to still be awake, and at that volume selfish too. After Sarah's mother had left, they would fall quiet, but a few minutes later Sarah would feel Veronica creep into the bottom of her bed, and with feet next to faces, they finally drifted off.*

Who knows whether TCR would have continued to house their pre-pubescent dalliances if Eliza had not had her evening in. But the day of the party, instead of camping out again in the pool house, Sarah's mother took them shopping and bought them each a new 'body' – bodies being a glorified leotard with poppers at the crotch, the uniform of the teenaged cool. Veronica's was pale peach, complementing her tanned skin and bright blonde hair. It had been Sarah's first choice too, but her mother insisted that it washed her out and steered her towards a deep red. Eliza had selected an electric blue one, ribbed with a low neckline that showed the brimming contents of her push-up bra. Veronica expressed her admiration at this. Sarah rolled her eyes.

She rolled her eyes again when Eliza appeared that evening fully dressed, her beautiful dark hair curled in a variety of spirals and crimps, her newly pierced ears sporting dangly blue earrings, her eyelids delicately shaded to match. Suddenly Sarah wished she had borrowed the lipstick Veronica had offered her, and dried her hair properly after her shower, and not chosen a body that was quite so flattening. Not that there was anything to flatten.

She rolled her eyes a further time when Eliza's friends arrived, coolly excited, chewing gum and flicking their hair. And again, when the boys turned up on mass. Amalgamated sharpness quickly over-scented the living room. Puffy bomber jackets and curtain-cropped hair clustered on one side of the room, bodies and jeans on the other. Pizza, coke and crisps – and nothing else Mum, really, please don't – stood brave in the middle, occasionally luring a couple of opposites in. Saranveronica stood in a two on the edge of Eliza's huddle.

Until, halfway through the evening, one of the boys meandered over and said hi to Veronica. And Veronica didn't seem to notice Sarah roll her eyes at that, or at least she didn't respond to it. And by the time the games began and the lights were turned down, and they were spinning bottles and declaring themselves 'nervous' and engaging in an array of other pastimes that brought lip to lip, and hand against padded bra, Veronica was altogether part of Eliza's coven, and Sarah had either to join in or not, and found herself retreating upstairs with a 'headache', to climb into bed with her parents who were watching TV, every now and then her father declaring it 'a load of rubbish', her mother hushing him, and Sarah tearing the crusts off his pizza.

When Veronica finally came up to bed, with Eliza, Sarah was back in her own bed and heard the two of them whispering feverishly outside her door. She strained her ears until at last her friend entered the bedroom. For a minute or two Sarah allowed Veronica to believe her asleep, fumbling around in the dark for her pyjamas, but after a while she switched on her bedside light and sat up, and waited for Veronica to talk.

"I got off with Adam," Veronica grinned almost at once, flopping onto Sarah's bed.

Sarah furrowed her forehead. Immediately, she wished she'd remained in the dark. "Which one was Adam?"

"The really fit one with the blue t-shirt. The one I was talking to. Eliza says he's really cool."

"Don't remember."

Now Veronica frowned slightly. "How's your headache?"

"Bit better." Sarah rubbed her temples for authenticity. "So?"

"So?"

"So? Go on then. What was it like?"

"Did you really have a headache, Sarah?" Veronica sat a little further back on the bed and stared at her seriously.

"Of course I did."

"You weren't just scared of playing those games?"

"Don't be stupid." Sarah threw a teddy bear at Veronica. A little too hard. It hit her on the neck.

"Ow."

Veronica stood up and moved to her bed where she set about taking off her shoes.

"So?" Sarah prompted again.

"Eliza said you were scared. But you know you could have just said 'nervous', if you didn't want them to touch you."

"I had a headache!" Sarah barked.

"O-kay." One by one, Veronica removed a row of bangles from her wrist.

Sarah gritted her teeth. "Sooo?"

"I'll tell you about it tomorrow," Veronica answered flippantly, pulling off her jeans and unbuttoning the ridiculous body with the stupidly placed poppers, that made Sarah feel like she was in a babygro. "Too tired now," Veronica softened,

yanking on an oversized t-shirt and crashing her head against the pillow. "Night."

The next day, however, and for the remaining three that Veronica was there, she didn't tell Sarah what it had been like to kiss someone. And Sarah didn't ask again. Although they still swam, and played cards, the long, expansive days of summer seemed to have lost their openness, their wile-away-ness. Things felt fissured, the first cracks of childhood. And Sarah noted that Veronica spent much of her remaining time either on the phone to Adam, or giggling from inside Eliza's bedroom. The two of them seemed suddenly to have secret things to discuss, and if Sarah appeared at the door, they would go quiet and sullen. One afternoon, Eliza crimped Veronica's hair. Another evening, Veronica borrowed Eliza's top when they all went out for dinner. Sarah spent a lot of time rolling her eyes. They didn't return to TCR. Or mention it.

Until, on Veronica's last day, they were packing up down at the pool, Sarah long-sufferingly listening to another idiotic detail about Adam with what she hoped was unspoken but noticeable disapproval, when she remembered that her favourite swimming costume was still in TCR, and ran through the pool house to get it. She had only been inside the room for a second, when the door slammed.

Sarah's first thought was that it was windy, and the door did that sometimes, so it was with a vestige of calm that she tried the handle. But the door wouldn't budge.

Sarah's stomach clenched. Already, the single window seemed tinier, and the switch for the light a million miles away in all its good being outside the room. She tried the handle again, pulling hard, imprinting the shape of it deep into her clutching palm. For a second, she thought she felt somebody moving it from the outside, then there was definitely the sound of a key turning, and for a moment she felt her body flood with cool relief. She even stood back to wait for the door to open.

But instead, a few seconds later, she heard Veronica's voice, not just beyond wood, but far outside: "Just going up to hang with Eliza!"

"No!" Sarah called after her, her fingers scratching at the door. "No! Veronica, wait! The door's stuck! Veronica! Veronica!"

But there was no answer, except for perhaps a giggle, wafting on the wind.

And then, nothing at all – no pulling on the door, no Veronica raising the alarm, no Eliza. No parents coming to help. They were going out, Sarah remembered frantically. For the first time, they had agreed to leave Eliza in charge.

Second by frightening second, the room shrunk to suffocation.

And Sarah screamed.

She screamed until her throat hurt and her voice came out in muffled wheezes. She banged against the door until her knuckles bled. In vain she tried to climb the bunks and squeeze through the miniscule window, but her face scratched against the splintered frame and her shoulders wouldn't fit. Tears arrived. Great heaving ones that she hadn't felt since she was much younger, and grabbed at her lungs. She gasped for air. She worried she was choking. Nausea gripped her stomach. Her ears rang. And on and on it went, on and on and on, until so much time elapsed that she collapsed onto the bottom bunk and drew her knees up to her chest and lay there, whimpering, shaking, trapped. As she cried, the sound of her feebleness, the physical proof of it, both angered and disgusted her, but she couldn't stop. She couldn't stop. She couldn't do anything. This time it wasn't a consensual dare, this time she couldn't say no, this time she was truly out of control. A timid sheep leading no one.

The pale light from the window began to fade, panic swelled in her throat, and she trembled more. Because now came the darkness. Not the soft bedroom kind, filtered by street lights through curtains, or hallway lamps. Not the moonlit, stargazing kind. But absolute, devil-shaped darkness, where even one's own limbs cannot be deciphered, and so detach, like a part of oneself lost. On the bunk, Sarah backed herself into a corner, the feeling of wood against flesh anchoring her at least to existence.

But then came the thirst. And the hunger. And then a need for the loo. She couldn't move, she couldn't bring herself to move, so soon there followed a liquid stench that wrapped itself around her legs and turned to paralysing coldness.

Finally, there was a slipping into oblivion.

By the time the door opened, it was light again outside, but the darkness had settled deep within.

"Here you are!" exclaimed Veronica cheerfully.

Veronica led her by the hand up to the house. She kissed her on the cheek as Sarah changed silently for breakfast, neither of them mentioning the 'accident' to her parents. All through that meal, Sarah stared with red, sore eyes at her sister and her best friend, their hair freshly braided to match, one dark, one light, both sleek and smooth, her own colour an in-between nothingness, matted with tears.

"I love you Sawah," Veronica said that night in bed.

And then, Veronica left. She and her parents retreated to Brighton for the rest of the summer. And when almost a month later they were about to return to school, Veronica phoned to say that her parents were moving to Oman and she was going to boarding school, and could Sarah please also say hi to Eliza.

That autumn term, Sarah was not in a two. Neither was anybody else. Somehow, without discussion, the old pairings had dissipated. A number of the girls in her year had met boys at summer camp or on holiday, or at an elder cousin's evening in, and some were now the overt holders of boyfriends.

Liaisons lasted a week, two. At a month they were relationship veterans. They figured out their lasting compatibility by writing their names and crossing out the letters that corresponded to the word LOVE on the backs of their homework diaries. Occasionally a particular bomber-jacketed boy would turn up with a few friends in the school car park, and then they would untie ponytails and borrow each other's hairbrushes and lip gloss, before sauntering arms hooked down the path to meet them. And coolly flicking their hair. At somebody's Bat Chayil that December, a boy with floppy brown locks and unfinished stubble asked Sarah to 'pull' him. And she did.

Nobody mentioned the drama and fascination they had felt just months earlier in the friendships of twelve-year-old girls. They still had friends, and best friends, and took time to make the distinction. But they were no longer practising for other things.

Veronica did not stay in touch. She might as well have moved to Oman with her parents for all the difference it made her being in Kent. Letters trailed off by Christmas.

Yet Sarah had thought of Veronica. She thought of her when she closed the door to a too-small toilet cubicle, when her mouth went dry in a lift, or when panic struck her on the tube. She thought of her when she saw a flash of blonde hair, or tanned flesh diving into a swimming pool. She thought of her when she saw her own naked reflection on the bathroom wall.

She thought of her now too, eyes firmly shut so as not to see how close the MRI machine was around her. Of course the pool house had been the trigger. Of course it was Veronica. Of course the impact was material. Before then, she and Eliza had laughingly hidden themselves in the linen chest at the end of their parents' bed; and they had buttoned themselves into duvet covers, delighting in losing the opening. She and Eliza. Eliza.

Sarah's breath stuck suddenly in her throat. She had spent

so long pretending not to blame herself for Eliza's accident that she hadn't even let her mind reach the logical conclusion of that thought.

Who had caused the claustrophobia that called for a car instead of the tube?

Who had put Eliza on the road that day really?

Who had pulled that trigger?

Veronica. Veronica.

Of course it was Veronica. She'd pulled Eliza away from her that summer, and then she'd taken her forever.

Veronica.

For twenty-odd years she'd been the source of all Sarah's nervousness and fear and self-loathing. The reason she'd declined a university sports trip, unable then to summon the courage to fly. The reason she'd had to rush out of an interview after a revolving door sent her into panic. The reason for nights and nights of insomnia in the dark. And Eliza. The reason she had lost Eliza. Her sister. Her always.

And Veronica didn't even seem to remember.

That had been the thing about her from the beginning, the thing that Sarah most hated and envied: the girl was oblivious. Beautiful naturally. Confident without trying. Wealthy for generations. And more than anything, she was free, bold, wild. That was what captivated people, that was what had hypnotised Sarah, that was what sometimes still, she wished she could be, rid of the long lists of morals embedded within her, the responsibilities of an immigrant family, a wandering people, parents who instilled these things. What would it be like, she wondered, to be free to do something deliberately bad, or not even bad, but foolish, unguarded, careless? What would it be like for the world to come so easily, to be as oblivious as her friend?

Keeping her eyes shut tight inside the machine, Sarah asked her mind to imagine it. But she couldn't, because even at university, even in that great wildness of youth, Sarah had remained 'true to herself'. She had drunk only in moderation.

She had never woken up in a surprising bedroom. She simply was unable to be that girl who could get up in front of other people to sing or dance with abandon, who didn't care. Only once, it had happened. Just once: at her parents' house that summer, under the blanket of night, and the sticky wood of the pool house, and the indifference of her hero sister. Watchful margins had somehow rubbed away, and awakened things. She had been emboldened, by Veronica, loved by her, illuminated by her gaze.

Until all light disappeared in the tiny room at the back of the pool house.

Sarah opened her eyes, then seeing the proximity of the machine, snapped them quickly shut again in a surge of panic – familiar and debilitating.

How dare Veronica do this to her? And to Eliza. And not even deign to remember it. How dare she invite them to dinner and then undermine her, manipulate her, visit David. How dare she make trouble now for Amelia. Suggesting there was something wrong with her. Hold that over them. And why did Sarah put up with it? Why had Sarah never called her to account? Why had she let it go back then? Why hadn't she told her parents? Why had she 'risen above it' and 'walked away' and not done something to take revenge?

Finding her, days later, crying in the bathroom, Eliza had hugged her, and hugged her, and made her tell her everything. Then she'd told Sarah that she'd had no idea what Veronica had done – Veronica had said Sarah was ill in bed. And she didn't care what Adam thought, she'd never liked Veronica anyway, she'd only been hanging out with her because she was there, and she knew it would annoy Sarah. 'Sorry,' she'd added. Her tanned arms squeezed Sarah's tiny frame. She smelled of coconut sunscreen. And bubblegum lip gloss. Sarah breathed her in, and Eliza squeezed tighter. Then she told Sarah – softly, sincerely – that she knew the two of them had been fighting lately, that things were different, but Sarah was still her sister, always her sister. Always. So she would always be in her corner, on her side. And at least Sarah had been the bigger person, and done nothing of which she should feel ashamed

Despite teenage-dom, Eliza was as fluent as Sarah in the family mantras.

People evolve though, don't they?

They meander.

Simone

Simone dresses in jeans, a simple white t-shirt, and a blazer she bought a few years back from a thrift shop. Outside the school gate, she stamps out her cigarette. She remembers how to play this part, though now it feels like dress-up. The teachers don't seem to notice. In the head's office, they are easily convinced. They tell her about the 'incident', the morning after her fight with Terry – how Dominic arrived late, as he does most mornings they add, then kicked over a classroom chair when the teacher asked him a question about the homework. In turn, she promises to have words with him, agreeing with the school that boundaries need to be set. It's that age, isn't it, she volunteers, when they start to act out a bit; she'll talk to him. Also, there's the general lack of concentration, the panel of teachers persist – more politely now that she seems one of them – and the detachment, has she noticed him tuning out sometimes? Because it's not that he doesn't have potential. But he must make an effort, he must stay on top of things, and of course any kind of violence cannot be tolerated. Simone smiles and agrees and bemoans that she doesn't know where it has come from.

A nod to the secretary as she exits the building completes the exchange of adult exasperation. Simone makes it through the heavy door and down the steps, her palm slowly stroking the railing, flesh finding fortification in cool iron.

But at the bottom she has to let go, and it is before she has left the playground that she collapses into a torrent of tears, unbefitting of her blazer, crouching on the concrete. She has told Dominic's teachers exactly what her parents would have said about her, what they did say, to her – they didn't know where it had all come from.

Simone stares at the closed wooden door. The scratching is there, like a mouse between floorboards. She is sixteen. Her father's pen works to fill the pages from which he'll speak tomorrow, delivering a lecture, enlightening a class, filling his students with the passion he does not hold for his wife and cannot muster for his daughter. If she knocks, he won't answer. If she enters, he will usher her away. If she stands in the hallway and screams and hits the walls and knocks over photographs, perhaps he will emerge for a moment and look at her with disappointment, or worse, puzzlement, confirming how unknown she is to him. If she keeps it up for long enough, perhaps her mother too will come out from her bedroom where she might be sleeping, is always sleeping, the research fellowship having disappeared without explanation some years back. Then, her mother will stare at her disdainfully, as though perturbed by the intrusion of sound. There is no point in any of these things. So Simone moves from the hallway into her bedroom, where she closes her own door, and gently scratches her skin instead of paper. She watches the way the blood trickles past her wrist, taking comfort in the certainty of that, proof that her actions do cause an effect, even if only on herself.

It is winter, but she wears short sleeves around the flat, waiting for somebody to notice. The multiplying marks on her arms are like breadcrumbs, but her mother leaves her dinner for her in the oven, and her father eats his behind his closed wooden door, and they miss the clues they might have otherwise used to track back to her. Or to each other. They are sleeping separately. There is no spare room, but Simone notices the blankets hidden behind the sofa and the way that the living room has come to have a slept-in morning stench. Nobody has told her anything. Nobody speaks at all. She feels as though she will be deafened by the silence.

At school there is a new student who doesn't yet know that Simone is not one of the popular girls. They find themselves next to each other in A Level English and she asks Simone where you can go around here to party. Simone doesn't know, but she pretends she does and takes the new girl, Kara, to a pub she walks past sometimes and seems busy. Kara looks around disdainfully as they enter. The clientele is far older than they are. There should be blow-dried girls in flared jeans, and men ordering copious rounds of vodka shots. There should be trendy light fittings, and menus describing humorously named cocktails. Instead, a gang of long-haired bikers look up from their beers. The other sticky tables are populated similarly disappointingly: middle-aged alcoholics; younger, pasty-skinned girls unsophisticatedly revealing both leg and middle; guys with shaved heads and gold teeth, all of them laughing too loudly, too coarsely. Kara goes to the bar and orders a gin and tonic. Simone, who has never drunk alcohol, copies her. The liquid feels at once cool and hot. Within a second, she can feel it flowing through her veins. "You sure about this place?" asks Kara, and Simone assures her that usually it's really buzzy and maybe they're just there a bit early, and anyway the drinks are cheap. Kara nods but isn't convinced. When she has finished her drink, she pretends she isn't feeling well and suggests they leave. Simone laughs loudly at this and tells her to go. By now, the gin is pumping hard, she can feel it coursing through her.

"Lightweight!" she declares, then she taps a man on the shoulder and points at Kara: "She's a lightweight!"

Kara does not really know Simone yet, they're not really friends, she doesn't feel the weight of obligation. So she leaves.

Left, Simone orders another gin and tonic, and then

another. Music sings in her spine. The too-loud laughter is contagious and she sets about giggling. The barman asks her if she's alright, and she shouts back to him: "I'm laughing!" He nods, that you are, love, that you are. "I'm laughing," she repeats to a table of people nearby. And they find this hilarious. They laugh with her. Or maybe at her. They hear what she has said and they laugh in response. One of them moves up on the bench and invites her to join them. They are only a few years older than she is, mainly men, but there's a girl on one of their laps. Somebody orders her another drink. That too feels good; it blurs things. She laughs again. And the group laugh again. One of the men puts his hand on her thigh, and she points at it: "Look what he's doing!" And everybody laughs again at that.

It might have been minutes or hours later that she feels movement in her stomach, a curdling of something. She runs to the door of the pub and throws up outside it. One of the men from the table joins her. He puts his arm around her waist. "You want me to take you home?" he asks. She shakes her head and stumbles away. She is unnerved suddenly, weakened by her stomach's frailness, alerted to the realisation of something shifting inside. She wobbles, slipping off the pavement. "You sure?" the man asks again. But she nods convincingly, and he doesn't follow, and somehow she finds her way back home, where nobody is waiting.

That night she doesn't even register the silence in the house. She sleeps without waking, well past the single, persistent sound of her alarm for school. When she hobbles into the kitchen for breakfast, still nobody is there.

It is almost two months before she starts singing on the doorstep. They can't ignore that, can they? Neighbours complain. But by then she has met Noah and she only wants her parents to notice so that she can tell them it's too late.

Noah is six foot tall, skinny, his hair long and locked in

dreads. He is more reserved than his friends, but he notices everything. He noticed her. On the night they first kissed, he ran his thumb over the bumpy tracks on her forearm, then he covered them with a strong, large palm, as though he was bandaging her, shielding her with protective wrap. His mother is a nurse in A&E. His father works in retail. She discovers later that this means he is a sales assistant in Dixons, but Noah is following neither of his parents' paths, and they don't want him to. He is studying for his NVQ in accounting, and he writes songs that he is beginning to gig. That is his passion, he tells her, his dream if ever he can afford to pursue it. His friends believe he will. They raise him up as special, a towering talent in their midst, only there among them until the world discovers his gift, although each of them have whispering aspirations too, growing louder. He plays his creations to Simone and she wants to cry for the way in which she feels he knows her. He thinks she is special too. He tells her to stuff her parents, but not to stuff up herself and urges her to do her exams that summer. She won't. They'll notice that. And besides, Noah is doing fine without A Levels. Exams aren't what matter. Money isn't even what matters. 'What matters then?' asks Noah.

His mother spends all day Sunday cooking Nigerian food that she stores in Tupperware and produces throughout the week. Simone regards the way that together the family sit to eat it. Between bites, they exchange stories, they offer ideas, they try out parts of themselves. Safely. Attentively. For weeks Simone watches it all with fascination, until finally she articulates something first to herself and then to Noah – her longing to be part of a family like that, an insider. Noah welcomes her into their close unit, understanding how much she needs it, putting his questions to one side. He doesn't drink, but he sees that, for now, she needs that too.

She wraps his estate around herself. They hang out on the Concourse. Noah steers her away from the guys who try to sell her drugs harder than weed, and the girls who sneer at her Zara jacket. They stay amongst his friends, who are fun and interesting and fiery and ambitious, feeding off each other like lit flames. They all want to change things. They all want to make an impact. They do things like writing spoken word, or training at athletics clubs, or joining political parties. They understand about being seen, being heard. Simone practises talking like they do – straight, blunt. Her parents would be shocked if they saw her. But they do not see her.

One night, returning from the estate, she trips over the top step to her flat and starts wailing in the street. Wailing as though she is a toddler and needs to be picked up, hands brushed, knee kissed. They leave their beds, come to the door, and this is the first time they pass comment on her behaviour. They didn't think she'd be so stupid, they tell her. She is seventeen, it's not even legal for her to be drinking. The next time, they put the chain on the door and lock her out until she can come home sober. Her mother starts slipping into the sacred space of her father's office and she hears them muttering. They don't know what's going on, they say to each other. They don't know what's going on, they say to her. They don't know where this has come from.

A week later she finds out she is pregnant. By a black guy from the estate, she tells them. And she is locked out until she can sober herself out of that one too.

It is then that she notices the grime. And the firmness of the walls around her.

Still, she tells herself, she is free. Free from the oppressive silence. Free from the stranglehold of invisibility. Free from the hypocrisy of a flat with a proudly decreasing mortgage, and balanced meals, and civic engagement, and nothingness.

Noah is real. He makes her feel part of something.

She drops out of school. Noah's mother, Lewa, tries to talk her out of this. It is not necessary, she says. They can help with the baby, studies are important, and her GCSEs were so good. But Simone wants only what they have, not the toxic veneer of letters after her name, false validations of worth. She washes down this decision with wine, beer, schnapps, gin, waiting for her parents to come after her and pull her from the filth.

Lewa gently suggests that it would be better, for the baby, if she lay off the alcohol, at least those first months. Concern unfolds itself across the room and finds Noah, nodding. Simone sees this, and so she does cut down, but not stop altogether. She can't now, she realises. She can't stop. She didn't know how quickly that could happen. She begins sometimes to drink in secret.

But Noah loves her. He writes songs about their unborn babe. He cleans the flat and paints it, he looks up on the internet how to tile a bathroom and he makes a good go of it. He takes on a job as a security guard, which they laugh at because of his skinny frame, and joke that with her expanding belly, she will soon be more threatening. He observes her carefully. It is Noah who notices her moods. It is Noah who delves deep to locate her desires. He goes one day, alone, in secret, to her parents' flat and asks them to reach out to her. They tell him that he has no right to stand there, that he has corrupted their daughter, that they want nothing to do with him, or her, so long as she's with him.

Nevertheless, when the baby arrives, they come to the hospital. They tell Simone that she cannot come home, but if she wants, they'll take Dominic.

It is Noah who persuades Simone not to cut them off completely.

He is a good father. She watches through blurry eyes as he gets up in the night and mixes bottles. She sees him change nappies and run baths in the sink. She notices the way that a sound or a movement from the baby seems to make a smile spread from its origin in Noah's mouth, into his eyes, and then all the way through him, dancing later in the notes of a new song, strummed softly on guitar next to the crib. She wonders how he has managed to capture such delight, for she does not feel it. She holds the baby because she has to, but she doesn't experience the rush of love she had expected. Dominic is a slight, sallow child, with small eyes. To spite her parents further, she had hoped he would be unmistakeable in his darkness, but he bears little resemblance to his father. She cannot see herself in him either. Lewa tries to show her how to breastfeed, but it feels unnatural and repulsive, a foreign creature tugging at her flesh. When Lewa arrives at the end of her nursing shift, Simone pushes the baby gratefully into her hands and sinks onto her bed, unable to comprehend how her body has become so heavy that it feels weighted with iron. Perhaps she is lacking iron, suggests Lewa, noticing her lethargy, bringing her supplements, singing soft gospel to Dominic as she dances him around the room, scattering about her an interminable scent of nutmeg. Dinners arrive in Tupperware. Noah heats them up and while the baby sleeps, she sees him trying to talk to her, trying to recapture that expanse of understanding between them. She sees him doing this, building that same family closeness she had envied; but she cannot join him in it. She no longer feels like an insider to his life. She only wants to sleep, to escape. But in the day there is the baby. And at night her mind will not stop. One afternoon when Noah is on security, she leaves the baby with Lewa and takes herself across the Concourse to the alcohol shop where she buys a bottle of wine. She plans to drink it all before returning to the flat so that Lewa won't judge her, but on the way back, somebody asks her if she's after an upper, and of course she is, anything to lift that iron weight from her bones. And after that, wine seems an immature, foolish flirtation.

It is almost six months after Dominic's birth that Noah's father, Robert, is diagnosed with stage four pancreatic cancer, and dies four weeks later. Lewa's nursing credentials are of no use. Noah's songs are of no use. And Simone's baby merely emphasises the great disparity between new life, and the ending of it. Noah's father spends his final days in a hospice, slipping in and out of morphine-induced oblivion: there, not there, there, not there, not there, not there, not there. The permanence is ultimately what slashes at Noah's soul. Life had poured through him before, fluid in its promises; but absence, nothingness, these are immobilising realities. The guitar music stops. The bath-times stop. He stops noticing how desperate and detached Simone has become. One evening, the baby crying, both of them hungry, neither moving, she offers him a line she had hidden in her sock drawer. She'd thought by now he must have guessed her habit, but he turns to her with a slow look of disgust, as though observing a ballerina taking off her costume to reveal that beneath the glittered skirts, there is only humanity: bloodied toes, bruised bones. And she watches his face as every last illusion of beauty is shattered.

That night, Noah leaves Simone alone with the baby who cries so much that she is forced to drag herself from the bed to mix his formula and to change his nappy. Without his father, it is her shoulder that the baby must fall asleep on, and despite the melancholy of the day, inhaling the soft breath of her boy, she feels just the smallest whisper of love sprouting. It is not developed, just a hint, but enough to see her through this first night that Noah is missing. When he returns the following lunchtime, he stinks of alcohol and marijuana. He sleeps through the day.

Now it is her turn, Lewa tells her.

Only a year has passed since Robert died, but Lewa is not the kind of woman to let the world crumble around her. Her flat remains immaculate, Sundays still spit out smells of spices, Tupperware is filled as ever with jollof rice and deep-fried yams. At the hospital, she does not miss a shift. Bills are paid, bins are taken out, and she turns up as often as before to sing nutmeg infused gospel-turned-lullaby to Dominic. While she is there, she urges Simone to eat, tutting at her skinniness. She tidies their flat, and she looks at her sunken son through eyes that betray sorrow and regret, as though his unravelling is her failure and not Simone's. But it is Simone's turn now, she tells her again.

Dominic has pooed through his nappy and Lewa is showing Simone how to bleach the material of his tracksuit bottoms. Their voices are low under the auspices of Dominic napping, but in truth, Lewa is grabbing the flash of muted air between them to fill it with obligation.

"Now he needs you," she is saying. "He is too young to give up on living. You are both far too young. It isn't too late."

But it is. Too late. Simone is disgusted by the pathetic lump that Noah has become. He is useless, defective, merely a bulging bulk in her periphery, like a tumour sapping them, almost as fast as it sapped Noah's father. He drinks more than she ever did, and now that she chooses to be up instead of down, she cannot stand to see him lying lifeless. Sometimes he collapses unmoving on the floor of the living room and she has to step over him to reach the sofa. She kicked him once when he was laid horizontal like this, kicked him like a bag of rubbish, or a defective machine, as though with one sharp nudge she might be able to knock back into him the energy he once discharged so keenly. Still, he lays motionless, and her stomach twists with resentment and revulsion. By the end of the year, she has asked him to go.

A space unfurls itself. A cold, beautiful, serene moment that lasts as long as it is able, though she feels its transience even as it is around her, aware of its fragility. She imagines herself during this time as an ice skater upon a frozen lake, pushing herself effortlessly across the dark, solid liquid beneath, gliding, gliding, walking, impossibly, on water. The wind is in her face. Frost nips with friendly tidings at her fingers and toes, and feel this, says the breeze, feel everything. She does. She feels with an intensity she's never known. No longer content with walking she spins and leaps and flies through the chilled air, not noticing the cracks opening beneath her sharp, razored feet, snow cut into thin, dangerous lines.

Into the space, Dominic grows and though the weeks and months are jumbled, there are moments of clear euphoria. Love has arrived now, fierce, boundless, finally imprinting itself into her bones. Even in her sleep she smells Dominic's infant skin, she can feel his warm, clutching arms wrapped around her neck, and she accepts the stabbing in her heart as the price for such pleasure. The stabbing comes most often when she is in the living room with a friend and a line, and he, her son, is locked asleep, or crying, in his room. It comes in waves that wash over her, lifting her high, dropping her low. It comes and comes. But even this is not strong enough to pull her from her other love, the substances that not only lift her high but stop her from falling. Only they can keep her standing up as she needs to. The ground beneath her is slippery. It is made of ice.

Even with Noah gone, Lewa comes for Dominic. She takes him to the family home his father has returned to, eyes glazed by booze and life, and she sings to them both at once. When Simone arrives to pick Dominic up, she stands sometimes at the window before knocking, watching, stifling a yearning deep inside her for the warmth she used to feel in this place, for the energy, for the reassuring sense of the insider, of wholeness. Sometimes she catches a glimpse of Noah side-on, and she doesn't see the vacant glassiness of his stare; instead she remembers how fast and how deeply she fell for him, and loved him, and loves him still. But she hasn't the strength. Not now. Not yet. She is only just staying standing. She is not strong enough to hold up another.

All she can do is glide.

Glide.

Ignore the splintering ice beneath her, slow in its expansion.

Hope she doesn't fall into the cracks.

And then Noah goes and gets himself killed in a car crash. Drunk at the wheel. And she cannot bear it. She cannot glide. She cannot balance. She cannot breathe. And everything collapses around her.

Lewa pounds on her door.
Lewa demands to see Dominic.
Lewa cries as Simone has never witnessed before.
Dominic cries too, for Lewa, from the other side of wood.
But Simone cannot bring herself to answer. If she does, then Lewa will judge her: for the overflowing bins; for Dominic's unclean clothes; for not taking her turn. She will stand there and judge. As her own parents did. And she will do so with Noah's dark, dreaded hair, and his dancing eyes, and the determined gaze that, perhaps, if it wasn't for Simone, could have done anything
"He's not yours," Simone tells Lewa eventually, calmly, resolutely through the door, many weeks after the funeral she didn't attend. "He wasn't Noah's either. Couldn't you tell? Never looked a thing like him."
A few months later, Simone hears that Lewa has moved to another estate somewhere south of the river.

It is another few months after that, that Simone's father turns up on her doorstep, her mother cowering in a parked car nearby. Simone is not so much surprised by their appearance, but relieved, as though the necessary thing has finally happened, and she lets them take Dominic for the weekend. Dominic is four years old then and doesn't know his grandfather at all, but he'll be alright, she tells him, he'll be alright, she tells herself. He has to be, because her parents don't invite her to go with them. Besides, she needs Dominic gone, if only for a day. She needs space again. She needs to scream and she needs space. But she is walled in tight by concrete.

The creeping darkness of the stairwell feels colder. The stench of piss smells stronger. The pumping flesh in her mouth tastes rancid. But he gives her a tenner, and that's almost enough for half a gram.

"You're Noah's bird, aren't you?" he asks, zipping up his trousers. "Always talked like you was something special, didn't he? That's a laugh, innit?"

She wipes her mouth, but stays crouching.

Pressing her hands against the concrete of the playground, Simone stands. Air pushes painfully through her lungs, but she forces herself to breathe deeply. She wishes Terry was there, the sheer force of his presence enough to sweep away her memories. He wouldn't have agreed with the teachers as she did. At home he'd have swiped Dominic about the legs with the metal end of his belt, and it is for this reason that she did not and will not mention the meeting to him; but here, he would have given the teachers what for.

Simone puts her hands to her face. Her make-up is smudged, but she'll stop in a café on the way and tidy herself. The staff at the gym won't notice. It's an easy part to play. She remembers this one too. She remembers it. All of it, suddenly, with growing colour, free from grey walls. It's easy. This is nothing.

Also, it is everything.

Terry's seen it. He's seen it in her, he's seen her desire for the things he despises, and he's watching. Watching her.

Simone longs for him, and she longs to be free of him.

She has no idea where it's all come from.

Sarah

"Look, it's not set in stone. At this stage, as I explained to David, it's just a concern," smiled Veronica.

"Do you usually track parents down outside of school?"

Sarah had appeared, uninvited, after school that Monday, on Veronica's expensively-tiled doorstep. A last-minute change to a case had prevented her normal Monday pick-up, but she had been seething all weekend, making David repeat again and again exactly what Veronica had said. Veronica's face looked pale at the intrusion, caught off guard perhaps. This was a meandering, not what she expected of Sarah. But if Veronica was going to snake her way across town to David, insert herself into their personal sphere, then Sarah could do the same. Besides, they were friends, weren't they?

"Of course not. Only because of our relationship. I didn't want to spring it on you with a formal letter."

Sarah nodded with what she hoped Veronica would realise was absolute scepticism.

Veronica stood up slightly from her leaned stance against the doorframe. "Do you want to come in?"

"No thanks. I have to get home to my kids."

Veronica smiled more broadly, but an unnerving coldness crept now beneath it. She never did like to be refused.

"Okay. Well, why don't we set up a formal meeting then? As I mentioned to David, I'm required to give a report of each child before they go up to the Juniors next year. So that their, *needs*, can be met."

"Amelia has no special 'needs' if that's what you're suggesting."

"Perhaps. Perhaps not. That's what we need to determine."

"Veronica, you know she doesn't."

Veronica smiled again. "Sarah, I don't mean to be rude, but I spend a great deal more time with your daughter than you do really, don't I?" She looked emphatically at her watch. "So, let's start with a meeting. You'd do that, wouldn't you? I mean, what would you do… for your daughter?"

Sarah felt her breath catch in her chest. "What? What did you say?"

Veronica continued to beam innocently. "What?"

Sarah didn't know how to respond. Should she hit her? Should she berate her? Should she plead with her? What on earth did Veronica want?

"Dinner sometime?" Veronica said eventually into the blistering air. "When you don't have to rush away, to your children. We can reminisce properly then. There's still lots to tell, I'm sure."

Sarah didn't nod, or agree, she couldn't. But she didn't say no either. "Goodnight, Veronica," she made herself utter. And forced herself again not to glance back to see Veronica's triumph at the open door.

Simone

Dominic is late.

Terry has been home for hours.

As soon as Dominic opens the door, Simone notices him noticing this – Terry's presence. It is tangible today, viscous. Terry has not yet looked up. The TV is blaring as usual. For a moment, Dominic glances back towards the hallway and Simone wonders if he is going to slip back out into the flower-boxed street, while he is still able. But he shuts the door silently and remains inside, his eyes searching as always for his sister. Jasmine is sitting on the carpet of the living room playing with her princesses. Wearing only a nappy and a t-shirt, her face is smudged with some kind of snack and she sings unintelligible words to the plastic figures in her hand, softly, as though she is soothing them. She has learnt this melody from Dominic, who despite his increasingly teenage demeanour, continues to dote on her. And watch over her. And shield her, when he can. Dominic takes a step towards her now and the floor creaks. Jasmine whips her head around, shrieking with delight at the sight of her brother. He smiles and stretches out his arms. She leaps up. But before she can get close, Terry turns.

Despite his own shortcomings in size, Terry is far bigger than Dominic, so when he stands square in front of him, when he lifts Dominic's chin in his palm, and when he lowers his face close to Dominic's ear, it looks threatening.

"Where the fuck have you been?"

Dominic coughs as the smoke on Terry's breath engulfs him. "Nowhere."

Like a bullet rebounding, Terry slaps the back of his head.

"I was just with Jakub. In the park," Dominic corrects quickly. "Weren't *doing* anything, I meant."

"That stinking Pole? You still mates with him?"

Dominic dares a glance at his mother. He's looking for help. But she doesn't like Jakub either. His mother is only a cleaner, but Dominic used to regale Simone with descriptions of how she sets Jakub extra homework, and teaches him piano, and sews his clothes, and how they have a bowl on their kitchen table always teeming with fruit. Jakub is Dominic's best friend and she knows he goes to his house, despite her disdain, pretending to be elsewhere. He doesn't invite Jakub back to theirs.

"Leave him," Simone tells Terry gently.

"Gotta be careful with Poles," Terry says. "Only gonna shaft you. You see them, don't you, Dom? In collaboration with the capitalists? Working cheap, ten to a flat, sending the money out of England, making it so that we, the English, we can't get a proper wage, feeding the fools at the top, just like they planned it. Hand in hand, aren't they? You best be careful with your Polak."

Dominic doesn't answer. He stands with his shoulders hunched, making himself even smaller.

"You're meant to be home anyway, aren't you? It's your day to do laundry. See, he's already steering you wrong, that Polak."

"Sorry," Dominic says now in dangerous monotone. He goes to the bedrooms where he gathers clothes from the floor and the wash baskets and brings them back to the kitchen where the washing machine is and where Terry is waiting. Carefully he sorts the clothes, and loads a pile of light-coloured items into the machine. Simone is making dinner a few feet away and attempts to stroke him on the back as he passes her. He responds with a small smile, an attempt at assurance, *Don't worry Mum*, but she should have known better, she should have left him. Terry is still watching.

"Know where this dense cow's been today?" Terry asks him suddenly, looming over the kitchen counter. "Know where? Ask her, go on, ask her!"

Dominic glances fearfully now at his mother. The panic in his eyes is sudden and clear, and she knows why – he thinks she's told Terry about the meeting at school. He thinks she's betrayed him.

"Where've you been, Mum?" Dominic asks, his voice quiet, trembling.

Terry prods her, laughing. "Go on, tell him, tell him."

"I started my job," she says, almost as quietly as her son.

"In a fancy blazer no less, didn't she, for a gym. Ooh, look at Miss Hoity Toity. Bet that's what you wanted them to think, didn't you? That you're something special? Eh?"

Terry begins to prance around the room in a crude imitation of her. She gives a forced laugh, and Dominic does too, his panic retreating just a little.

"Yeh, well, I learnt my lesson, I'll wear a tracksuit next time. It was a bit much."

"Fucking 'course it was, dense cow," Terry bellows. "That's what they want though, don't they. All these twats round here. Come join our dim-witted dance into oblivion. You ever seen anything so contrived? How easily manipulated do they think we are? Stuff us in holes and put bright lights around us, and we're gonna think our dark pit's gonna get some of that brightness? Yeh right. Whose plan was that anyway? Bloody Zionist bankers probably. Think they can control us. Think we don't notice, but I do, don't I? Don't I?"

Simone is not sure which of them this question is directed at. She dares to look away from Terry towards her son. Dominic may be off the hook about school, but he is still standing as motionless as he can, his eyes fixed on the older man, nodding whenever he pauses. Simone's breath relaxes a little. So long as they both stay listening, stay respectful, Terry's rant will run itself out. Minutes tick by to the beat of the whirring washing machine behind them. Every now and then there's a pause, and Simone and Dominic nod, before Terry carries on unabated, ignoring Jasmine's sporadic bursts into the kitchen area, which are warded off by Dominic passing her a Kit Kat. Simone tries hard, but she can't quite follow Terry's jumbled tirade. He's jumping from one subject to another, too fast for her so that it's impossible to follow the connections. There are frequent references to Toffs and Dirty Politicians and Jews and Fucking Primrose Twats, but she loses the thread of it. At one point there's something about 9/11 and the banking crash and how they're related, but she doesn't catch on to that either. Terry is talking at speed and loudly. There are few breaths. He's sat himself on a chair at the counter, but neither Simone nor Dominic dare to move. Her legs begin to stiffen. She sees Dominic's shoulders tightly raised. Now Terry asks Dominic something. What has he asked? Simone wasn't listening. Dominic glances at her, his eyes bright again with terror, but she can't help her son. Her own stomach contracts. She can see Dom's shoulders trembling. What has Terry asked?

"Do you think so?" Terry repeats, to Dominic.

Is he supposed to say yes, or no? Simone has no answer to mouth him.

"Well?"

"I dunno," Dominic answers finally, quietly, head bowed but eyes still dutifully fixed on the larger man. "Sorry."

There is a pause. A brief silence amid the thunder. Terry is staring at Dominic. He is close enough to hit him. Simone thinks he is about to. Not the face, she pleads internally. Not his face. But, suddenly, Terry laughs. "You're as dense as your dense mother."

Dominic says nothing. He keeps his head low.

Terry laughs again, this time louder. Then he leans over the counter and flicks his fingers sharply on Dominic's forehead. One, swift, ping.

Is that it? At the silliness of this gesture, it is all Simone can do not to laugh herself. Is that it? She thinks so. Terry is beginning to return to the sofa. It's over. It's over.

Then, however, the washing machine beeps. And once again, Terry turns.

Now, he watches Dominic take out the wet clothes. He's waiting for a mistake, Simone can feel it, it's not over at all, he's gunning for a fight. There's a drying rack behind the door and Dominic's meant to put a towel underneath it to catch drips. He remembers, thank God, he sets it up carefully, making sure to shake out each item to minimise creases, painstakingly ensuring there is breathing space between them; but suddenly, Terry rounds the kitchen counter and thuds him sharply in the small of his back.

"Where're my things then?" Terry is demanding, shouting. "Are yours more important?"

Dominic has had the wind knocked out of him, and between strained breaths, Simone sees him looking frantically at the clothes on the rack. They are a mixture of his school shirts and Jasmine's dresses and some underwear of her own. He has clearly sorted them by colour, just as she would. Terry's jeans and other stuff are in the pile of dark items he has not yet washed.

"I was just starting with the light stuff," Dominic says, inhaling sharply. "I'm doing yours now."

Immediately he turns to the dark pile on the floor and loads it into the machine, but Terry has already begun rummaging in a drawer behind him. Dominic turns. In his hand, Terry has a pair of scissors, the kitchen sort, large, sharp. Instinctively, Dominic puts his arms in front of his face.

"Tel," Simone intervenes quietly, but he shoos her away.

"Give me your clothes," he instructs Dominic.

Confused, Dominic lowers his arms and hands him the wet shirts he has just hung.

"You've got to respect your elders," Terry says, shaking his head. "You've gotta learn that, Dom. Don't forget who pays for your clothes, who pays for everything, who sorts out everything round here." He cuts through one shirt, and then the other. "Get the rest," Terry tells him.

It takes a while for Dominic to understand, but Terry explains it for him. He marches Dominic into his bedroom and one by one slashes every item of clothing he owns.

It is three hours later that people start arriving. It's not late, only around eight-thirty, but Dominic has been in his room since Terry left him there and the dinner Simone had been cooking never got served. She's left it on top of the kitchen counter, but she doesn't dare move from Terry, who is now all over her. Simone can hear Jasmine crying in her cot – she must be hungry, but Terry won't like it if she sees to the baby instead of him. Simone's only hope is that Dominic will go to her.

Things were worse for Dominic when he was a baby. Simone comforts herself with this often. At least Jasmine has a brother. At least Jasmine's dad is around, alive. At least Jasmine gets cooked for, usually, something she can't remember ever doing when Dominic was little. And at least this abandonment to her cot isn't regular. Dominic used to get left for hours when he was that age, if she had a friend round who'd brought some charlie. Simone winces when she thinks of that. Yes, in many ways, Jasmine has it easy.

The crying continues. There is a wrenching, wretched sorrow to it.

"Come sit with me," calls Terry.

The room is rowdy now and Terry is at the centre. Simone perches on one side of his chair, accepting the joint he passes her. Beneath the fog of that, and the din of music, and the chatter of the people, Jasmine's sobs are softened. Simone forces herself, or allows herself, to focus on the crowd.

There are nine or ten people in all, friends from the estate, and Terry is magnetic amongst them. He is holding court. Refuelling, Simone laughs at something he says. He kisses her smack on the cheek. Somebody passes her a beer. She feels herself relaxing.

Until suddenly, in her periphery, she catches sight of Dominic darting into the kitchen at the far end of the open plan living area. He doesn't know that he has been seen and grabs a few slices of bread and a chunk of cheese. He is like a mouse, scurrying close to the floor. With a sharp knife he starts cutting the food into edible pieces, then Simone notices him spy the baked potatoes she cooked earlier. Body still lowered behind the counter, he reaches for one and hurriedly slices this too. Then all at once there is a clatter. Simone looks to Terry with apprehension, but he hasn't clocked. The group have broken into song, and Terry's voice rises at the top of it. Dominic peers silently over the counter and sees Simone watching him. He lifts his hand. There is a trail of blood running from his finger down his arm. Simone tries with her eyes to ask him if he's okay, but he doesn't respond. He slips a dirty tea towel off the counter and wraps it around the blood. Then he looks at her, waiting.

Terry's hand is on her thigh. She doesn't move. Instead, she nods at Dominic again. But he merely waits. Silently. Testingly? She starts to feel agitated. She nods again, more firmly. And again. Until finally, he nods back. "Jasmine," she mouths to him now. Still he doesn't answer. Still he waits. And she waits. But eventually, he does slip silently away. A few minutes later, the sound of Jasmine's wailing ceases.

An hour after that, Simone hears a piercing scream. It sounds distinctly like Dominic. For a moment, her body tenses, air slicing her lungs like the knife sliced his finger, but then she realises that the shout hasn't come from his room at all, or from Jasmine's. She strains her ears through the music and when the noise comes again, she realises that the scream is not even within their flat, but coming from outside, and growing quieter as it moves away. Just somebody stupid, or drunk, like them, running in defiance down the civilised street.

Simone accepts another joint and slides her hand beneath Terry's t-shirt. He squeezes her round the waist, and she listens as he regales the room with another story that lifts them high into the night.

Veronica

It slipped like loose thread. Time. Memory. The blurred edges of reality. Veronica had been sat at the table for over an hour, twenty accounts of favourite hobbies spread out before her, not one read or corrected. From the house next door, music was pumping even beyond the usual decibel, and voices were raised – Terry's in its loutish tenor discernible amongst the multitude. Thank goodness the crying of the baby had stopped. Toddler, she should say, not baby. When she'd finally seen them all together on the street, Veronica had been surprised by how old the child had turned out to be. She hadn't considered that a little girl who could most likely talk and move and climb from her crib, would have cause to cry for so long nor so loud. But she did, often, and every sob that seeped through the walls continued to feel like the universe mocking Veronica, reminding her that this disgusting couple had easily, flippantly, manifested the very thing she hadn't, and couldn't. Same as Sarah. Sometimes Veronica longed to break through those walls and scoop the child up, and then run with her as far away as she could manage. She didn't know what would come after that though. It was only this one moment about which she fantasised.

She poured herself another glass of red wine. George was in bed. With earplugs. He'd arrived home just after ten and headed straight up, but Veronica had mumbled excuses about marking and lesson plans, not mentioning Sarah's surprise, unnerving visit, and remained at the table with her papers and her wine and a new level of relentless itching. It had been three days since she'd told George there was no baby, three days since she'd slept more than an hour at a time, and the dark wakefulness of the bedroom loomed terrifying. All weekend George had tight-roped between apology and cheerfulness, an impossible attempt, she realised, to sympathise with her disappointment, yet not seem too disappointed himself. In return, she accepted sushi and alcohol, and hated him. Hated him for saying nothing, for pretending that the hole inside her and the canyon between them didn't exist.

Like the baby that wasn't.

The celebration that wasn't.

The future that wasn't.

The marriage that wasn't.

The friendship that was, once, but no more.

The girl, herself, dancing with eternal pre-teen verve, just beyond articulation.

She could barely remember that girl. Not really. All she could recall was that during those last days at Sarah's house, she had felt powerful. Is that what they had argued about? She had remembered recently that there was something, something that had caused a rift between them, though she was sure they'd parted happily in the end. After all, that summer was her calm time. Her content time.

Still, there had always been a certain patchwork element to Veronica's recollections. Sometimes she put this down to the piecemeal chronology of her childhood and whenever she was asked about her youth, it was in this fashion that she deliberately rolled the quilt out for the listener: here was her flat in Holland, there was the market in Oman, here the New York subway, there the handsy English teacher. Described this way, she sounded worldly and exotic. But the threads that held this variety of pieces together were darned hastily and sometimes they seemed to split inside her. She couldn't gather them or hold them all at once. She couldn't order them or pull from them a sense of progression. She could barely even locate herself within them. And so they slipped, untethered threads.

Why did Sarah hate her?

Veronica took a long gulp of her wine and looked out to the street, as though solidity lay somewhere in the lamp-lit throws of prettily painted Primrose. Her mind spun. She had to still it. It had been many years since she'd felt this out of control, and she had to regain it. She'd grown up now. She didn't want to pilfer. The thought of what she'd been doing to Amelia was sickening.

But resentment burned in the empty space where a baby should be.

No. She'd been enough, once. She had to remember that. She'd been enough, without a baby, without Sarah, just as she was. Of all the misshapen, untied, jumbled memories, that's what she had to remember and cling on to. She'd been wrong to return to pilfering, wrong to taunt her old friend, wrong to go to the museum, wrong to use Amelia. There was no need to tear at the hem of Sarah's life just to darn her own. It was far better to be mending, patching, fixing.

She would lay off Amelia. It wasn't necessary to explain, she would simply find an excuse not to have the meeting.

She would lay off Sarah too – not force the friendship, not force herself to confront her envy.

She would busy herself – with other friends, with her husband, with their new home. Except of course, that as soon as she glanced again to the street and considered their perfect, pastel dwelling, she remembered that, unlike Sarah, she had no family to fill it.

Then, a face appeared at her window.

It was wrong to feel so unnerved by the sight of an eleven-year-old. Veronica realised this at once and was reprimanding herself for it before the thought was even fully formed. But the intensity of Dominic's beady, too-close eyes had a way of disquieting her even on the street in daylight; and this time, it was not day but night, and he was not innocuous on a public street, but peering through her window, at her. As soon as he saw her see him, he backed away a little, squirreling again, but as he did so she noticed a towel wrapped around his hand, darkened by something she could only presume was blood.

Afterwards, she would wonder why she hadn't thought of calling up to George. Afterwards, she would wonder a lot of things. But in that moment, all that occurred to her to do was either to shut the curtains and shield herself from the boy's strange probing eyes, or to open the door and ask him in.

He lowered himself into a chair at the great oak table where moments before she had been sitting. He appeared to be waiting for something and so, without being asked, Veronica brought him a mug of hot chocolate and a sandwich. The sounds of slow chewing nibbled at their ears.

"What's happened, Dominic?" she ventured finally, nodding towards his hand.

At first he shrugged in habit, but then, perhaps realising the obligations attached to his sitting there in her kitchen, he mumbled, "Nothing. Cut my finger on a knife."

"What were you doing with a knife?"

For a moment, Dominic only stared at her, but when finally he did answer, his voice came out far bolder than before. "I was cutting a potato, wasn't I?"

"Oh."

Indignant, Dominic seemed a little taller to Veronica. She began to study him afresh, but as she was doing so, there was a roar of voices from next door, from his flat, and as quickly as he'd grown, Dominic sunk smaller.

"Does your mum know you're hurt?" Veronica persisted. "Did you do it at home?"

Dominic slunk further into his seat. Again came the shrug.

"Dominic, is everything alright?"

This time, the boy's beady eyes fixed firmly on the table, scanning the papers still littered across it.

"Dominic," Veronica urged, after another protracted silence.

Nothing.

"Dominic—"

"I used to do colouring on a table like this," he said suddenly. "At my grandparents' flat. When I was little. Gram always made a roast dinner, and there was gravy in a little china boat. We never had a boat like that. Gramp let me pour his. He was a teacher, too, like you, but at a university."

Veronica accepted this outpouring carefully. She smiled, told him how lovely it all sounded, admired his grandfather's position. Then, "Don't you see them anymore?" she asked slowly.

"Nah. They fell out with my mum. And Terry said I'm not allowed."

"Oh. I'm sorry. But you know they are your grandparents so you probably could—"

"No I can't," interrupted Dominic, with what Veronica suspected was a slight tone of condescension. He placed his injured hand gently on top of her sheets of marking.

The reminder of schoolwork made Veronica wonder fleetingly what the time was, but not wanting to fluster Dominic, she resisted the desire to look at her watch. There was a peculiar detachment to the boy's demeanour. Quite plainly he was there by choice, sitting at her table, eating her food; but he seemed also not there, not quite present. Briefly, she contemplated what George would think if he stumbled downstairs upon them – spawn of the thorn in their tranquillity, sitting at their table. But she pressed on.

"Let me look at it," she said.

Standing up, she moved authoritatively to the medical box they kept in the kitchen cupboard and then over to him, where she held out her hand and, to her surprise, he placed his own within it. Unwrapping the towel, Veronica noticed again how small this boy was, how skinny and light, a fact that seemed cloaked by the bulky mass of shadow that emanated from him. When she reached his hand, she could have been holding a small bundle of twigs, easily shattered. She looked closely at his injured finger. The cut was deep, the skin either side still separate, but the blood had begun at last to congeal. It clearly had not been washed but the towel was thick with an unfathomable amount of blood and she was afraid of water starting it off again, so instead she applied a hefty blob of antiseptic, then placed a gauze over the wound and wrapped it carefully. Still the boy said nothing, but he turned his finger over as if to admire her work, and Veronica felt a sudden surge of gladness, usefulness. "Careful next time," she smiled. "Cutting potatoes."

At this, Dominic half-smiled back at her. He lifted his eyes and again she was struck by the intensity of them, the darkness that hid within. She found herself wondering what he had wanted, coming to her home so late at night. Perhaps he was in danger – should she be calling somebody? Social services? The police? Or perhaps he'd needed somebody to confide in. Or maybe he just needed somebody to bandage his hand. Clearly he needed something.

Fixing.

There was a sudden surge in Veronica's chest.

"Are you alright, Dominic?" she asked again, pointedly this time, an unbidden image of saintliness trickling its way into her mind.

But his smile dissolved. "Thanks for this," he said, holding up his hand and standing to leave.

"Are you going home?" she queried. "It sounds like there's quite a gathering tonight. Is Mum there?"

"Yeh," he nodded.

"You can stay here for a while, if you like," she urged.

But he was already at the door, already not listening, already somewhere else. "Yeh."

And then he was gone, out into the night, hovering for a

full minute on his own doorstep before pushing open the door to a roar of trance music and other adult things.

"Did I hear the door go?" George spoke sleepily, removing one of his earplugs as in socked feet Veronica crept into the bedroom. "Not that you can really hear anything with this racket going on."

"It was just me trying to lock up. The latch is playing up still." For some reason, Veronica had decided not to tell George about Dominic, and his queries irritated her. She turned away.

George half sat up against his pillow, cradling his earplugs in his hand. "We need to do something," he said.

"I'll call the builders tomorrow."

"Not about that, about this." Veronica looked at him and he nodded towards the wall that adjoined the neighbours' flat. Dominic's return had clearly done nothing to quiet the din or bring the gathering there to a close. "We can't go on ignoring it," George said. "It's our lives, our wellbeing. We've put everything into this house, into making it a family home, and we're blighted constantly by an ignoramus who doesn't work, doesn't give a thought to anyone but himself, screams at his family, must be on drugs otherwise I don't know how he raves till God knows what hour in the morning, and ruins our lives. He's not going to just stop. We need to do something."

Veronica's first thought was to point out that actually, it wasn't only the neighbours ruining their lives, it wasn't solely their fault that this wasn't the 'family home' they'd dreamed of; but she held the musing back, wondering why such barbed bullets shot from her so frequently. She set about undressing. And now came her second thought: George had actually acknowledged a flaw in their existence. Even if he was talking only about the neighbours and ignoring the bigger, baby-shaped blemish, until now, such an admission had been beyond him. His bravery touched her, and, "The boy was here," she told him.

"What?"

"The boy from next door. Dominic. He was here just now. I didn't want to wake you."

"Are you crazy? You let some strange kid into our home in the middle of the night? Are you alright? What did he want?"

"He was injured. And he's not strange. Actually, that's not true, he's very strange, but he's not a stranger. I've spoken to him a bunch of times."

George sat up properly now, resting against cream waffle, and switched on the light. "What do you mean he was injured?"

"He'd slashed his hand. He said it was from cutting a potato, but who knows. There certainly wasn't an adult looking after him. Nobody had helped him with the cut. He's only eleven you know."

George looked towards the adjoining wall. "Do you think Idiot Man did it to him?"

"God, I hope not. I've no idea. But he's gone back there now. And—" she paused to let the noise from next door make her point. "Well, they're still raving."

"I think we should do something," George said again.

"About the boy?"

"The boy, the baby, the woman, the noise."

"Maybe the woman's part of it," mused Veronica. "I thought, after that first night, that she might be the one in trouble, but why doesn't she comfort the baby? Why isn't she looking after her son? Or maybe she *is* in trouble and that's why she can't look after them."

Female shrieks resonated on cue through the bedroom wall. "It doesn't sound like she's in much trouble," said George. "But now we know the boy's been hurt, I think we have a duty to do something. Maybe that's the reason we're next to them, the reason for all of this."

Veronica smiled fondly at his attempts to rationalise the universe. "I agree. I keep thinking about that too, but you know, once you make that concern a formal thing, you set a whole process in motion. There'll be social workers and potential intervention, and what if it ends up splitting the family, and we're wrong?"

"What if we're not wrong?"

Veronica sat on the bed next to George, her stomach tightening. "That would be bad," she said. "If we did nothing." There were other times in her life when she'd done nothing, too. Her father's friend from Oman sprang again, uncalled into her mind. So did her English teacher. And a boy from the sixth form. And– "I don't know. I don't know what we should do." She looked to George.

"The thing is," he said. "Even without that question, even if things are okay for the boy, and in the family, we can't live *our* lives like this, we can't live scared, we can't just let them do this to us."

"I agree," said Veronica again. "It's better to be doing something." She said this pointedly, and for a moment both of them were cut short by a joint awareness of other things un-acted upon, unsaid. But they pushed it together aside.

"Let's go round." George took her hand and pulled her gently to the side of the bed.

"What? Now?"

"Yes. Let's go together. Let's be calm and pleasant, but let's let them know that this isn't okay. And that we're not frightened of them."

"Um, I am a little bit frightened of them," laughed Veronica nervously, confessing.

Like George, it was rare for her to acknowledge any vulnerability. Like George, she hadn't for the past year been able to do it. Even in the midst of their conversation, the epiphany of this caught Veronica's breath a little. For months she'd been waiting for her husband to notice her tears, her darkness, to acknowledge it, her failure, their failure; but she had seen his darkness just as plainly as her own, and had also said nothing.

"I am scared," she dared again.

The simple statement of this was transforming. George's face altered in a way she hadn't seen for a long time. Softening. He looked at her with a fresh attentiveness.

"That kills me," he said. "I hate that you feel that way in our home. I wish you didn't. But, it's all the more reason to confront them, I think. Come on, let's do it together. I won't let anything happen."

He was squeezing her hand as he said this and she felt that old surge of faith, and hope, and solidity.

"Okay," she breathed. "Okay, but I'm taking the panic button." It had come as part of their shiny new alarm system, no extra charge. When the security company had offered it, she'd thought it reminiscent of heist movies, or futuristic novels, but apparently for such houses these days, it was standard.

George shook his head, amused. "You're not going to need the panic button."

"I hope not," she smiled, pulling on some tracksuit bottoms, but she slipped it off her bedside table and into her pocket nonetheless.

They stood on the doorstep. They had already rung twice and George had just pressed the bell again. The night had turned cold and Veronica was pleased she had a jumper, an extra layer of padding between herself and the elements. Her legs itched beneath the cotton, but she kept hold of George's arm.

"How do you think he stands it?" she whispered, gesturing to the downstairs neighbour's flat.

"There's a floor between his bedroom and their living room," George replied. "We get the worst of it."

"Still," she shrugged.

The door opened. Bleary eyed, just inside the threshold, Terry leaned against the frame, his chest emblazoned red with an Arsenal strip, his feet bare. "You're not pizza," he laughed loudly, a slight spray of spit winging its way towards them.

"No," said George. "Definitely not pizza."

"Fuck off then," laughed Terry.

"Excuse me?"

"What are you disturbing my party for, if you're not pizza?"

"*Us* disturbing *your* party?" fumed George, quietly.

Veronica flashed him a restraining look. "Actually, you're disturbing us," she intervened. "We live next door and–"

"I know who you are," slurred Terry.

"Yes, well then, you should know that you disturb us quite often, actually."

"Pipe down love," Terry laughed again, "It's my house isn't it? I can do what I like in here."

"Actually, you can't," said George, stepping onto the higher step, a little closer to Terry who immediately straightened himself from his leaning stance. "There are laws about noise. And it's late. You're breaking the law."

Terry sniffed a few times and rubbed his hand against his nose. His hair was thick with grease, his eyes bloodshot. "Call the coppers then." He raised his chin at them, seemingly amused, and reached for the door, making to close it, but George put his hand in the way. This surprised Terry. Veronica saw the shock dart across his face and into his frame, but there was no contest in strength and the door fell open. Terry took a clumsy step backwards, rescuing himself with an Oscar worthy pretence of purpose.

"Maybe we will call the police," interjected Veronica, thinking of Dominic, boldness flashing. But George squeezed her hand.

"We're here, talking to you," said George calmly, firmly. "Because we're trying not to involve the police. Or other authorities. But as I'm sure you're aware, our bedroom borders your living room. We can hear everything. It's not reasonable to be so loud, so late. We have jobs to get up for."

"Well I wouldn't want you to be too knackered for your

fancy jobs, would I?" jeered Terry, his voice taking on the mocking tones of a teenager. He peered past George towards Veronica. "Getting a bit tired are you love? Looks like you could do with some beauty sleep."

"I'd stop right there if I were you," said George, his frame somehow broadening without moving.

"Actually," said Veronica. "I could do with some sleep. I could do with it being quiet enough to—"

But Terry ignored her, his eyes locked on George. "Look, if you're not pizza and you're not the cops, trot back off to your prissy little house and fuck your prissy little woman and leave me alone," Terry spat.

This time Veronica squeezed George's hand. "George."

But George was already letting go, moving closer to Terry, squaring up to him. He placed himself inches away from Terry's face. "Do you want to come outside and say that to me again?" he asked slowly, softly.

"Fuck off," said Terry.

"Come on," George practically whispered. "You're the big man, we hear you being the big man. Yes, you know what I'm talking about. Why not come on outside, let's chat, big man to big man."

Their eyes remained locked – Terry's raw and angry, George's black with resolve. For what seemed like an interminable moment, Terry tried to hold George's stare, as though the world was watching, as though his entire manhood rested on it, but finally he lowered his eyes. As he did so, his whole body shrank, the skinniness of his arms and his pallid complexion slipping into the space where a moment before there had been belligerence and venom. For an instant, Veronica even felt sorry for him. She knew that George would never actually hit Terry, but Terry didn't know that. Clearly he had weighed things up, considered George, considered himself, and found himself inferior.

"Keep it down then," said George, after allowing Terry's submission to register fully, to imprint itself upon him. He continued to stand close to the cowed man. "Or next time we will be calling the police."

Eyes still lowered, Terry said nothing as George stepped backwards onto the pavement. He said nothing as George turned towards Veronica and took her hand. On the stairs behind him there was a creaking, and Veronica saw Simone appear. Eyes almost as blurry as Terry's, she held one hand against the wall to balance herself. "Everything alright, Tel?" she asked, slurring considerably. But still he said nothing.

Until, as George and Veronica were navigating around the railing onto their own step, suddenly he leaned out of his doorway, and like a beaten animal made one last, defiant cry. "I'll have you begging! I'll have you on your knees and broken! Fucking toff wanker!"

And then he slammed the door, and George laughed, and Veronica felt her stomach contract with terror.

Simone

Even from the bedroom, the stench of alcohol is stale and sticky. Next to her, Terry lays naked, one skinny arm draped over the side of the mattress as if pointing down to oblivion. There is a nightstand next to their bed, and on it is an empty plastic packet smeared very slightly with the remnants of white powder, like stratus clouds. Simone has been staring at that packet for a good few minutes, recalling her GCSE Geography trip to the sand dunes in Studland Bay. They were taught there about longshore drift, and spits, and different types of cloud: cumulonimbus, cumulus, stratus... The powder is definitely stratus. She got an A* for that project.

Exhaustion comes in waves, shifting the sands, lapping her eyelids open and shut, and Simone finds herself jolting awake at least three times before she manages to pull herself up to sitting. She doesn't know what time their friends finally left that morning, but it feels as though she can't have been asleep for more than a few hours. Luckily, she set her alarm. It is only her second day at the gym and she wants to make a good impression, but it was necessary for Terry to blow off steam. He'd needed it. For weeks now, she has seen the street creeping like poison under his skin. Not that he's actually envious. He genuinely finds four-pound kale juices, and jobs that keep people locked away in offices either side of daylight, a stupid undertaking. But if he ever did want those 'ridiculous' things, or that 'mindless' corporate job, like his father, he wouldn't know where to begin. And that's the crux of it, the winning blow, the thing the rugby neighbour was able to knock Terry down with without even touching him: Terry has no choice, no power, not really, and the fact of this taunts him on this street, with every perfect piece of paving. Simone does not, however, suggest that they leave the flat in Primrose Hill. She doesn't consider it for even a minute.

Jasmine is asleep. A dirty plate from the dinner Dominic smuggled in to her lays on the floor next to her cot, and so does Dominic. Curled around the little girl, their fingers intertwined. Simone notices at once that Dominic's hand is bandaged and she wonders how he managed that on his own, worrying immediately where he got the wrapping from and if he told anybody why she wasn't seeing to it. Only after this thought does she wonder if he's in pain, or if his finger is damaged badly, and in the next breath, guilt about the order of these thoughts sends her into a spiral of self-accusation. Terry is right, she's a bad mother. She misses things on her own, she always misses things, she doesn't see what's in front of her. Simone bends down and fondles Dominic's hair, gently brushing it off his face. She feels him waking beneath her touch, but for a full minute he doesn't open his eyes. He pretends sleep, and she pretends not to notice, and continues to softly stroke his head.

"Dom," she whispers finally.

He opens his eyes. They are red around the edges, either from tears or tiredness.

"Dom, I've got to go to work. Can you see to Jas?"

He nods groggily and sits up. "What's the time?"

"Eight-thirty."

"Oh. I've got to get to school."

"Just see to her quickly will you, sweetheart? Then give her to Terry before you go."

He looks at her sceptically. They both know the farce

that this is, the great nonsense of such easiness. But he nods anyway. "Is the job going well?" he asks her.

"It was good yesterday," she says. "I did well. They like me. But it's only Day Two."

"I'm glad," he tells her, and waits a moment, perhaps for her to reciprocate with some nicety, or to kiss him, or to squeeze his arm, but she'll be late soon.

The cold snap is over. The night before was cool, the air tinged with deceptive chill, but this morning there is a humidity already creeping back to wrap itself around her. Today she wears black leggings that hang too loosely from her legs, a vest top, and a baggy grey sweatshirt that used to belong to Noah. The gym provided her with two turquoise logoed t-shirts, but she left them behind reception to change into on arrival. She doesn't want to flaunt her aspirations before Terry, or to hear him confirm her own nagging suspicion that they are, after all, ridiculous.

Simone dips down next to the fancy restaurant on the corner and walks under the bridge next to the canal. She knows a bizarre and useless amount of information about this canal. It was a pet fixation of her historian father, and there was more than one occasion as a young child when he brought her here to walk with him as far as they could by the water's edge. Even now she remembers detailed descriptions of the workings of the hydro-pneumatic lock, and her father's ponderings about the great Nash arches.

It was a long time before she let her father meet Terry. She'd kept him out of sight at first, when her father turned up on a Friday – a routine that had begun after Noah's death and developed more easily than she would have imagined possible after all that had happened. Sometimes her mother was with him, peering out from the car, but usually it was to her father that she spoke – he who for so many years had kept his thoughts private and hidden. She would always have

Dominic ready. Wearing his best clothes, he'd have a rucksack with enough outfit changes for the weekend, his toothbrush, a hairbrush, and also a few coins in case he wanted to buy them all an ice cream. As a child herself, whenever Simone had been sent to people's houses, it was always with a few coins in a small purse, and the instruction by her mother that if she was taken out, she must make sure to offer ice cream. Although Simone didn't like to admit it, she hoped her mother would notice that she had remembered this nicety. In fact, she hoped that both of her parents would notice Dominic's carefully packed bag, and his brushed hair, and induce from it that she'd done something right.

They never did notice that though. They noticed that Dominic was too thin, and that he ate as though he was never fed at home – was he fed at home, they asked her. They noticed that he had coughs constantly, and glue ear twice the same winter, and that he seemed smart enough, but not able to concentrate, not the way a child his age should. They noticed that he often seemed anxious when they first got him home. That he cried a lot in his sleep. That sometimes it seemed as though he couldn't tell the difference between the bedtime stories they read to him, and the real world, and they weren't sure if that was because of some blurred lines in his cognition, or simply because he was trying to escape reality. They asked her, weekly, if she'd thought again about letting Dominic live with them.

Simone always made sure to hurry Dominic away before they could trudge too deeply into this conversation. She despised the way that he looked forward to Fridays. She despised the way he talked about her parents with such awe, telling her about a game of chess with her father, or a rainy afternoon baking with her mother, or his latest acquisitions from the book-laden office she had never been allowed to enter. She despised the way he returned as if infused with new life. And she despised him, her son, for the opening he seemed to have so easily forged into hearts that had always been closed fast to her.

Even more than she despised Dominic, however, Simone hated her parents. Hated them, with a consuming, sucking, ravaging force. She hated them for noticing things about her child that she didn't. For having failed, when she was young, to notice anything about Simone herself. For even now seeing only her flaws. Or worse, not seeing her at all. For never inviting her to spend the weekend with them. Never asking her what she did those days when she was alone. Never wondering why she was thin, why she couldn't concentrate, why she needed to escape from reality too.

It was no wonder really. How could they understand her reality when they had no comprehension of it? They'd thought – when she was seventeen, when she'd started drinking, when she'd met Noah, when she'd gone off the rails – that that was when she'd sunk from the dizzying heights of civility. But it hadn't been like that at all. Noah was normal. His family were normal. The people who lived in his building were normal. Same as them. There was nothing, in the end, that was so foreign or alien or exotic about these people who lived on the other side of towering walls, other than the walls themselves. The realisation of this had been a little disappointing to Simone at the beginning. Wrapped up in Noah's family, she had at last the feeling of connection for which she'd been yearning; but in the months that followed, after the first grand gesture of her pregnancy and departure from home, she hadn't felt as though she was doing anything so desperately wild anymore, anything that would really stick it to her parents. She had swapped a clean, private flat for one in disrepair, ease for urgency; but she had good people, she had support, she couldn't blame the estate for the pain she continued to feel.

Perhaps that was why she had let herself sink lower. Perhaps it was intentional. A way to shock them. A way to shock herself. A way to attach her hurt to something tangible.

Terry was tangible. Terry was at last the archetypal estate boy her parents imagined. And there when she was at her lowest. Seeming to need her. Seeming to understand what she needed. Seeming able to sweep everything else away.

Simone rubs her head. It feels groggy. She has not eaten and in the growing heat, with the lack of sleep, and the after-effects of alcohol, her legs feel like jelly. Pungency wafts from the canal into her nostrils, but at least there is shade down here, and the cyclists whizzing past her fan sharp bursts of welcome air into her face. A number of pedestrians overtake her. Her father used to walk quickly too, his legs, or sense of purpose, sturdier than hers alone. Still, if she sticks to her pace, she will not be late, and she continues on, wondering if Dominic has managed to change Jasmine's nappy and give her some cereal; and wake Terry.

She does not hear him behind her. Not even a second early. She does not see his arms reaching. She has no idea he is there until her body is yanked forcefully around the side of a stone, Nash archway, and her throat is gripped within his hands.

This is not the first time she has been pinned against a Camden wall, staring into blistering blue.

It was overcast, the first time, the sky seeped in grey, like a pencil smudge somebody hasn't bothered to properly erase. But Terry's eyes had been bright, and mad, and piercing. Twenty minutes earlier, they had set off for the courthouse together, chatting jovially. By then, he'd been sleeping on her couch for three weeks, and they'd been flirting a little, staying up late to chat, or party. He hadn't asked her for the alibi, she'd volunteered it, casually over a pint; but she'd liked the way that he seemed surprised by the suggestion, like a child who's given a present unexpectedly, and it made her want to give herself to him more, again and again. If she took his word for it, he'd been set up anyway; but even if that wasn't the case, who cared really if he had robbed somebody at knifepoint? He hadn't hurt them. And everybody did things sometimes that they didn't mean, didn't intend, didn't imagine they'd ever stoop to. The forces that drove people couldn't be explained the way her parents imagined, in black and white, in scrawls made in ink against paper. Terry's hand had squeezed at her throat as though he were extracting the juice from an orange. "You're not gonna make a mug of me in there, are you?"

Simone had never been manhandled like this before. Even amid everything she'd done for men, for money, there hadn't been violence to it, not like this. There had been choice still, not a great choice – not with a lease and a son and the need for a fix, and no Noah to help her – but choice nonetheless; she could always have walked away. Pressed hard against stone, hypnotised by the intensity of Terry's eyes, she understood now that she couldn't. She felt the coldness of the wall against her bare shoulders, she felt the roughness of the stone, she felt each distinct finger of Terry's hand driving into her flesh.

"I'll kill you," he warned, pushing his face close against hers. "I'll kill you if you don't keep your word, and I'll kill your son, I promise you that."

She shook her head as best as she could within his grasp, feeling her throat throbbing and constricting. He looked her in the eye a moment more, then loosened his grip.

"I know you'd never do that though, would you, Simone? You're a good one. Sweet. Clever. And you've got a good heart. You look after me, and I'll look after you, won't I?"

He let go of her throat and Simone nodded. Never in her life had she felt so powerless, so controlled, so removed from choices. There was something liberating about that.

Simone closes her eyes now and feels the cold of the stone behind her. Her head lolls against the Nash arch. The familiar grip of Terry's fingers encloses her throat. If she remains very still, it will be easier to grasp at the tail ends of breath. But he won't start speaking until she opens her eyes, until she looks at him, until she gives him that respect. She forces her eyelids open.

"Where are you scurrying off to then?"

Loosening his grip enough for her to talk, he leans in close, and she speaks quickly, with scratching breath. "I've got work, Tel. At the gym. I didn't want to disturb you."

"You're gonna leave me, aren't you?"

"What?"

Simone shakes her head and tries to look convincingly into the intense blue. Rimmed in red, his eyes are darting across her face, a fusion now of menace but also panic. This happens sometimes. At the very height of his dominion over her, of his power, he reveals his own utter vulnerability. He thinks she wants to leave him.

Simone's mind scrambles, tripping over itself. Despite the hand still around her neck, this raw display of weakness does something to Simone. It always does. It makes her want to comfort Terry. To make up for the damage his family has done. But at the same time, she is scared. Terry thinks she's plotting against him. Cornered creatures are dangerous.

"I'm not gonna leave you, Tel," she manages to say. "I don't want to leave you."

She has told him this same thing many times over the years, she has promised it and she has meant it. Today, however, as the words slip in habit from her tongue, she notices that they taste different. There is an unfamiliar, sour edge to them. She no longer feels liberated.

"What's the job for then?" he spits at her. "Why d'you need a job all of a sudden? Do you want me to buy you something? Is that it? Or what are you hiding?"

"It's not about the money, or not only, I haven't even got my first paycheck, Tel," Simone soothes, daring to touch Terry's grasping hand. It is a mistake. She had hoped to coax his hand away from her throat, but it makes him grip harder. "Tel, Tel, please let go," she gasps.

There are footsteps on the other side of the arch and, still gripping, Terry manoeuvres his body in front of hers so that to anybody passing they look like an ordinary couple locked in close conversation. Even in public he can control her; he wants her to know this. Breath evades her. She could kick him, but he'd punch her for sure. She could flail her arms and legs and try to at least grab somebody's attention, but what stranger would stop to save her?

"Plead again," Terry whispers.

Obediently Simone mouths the words, but no sound comes out.

Finally, when the pedestrian has passed, Terry loosens his grasp. Simone splutters and he stands there watching her struggle. Watching. Watching. His face is full of disgust, and maybe pleasure.

"Don't whimper," he spits. "It's ugly."

Simone attempts to struggle more quietly. When at last she catches her breath, she says softly: "I wouldn't leave you. I just want to do something for myself, Tel. I just wanna try the job."

For a moment, relief washes over Terry's face. She sees it coming, growing. For a moment he believes her. But only for a moment. The next second his jaw is clenched again, his eyes locked. He speaks slowly. Smoothly through his fury. "I know you wouldn't leave me, cos I'd kill you if you did. I'd kill you and your fucking son. And Jasmine. I'd kill all of you."

If somebody threatens you enough times, you believe it.

Simone nods.

"I'd kill you," he repeats.

Simone nods again.

He lets go of her and she reaches tentatively for her neck, stroking the angry skin.

Then, "I love you," he says suddenly, as fiercely as his threat of death. "You know that."

Simone nods once more. "I know, Tel. I love you too."

It's true, but the sour taste comes again.

Terry doesn't seem to notice. Gently, he touches her on her

190

shoulder, and for a moment she thinks he is going to hug her, but he is only reaching for the strap of her handbag and then lifting it away. Opening the zip, he pulls out her wallet and removes her bankcard and the thirty pounds of cash, then grinning with bizarrely abrupt merriment, he thrusts the emptied wallet back at her. "Go on then, scurry off to your job."

A switch has been flicked.

His anger gone.

On. Off. On. Off.

Simone knows that she shouldn't say anything, but a snaking thought creeps through her mind and she cannot help herself. "What do you need the cash for, Tel?"

On again. His face leers, centimetres from her own. "None of your fucking business."

"But Tel, you're going home to Jasmine aren't you? Who's got Jasmine?"

Terry looks at her again. His eyes are dancing dangerously now and he holds her gaze for a long time. When finally he answers, he doesn't answer at all. "Go on, job to do," he taunts, and waves her away.

She can't move. Not in either direction. The canal path feels precarious, as though with just a misplaced foot she could slip and drown. A goat on a cliff edge. Jasmine sits frozen before her eyes. Terry watches her amusedly, enjoying her terror. The moment flows on and on, slowly, like the canal. Eventually she gathers herself enough to respond, but even as she does so she feels the smile she has fixed onto her face faltering at the edges. Terry laughs even before she has started speaking. "You know what," she coughs anyway, with absurd levity. "Maybe I will miss work today after all. I'll come home with you. See Jas."

"No no." Terry turns her shoulders back towards the canal, grinning at her wildly, eyes dazzling blue. "No no. Go on, you don't want to be late. Your grand job's awaiting."

Veronica

Somehow, Veronica slept. Not at first. It was past four in the morning when she pulled herself out of bed, legs itching incessantly, to email the school with excuses of illness. A little before six she was still awake enough to notice George showering and dressing and creeping out of the house. But sometime after that, she had successfully slipped into oblivion. When she woke, it was almost midday. Long bands of light had nudged their way through the bedroom curtains, pumping like bold veins across the room, mocking her cowardice. It had become too warm under the duvet and in her sleep she had thrown it off, but she lay nevertheless in a narrow, contained strip right on the edge of the mattress. Even in slumber she seemed to be curling inwards, making herself small.

No matter how much George had attempted the night before to reassure her, she couldn't help but feel terrified of Terry. Rarely in her life had anybody spoken to her with such venom, and what made it most disconcerting was that she couldn't fathom what had caused it. There had been plenty of times over the years when there had been a valid reason for somebody to take issue with her, whether they did so openly or only in whispers behind her back, like Sarah now; but she had barely even brushed shoulders with Terry. She had heard him enough, suffered his vileness, pondered what a disgusting man he must be; but she had never said so. George did square up to him. Still, that hatred – that was something that neither she nor George could possibly have caused in the space of one conversation. In some ways that was a comforting thought. It meant that it wasn't really because of her. But on the other hand, having not caused it led Veronica to conclude that she had little power to fix it. And it was this thought, this maddening, recurring helplessness, that kept Veronica awake into the small hours, even after the music next door had finally stopped.

In the end, there had been only one remedy to her wakefulness. It was obvious really and she should have thought of it weeks earlier: the only way to combat a feeling of powerlessness, was to reclaim the reins of power. Not half-heartedly. Not through resentment-led pilfering, or even the unreliable fixing of and fixating on others. But boldly and head-on. Of course, to do that, one must acknowledge that there is a lack of power to start with, a vulnerability, a flaw – but they had begun now, they had begun, she and George both.

Veronica pulled her laptop onto her bed and set about googling. Within twenty minutes, she had booked an appointment with a fertility specialist, a nutritionist, an acupuncturist, and with the housing officer at Camden Council. The fertility doctor had a cancellation that afternoon, and the housing officer would see them two hours after that at four. Putting down the phone to the council with a feeling of invigoration, Veronica fired off an email to George. She didn't mention the doctor, not yet. But George replied seconds later confirming that he could make the council appointment, and also that he was glad they were taking action, with three kisses

an excess of emotion which he only appended to messages when he knew she needed them. Veronica slipped those kisses around her like a chainmail vest, conscious of how potent the sharing of truth between them had been.

Dressing in a bold red summer dress, bias cut and nipped in at the waist in ode to Hepburn, Veronica stepped onto her doorstep with a surge of confidence. She had almost forgotten this feeling, but it tasted familiar and wonderful. At the sight of the house next door, her stomach traitorously contracted a little, but she threw her chin up nevertheless, pausing only to lock the door. The latch was still sticking. It seemed to close and then pop open unexpectedly. In spite of her morning of activity, she had forgotten to call the locksmith. Making a mental note to do so when she returned, Veronica spun back towards the street, and it was then that she spotted Dominic.

Hand in hand with his little sister, it was with seeming lack of hurry that he strolled down the paving, though his shoulders were hunched peculiarly upwards as though pulled taut with tension. Veronica checked her watch. One-thirty. Clearly he was missing school. Perhaps, she considered, he was ill. Or maybe he'd been to get his hand checked at the hospital. Dominic kissed the top of his sister's head, receiving hot, clammy arms around his neck. He smiled and looked up.

Again, Veronica's stomach contracted. At the back of her mind, came an instant, worming whisper, a nagging that told her this boy was trouble, and not her problem, to get on her bike, to ride away, to focus on her own challenges as planned. In prudence, she knew that she should listen to that whisper. But there was another murmur too, telling her to make sure Dominic was alright, telling her to help him – that old desire to fix. Risky, unreliable, but so enticing. Veronica repaired her bike key to her bag and stood solid on the pavement, ignoring the itch at her thighs. Dominic stopped directly in front of her. He turned his eyes towards the ground and lifted his sister into his arms, kissing her neck.

"Hi," Veronica offered.

Raising his gaze, Dominic smiled at her, hesitantly.

"How are you?" she asked.

His cheeks were flushed from the heat, improving his sallow complexion, but dark shadows pulled at his eyes, blackening them with a heaviness not meant for children. His smile wavered at the edges. He gripped Jasmine tight. Veronica suppressed an unbidden urge to reach out and hug him.

"It's much better today," he said, holding the bandage up for her to see. Then, after a slightly too-long pause, added. "Mum would've done it, she said."

"Is your mum home?" asked Veronica.

"No. She's at work."

"What about your dad? Sorry, your step-dad?"

Dominic looked down for a moment at Jasmine as though consulting the toddler, or contemplating her, then slowly back towards Veronica. "No."

"Where is he?"

Dominic shrugged.

"So you're looking after your sister, are you? Don't you have school?"

Dominic shrugged again. Veronica didn't expect more than a shrug in answer to this – it wasn't an easy question, and there could be legal ramifications. But the boy didn't move with his shrug inside. He didn't disappear. He wouldn't confirm Veronica's suspicions, but he didn't deny them either. He stood looking at her, the adult, the only adult there, as though waiting for something, waiting for her to say something, for her to do something, for somebody grownup to take control. Just like she had waited – in Oman, at school, forever – for somebody to notice and act for her.

Her bike was within touching distance. Her appointment was soon.

"Shall I come up and wrap it for you again?" she asked finally.

What a stupid, stupid, stupid suggestion. After the altercation the previous night, what would Terry say if he found her standing in his flat? What would he do? Before she'd even moved from the pavement, terror gripped her. In her pocket was her mobile phone and she slipped her hand against it as though it provided safety, knowing even as she did so that if she needed to act fast, it was useless. She would have liked to call George, but how could she? With Dominic listening, what would she say? As he let them in, she couldn't tell if the look on his face sat so strangely because he was apprehensive too, or relieved, or perhaps something else entirely.

The inside of the house next door was altogether different to her own. It reminded Veronica of what their building had looked like before they'd done the work to it, at the stage when she and George had declared it to be uninhabitable. A threadbare carpet lined the entrance, nipping the edges of stairs like grass that needed trimming. The walls were snaked with cracks and patches of yellow. A smell of mould or mildew hung over it all. Once they were up the stairs however, and inside Dominic's flat, all of this faded to nothing, smothered immediately by the overwhelming stench of marijuana and spilled beer.

It was impossible to know if the state of the place was the result of the previous night's party, or if it was the norm. While Dominic went to the bathroom to find bandages, Jasmine gripped hold of Veronica's hand, peeking up at her from behind her legs and giggling gleefully when Veronica reciprocated her smile. Veronica examined the girl carefully for signs of alarm at the state of the room, but she didn't seem to see, or notice, or find unusual the piles of empty beer cans, the array of unwashed plates encrusted with food, the cigarette ash that speckled the furniture and floor, the sticky patches beneath their feet. Veronica's mind flew to the council meeting she had set up for that afternoon and, hand still caressing her phone, she wondered if she should take some photos of the mess around her. She shouldn't be there, she knew she shouldn't be there, Terry could return at any moment; but surely she should do something.

Veronica's mind shifted suddenly again, this time to the daydream she sometimes still had, where she scooped the girl up in her arms and carried her away. Was it this girl in particular who she wanted to save, Veronica wondered, or was it any child she could lift up in her arms and claim? As though reading her thoughts, Jasmine reached upwards with a series of grunts in a clear desire to be lifted. Lifted away? Veronica lifted her, Terry's child.

The girl was warm and softly rounded. She manoeuvred herself around Veronica's waist like a clinging koala and Veronica responded, her arms cradling the girl's back, the stance of it instinctive and natural.

What was she doing?

As Jasmine nuzzled closer, Veronica felt her arms begin to tremble. What the hell was she doing? If Terry found her holding his daughter like this, she didn't know what might happen. The thuds that had once reverberated through their bedroom wall now began to echo like a pulse around her head – thud, thud, thud, thud. *Get out*, they warned her, a beating, wartime drum *Put the girl down. Leave the boy. Get out. Get out. Get out.* But she felt stuck, as though somebody was clamping her thigh to a bed, or muzzling her mouth. Jasmine burrowed gently into her neck, and Veronica found herself kissing the top of her head as she had seen Dominic do earlier. Somewhere in the back of her mind she considered that she barely knew this child, and not only was it strange for her to be holding her this way, but it was strange, too, for the girl to give such affection to a person she didn't know. Yet the girl was snug, and yearning, and Veronica could not put her down.

Dominic arrived back in the room carrying a shoebox of disordered medical supplies. Seeing the two of them in embrace, he strode forwards, and with an almost accusatory stare, held out the shoebox to Veronica. "What are you doing?" He lifted Jasmine away, but the girl lurched forwards, clinging in protest to Veronica's hair. Her brother untangled her quickly, skilfully, and levered her down his body onto the floor where he gave her a biscuit to quieten her.

"Sorry," said Veronica, still feeling the weight of the toddler, and the accusation. "She wanted to be picked up. You two are close, aren't you?"

Dominic shrugged.

"I see you're very protective of her. That's lovely."

"I can't protect anyone," muttered Dominic, and Veronica immediately raised her eyebrows.

"What do you mean?"

But now he only shrugged again.

Veronica looked into the box. An insufficient offering of plasters and bandages fought for space with unmarked pills and copious bottles of medicine, and an open pregnancy test, one of two sticks remaining.

"There're bandages in there," said Dominic.

Veronica nodded. "Yes, I see them." She smiled at him, but as she did so she noticed that Dominic's eyes were no longer on her. Instead they had moved to the door, static in watchfulness, his pupils wide and apprehensive. Had he heard something? At once, her stomach contracted again. Had he heard someone? *Get out.* Breaking off from her rummaging, she strained, as she imagined Dominic was straining, to hear movement on the stairs. She listened intently, as he did. She stared with him at the flaking wood. But there was nothing, and after a minute or so, she saw the tension slowly release from his body. Now he smiled, a forced, awkward expression and Veronica felt her heart lurch. Over the past few minutes she had been thinking only of the precariousness of her own situation in the flat, but what would Terry do to Dominic if he found her here with him? What must it be like for Dominic, she wondered, to live all the time with such trepidation? He was only a child. In a patchwork way, she remembered being a child too.

She wrapped his hand. For the entire time that she did so, her ears pricked at creaks in the walls and unexpected car horns. And thuds continued to sound inside her head. Like the knocking on a dormitory door. Her heart raced. Every second or two she was convinced she had heard somebody on the stairs, and at one point she dropped the end of the dressing so that it unravelled into one the sticky patches on the floor and she had to start again. But at last she finished. Dominic hadn't moved his eyes from her since she'd begun, and part of the way through, Jasmine had reattached herself to her leg. With the job done, the three of them found themselves standing uncomfortably close, in uneasy, unoccupied silence.

Thud. Thud. Thud. Thud.

Veronica needed to leave. She needed to get out of there. But the act of that suddenly felt like desertion. Casting her eyes around the room again, she noticed a sharp kitchen knife on the counter. On the wall there was a nunchuck, and a pair of boxing gloves. The girl was two. The boy a small eleven.

"What time will your mum be back?" she asked Dominic.

"Not sure. Later."

The council meeting was later. Veronica stroked Jasmine gently on the head, then looked apologetically to the boy. "I've got to go."

Dominic nodded without resistance, but he didn't move. He looked up at her. And she hesitated.

"Could we try to contact your grandparents?"

Dominic shook his head. "I don't know their number, and I can't remember where they live. And anyway, Terry said he'd kill me if I tried."

"He'd kill you?"

Veronica watched as Dominic's eyes startled, as though aware too late that he'd let something slip. The boy forced a little laugh. "I mean, he'd be annoyed. And Mum would be. I'm not allowed to see them."

"What about your dad's parents? Your real dad's, I mean?"

"Dad's dad's dead. And his mum didn't want a bar of us after Dad died. I don't remember her anyway. Only her voice, I think. She sung gospel or something. And she smelled of something sweet."

There was a creak and immediately Dominic went silent. Veronica had never heard him say so much at once, nor tell her anything so personal. She didn't want to leave him now, but the minutes were ticking by, increasing the likelihood of Terry's return. Besides, she wasn't supposed to be fixing others.

"I'm so sorry, but I have an appointment," said Veronica. Dominic nodded, as he had before.

A car door slammed on the street and instinctually both of them listened.

"I'm right next door," said Veronica. "If you need anything."

Again the boy nodded, his beady eyes never leaving her face – unmoving, unreadable. Veronica looked away from him towards the door. Thud, thud. She was unsure if the noise was in her head, or outside that piece of wood. But she was unable to move. While he stared at her like this, she was unable to do anything, as though caught in a spell, or a web of dark, unknowable things.

Abruptly, however, Dominic shook his head. He grabbed Jasmine up from the floor and away from Veronica's leg. "We don't need anything," he told her.

Dr Shirazi filled in a blood test request and handed it over his vast desk towards her. The table top was a physical manifestation of chaos. Brown paper files towered in one corner, post-it notes littered the surface, and atop it all, was a scattering of dropped shells from the nuts the doctor was steadily eating. He was, she had heard, the best in the business.

"There's probably nothing wrong," he told her, with a slight accent she presumed was Middle Eastern. "The itching, that's the key, that's what tells me the problem."

"What is the itch?" she asked. "I was thinking some kind of nutritional thing?"

"It's unlikely to be nutritional," he smiled.

"Oh."

"More likely, your mind is telling you that before you're ready for a baby, there is an itch you need to scratch."

Veronica raised her eyebrows. "Excuse me?"

"It's quite physical sometimes, the goings-on of the mind. And now it's telling you, quite clearly, that there is something you need to deal with. Something you need to let out. Something stopping your body from doing what you want it to do. Maybe you don't actually want your baby quite yet."

"I absolutely do want a baby. Now."

Dr Shirazi manoeuvred another nut into his mouth, gathering the shell into a growing pile and regarding her closely. "You had a miscarriage, how long ago…" He checked his handwritten notes. "Almost a year. Have you said goodbye to that baby yet? Have you let go of your fear that it will happen again? Have you acknowledged the disappointment? How are things with your husband?"

Without warning, tears threatened at the corners of Veronica's eyes. Missing nothing, the doctor handed her a tissue and she laughed with embarrassment, forcing a cough to keep the tears at bay. "Things have been tricky," she admitted, intensely uncomfortable. "Strained. But improving now."

Dr Shirazi nodded. "The body has to be ready to receive something new. You need to scratch the itch. Metaphorically," he clarified. "Don't actually scratch or you'll damage your skin. Further. I see it's already very raw."

He picked up his voice recorder and spoke into it a rambling series of notes for his secretary: *book follow up appointment for Veronica Reddington, inform me as soon as bloods are back, attach information for grief counsellor.* Veronica looked at his pile of shells and attempted not to raise her eyebrows again. She had been after action that morning, not airy fairy chatter, and she wasn't sure she would be able to take seriously the mystical ponderings of this nut-eating man. On the other hand, if she did take him seriously, then she was now both affronted and infuriated. How dare he suggest that she was sabotaging her own chances of pregnancy, as though through some kind of emotional deceit, it was her fault? She longed for a baby with at least part of her consciousness every minute of every day. There was no part of her resisting. She was ready. But people swore by him.

"We'll run all the tests anyway," said Dr Shirazi, as though sensing her hesitation. "Your scan was fine, all normal. Pop across the road on your way out and we'll take the bloods. Then we'll have all the information. It'll take a few days for the results."

"Okay," she agreed, thankful for this sturdier, more medical ground.

"And in the meantime," he winked. "Try to scratch that itch. You might even want to talk to it, find out what it wants, give it a name."

Now Veronica couldn't help but raise her eyebrows once more – her legs itched at that very moment, physical, real. He wanted her to name it? The man was clearly deranged. Still, she couldn't resist the warmth in his eyes and as she stood up, conceded to a sceptical smile.

"May I hug you?" he asked as they reached the door.

She smiled again, almost laughing at the absurdity of it all, but, as his arms wrapped around her shoulders, firm and engulfing, and not straying anywhere they shouldn't, the tears that had been threatening earlier saw their chance for escape. Within a minute, the doctor's shoulder was flooded. Coincidentally, the itching stopped.

The clinic was nestled in a converted church in a leafy crescent of St John's Wood. It was only a few streets away from the school where Veronica worked and was today absent, so she cycled quickly. *Name the itch. Name the itch.* What a ridiculous suggestion. What should she name it? Immediately, names tumbled through her mind – Rosie, Matilda, Sophia, Oliver, William – names that she realised at once had been on her premature list for the never-meant-to-be baby. As she pedalled, the names rolled like noisy spokes around her mind and the subdued itch began to start up again as though demanding a decision, so she settled on Rosie. Rosie clearly wanted her attention. Rosie was incessant. Rosie was consuming and infuriating. Perhaps she did want to be 'named' after all, acknowledged, talked about, released.

Veronica knew that already. She hadn't needed Dr Shirazi to tell her that she and George needed to talk about the miscarriage, the baby, the absence of it. She had longed for that communication, she had longed for them to unload like they used to, to tell each other how sad and disappointed and thwarted and exposed and powerless and guilty and vulnerable they felt. But it had been easier to believe in the freshness of the house. It had been easier, in the move, to pack her problems with their belongings in carefully sealed boxes.

Only, boxes need unpacking eventually.

The neighbours were a beginning. One problem at a time. One box. One memory. One fear, one confession.

Coming to a stop next to a bike rack, Veronica locked the frame of her bicycle to the street-side metal bar, and scratched the itch.

She had no idea where she was. The maps app on her phone had directed her back through Primrose Hill, past Chalk Farm and to what seemed to be a housing estate somewhere in Kentish Town. Supposedly, this was where Primrose Hill's social housing offices were located, but she'd been imagining an official-looking building on a main street, not a maze of difficult to distinguish towers. In the morning's spirit of boldness, she'd told George she would meet him there, but in hindsight she should have waited in St John's Wood and shared an Uber. On the corner of the estate, a group of teenage boys gathered, hooded despite the summer heat. They hadn't seemed to notice her yet, but there was something forceful and threatening about their sheer multitude and youth. It was probable, she realised, that the boys were simply spilling out of school, loitering here for a game of football, but she left her bike and walked quickly away from the estate, round the corner, and out onto the main road. She was half an hour early anyway, she told herself, why not grab a coffee and get George to meet her at a café?

Had she not been wearing red, she may have felt entirely differently, but as she walked along the row of shops, the boldness that had inspired such wardrobe choice transformed into a sense of conspicuousness. On the other side of the street, she noticed a man in tracksuit bottoms and a bare chest. Veronica's chic midi dress and pointy pumps felt highly out of place, and she became convinced that the people around her knew what she was about to do, knew she was about to snitch on the neighbours, one of their own. As soon as this thought entered her mind, she dismissed it reproachfully; there was nothing to say that these people were anything like her vile neighbour. Still, anxiety snaked beneath her strength. Gratefully spotting a café, she located herself on her maps app and sent it via text message to George.

The social housing officer was, Veronica guessed, about a decade older than they were. Everything about him was greyed around the edges, but he possessed that earnest, vital passion that some people have about them, even if worn slightly. People used to tell Veronica that she possessed such an energy, a charisma, but in her heart she knew all the time that hers was false and born only from two sources: Either, it was counterfeit confidence, pilfered from others. Or else it was the yet more shallow thing: the good fortune of having been born blonde and slim and curvaceous.

It was amazing what she had been able to accomplish with that one power, with the simple understanding of her formidable, reductive, hazardous sexuality. Of course, it would disappear one day. She'd looked at her mother and known this. But she had never imagined the reality – that it would hit her from behind like a truck, not from a gradual creep of age, but from the instantaneous vanishing of a very specific part of her womanhood, the ability to bear a child, the one thing that all that beauty and sensuality and flesh was there for. The thing that even a stupid, abusive man and his stupid, doormat wife could do without even trying.

Inviting them into a small meeting room, the officer opened

a thin folder and consolingly asked them to sit. Between the café and this office, she and George had discussed the reaction the council might have to their complaint. They had done this in engaged, united tones, boosting Veronica's optimism and recapturing a little of the day's thrust for action. But it wasn't simple. The issue was sensitive and threefold: first, the noise; then the hostility; and then the most delicate matter, which was the safety of Simone and the children. About the latter, after much, much discussion, they had decided to say only what they knew for sure. Focussing on the noise had to be the main issue, for them. Besides, George had pressed, they wouldn't be able to live with themselves if they ignited a process that ended up removing children from their parents. Both he and Veronica knew what that was like.

She could not, however, quite dislocate her mind from the flat she'd entered that afternoon, nor the fear that had washed over Dominic's face at the creak of a wall, or her own panic. George had been horrified. Despite her obvious survival in standing there next to him, he had clutched her shoulders with both hands, as though to check that she was not in fact dismembered. "I'm alive," she had smiled at him, and he had smiled back, their eyes locking for a moment while the world continued around them, like the early days.

Smiles, however, had turned to disgust when she described the state of affairs next door. But they couldn't act on it, George had worried – how could they without detailing her unsanctioned visit? *How could she have told her father about his friend in Oman without mentioning her own flirtations? How could she have blamed her English teacher without blaming herself?* George was probably right. They might still have the wrong idea anyway. And if they overstepped, they could well make everything worse.

Nevertheless, indecision twisted Veronica's veins. Untethered threads tangled. Dread stomped upon boldness. Rosie itched.

The housing officer asked them to begin. His expression

seemed understanding, but Veronica worried. Council workers were usually socialists, weren't they? What if he thought them simply privileged complainers? What if through the shine of their watches and the polish of her nails, he couldn't see how terrified and vulnerable she and George were, how crucial for them this moment of action, how mammoth coming to see him had been?

"I'm very sorry you're having to deal with this," the officer said when George had finished his initial explanation, Veronica chipping in every now and then to add her impressions and some details from the encounters she'd had. "I can't give you much information at the moment, but we are aware of this family. We've had another complaint already."

George and Veronica looked at each other.

"In fact, more than one. Now, what would be helpful is if you could describe to me exactly who you've seen going in and out of the flat. It's registered to a Miss Milly Peck. Is she somebody you've met?"

Veronica shook her head in surprise. This was not at all what she'd been expecting. They weren't the only complainers! The result wouldn't only be their doing! At this, relief and hope trickled through her, untangling. Next came intrigue: "No. Who's Milly Peck? There's nobody called Milly living there."

"You're sure?" asked the officer.

"We can hear everybody," confirmed George. "We're sure."

The officer nodded and made a note in the file, but before he could ask anything further, George redirected.

"What can you do about the noise?"

Now the officer sighed heavily. "It's a process, I'm not going to lie. It would begin with a warning, and could ultimately end up in court."

"I'm quite worried about increasing hostility," Veronica ventured, glancing across to George. "I presume they'd know a complaint had come from us?"

"It would be anonymous to start with," said the officer. "But then yes, if it progressed to court, it would become clear. After your encounter last night, and the man's threat, I imagine he'd expect it came from yourselves anyway, though of course there have been those other complaints."

George put his arm around Veronica's shoulders. "We can't be afraid," he said solemnly. "That's not us. We have to take control of the situation."

Through her fear, Veronica nodded.

"It may be," interjected the officer, "that we don't actually have to go that route at all."

"Excuse me?"

"We may be able to move the family on, you see, if they're not the registered tenants, who of course is supposed to be this Milly Peck. From the sound of things, they're not a suitable, family, for this, property."

George raised his eyebrows and exchanged a glance with Veronica, both of them noticing the slight, knowing inflection in the officer's words. Not, apparently, a socialist. But it was true, they weren't suitable. There was drugs, and they drank, and they fought, and they screamed, and they didn't work, and they were dirty; these were not the kind of people she and George and the rest of the residents on the street had paid millions to live next to. Now, here was a chance to move them on without personal dispute, without culpability.

Nevertheless, "Move them on to where?" asked Veronica. "Where would they go?"

"That's to be determined," said the officer.

"And what about the children? The woman?"

George shot her a warning look. "As we said, we can't be sure about what's going on, with the children, we didn't actually see any violence," he hurried.

"But we do hear things," pressed Veronica, patchwork pumping her blood. "And the boy did have a cut. And was alone looking after the toddler when he should've been at school. I don't think it can be a very, wholesome, place for them."

"Yes," said the officer. "Yes, that's all noted. It's not so unusual in some families I'm afraid, but I'm going to pass it on to our team and if they determine that there's a critical threat, then they'll act immediately. Otherwise we'll tread more gently, perhaps through the older child's school."

"Okay," said Veronica.

"And meanwhile we'll look into the tenancy issue."

"Okay," she agreed again.

"We weren't actually sure whether to say anything at all," said George.

The officer nodded understandingly. "It's always better to say something."

She should have felt invigorated, assured, but Veronica padlocked her bike quickly and checked the latch twice as she closed the door to their house. Despite leaving the council building at gone five, George had had to return to the office, so here she was again, arriving home alone. Throughout the afternoon, the temperature had risen even higher and the windows of the kitchen begged to be opened. If she unbolted one at the back of the house as well, she might just harness a cross-breeze to temper the stickiness of her skin. But Veronica left the windows shut. Instead, she half-filled a glass with ice, plunging water on top of it, and only after a deep, fortifying sip did she consider the window again. In all of their design meetings with the architect, they had talked in length about maximising light, and letting the space flow outwards, but never once had they mentioned the opposite current – the way that the street could spill in.

Despite the day's action, and her enduring conviction that power must be reclaimed, Veronica couldn't escape the dark feeling of dread that crept into her as soon as she was inside this house, near to Terry. He was there now, probably, a matter of feet and bricks away, so close that she could almost smell him. When she'd come in, she had set the house alarm immediately, and the panic button sat now on the coffee table next to her, but how quickly could the police respond?

Veronica took a sip of her water and let the cold liquid run through her. Perhaps she was being overdramatic. Perhaps Terry wasn't as volatile as she was imagining. It was possible that the previous night's rage had been exaggerated by the simple fact of his having been drunk. Perhaps he didn't even remember it. Perhaps he wouldn't care that she'd been in his flat that afternoon. Perhaps it hadn't occurred to him that she and George might snitch. Perhaps he wasn't even home. Veronica was relatively certain, however, that he was home. Although she hadn't yet heard him, when she'd arrived at the house – locking up her bike, finding her key – she'd had a strange, compelling sense of being watched. It's a specific feeling that, not easily confused. She'd looked up and found the neighbours' curtains drawn, but who knew if somebody was peering out from behind them.

Veronica took another long, measured sip of the icy water. It could have been Dominic looking. Or little Jasmine.

Her upper lip tingled. Although the water was helping, without a breeze, she was still far too hot, and like a muscle memory, recollections of Kenya percolated her pores. By the coast, it had been especially humid, but at least there had been fans. And open windows. She had never felt afraid there – different, conspicuous, but not afraid. Setting down her glass, Veronica reached for the window blind; if she couldn't open the glass, at least she could shut out the evening sun. On the street outside, she noticed a handsome young couple, arms interlinked; there was an elderly lady pushing a floral shopping trolley, eggs balanced sensibly on top; and a middle-aged man in a suit. Nobody threatening, nobody ominous. For a moment, Veronica felt foolish in her obsessive overthinking. Irrational, and weak. But the very next moment, standing there framed by the window, once again there came that overwhelming sense of being observed, surveyed, scrutinised. With sudden, defiant impulse, Veronica had a thought to throw open the glass and crane her neck into the muggy air. Let them look

– she could look back. Why should she cower? Why should she be afraid? The power was hers to take.

She almost did it. Almost. But in the end, she pulled hastily at the blind, and once closed, encased it further in the white wooden shutters she and George had so carefully had restored.

In semi-darkness, she sat on the sofa, a brief memory of another time flitting across her eyes – another room dimly lit and sealed in wood, though she had not felt trapped then, but liberated. She should feel liberated now. It was ridiculous to feel so vulnerable. She wanted to shake herself. That was what Dr Shirazi had been getting at though, wasn't it? The fear? That's what she had to confront and let out: the ways in which she, and George, were not all-powerful, were not able to control the world around them, and how this failure had rocked their confidence, rocked their cores, rocked the foundations of everything.

Abruptly, there was a sound from next door – the front door opening and shutting. Veronica sunk further down into the folds of the sofa. She was afraid, she admitted it! She would, if anybody asked her to, say it out loud, scream it even! She was afraid of Terry. She was afraid for Dominic. She was afraid of all the things she had never said. She was afraid she had gone too far with Amelia, and Sarah. She was afraid George didn't love her like he used to, or her him. She was afraid she would never have a child of her own.

Nobody, however, was there to hear her confession. Screamed or otherwise. Looking at her watch, it would be hours still until George would be home. At least the water was cold, bracing. Sipping it slowly, thoughts trickled.

She wondered what Dominic and Jasmine were doing. She thought of Amelia and the rest of the class she had abandoned in concession to 'action'. A number of times she pushed away visions of 'not pregnant', and ovulation sticks, and George trying to act strong and un-skewered by them. Twice, she calculated the number of days till she would be ovulating again.

It was hot, so hot. Suffocating her like unwelcome hands. Another sip.

Somebody slipped something through her letterbox and she flinched at the sound of the flapping metal before reasoning that it was probably just a pizza menu. Terry had ordered pizza.

With Terry back in her mind, she wondered again and again about Dominic, Jasmine, Simone.

She waited for George.

She waited for George.

She scratched at Rosie.

She reminded herself to let Rosie out. To take back her power.

And all the while she felt, even through the blind, even through the shutters, a nagging sense of somebody there, somebody nearby, some malign presence hovering.

Sarah

Sarah had not told David about visiting Veronica the day before. Instead, she'd rearranged meetings and turned up at school to collect Amelia that Tuesday not knowing what she intended. She knew only that she intended something. But Veronica wasn't there.

On the journey home, she found herself consumed by silent thought, and when they arrived, instead of unwinding with David and the children, she rummaged through Amelia's school bag, unsure what she was searching for but noting the stark absence of a letter requesting the threatened parents' meeting. A further taunt from Veronica – making them wait. Sarah rummaged on, and that's when she discovered a string of barbed comments over the past week in Amelia's reading record book – tiny, barely-there digs, that David had missed because only Sarah would understand. '*Amelia read fluently, but is too fixated on the rules of grammar, it is holding her back.*' '*In choosing longer books, Amelia needs to dare a little.*' '*I did not have time to hear Amelia read today.*' '*I'm afraid I did not have time for Amelia again today.*' Now, seeing them, Sarah started spiralling. What else had Veronica done? Was she the cause of all the disappointments poor Amelia had faced that term? Was she the cause of everything?

It was the lack of consequence that ate at her. Bad actions were supposed to come with penalties. That's what the law prescribed. Even if it took three months to get a judgment, careering unbidden into an unrelated day, the judgment always came in the end. The beautiful order of this is what had made law so attractive to Sarah. It was what, at the bar in her mid-twenties, had finally set her free from sealed wood: justice. Designed neatly, if not always clearly, in the spirit at least of fairness and right. In court, she'd grown bold in her defence of this. Not that she'd been timid before. 'Spitfire', her university friends had called her, 'Sarah Spitfire', because she was inevitably the one who went to rallies, the one who called out the lecherous professor and in clubs slapped men's hands away from bums, the one who started protests – a natural evolution of her family-ingrained sense of Right. Not daring at all.

Veronica wouldn't have a clue what was 'right'.

Sarah steadied herself with a deep breath and repaired Amelia's reading book into her bag. Glancing over to the table, she found David watching her. David valued Right.

"Are you okay?" he asked her.

When she and David had first met, he still wore his bar mitzvah ring. At Caius, they had both, individually, made the inevitable university discovery of a different sort of ring – crests worn on pinkies (usually by somebody named Figgy or Aubyn or Octavia) – the mark of the aristocrat, the Anglo-established, the land-entrenched. Until then, the only person Sarah had known who owned such a trinket was Veronica. Sarah had remembered her then, as she embarked on her university adventure, thinking how well she would have fitted in there, how quickly her slim limbs and blonde hair and magnetism would have enchanted and fooled them all. It was an apt time to remember her friend. Their shared, long ago summer had been the last time that boundaries seemed to blur, but now here Sarah was, away from her family and their mantras, away from the community she had been a part of, away from everything she thought she knew. Unchained and free.

Unlike some of the other North London boys who had come up to Cambridge with her, David did not disown the gold-embossed capital letters that spelled his initials and looped around his finger. It didn't matter that next to the intricately engraved Oxford ovals of their new peers, his band seemed nouveau and gaudy. To David, it signified a choice he had made and an identity he had chosen – choosing to be one of the chosen; a semantic that Sarah of course loved. Back then, however, sitting in the Caius bar sometime during their second term, all she had observed was an interesting looking guy she had never noticed before. She remembered describing David this way to her friends – an interesting guy. It was a murky period of transition in which she was never sure whether to call people girls or women, boys or men, so she often landed on 'guy'.

This guy was sitting alone, entirely unembarrassed by his solitude, wearing a t-shirt and jeans instead of a linen shirt and chinos, drinking a coke instead of something alcoholic, and wearing a kind of ring that Sarah recognised. Her own parents being a mixture of non-believing Jewish (her mother), and culture-clinging half-Jew (her father), Sarah herself had never had her own day of reckoning in synagogue; but she had tried getting drunk via invitation to a drinking society, and couldn't, she had tried fitting in with her jolly hockey-sticks sports teams, and didn't, she had tried joining the naked run around the quad, and returned fully dressed to her bedroom. Here at last was a frame of reference that she recognised, poised upon the hand of the most arresting 'guy' she had ever encountered, his strength immediately startling in its softness. Brown eyes crept out from beneath an unkempt head of floppy locks, earnest words followed; and she was his. Two true-blooded Jews finding each other long before either could collect the usual university dalliances, and in their union pleasing hordes of dead great-grandparents, despite the best efforts of rebellious intervening generations.

Found, with David, perimeters erected themselves around her again. It had only been a brief interlude of aimlessness, a matter of weeks really, and now Sarah began again to soar. That was the thing about David: he was so substantial, so constant, so unwavering in his faith in her and in himself, that it was impossible not to feel secure in his arms. He made her laugh, and he laughed with her, getting her jokes, noticing the small witticisms she'd thought were only funny within the confines of her family who had created them, making her feel entertaining and shiny and seen. Validated, she was able to take this shininess and radiate it outward. And his roots were so deeply dug, so firmly fixed, so akin to her own, that protected by the borders of their relationship, no matter the condescension she encountered elsewhere — *what does your father do, where do you summer* — Sarah felt safe, free.

"Are you okay?" David asked again. "Is it Veronica?"

That was the other thing about David, he had a knack for seeing through to a person's soul. Many times now since Veronica's visit to the museum, he had urged Sarah to breathe, to not worry, to realise it was all just a petty attempt to annoy.

But David didn't know Veronica, not properly. He didn't know what she had done that summer, or the lasting impact it had had. He didn't know what she was capable of. He didn't know how Veronica had hurt Eliza. And the thing about David's perimeters, was that though strong, they were never enforced by him, never imposed, not a court-ordered requirement, only there, without pressure, without threat, to shield those that chose to reside within them. Amelia. Harry. Her. A force-field of principles, just like the ones Sarah's family had wrapped her in so tightly and which she hugged against her chin.

"Don't obsess," he cautioned now, again, across the room "Just be present." He nodded his head meaningfully at the children.

But she was meandering from the edges of his protectorate. Hiding things. He could see it. Even before she'd done anything. And Sarah could see it, and she could feel it. Not confiding in him was like suddenly being devoid of oxygen, or holding one's breath.

"What are you even looking for?" he asked her.

Sarah shrugged. She couldn't answer. But she couldn't stop. Only that afternoon she'd looked like an idiot needing to 'go to the ladies' instead of accompanying a senior partner and an important client downstairs in the chambers lift. Panic had mingled with fury. Thoughts of Veronica had become consuming. It was as though she'd finally realised that this one childhood injustice was the source of all injustices in her life. The reason for all losses. Hers and Amelia's too. It was the reason they'd lost Eliza.

There had to be a consequence. There had to be. She could no longer cower behind blurry 'right-made' walls. Not when the transgressor remained so juvenile, so brazen and untouched. Not after twenty years of cold sweats, and a racing heart, and avoiding things. Not now that Amelia was being dragged down by it too.

She just needed a little leverage. Something to entrap Veronica with.

Sarah closed Amelia's bag and smiled apologetically at David, lifting her phone up to feign a sudden message. "I'm so sorry," she said. "I have to go back into the office."

"Now?" he asked.

"No!" moaned the children.

But Sarah left. And nearly an hour later, she found herself walking through the city: watching the commuters rushing atop hot pavements; watching young professionals drinking outside bars; watching time tick by and the heat still rising. Watching grand Elizabethan architecture give way to royal gardens and pastel homes. Watching urban villagers navigate pretty, tree-lined streets. Watching red-robed cyclists with flowing Hepburn skirts dismount from blue pedals, and hastily enter their homes

Simone

There is nobody to phone. For hours at the gym, Simone thinks about this. If only there was a friend she could call upon to pop into the flat and check that Terry was there, looking after Jasmine. A friend, or a neighbour, or her mother even. But after Noah died, most of the friends he'd once shared with her seemed to dissolve into the shadowed stairwells of the estate, as though she was a burning flame who might turn them, like Noah, to ash. Once Terry was on the scene, the few that had remained soon vanished too in a puff of disgust or disappointment. One of them, Fiona, tried to pull her aside around that time, making one last attempt at anchoring her, on behalf, Simone presumed, of Noah's tribe, or as part of his legacy. Fiona was a few years older than they were and already finished a course in film studies at Middlesex University, now a production secretary at a TV company with trendy offices in Camden. She had arrived in a cloud of purpose and whisked Simone out of the flat to a café. Over tea and cake she'd spouted something about the strength of women, and the specific strength Noah had seen in Simone, and the different kind of power that only pretended to be strength in Terry, and the strength that was needed now. But Simone hadn't wanted to hear any of that then. She'd eaten the cake, but barely nodded at the young, together woman opposite her, and after a while Fiona had resorted to appeals about what was good for Dominic; but Simone still hadn't nodded, or agreed, or been suitably reformed or inspired, and Fiona never called again. She spotted her occasionally on the Concourse, but Fiona was always hurrying. Away. Not long after that, Simone and Terry had pushed her parents into the same oblivion, and she had seen to Lewa's departure herself long before. As far as childhood friends were concerned, she still had the phone numbers of a few from school, but she'd never been popular, and those that she'd once counted as loyal were not the type to envy or admire a descent into poverty and recklessness, nor wanted it to rub off on them. So there was nobody. There is nobody.

Except Terry.

She can't phone Terry. The not knowing is exactly what he intended for her, and she can't go home in case he's there, waiting for that. But all morning, with every smile she gives to a gym member, with every swipe of their cards, every tap of a keyboard, she feels the betrayal she has chosen, the treachery she's inflicted upon her daughter, leaving Jasmine with Him.

The crystallisation of this thought comes as a surprise to Simone. She'd understood a long time ago how volatile Terry could be. She'd realised that the anger beneath his skin sometimes exploded out of him. She'd seen that he had always to be right, which meant she would spend her life wrong. But she had also always believed that he didn't mean to hurt her, them. It was only because he was so hurt himself. And besides, he loved her, he did. It all came from a place of care. Jasmine in particular was his blood. Is his blood. He dotes on her, sometimes. But suddenly, the thought of leaving Jasmine with Terry fills Simone with dread.

Why? Simone has no idea: why she is questioning him; why her mind is racing to crazy ideas – that he might not be with Jasmine, that he might not have gone home; why she has never worried about this before. Yet even the thought of returning home herself, makes her lungs constrict.

Dominic at least is at school, away, but all morning at the gym, Simone imagines Jasmine screaming, wet and hungry in her cot, or worse, wondering alone around the flat where there are things she shouldn't touch, or worse still, making too loud a noise at a moment inconvenient to her father. Is this why her daughter has learnt to freeze, to become invisible? As she works, she finds herself touching her fingers to her throat, where a thick layer of make-up masks deep red imprints in her flesh.

It is well past lunchtime when she finally makes it back down the canal, up the steps just beyond the Nash arch, and to the flat where she both fears and hopes that Terry is waiting.

As soon as she enters, she knows that he is not there. The TV is on but the air is otherwise unsullied by friction. Frantically she glances around for Jasmine and with a surge of relief spots her quickly, in one piece, on the sofa. She is hypnotised in front of some cartoon, and next to her, arm around her shoulders, is Dominic. He wears his school uniform, but he has clearly not been to school. He catches her eye, and in an instant Simone understands what has happened – Terry left, so Dominic couldn't. With a deep, tear-tinged exhalation of breath, gratefulness sweeps through her. Thank goodness for Dominic. Thank goodness her son was there for his sister. Thank goodness Jasmine has not spent the day alone. With the same breath, however, there is guilt too, for Dominic has been sacrificed once again. By her. With a nod of her head, Simone tries to convey the shame she feels about this, the remorse, and the thanks. She wants to go to him and engulf him in a hug. But Dominic shakes his head at her, contempt spilling from his eyes like years of untended teardrops.

Simone's arms ache with emptiness. For a while she busies them in the kitchen, then delivers a snack of toast with jam to each of her children, Dominic accepting his begrudgingly, Jasmine pulling Simone tight towards her until their cheeks are locked and jam somehow makes its way into Simone's hair. Untangling herself from her daughter to remove it, she notices the pile of pizza boxes next to her children on the sofa, prompting Simone to turn her attention to the other remnants of the night before. The flat is as she left it: the rank stench of stale beer and festering leftovers, bottles and glasses everywhere, overflowing bins, a grimy floor, the lingering smell of smoke that is not pure tobacco. Simone rarely cleans the place properly – there seems little point when each day ash renews its claim on the carpets – and often she stops noticing the grime of it all, but for some reason she feels now that if she can just rid the rooms of the dirt, the ingrained filth, then perhaps when Terry returns he will feel cleansed too, unburdened, washed free of fury. And she will be washed free of doubt.

She cleans with an almost wild passion. It is hot, the heat wave of the last week unrelenting, and stickiness snakes over her in efforts to slow and dissuade; but she strips to a vest and shorts, pulls her hair into a tight ponytail, and carries on. Black bin bags bulge with rubbish, the windows are thrown open despite the breezeless air, the surfaces are scrubbed. It takes three rounds with the hoover to remove the greater part of the ash from the floor, and when she is done, she empties this bag along with the contents of the ashtrays straight into the outside bin. Pausing for a moment by the doorstep, she cannot help but notice the house next door with the newly painted railings. The neighbours' boxes must all be unpacked by now, she supposes, their quiet, perfect life begun. Except of course for the noise invading their haven through her own wall, a thought that still fills Simone with acute shame, but also just a little triumph. She barely remembers the encounter they had the night before – she had been way past drunk by then – only that Terry had been livid with the man, riled by the 'smug' woman, and it had taken a number of drinks more to placate him. She wonders what Veronica is doing now – maybe getting herself dolled up for a party, or maybe, with a real job that lasts all day, giving a presentation in some high-powered meeting, or maybe just strolling somewhere, un-set-upon, unburdened, free.

Locked, herself, in daydream, Simone stares for a moment more at the neighbours' front window. The blind is down, the shutters closed. Still, she watches the impassable blankness, and as she does so, flashes of other things shut to her, force their way into her mind: her father's study door, then her parent's front one; the car with which they used to drive Dominic away; the grief that sealed itself deep inside Noah; the maternal joy that came too late to save either of them.

She is going to send a letter to Lewa. Or an email. The thought comes to her abruptly, but she means it. Somebody on the old estate will have her address, though she doesn't know what she will say. The truth, she supposes. That Dominic was, always, Noah's. That Dominic is, still, hers. She will not ask the woman for anything material. She will not even ask for forgiveness. Only for her phone number, in case one day there is need again for a person to call. Everybody needs one number, one lifeline.

Lewa told Simone to stay in school. Lewa told her she was too young to give up. Lewa told her it was her turn.

Simone shakes her head. Guilt is not helpful. It laps around her, tempting, seducing, but she has seen already its paralysing results. Besides, it would be hard for her to feel worse about herself than she already does. It is all her fault and she knows this. She made her bed, as her parents would tell her, and did.

With one last glance towards the neighbours' closed window, Simone turns back towards her own. In the front room, a shadow darts, but Dominic moves before he can notice her noticing.

In the living room, there is a large clock that Simone presumes was purchased by Milly, or a tenant before her. It is not wooden, nor does it boast intricate mechanics of spinning wheels that can be viewed through glass – in other words it is not like the one that Simone used to spend time gazing at in her parents' hallway – but it is large and loud, and the ticking of seconds is strident and unmissable. By four o'clock, Terry is still not home. At creaks, and slams, and imagined sounds, she and Dominic take turns in snatching their heads towards the door, but more minutes pass intact. Until at 4.15pm there is finally a ring on the bell. When Simone sees from the window a woman accompanied by a pair of police officers, her constricted lungs give way to the heat, and the activity, and the lingering smoke, and for a full minute she cannot breathe.

The woman turns out to be a social worker named Polly. She wears a pair of loose black trousers, a short-sleeved blue blouse, and her cropped blonde hair sticks slightly to the sweat on her brow. Her cheeks are flushed by the heat of the day, but a red lip brightens the effect so that the colourfulness looks almost intentional. When Simone creeps tentatively down the stairs and cracks the front door, Polly smiles broadly, introducing first herself and then the officers, allowing Simone one last pretence of choice in asking politely if they may come inside. Simone doesn't have to let a social worker into the house, she knows this, but police is different.

Simone invites them to sit at the kitchen table. The TV is still blaring, and despite being well used to its constant presence, a remembered etiquette flits through her fingers. She feels embarrassed to leave it on in front of company, though not enough to turn it off. She is too grateful for the shield it provides, the distraction that will stop Jasmine at least from hearing whatever it is these people have come to say. It won't work quite the same for Dominic. Dominic is listening.

What are they going to say?

Simone imagines that Terry has gone and done something stupid, that he's hurt somebody, or done something to himself, that he'll need an alibi again. She braces herself for this. But

Polly does not want to sit at the table or whisper to Simone by the door, and begins instead by asking if she can speak to Dominic, alone, in his bedroom she suggests. A glance to the police officers confirms to Simone that this is not a request, so pasting on a forced smile she ushers Dominic over. "What's going on?" she asks Polly as breezily as she can, putting her arm around Dominic. But beneath lowered eyes, she and her son exchange bewildered glances, and before he disappears with Polly, Dominic grasps his mother's hand as he has not done in a very long time, and Simone squeezes his palm back. Through interlocked fingers, their panicked thoughts mingle wordlessly, tensing flesh, tormenting bitten nails, conspiring together to maintain the pretence they both know is the only way to protect each other. And then he lets go, and with Polly is gone.

Simone's mind races – what does the woman want with Dominic? Who's reported them? For what? Maybe Dominic's done something. She should have come down on him harder after the incident at school. She should have asked more questions before allowing Polly to lead him away. She should have insisted on remaining with him. Terry would have insisted. Terry wouldn't have been mild and meek. She wishes he was there. She was trying to seem flippant, amenable, innocent, but there she was caring too much again about what others might think. She offers the police officers tea. Employing the polite tones of her childhood, she sashays around the kitchen with inquiries as to milk and sugar, muttering niceties. But the police officers are young and slightly awkward. They won't join her in the charade. Their answers are courteous, but she can see their eyes darting about the flat, looking and judging. Mostly, they sit without talking, sipping tea despite the heat. She listens hard for clues to emerge from beneath Dominic's closed door.

Finally, Polly returns. When she does so, she nods to the police officers who stand and occupy themselves by the window, then she pulls out a chair and sits across from

Simone. Dominic has not come out of his room. Hands placed on top of each other on the table, Polly exhales heavily, as though she and Simone are not on opposite sides of authority, not here because it has been ordered, but old friends sharing the day's woes. "How are you doing?" she smiles.

"Fine," says Simone, more perfunctorily. "What's all this about?"

Polly smiles again, relaxed, easy. How does a person become this way? "Has everything been alright lately, in the family? Dominic tells me you've got a new job?"

"Yes," says Simone. "Just on reception at a gym. Nearby."

"Great." Polly keeps smiling. "How's that going?"

Simone hesitates, searching for the condescension in Polly's tone, but she finds none. "It's good," she answers. "It's going well. I've only just started."

"Wonderful." The smile never seems to leave Polly's face and Simone finds herself wondering if the woman sleeps this way, her cheeks plastered upwards. "And how are you managing balancing the job with your young family? It can be tough." She nods towards Jasmine whose eyes haven't left the TV. "Do you have help from Dad? Or your family maybe?"

"Jasmine's dad is wonderful," says Simone quickly. "Terry loves spending time with her, and he's not working right now, so he's usually around. He's a great father." She pauses. "Dominic's dad passed away a number of years ago. Unfortunately. He was a great father too."

"Sorry," says Polly. Her eyes don't move from Simone's for a second. She is still smiling. "And your partner, Terry is it, is he good with Dominic too?"

"He loves Dominic."

Polly nods but doesn't speak.

Simone attempts to be similarly reserved, but the silence seems to draw words out of her. "They're boys, aren't they? They play footie together and stuff."

"Where is Terry now?" Polly asks.

"Oh, he just popped out. I'm sure he'll be back soon

for his dinner. Actually, if you don't mind, I'll have to get cooking soon…" Simone half lifts herself from her chair in a gesture towards the kitchen area, but Polly holds her stare patiently until Simone sits back down. Suddenly, the woman's seemingly endless smile transforms, and she leans across the table – there is concern in her eyes, sympathy, knowing.

"Have there been any difficulties for you lately, Simone? Drugs? Alcohol? Violence maybe?"

"What are you getting at?" Simone knows at once that she has said this too quickly, too loudly, too defensively, but she steadies herself. Her abruptness could as easily be cultivated by indignation, as fear.

Polly nods, clearly understanding those twin possibilities. She looks at Simone carefully, then takes a breath, as though she is getting ready to level with her, or confide something, or make a decree. Simone waits. The two women are around the same age, and somehow, despite the difficulty of the situation, Polly continues to wrap her questions in the guise of an old friend. If it weren't for the police officers by the window, they could almost be at a café together somewhere, like the one Fiona took Simone to once, swapping the secret stories of their lives. Beneath Polly's gaze, Simone resists an urge to touch her throat. She hopes that the make-up she applied earlier is holding. "I'll get right to it," says Polly at last. "We had a report that Dominic's been hurt, so we always need to check those things and see that his home environment is safe."

"Hurt?" Simone declares with surprise – real, but also heightened for drama. "Who told you that?" She shouldn't have asked who told her. She should have asked how he's been hurt. But Polly appears to have conjured for herself the should-have-been question.

"His hand," she says.

"Oh, that. Well that's silly, he cut it on a kitchen knife," objects Simone with what she hopes is convincing flippancy.

"That's what he said, too," Polly nods.

"Because that's what happened."

Polly pauses, as though waiting to see what else Simone is going to say, but she is not going to fall into that trap again. Dominic did cut himself; it is actually what happened, this time. There is no need to reveal more. "Who reported it?" she asks crossly, attempting to keep the unsteadiness out of her voice.

"I'm afraid that's confidential," says Polly. "But I can tell you that one report came through Dominic's school."

"One report? There was more than one?"

"Yes, over some months." Polly watches Simone as this registers.

"He cut it on a knife," she says.

Polly pauses for a moment, then leans forward again – friends, confidantes, informant? – and she speaks softly. "Why wasn't Dominic at school today?"

"He wasn't feeling well."

"Why are his clothes torn?"

"You know boys," smiles Simone. "Always climbing."

"Does Terry hurt him? Or you?"

This is what Simone has been waiting for. Preparing for. On cue, she pretends to be aghast. She shakes her head as if astonished, indignant, and pushes her mug of tea away from her. "Of course not!"

"Are drugs a problem? Or alcohol?"

"Of course not!" Now Simone flaps her hand dramatically around the room. Thank goodness she has just finished cleaning it; she cannot imagine what the woman would have thought if she'd arrived an hour earlier. "Does this look like a drug den?"

"It looks very nice," concedes Polly. "Which brings me to my next question – are you the registered tenants of this flat?"

Simone freezes. This, she hadn't prepared for, and she doesn't know what to say. She wishes again that Terry was there to help her, to think for her, to tell her what to do. They can't lose the flat, she can't give it up, she can't go back to the estate. "It's Terry's cousin's," she answers carefully. "Milly. Her husband died, so we're staying with her for a while, keeping her company."

"Oh? So you have help from an auntie type too?" Polly's smile returns at this, clearly pleased with such a development.

"Oh yes, of course," confirms Simone. "Did I not mention that? She's on holiday though, this week."

Now the smile dissolves just a little. "Okay. Well, I'll leave you my card," she says. "And I'll be in touch with Dominic's school, just to check on his progress there. Would you be open to setting up a plan with us, together with his teachers? Aside from this, knife injury, it seems he's struggling a little with some aggression in the classroom."

Simone nods and quickly dons her now familiar 'good parent' costume. "Yes, I know. I've spoken to his teacher about it already. We need to get that sorted, of course. I've no idea where it's all come from."

Even as she speaks it, this line, this lie that she has repeated now twice in a week, she can hear her own parents' – they have no idea, no idea. Their denial twists itself around her throat. But she has delivered the sentiment as convincingly as ever, so it is surprising when Polly continues to stare, to wait for more. Testing her? Challenging her? Defying her? Offering her rescue?

Simone doesn't flinch. Inside, she imagines herself breaking down, telling Polly everything, flooding and fouling the newly cleaned flat with the filthy truth. There is a surging pulse somewhere in that thought, thumping, pushing her to do it. Do it. Do it. But she doesn't know if she can trust Polly. Terry always says it, they can't trust anyone except each other. She imagines Dominic and Jasmine being dragged away from her. She imagines Terry's reaction when he arrives home. She takes a breath. She imagines something else: herself mustering all the passion and certitude that is necessary in order not to fall into the abyss. And she doesn't flinch.

"I'll be in touch with the school then," says Polly finally, satisfied at last by Simone's un-crumbling. Either that, or the wall of denial has tired her. Or else it is six o'clock, and she's hot. Polly takes one last, long look around the flat, letting her eyes linger for a moment on Jasmine, then she smiles at Simone, that unfailing smile, exhaling deeply, heavily, as she did at the start, two friends who have exchanged woes.

It is only as the door is closing, only as the absence of Polly and the police officers creep through the room, stripping with it the shiny veneer that she and Dominic have together conjured, does Simone realise that instead of relief, she feels a sudden, searing loss. At the sound of the door, Dominic has come out of his room and is standing next to her. He has done his part, as she has done hers. But all at once she realises what in their fear they both have missed: an opportunity for escape.

Simone feels dizzy. She raises her arms into the air next to her, and Dominic takes her hand, but the realisation continues to disorientate, because it is only in this moment, this very moment, that she understands the truth of it, the obvious, complicated truth: that escape is what she longs for. Until now, she has not even seen how trapped she is. They are out of the estate, they have broken through the grey, towering walls, and she had been imagining this to be freedom; but amongst the free she feels more trapped than ever. It hits her now with the full weight of epiphany.

Has she missed it?

Most days, Terry would have been home with them. But just then, there had been a chance, there had been a rare chance. Terry was out, and she had both the kids, and still marks on her neck, and surely if she'd told Polly or the police officers the other things that Terry does, they would have done something. An overwhelming surge of panic shoots through Simone's chest at the loss of it – what if this was her only chance? What if she waits for things to improve with Terry and they never do? What if things get worse? What if she has realised two seconds too late that they need to get away?

Listening for a moment, she can still hear footsteps on the stairs. Perhaps it is not too late after all. Perhaps if she calls Polly back...

Without thinking further, Simone reaches for the door handle, but she pauses for just a split second to look to Dominic who is standing stock-still next to her. She should not have done this. When she looks into Dominic's eyes, she sees clearly the same panic that is pushing at her own lungs and squeezing hard against her throat, and it makes her waver. "It's a chance," she tells Dominic, urgently. But he shakes his head. He is terrified. And of course he would be. Chances are risky. By their very nature, they are a gamble, and she hasn't even planned it properly. She isn't even sure if Polly could protect them. She doesn't even know if, should she make it to Polly, she would be able to snitch on the man she has loved.

There is a part of her that loves him still.

That's the joke of it all. She needs him. She depends on him. She wants him, even now.

But wanting him has destroyed her. It is destroying her children too.

Forcing herself to turn away from Dominic, Simone opens the door just a crack. The front door to the street sounds from below, they are almost gone, but she could still run down the stairs and catch them. There's still time. She could still tell. She could tell. She could tell.

It's not only Terry though, who might be told on. There are plenty of things that could be said about her too. Terry could say them. In his clever way, he could make her the villain. Then she could lose not only him, but the children. She could gamble, and end up with nothing. But what if she does nothing?

Glancing again to Dominic, she hesitates for a moment more. Her mind flitting back and forth. His eyes seem to lock her into immobility. They are so intense, always so intense and unreadable, so dark and tormented. That's what she's done to him, she realises. That's what Terry's done to him tenfold.

It was Terry who flushed Dominic's head down the loo. It was Terry who stood on the doorstep arguing with her parents. It was Terry who put the final stop to their visits, leaning far into the car to make certain they understood. It was Terry who told Dominic he'd kill him if he tried to see them. He shouted this while holding his face hard against a pillow. It was she who stood by and did nothing.

She throws open the door.

And runs straight into Terry.

"Who the fuck were they?"

Terry's mouth is close to Simone's ear as he pulls her inside, slamming the door behind them. Dominic's eyes dart anxiously to his mother, but from behind Terry, Simone shakes her head. She and Dominic have performed many roles today, they can do this one too. "Bloody social worker," she tells Terry. "And some cops. Apparently somebody took issue with our noise last night."

"Fucking wankers next door," he spits. "I knew they'd do that. What did you say to them?"

"That it was a one-off party, that we're usually quiet, having the kids and everything. That we're really surprised by the complaint."

"Hah!" laughs Terry, his mouth wide and wet. There is a blurriness to his gaze. He has been drinking, or smoking, or something. "That's what all those exams of yours were for." He grabs her around the waist and plants a moist, lingering kiss on her mouth. It is as though their encounter by the Nash arch never happened. It is as though he has never hit her or threatened her or taunted her, it as though they always love each other this way. "Did they buy it?"

"'Course," she smiles. "I used my posh voice." Then for authenticity she adds, "Bloody interferers."

Now, Terry gets a different look in his eye, as if a new thought has traced itself in the muggy air in front of them.

"I'm gonna lay into them, I tell you," he mutters. "Bloody rich wankers. You should've heard the way that idiot talks, so far up his own arse. And her, with her smug, prissy face, I'd like to smash that in."

Simone's chest tightens, but she tries to remain breezy. "Maybe just leave it, Tel. Don't play into their hands. It's probably what they want."

But Terry has already stopped listening. He has turned and stumbled back down the stairs onto the street where Polly is possibly just a road away. When Simone and Dominic look down from the window, hands again interlinked, they see Terry curling himself around the railings that separate their doorstep from their neighbours'. He steadies himself with the shared black iron, then raises his fist, using it to pound hard upon the neighbours' door. With the window open, they can hear the noise even from upstairs. But they watch calmly. This pounding on wood is less dreadful than the sound of pummelling flesh.

Veronica

There had been nothing to do but ignore the thudding. Veronica had been too scared to move from the couch or look out from behind the shutters, let alone answer the door, but she had also been too proud to call George, and too worried about Dominic and Jasmine to press the panic button or phone the police. So she had sat, listening to Terry hammer at wood.

It crossed her mind that she may have misjudged things. The previous night, watching Terry shrink into himself in front of her husband, the matching of men had felt so simple and animalistic. Outclassed at every turn, Veronica had almost felt sorry for Terry in the inevitability of it. And the hammering now was proof. He was so witless. There was no logic to it. It was broad daylight so the best he could do was what? Assault one of them, or kill them she supposed; but then his life would be over too. It was all so stupid.

The problem was, in Terry's stupid, reckless battering of her door, there was still a chance she might answer, or the dodgy latch might cave in, and then all at once it would be just him facing just her, and everything would be animalistic again, wit irrelevant. He was bigger, stronger, angrier, and a man with something to inflict, while she was a woman, forever a recipient of things forced.

It had not been a conscious intention to protect her parents, but hallway-hung telephones never seemed like the place for confession. Besides, she could cope without them, and aged thirteen, she could never be sure anyway if a young, male teacher complimenting her on her legs was inappropriate, or just flattering. She'd liked that teacher – the smell of his cologne when he leant over to read her work, the jokes he threw about the classroom, the heat of his body pressed ever so slightly against hers. At first, she looked forward to his lessons, sat in the front and tried to catch his eye to smile at him. But then one day in the lunch queue, his hand found its way beneath her pleated skirt, grazing her bottom. Only briefly, only faintly. But something had felt different about that, and in the lessons that followed she'd sat in the last row at the very back. Somehow, however, everybody had already clocked the vibe between them, and whether or not she joined in and confirmed it, they made jokes, and passed notes about it, and watched for sparks. She could have flat out denied it, but there was a certain admiration attached to such attention, and besides it was only talk, which died down eventually. Until she turned sixteen, and then suddenly she was 'legal', and either the teacher or one of her classmates started the rumours up again with a new, rampant energy, so that by the time of the Christmas dance, when they were all dolled up in tiny dresses, and he was there as a chaperone, it seemed inevitable and expected that she should consent to his hands beneath her bra. And later, more than once, in the darkness of dorms, more.

It was expected, a while after that, that since she was now dating a sixth-former, she laugh along with their banter, parry it, raise the stakes. And she did.

It was expected that being the recipient of such attention was an honour, a coveted thing. And it was.

It was expected that she knew exactly what she was doing with her body and her smiles and her provocations. And it was true, kind of.

It was expected that popular, beautiful, clever, admired, she had the whole world in her hands. At her feet. And she did.

By the time she was entertained by her father's friend in Oman, so much was expected.

It was expected too, she supposed, that she remain cowering on the sofa. And at first she had. Gradually, thuds had turned to slow, tired thumps, like a cat playing with a dead mouse, then eventually they had stopped altogether, and still Veronica had not moved from her spot behind the shutters. But perhaps it had been one thud too many, knocking the fear clean out of her. Or perhaps the confession of that fear, if only to herself, had restored an element of control. Or perhaps it was the action of the day, or the glimmer of reconnection with George, or Dr Shirazi's bizarre suggestion of naming Rosie, or a final infuriation with doing nothing, but suddenly, Veronica stood up from the soft folds of her seat, and opened the shutters, and then the blinds, and then the window, and then her laptop.

George arrived home three hours later. She revealed nothing to him until after their takeaway had arrived – the usual assortment of sushi from the place on the high street that didn't do spring rolls but made up for it with a broth-based soup that was the cottage-pie-comfort-food of their generation. And between slurps, she told George everything.

"We're reporting it," he said immediately.

"I already have."

"Oh." He paused, surprised. "Good. We may get him in trouble you know?"

"He should be in trouble."

"Precisely."

George squinted at Veronica slightly.

"We can't just allow this idiot to harass us," she explained plainly. "Or his family. He's a psychopath. There's just no knowing. I don't feel comfortable being home alone. And that's not okay."

"It's not okay," he agreed, smiling tentatively. "Are *you* okay?"

Veronica put down her bowl of soup in order to answer, as though the weight of what she was about to impart needed both hands to carry it. "I was utterly terrified," she confessed. "But I can't let fear control me anymore. I just can't. It's too tiring." And before George could answer, she pressed on. "We will manage to have a baby you know. I went to the doctor today and got tested. And I've just booked you an appointment to be tested too. If we need help, we'll get help. If it turns out it's impossible, we'll consider other ways. If things are fine, we need to bloody well stop worrying about it, and stop hiding our worry from each other, and stop being so bloody afraid."

George opened his mouth to protest, but Veronica stopped him.

"You are afraid, George. I know it, I see it. You're afraid of letting me down, you're afraid of failing, you're afraid of what it's all been doing to us, you're afraid of even talking about it."

"But you're not?" said George, part question, part statement, part awe.

"I was. Not anymore."

Now, George part-laughed, a smile slowly finding its way across him. "I knew you'd be back," he winked.

"What?"

"There's the woman I married." He stretched out his hand over the sushi. "Hi there, nice to see you."

Now it was Veronica who laughed, wholly. "And the man?" she asked, taking his palm in hers, feeling the warmth of it. "He's been AWOL too, you know. I've missed him."

"Working on it," George nodded. "Working on it."

Their hands hovered over the table top. Despite the muggy air, neither one wanted to let go, savouring the heat of forgotten skin. Eyes locked, they stayed this way. While a breeze slipped through the open window. While their soups grew cold. While the TV blared next door. Until eventually, sincere gazes turned amusing, the physical display of it striking them both at the same time as acutely comical, and in a way they hadn't done in almost a year, together, they creased into hysterics.

"Maybe this was the reason," breathed George, when finally they managed to stop. "For the neighbours. Maybe it was the universe's plan."

Veronica smiled at him tenderly. "Let's go away," she said. "Let's just be us, somewhere else for a minute."

"France?" George concurred. "Saint Paul? Colombe d'Or?"

"This weekend," she nodded. She was unable to stop smiling now, unable to stop smiling at George, and it was only absentmindedly that she noticed it had been hours since Rosie had itched.

Simone

Just like that, he is magnificent again.

It is as though the last of his anger has fallen from fist to wood, and when Terry returns home, it is to kiss Jasmine, and joke around with Dominic, help with dinner, compliment Simone on the cleanliness of the flat and her quick thinking, and then envelop her in a long, meaningful embrace. That night, he pushes the hair away from her shoulders and traces his fingers over the imprints that remain around her neck.

"I'm so sorry, Simone," he whispers into her cheek, tears daubing her skin. "I didn't mean it. I love you. You know I love you. I just get so mad trying to protect you. I know I need to sort out my anger. I know it. I won't do it again."

He has promised this many times, yet there is part of her that longs to believe him. Still.

"I'm not my father," he says.

"I know."

"I'll sort it out."

She kisses his head. Simone does not possess the confidence to affirm that yes, he must sort it out, or to suggest he lay off the substances that trigger the worst of it, stop spending his money on that, start investing his self in them. He's not looking for this. He wants affirmation of his remorse, he needs to be forgiven, absolved.

"I love you," he says again, waiting for her reply, her assurance, his hands still on her neck.

Maybe he means it. Maybe things will be better, this time. She has missed her chance anyway.

"I love you too," she says.

Sarah

It had been almost a week, and still there was no note from Veronica, no request for a meeting, no judgment about Amelia. It felt to Sarah as though she was trapped again, in that tiny room, with no knowing when she might finally escape. All week she had been probing Amelia for clues about Veronica's behaviour towards her – had she been told off, singled out, given anything different or extra to do, had she 'played' with any different teachers? But highly perceptive Amelia seemed oblivious to any change, and David said that Veronica had communicated nothing to him at the classroom door.

She knew it was all part of Veronica's manipulation. This is exactly how she wanted Sarah to feel – controlled, powerless, just as she had always been. Too weak even to stand and reclaim Eliza. The thought of this ate away at her, and on Thursday, she took the afternoon off, collected Harry from David who was appreciative of the extra time to prep the museum's new exhibition, and arrived at pick-up still without a plan exactly, but with a definite attitude. Veronica looked suitably unsettled to see her, but after a brief adjustment of her face, she smiled warmly.

"Can we have a word?" Sarah asked, just as warmly, as she leaned into the classroom door and Amelia flung herself into her arms.

"Of course. Just give me a moment."

While Amelia ran off to the playground, Sarah waited by the door. Veronica slowly saw the other children out of the classroom, then spent forever pretending to sort papers on her desk, before finally returning to her.

"Come on in," she smiled then, at last, and together, Saranveronica entered the classroom. "How strange, for us to be parent-teacher instead of classmates."

"Strange indeed," agreed Sarah. "I never would have pegged you as a teacher actually."

"Nor would I," Veronica laughed.

Harry wriggled on Sarah's hip. She placed him on the floor and wished Amelia was there to entertain him so she could concentrate on the woman in front of her, but she could multitask. She could, in fact, do anything. "Do you enjoy it?" she asked, stroking the fingers of Harry's hand as he hung off her leg. "It's a career for you I mean, is it, you treat it, *professionally*?"

Veronica eyed Sarah carefully. "Of course."

Sarah stared just as pointedly back. Then, "I've been waiting to hear about this meeting," she said abruptly. "I thought it was urgent, you said, to identify if there was anything you needed to report? About Amelia?"

"Oh, yes," said Veronica. "Yes it is."

Sarah waited. A long pause. Was Veronica scrabbling? Or enjoying the calm before the kill?

"But actually," said Veronica finally. "Over the past week I've been noticing more that…"

"Yes?"

Veronica paused again, with unnecessary length, stringing it out. And now Sarah understood – the bitch had decided already. She had unilaterally made her decree over Amelia's future. She'd condemned her. She'd sent the report. It was done.

"Over the past week," Veronica continued. "Amelia has exhibited—"

But before Sarah could hear exactly what her daughter had supposedly exhibited, Amelia burst screaming into the room. Her hand clutched at her elbow and a trickle of blood was streaming down her arm. Abandoning the conversation, Sarah leapt towards her.

"Okay, okay, oh gosh," said Sarah, forcing a peek underneath Amelia's resistant hand.

The cut was deep, a thick layer of skin flapping over a wound full of dirt and pebbles.

"Oh Amelia, you poor thing," cooed Veronica, leaning over Sarah's shoulder to look. Then, to Sarah, helpfully, "The nurse will still be here."

Even in the drama of the moment, the false sincerity in Veronica's voice made Sarah seethe. She wanted to slap her. To make her at least finish saying the words that proved her deception, her attack on Amelia and her future, to make her at least own her manipulation. But there was nothing else for it. She kissed Amelia's head.

"Come on Harry," Sarah called. "We need to get Amelia to the nurse."

Amelia was still screaming, but in the intervening seconds, Harry had discovered a box of tissue paper inside a cupboard and was pulling out the colours one by one. Holding Amelia by the shoulders, Sarah went over to him and lifted him up. But now Harry started wailing, and kicking his legs, and meanwhile Amelia was demanding to be picked up herself.

"I can stay with him," offered Veronica, sweetly. "While you sort out Amelia. He's fine here."

Sarah couldn't think of anything she wanted less than to leave her baby with Veronica, but Amelia's shouts were getting louder, and she was tugging at Sarah's neck, the blood was coming thicker, and Veronica was a teacher, wasn't she, despite her scheming, despite her other failings of character, she was confident enough with children. "Okay," mumbled Sarah quickly, lifting Amelia into her arms. "Thanks."

It took only ten minutes for the nurse to first wash, then disinfect the cut, to pick out a stubborn piece of gravel, and then to bandage it with just the right amount of flippancy to reassure Amelia that she wasn't dying, yet enough sympathy to bestow her with pride in her wound of war. But all the time Sarah found her mind flitting back to Veronica and her son. She itched to get back to them, hurrying Amelia out of the door as soon as she was able. Amelia skipped out proudly, a sticker on her summer dress. "Let's show Harry!" she smiled. "And Mrs Reddington."

Sarah nodded, and together they hurried back down the hall. Now that Amelia was tended to, Sarah brushed away the anxiety she had been feeling, attempting instead to listen to her daughter, who chattered loudly as she cradled her elbow, and in great concession to it, didn't cartwheel. When they reached the classroom, however, and Amelia stopped chatting to burst through the door, the quiet of the room was immediately striking. It was empty.

No Harry.

No Veronica.

Instantly, Sarah's stomach lurched.

Where were they? Where were they?

Where was her son?

An image of Veronica smiling duplicitously shot through Sarah's mind, but she breathed deeply and resisted the lure of it. They were grownups now; Veronica was a trusted teacher. Whatever hung between them, it would never reach so far as to put her son at risk. The playground. That was all. Surely they were at the playground. Harry had grown restless and Veronica had taken him out for some air. That must be it.

"Playground?" Amelia queried.

But they were not in the playground.

And they were not in the staff room, or the toilets, or any of the other classes into which she and Amelia peered with increasing haste. Sarah tried not to reveal her growing panic to her daughter, but her voice grew higher and faster as she hurried Amelia this way and that, and then back to the classroom, where she noticed that not only was Veronica not there, but her bag was missing too. Now Sarah couldn't contain her terror. Where the hell was the bitch? Where was Harry? What was she doing with him? She looked at her watch – it had been a good fifteen minutes since they'd finished with the nurse, almost half an hour altogether. Should she call the police? The school security? Or is that exactly what Veronica wanted? To make her look silly and paranoid. To paint her as a parent not in control. What was her plan? What game was she playing this time? Whatever it was, Sarah could no longer play it. Feeling tears welling, her courtroom poise by now far out of reach, Sarah took out her phone to call David, and she was just about to press the call button when suddenly, of course, she heard a giggle from the corridor. And they were there.

The first thing she did, was to bundle Harry so tightly into her arms that he wriggled from lack of breath. The second thing, was to turn violently towards Veronica. Despite the learned courtroom art of patience and control, this time Sarah found it impossible to hold back her fury. "Where were you?" she spat through gritted teeth, "Why did you take my son away?"

Veronica smiled, seemingly oblivious to Sarah's tone, and ruffled Harry's hair. "He was hungry. So we went to the staff room for a snack. And then we've been walking about all over the place. He's been leading the way. He's so adorable."

"Did you not think I might be worried?"

"I took my phone. I thought you'd call."

In her panic, Sarah hadn't thought of that.

"Sorry," said Veronica. "Did we worry you?" Then, without waiting for an answer, she cast her eyes at Amelia. "Well, that's a proper injury," she declared. "You're very brave." Amelia puffed up with pride, and Veronica leaned in to inspect it closer, before whispering to Sarah. "We can finish our chat another time. It's not urgent anymore." Then she painted on a broad smile, and went back into the classroom, where she was a teacher and Sarah was a parent, and she still held all the power. And Sarah was left, staring, with her children, at the closed wooden door

Veronica

Dominic knocked on Veronica's door three times that week. On each occasion, shortly after she'd returned from school, she let him in and made him food, and allowed him to sit in silence. Delivering a sandwich to the table and sitting opposite him, she waited for him to speak, but he never did. It was difficult not to fill the air with mindless chatter, difficult to resist the compulsion to fix and patch; but she tried hard, sensitive to the boy's need for quiet, for a place that didn't dominate or demand. Only once, that Thursday, did she press him.

"Your step-dad was round here the other day," she said, watching Dominic for reaction. "Hammering on my door. Is he ever aggressive like that with you?"

But Dominic had only given her a look then, as if to say 'don't patronise'. He knew that she knew. It was why he was there, without words screaming for rescue.

"How's your sister?" she tried again, a different angle. "You two are close, aren't you?"

"Not always. Today she was crying and I left her in her cot, came here."

"Why did you do that?"

"Let them look after her."

"Them? Your mum and Terry?"

Dominic reverted to a shrug.

"You know, it's not your job to look after her."

Dominic said nothing.

"And it's not your fault."

Still nothing.

"Any of what happens at home, I mean. It's not your–"

"What do you know?" Dominic interrupted, pushing the sandwich away from him. "You're a fucking teacher. You're all the same. You don't know anything. It is my fault."

"What is?"

Dominic said nothing.

"Something to do with your sister?"

Still nothing.

"Or your mother?"

Dominic looked up. "Sometimes, I only have to think things, you know, and they happen."

Now Veronica was the one silent. The boy's beady eyes were as dark and impenetrable as ever. And locked on her.

"I wanted my dad to die. And he did. And I wanted my mum to get hurt, I mean not really, not properly, but I was angry and I thought it. And then…"

"Then what, Dominic?"

He stopped.

"What?" Veronica moved closer to him, tried to touch his hand, but he drew it away.

"What do you know?" he repeated.

Veronica still wasn't sure what exactly she knew, but she reported each of Dominic's visits to the council. It wasn't enough, but it felt important, necessary, for her as much as him. Besides, what else could she do? She was unable to scoop him, or his sister, into her arms and run.

Like she'd scooped up Harry.

She shook her head, chasing away that vision. She wasn't sure why she had done it, or how she could have allowed herself. It wasn't from spite, it really wasn't. Since things had escalated with the neighbours, Sarah had all but slipped from her mind. She hadn't even formulated a way to roll back the demand for a parents' meeting. She wasn't pilfering. If anything, she was fixing, she was fixing Dominic, concentrating on him. But more than that, she was finally concentrating on herself. Retaking control. Yet, the little boy had found his way into her empty arms.

That evening, while she was putting out the bin, Simone confronted her in the street: "It was you, wasn't it?"

"Sorry?"

"You got social workers involved, didn't you?"

"What?"

"Don't play dumb."

They were in front of their houses, Veronica alone and without even a phone in her hand. She reasoned, however, that Terry must be out otherwise Simone wouldn't be talking to her, and it was still light, and the woman was hindered by babe on hip. "You saw some social workers?"

"Don't pretend," admonished Simone, spitting out the words as though the taste of them was disgusting, and all the while jiggling Jasmine who was reaching out for Veronica's hair. "I'm not stupid."

Veronica's first thought was to reach for Jasmine. She couldn't help it. Whenever she saw this child, the yearning inside her magnified. Just like it had with Harry, she supposed. It was as though her arms ached for a space to be filled, as though her body was only responding to a natural call. This time, however, Veronica kept her arms to herself.

Her second thought was to deny everything – the tentative disposition of the last year hard to shake. But instead, she found herself stepping forward, closer to her neighbour.

"Don't you *want* to talk to social workers?" she asked Simone quietly. "You know that we hear things. Don't you want to get out?"

"You don't know what you're talking about," the woman hurried, just as Dominic had proclaimed.

"It's not normal," pressed Veronica.

"You have no idea about normal. I know you, you know."

At this, Veronica felt a surge of caution. Often, she still felt that discomforting sensation of being watched, observed. Perhaps it wasn't Terry after all. Perhaps it was Simone. "You don't know me," she ventured.

"Oh yes I do. I know all about your type. Whereas you know nothing – you don't even know what you think you know. Terry's a good guy really. You don't understand. Besides, he adores me."

"It doesn't sound that way," persisted Veronica.

"Then stop listening," barked Simone. "Just stay away from us."

"Well that's a bit hard, isn't it?" Veronica motioned towards their houses, seamlessly connected, except for the distinct dividing line of pristine paint versus peeling.

Jasmine lurched towards Veronica again, and roughly this time, Simone yanked her back. "You are so fucking condescending," she laughed. "You have no idea. No idea. Just keep your nose out of our business, okay?"

She turned then, sharply, and strode for her door. Perhaps Veronica should have left it at that. Perhaps she should have stayed out of it. But instead, again, she found herself stepping closer, following. Simone's shoulder felt hot under her touch.

"Get off me!"

Veronica lifted her hand. "I just want you to know that I'm here," she said quietly. "If you need anything."

She said this, and then she braced herself, half expecting to be slapped in the face. But instead, for the briefest of moments, the woman in front of her dissolved, and a different person passed through her. Veronica nodded with what she hoped was encouragement. Softly, she opened her mouth to speak again. But then, as quick as it had come, the calm intruder moved on, and now Simone shoved away the hand that Veronica had risked again on her shoulder, and muttering "fucking condescending", bundled her wriggling daughter inside, slamming the door behind them.

At school the following day, Veronica watched the door for Sarah, hoping she wouldn't appear. Part of her did want to apologise, to explain – about Harry, about Amelia. Part of her wanted to tell Sarah how often she'd thought about her and her family over the years, how precious that time, how jealous she had been. And still was. How that envy made her do things she regretted. But, the greater part of her decided that it was better to simply stay away. To detach herself from her own unravelling. Besides, more urgent matters were occupying her mind.

Veronica avoided David when he dropped Amelia off that morning. She avoided him at pick-up too. And then all at once it was Saturday, and no more avoidance was necessary because she and George were no longer in the busy bustle of London but sat sleepily outside, in the glorious garden terrace of the famous Colombe d'Or.

Their table was perfectly shaded. A vast Fernand Leger mural presided immediately over them, peeking through ivy, and as always they basked in the legend of it all. This was why they loved it here – not for the simple, rustic charm of what was in essence a small hotel/restaurant in the South of France; they came for the art, for the history, for the folklore. Nestled just outside the walled village of Saint-Paul de Vence, myth had it that almost every artistic icon of the last century had come to this hotel to meet and play and work, and often, paid for their meals or lodgings with a piece of their own art. Now, original works by Matisse, Chagall, Braque, Picasso, hung casually throughout – up-lit in the restaurant, suspended over white sheets in the bedrooms, offering visitors a nonchalant slice of the extraordinary. George and Veronica had visited the Colombe d'Or together on at least four previous occasions, and now, unfailingly, it filled them with all the promised stimulus that such rare brilliance beholds. They held hands over the terrace table as they consumed Burgundy snails and rare-cooked steak, rich cheeses and dry wine. They allowed their legs to intertwine in the swimming pool beneath the Calder. They lay on fresh, soft sheets, staring up at a heavily gilded Chagall, and they felt their bodies turn towards each other like the easy brushstrokes of a master painter: confident, practised, surprising.

They felt like naughty schoolchildren. She was not ovulating, it would be another week until then, and the results of both hers and George's tests had not yet arrived, but their hands crept over each other. The prospect of sex, unrequired, titillated them as though it was a fresh discovery, pleasure pulsing back and forth in the empowerment of choice. They lay afterwards, heads propped on plush pillows, secrets spilling out of their mouths: how isolated they had each felt, how guilty, how sad, how fresh each month's disappointment, how strong remained the desire to grieve, how vivid their dreams of that room in the hospital and the blood on the floor of their old flat, how weak they felt in the wake of it all. Unpacked at last, their eyes met with the old openness, and in the air was a palpable scent of triumph: their childhoods did not rule them after all, they had proved it, there was always chance for escape.

They stretched unhurriedly into the expanse of white cotton. They raised their arms and pointed their toes, their limbs free from manacles. They exhaled onto each other's lips.

Rejoicing in her liberation, only a few times Veronica felt her mind slipping back to London, to Simone, to Dominic, to the entrapment she envisaged there, to the continuous question of if they should be doing something more; but mostly she nudged such thoughts away, finding room instead for lazy games of boules in the sand at the foot of the walled city, salted frites at the café, and hikes up the hills, all the while colluding with her husband in fresh determination to be bound together, and free.

Simone

You can threaten somebody too many times. You can tell them you'll kill them, you'll kill them, you'll kill them. And they'll be scared. And they'll be obedient. And they'll cower in a corner. But there comes a day when something snaps. And it just doesn't matter anymore. There's no energy left to care.

"If you're going to do it, do it already," she tells him.

Dominic is out. It is Sunday and he had nudged her awake to tell her that he was going to Jakub's, not meaning for Terry, next to her, curled into her body, to overhear. The result was an uninvited thirty-minute speech about the parasitical Poles, but she didn't intervene in that one. Remaining in bed, she rolled her eyes in discreet sympathy with her son, but Terry's lecturing was on this occasion verbose rather than aggressive, and it wasn't worth tainting the good atmosphere between them. There had passed five days with barely a raised voice, five days of gentleness and talk and laughter. Laughter! Besides, she doesn't think that Jakub's is where Dominic was really headed. More than once that week she has noticed him hurrying off in the other direction, and she followed him one morning down the road, over the bridge by Chalk Farm, the route that would lead to her parents' house. At first she was surprised that he remembered this route at all, he'd been so little, but he didn't actually reach the house. He walked up and down a nearby road – not the right one, but similar enough looking – and he knocked on three different blue doors that could have been a match. She had, however, been careful over the years with what she told him. He doesn't know her parents' full names. She refused him their phone number.

Watching from a distance that morning, there was a part of her that hoped serendipity would intervene and he would, miraculously, find them. But in the end, Dominic had given up, trudging back without noticing her crouched in a café, and instead, Simone had begun her own pursuit. She'd gone to the estate.

It had taken only a few minutes to find the old family friend and get Lewa's email address, and she'd sent the message immediately, from her phone, in a rush of determination before she could change her mind. She'd felt a little traitorous about doing this, particularly in the glow of Terry's good mood, and she made sure to delete the message quickly. He'd always been tetchy about Noah. If he found out, the seed of insecurity would work its way through him until it destroyed everything. That would be her fault of course, he would say so, and he would be right.

She shouldn't trust people with 'motives'. Like her parents. Like Lewa. Like the social worker, whose card is wrapped in a pair of old knickers and buried at the bottom of a drawer.

What she should have done, was intervene in the rant. At the time it had felt harmless, but maybe it was this that wound Terry up, like revving an engine, or lighting the long tail of a firework. While he was showering, she had fed Jasmine breakfast, prepared some for Terry, and then dressed herself for work. She was supposed to be doing a four-hour morning shift at the gym and she had told Terry about it days earlier, but when he emerged from the bathroom, naked and motioning for

Simone to follow him back to bed, he had clearly forgotten, or didn't care.

"I'll be late, Tel," she'd smiled, carefully adding, "though you know I'd rather stay."

"So stay. Fuck the gym." He was smiling too, flirtatiously, but there was a rough tenor to his voice, just tracing itself around the edges.

"I can't. You know I can't. Jas is all ready though, you can take her out or something. I'll be back by lunch."

"Are you serious?" He'd asked this sharply, the edges closing in. "You're gonna choose some dead-end job that pays a pittance over your husband? Don't you see how you're being manipulated? You've got to get your priorities right, my girl. Start making some better choices."

"Tel," she tried again. "It's tempting, obviously, but—"

"Here," he said, finding his wallet on the sofa. "Is it the money? Here, take this." He threw a wad of notes at her, either a fresh influx from his father, or gained she didn't know how. "Now, make the right choice."

"It's not just the money, Tel," Simone tried again, gently. "It's—"

"You'd be a mess without me," Terry leered suddenly, stepping closer. "You know that, don't you? You're nothing on your own. I'm trying to help you. I don't know why you don't listen. Already your deviant son is messing around with scum. And you're frolicking off to prostrate yourself for some wanky gym bunnies. Fuelling the system, both of you. Mindless. Idiotic. While you abandon us. Your husband. Your children. We need some family values in this house."

"I'm doing it for our family," she tried. But this was obviously the wrong thing to say.

"You're gonna do something for us," he growled, grabbing her abruptly by the hair. "You're fucking gonna do something for me."

Across the table, Simone noticed her daughter freezing, staring at them, unmoving. She felt her head being yanked backwards and couldn't help but let out a scream, but as she was being dragged to the bedroom, she locked eyes with Jasmine, and blew her a kiss, and hoped that would be enough.

"Do it already then," she spits at Terry.

He has finished fucking her. Her cheek is already puffing beneath her eye, and her arms are sore from being held behind her, but she is unable to submit as she usually would. He has promised to kill her, to kill Dominic too. At the mention of her son, her chest tightens and it is hard to breathe, but she cannot protect him, she cannot protect anybody. In that moment all she can do is submit or stand, and she is too bent already to stoop lower.

"If you're gonna kill me, just kill me."

She has never before said this to Terry and he seems unnerved by it, unsure how to respond, as though hearing his words repeated back to him has detached them from him somehow. His face clouds in puzzlement. But only for a moment. A new logic has worked its way into his mind. Grabbing first the belt of her dressing gown, and then the charger cable to her phone, he yanks her from the bed to her feet and then pushes her into a chair in the corner. "I don't want to kill you, Simone," he says wrapping the cable around her wrists and fastening it to the chair. "You think I like this? You think I didn't see you the other day talking to that posh slut from next door? What were you saying? What are you planning? You push me to it. I only want you to do what's right, I only want to help you, but you keep on doing these stupid, senseless things. You're hurting us, Simone. You need to start listening to me, don't you? I'm the one who's sorted things. I'm the one who looks after this family."

"You? You spend all your money on drugs or drink! Your *father's* money, half of it. You think I don't know? There must have been thousands of pounds of it by now – we could live a different life!" she explodes, struggling away from him.

"I don't need his fucking money," he spits.

"But you're just like him. You steal my benefits and you piss that away too. What do you do?"

"I saved you," he growls. "And don't you forget it. You think you're above me? You think you're so clever? I made the decisions you couldn't fathom. Me. I saved you from parents who treated you like the crap you are. I saved you from all that shit you were doing. So you can sit here and listen, to me, not your fucking friend next door, and think about that. And then we'll see about killing you." Her arms are bound tight now and Terry starts in on her legs. He has never done this before and despite no longer caring, she can feel herself starting to panic.

"Terry," she says, but he puts his hand roughly over her lips.

"No, no, just listen."

He presses his hand a little harder against her face, a gesture to hammer home his power, and then he crosses the room where he pulls out a pair of shorts and a t-shirt.

"Terry, please," she says.

Her eyes feel as though they are burning, but she cannot look away from him. He runs a dollop of gel through his hair and slaps on some aftershave. "Right," he grins at her, fresh, invigorated. "Wonder when Dom will be home. Maybe we'll see if he's any better at listening than his mother."

Simone's throat tightens, the panic building into an un-swallowable lump. The look in Terry's eyes is goading now, triumphant. She has seen that look many times before. Fragments of memories flash across her mind: Terry punching Dominic in the face when he was eight years old and splitting his skin; cuffing him around the ear, behind his head, in his stomach. Why had she done nothing then? Why had she let it happen? How had she made herself believe it was okay, right, the discipline Dominic needed? What is Terry going to do to Dominic now? *I'll kill you. I'll kill you. I'll fucking kill Dom too*. Without thinking any further, she opens her mouth and starts to scream. As loud as she can. At the top of her register.

Help. Help. Help. Everything she has been wanting to yell since she was sixteen. Voiced at last.

If only somebody could hear her. If only somebody could do something.

Veronica. Veronica can hear. Veronica will hear. Veronica has promised.

Terry's fist hits her hard across the mouth. Then he wraps a scarf tight around it, muffling her desperate shouts, catching the blood.

Simone

At some point, it struck Simone that nobody was coming to rescue her.

Not only from the chair to which she was tied. Not only from Terry. But from her life, from her choices, from herself.

No bell had sounded down below. There was no banging on their door. No benevolent, rescuing neighbour charging up the stairs. No social worker.

Or parents. No parents had marched onto the estate to insist she return to them. No parents had snatched her away from the drink and other substances. Nobody before that had noticed the scars on her wrists, or grabbed hold of them, or kept her above the ground.

Nobody was coming. Then. Now. Ever.

Simone had stopped screaming – a futile effort in any case given the scarf around her mouth. She had stopped trying to tip the chair and drag it to the window. And in the abruptness of the silence that followed, she found herself leaning her head backwards, searching through the ceiling for sky. She could have been in an empty field somewhere. Not a single noise crept under the door from the living room. A while ago she had heard the slamming of the front door, so Terry must have taken Jasmine out, and now it was strangely, piercingly, quiet. Simone absorbed the quiet. She allowed it to flow through her sore limbs, to soothe her bound wrists, to slip itself beneath her skin and take her back to a time before the volume of life blocked out everything.

Maybe this was why her father had hidden behind his own closed door. Maybe his life had grown too loud, too engulfing. Though they should have told her. Whatever was going on, they should have told her instead of shutting her out. Simone's mind flies to the years in which Dominic was a baby – locking him in his room, quite literally shutting him away. Which was worse? Perhaps her own parents had imagined that what they were doing was some kind of protection too.

It wasn't so awful really. In the dearth of parental love she hadn't seen it at the time, but as a child there was so much that she did have: safety, a flat, an education, options. Yet it had been so easy to shed those things, softer than they'd seemed. It had been so swift. So simple.

With a profound aching, she wishes she could go back and shake that naïve, sixteen-year-old girl and tell her that things could be a hell of a lot worse. She wishes she could tell her that okay, her parents weren't perfect, but hey, they probably had issues of their own, and she was wasting time trying to get them to notice her, or to save her; because nobody is going to save her. Nobody is going to rescue her. Nobody is going to come.

Nobody is going to come.

It seems bizarre that after over a decade, this thought is only just percolating in Simone's mind, but as soon as she considers it, it hits her like a fist: nobody is coming, nobody is coming. The rhythm of the words beat around her brain, undulating and hypnotic. She repeats it to herself over and over in the unusual quiet of the flat. And the realisation of it is unexpectedly, overwhelmingly empowering. If nobody is coming, then it is up to her to rescue herself. It is up to her to change things. To make decisions. It is all up to her.

She starts to make lists. The first priority is clear: she must get away from Terry. For the first time ever, this simple truth is razor-sharp, slicing effortlessly through reservations; but complications remain. She must get the kids away from Terry too, and they must go somewhere he cannot find them. She'll need money for that, but he's never given her access to his, and he commandeers everything of her own – it was years ago that he took charge of her benefits, 'helping'. Whenever she's attempted to put some aside, he's found it and spent it. Perhaps she can open a new bank account and start channelling her wages there. But he'll notice that. And there might not be time. What has she time for? If he's going to kill her today, then time has run out anyway, but if he doesn't, she'll need to be smart about things, play at compliance, act normal.

As she thinks about this, a nervous energy builds inside her, a fear-laced, hope-tipped momentum, growing exponentially with each passing second, a call to action almost bursting through her skin. It is powerful, that feeling. Unfamiliar. Dynamic. Nothing is going to stop her. Nothing will stand in her way.

Except that she is tied to a chair.

Simone laughs.

As though catching sight of her reflection in a mirror, she sees the futility, and for a moment there is a danger of everything unravelling, there is a risk of submission – habitual, easy. But no. She is laughing, not crying, and the juxtaposition of her mindset with the physical reality she finds herself in, only reaffirms the need for action. This is not a way to exist. This is not normal. This is not something that Terry can convince her was justified, or her fault, or the unintended upshot of love.

Simone does not know how many hours pass before Terry returns to the flat with Jasmine. She suspects he's been drinking because his voice is even louder than usual and for the first twenty minutes or so he is raucous and enlivened, chasing Jasmine around the living room with noisy delight, and then quite abruptly growing bored of this and turning on the television. For the next hour or two Jasmine is either inaudible, or crying, and he is either silent or shouting at her to shut up. Simone can hear hunger in her daughter's cry. She can hear fear in her silence. Until eventually Dominic arrives home and sees to her.

There is nothing she can do to explain things to her son. She can hear him asking Terry where she is, but even if he knew, he is too young and too slight to help her. Terry tells him she is out. 'Frolicking', he says. She used to go frolicking, leaving Dominic alone. Dominic will remember this. She wants to let him know that she hasn't abandoned him again, that she's there, here, right here. But if she has any hope of surviving this, if there is any hope of Dominic escaping unscathed, she knows she must stay silent, appear to submit. Soundlessly, she prays for Dominic to stop asking, to yield too, to not choose today, this moment, to take a reckless stand. It has, with pre-teen hormones, been building in him, and she can hear Terry goading – ordering him around, clipping his ear, calling him a runt, and stupid like his mother. *Say nothing*, she prays. *Bide time. I'm coming.* She hears Jasmine banging on the bedroom door behind which she is sitting. She hears Dominic asking her what's got into her, what she wants, soothing her, pushing down the handle of the door; and then a sharp thud, and Terry grabbing her, shouting at her, marshalling her away. A few minutes later there is the sound of Jasmine's bedroom door closing. She hears Dominic singing to her – a gospel-turned lullaby she is stunned to discover he remembers from Lewa. But this time Dominic is unable to soothe Jasmine, or unable to persist with it, or riled somehow by it, and suddenly she hears the slamming of the front door, and Dominic's feet fast on the stairs. Then, for hours, there are the rising and cresting waves of Jasmine's increasingly breathless sobs. When finally they cease, there is only the television. On, and on, and on.

Until suddenly, Terry opens the door to the room, walks straight over to Simone, lifts the scarf from her face, and unties the cords.

It is morning. Somehow she has slept.

"I'm sorry," he cries into her lap. "I had to do it. I'm sorry. I'm sorry."

Simone places her stiff hands onto his head and strokes his hair.

"It's okay," she hushes, soothing, reassuring. "It's okay."

It could have gone either way. But it is okay. She is alive.

Her children are alive too. Having slept, thus missing hours of potential doom, the confirmation of this hits Simone with a relief that rushes so fast out of her body she has to hold onto the doorframe to steady herself. When she peered first into Dominic's room, his vacant bed had sent her spiralling into thoughts of disaster – accident, injury, death. But a moment later she found him – only his knuckles stained red, as though he had punched a wall, or a window, or, she prayed not, a person. Still sleeping, he is curled now into Jasmine's cot, his head in her neck, holding the girl close. Holding her as Simone rarely held him. She will make it up to her son. Silently, she promises him this.

Simone closes the door to Jasmine's room softly. The morning is already bright, but it is early, not even the city workers have departed with Monday zeal from the street. Terry has gone for a shower and Simone picks around the living room, throwing rubbish into the bin, loading the dishwasher, sorting through laundry. Her body is stiff and she moves slowly. Wincing as she does. Her wallet and phone fall out of Terry's shorts pocket. There is no money left, but on her phone there is a missed call from an unknown number. Simone has an urge to call it back, but Terry may hear. She must act normal, she reminds herself, be careful, smart.

Simone opens the window. Below on the street, a taxi is pulling up. The door opens, and out of it steps Veronica and her husband. They are sunkissed and smiling. Each carries a small suitcase and their eyes dance as though filled with the sparkling stories of adventure shared. They do not even look up. They link arms as they weave their way from the pavement to their front door, then they tumble into their house, mere feet away from her own. They are happy, quiet, oblivious.

Sarah

Sarah was early for Monday pick-up. With Harry at home, unencumbered, she planned this time to pin Veronica down. Stuff niceties, stuff tiptoeing, she would make Veronica tell her exactly what her report had said. Through the glass window of the classroom door, Sarah watched Veronica sail between the desks handing out some art creation that the children proudly accepted, excited to bring home. At Amelia's desk, Veronica bent down and said something quietly to her, to which Amelia nodded her head slowly, before Veronica moved on to bestow joy to the next child. Sarah gritted her teeth.

Not this time. Not this time.

When Sarah had walked into Amelia's classroom the previous week to find Harry not there, the helplessness that had already been building inside her, expanded into untameable horror. It had stuck in her throat, paralysing and oppressive. And all week since then, it had sweated out of her, forcing her to avoid colleagues and cancel meetings, and sit at her desk as though wrapped tight in sticky web. It was the same way she'd felt when Eliza had died, and there had been no recourse, nothing she could do to turn back time. It was the same way she'd felt years and years earlier too, locked in a small wooden room, smelling chlorine, eyes blinking manically in the dark.

Helplessness: the inability to defend or to act effectively.

How quickly it had struck. How easily Veronica had unravelled her. Again.

Yet surely this was the opposite of what she was now. Her whole career was built on her ability to defend, to enact effect.

So not this time. This time would end differently.

Veronica was tanned, refreshed, glowing. Sarah waited until all the other children had departed, she waited until she'd enveloped Amelia in a hug and heard her explain that her lost piece of art had turned up, but too late to be featured in the school magazine, and asked her to go ahead to the playground. She waited until Veronica thought she had the room to herself. And then she flung the door open.

"What happened to Amelia's art?" she asked abruptly into the silence.

Veronica spun around. "Oh I know, I'm so sorry, I must have misplaced it somewhere." She smiled. "It was very good too so such a shame not to be featured in the magazine. But luckily it's turned up now. These things usually do."

"When are you going to tell me what you've put in your report?" said Sarah.

"Oh Sarah," Veronica sang. (It was almost Sawah, almost.) "I told you, it's not urgent anymore. All the parents will be receiving an email this week about next year's arrangements, so everything you need to know will be in there. We can chat after that if you like?"

"So it's written? The report. You've done it?"

"Yes," smiled Veronica. "And I'm so sorry, but I have to rush now, I have an appointment."

And she hurried away. Just like that. Without consequence. Without care. Without any idea what she had caused or what might be coming.

Simone

The social worker at the door is a mistake. Something must have got mixed up in the paperwork. It isn't Polly. This woman doesn't have a clue. Maybe there's been another complaint, something separate. But the woman sees the panicked urgency in Simone's eyes; she understands.

"I already spoke to Polly last week," Simone rebuffs, angrily for Terry's benefit. He is hovering behind her with his hand on her waist. "Who's called you this time? Was it the neighbours again? You know they're just wasting your time, just trying to cause us trouble." Only with her eyes can she communicate truthfully with the woman: *say nothing, say nothing, talk to Polly.*

Polly has arranged it all. She came to the gym the same afternoon that Simone called her, and she took her to the police station where photos were taken of her wrists and her face and the other places where bruises remained. It had taken three days for Simone to summon the courage to make that call, and because of the delay her injuries weren't as evident as they could have been, but she'd needed time. Even reclaiming Polly's card from the bottom of her drawer had felt like a dangerous act of espionage. Her heart had been racing as she'd stuffed it into her bra, listening for the sounds of Terry's footsteps, but somehow she'd managed it. At the police station, Polly had told her that there was a women's shelter in Camden that would take them, and she urged Simone to go at once, that day; but Terry had Jasmine. Since the incident over the weekend he had been making amends again – another turn of the never-ending wheel of promises that Simone finally saw in full colour – and it would have been impossible to reject that without raising his suspicion. He had made a whole show of facilitating her work. She could put in for a longer shift, he'd told her, he'd stay off the booze, and he would have Jasmine, properly this time. She had to seem pleased about that. She had to be grateful. She couldn't suddenly return from work early or take Jasmine out without him. Besides, by that time in the afternoon, she wouldn't have been able to intercept Dominic before he got home from school. And they had things to collect from the flat. Nothing irreplaceable, but enough to furnish what she imagined was going to be a stark if not run-down room at the refuge. She remembered how important those homely items had felt when she first moved onto the estate with Noah.

The problem was, now that Polly knew there was an imminent risk of violence, she couldn't leave the children unprotected. She told Simone this sensitively but firmly. She could send in a police officer to get them, she said, in fact, that is what she would have to do. But Simone begged her. She didn't want the police involved. Terry was wily, conniving, clever, he'd find a way to wriggle out of things, he'd get somebody to give him an alibi, or to somehow point the finger at her, he wouldn't go down. And then he'd come after her. He'd find Dominic. He'd kill them both.

If she was to do this, she didn't want the police involved. Give her a day, she'd begged Polly. She'd arrange things with Dominic. She'd pack a bag. She'd find a way to take Jasmine. Give her a day.

The woman should not be here. It has only been hours since Simone agreed things with Polly. The bag at least is ready, hastily stuffed while Terry was watching TV, squashed carefully underneath their bed. But the kids are unprepared, and Terry is here. Tomorrow, Thursday, is one of their friend's birthdays. She has told Terry that the gym has rearranged the rosters so that she has the day off, and he's thrilled that this means they can go to the pub together. She plans for Jasmine to have a last-minute onset of sickness, for the two of them to need to stay home. Dominic will be at school then, so while Terry's at the pub, she can pick him up and get him away. She still needs to prepare Dominic for this, but he hasn't come home yet, and when she tried to talk to him earlier in the week he would barely speak to her. He is angry. With her. He thinks she was out that night, that she abandoned him, again, even after he did his part pretending to Polly, even after they'd seemed to reconnect. He doesn't know she was there all the time, metres away, strapped to a chair.

Feeling Terry's hand growing heavier on her waist, Simone grits her teeth. The social worker holds her gaze probingly.

"Bloody bother the neighbours this time, not us," Simone says boldly, willing the woman to understand the warning look in her eyes. "Tell her, Tel."

Simone looks behind her to Terry who stares back at her with admiration. "Goodbye," he says to the social worker, and slams the door in her face. "You fucking stupid goddess," he whispers in Simone's ear, lifting her off the floor.

Simone steadies her breath. Eyes she used to think she loved are staring at her with desire. Hands she used to kiss, and cower beneath, are already working their way under her shirt. Every inch of her body tightens, repulsed and nauseated, but she forces another breath, one more breath. One more time. Terry shuts the bedroom door and climbs on top of her.

Simone prays that the woman at the door has understood. She thinks she has. She prays she has. She need only call Polly.

Terry grunts, and she forces herself to respond with the

heavy intake of breath she knows he likes – braving him, succumbing to him.

In the next room, Jasmine is watching TV.

Perhaps Dominic will come home soon. Simone prays for a chance to talk to him away from Terry. To warn him. To explain.

Terry is moving faster.

She prays that the bag does not come loose under the bed.

She prays the police don't arrive at the door.

She prays that she and her children will survive.

It occurs to Simone that she does not believe in God and doesn't know who she is praying to, but she prays again anyway.

One more day she needs. One more day till she is free.

Sarah

Sarah knew what she was going to do. Finally. This was her favourite part of any case: sifting the facts, finding the arguments, distilling them down to one, crucial key. Not that Veronica was a case, but her mind carried it that way, accompanying her to the office, and to dinner, and to bed. And just like other cases, the answer had come to her slowly, gradually, a gentle bubbling that had simmered under the skin until at last it was an idea fully formed, presenting itself to her like a pre-packed solution. Or a lightning bolt. When she thought about it, Veronica herself had practically handed the idea to her.

What would you rather? The game of their youth. The test of their depravity that started it all. Well, how depraved was Veronica now? More than she let on, Sarah betted, more than the wholesome staff or right-thinking parents at Amelia's school would expect. This was her leverage.

Veronica still hadn't sent the letter about Amelia – revelling, Sarah supposed, in the anticipation and the control, the joy of watching her squirm. Probably, she thought it didn't matter how long the letter took, and it didn't matter what lies her report contained, because Sarah would never do anything about it. Like always. But she should have been listening more carefully all those years ago. Sarah would do anything to protect her family. Anything. So now, what would Veronica rather?

The plan was straightforward: arrange to see Veronica, get her drunk, get her more than drunk, wasted, and then… play. Just like when they were children. Except that these days there were phones with cameras, and there was social media, and consequences. Especially for a teacher.

Nothing illegal. Nothing harmful.

Those had been Sarah's self-prescribed parameters, outside, as she was now, of David's.

But she would make Veronica tell her what she'd put in the report; she would make her tell her why. She would expose how Veronica had singled out her child, 'lost' her work, lied about her, shamed her, pretended she had 'issues', used her as bait. And then, then, she would make Veronica understand the other things she had done. She would finally make her see how it felt to be manipulated and trapped, to have one's confidence stripped and trampled upon, to feel humiliated and small. She would, just for a moment, take away that infuriating Veronica-boldness, that maddening power, and hold up a mirror so that Veronica would be forced to see the weakness that lay within. As Sarah had had to see. To know that actions had impact. That there were consequences. In this case, the consequence would be Veronica staying the hell away from Amelia.

Lightning-struck, Sarah lay awake in bed. Harry's podgy feet were nestled in her armpit, his head tucked perfectly into Amelia's neck. Amelia's own feet were resting on David's cheek. Real lightning had been raging for hours, prompting the children's sojourn into the parental bed, though it was not unusual for them to end up there unprompted. The curtain of the bay window was drawn back slightly and outside, an otherworldly darkness beset the summer dawn. Sarah didn't know how long she had been awake. Amelia had been the first to come in, sometime around 4am, Harry shortly thereafter, and it was during the alert wakefulness that followed that her plotting had begun. A storm brewing. Atoms crashing. Friction exploding and finding its target on Earth. Sarah appreciated the emblematic appropriateness of the weather, the supernatural might it enabled her to imagine, as though she, a god-like judge, was the source of the obliteration in the air.

Sarah craned her neck, trying not to disturb Harry's feet as she searched for the time. The clock on her bedside table showed 5:55am. She often seemed to see a run of repeating numbers like that. When she looked at the time, it would always read 11:11, or 12:12, or some other strangely conspicuous combination, and after a while she had googled it. One explanation was simply that the repetition made the number visually pleasing, so that it was more consciously noted than other permutations, and not really more frequent at all. But there was another account that described spirit guides and guardian angels, using these numbers as a way to grab human attention and impart something important to the viewer. And when Sarah read that, she had immediately thought of Eliza.

When they were children, her sister had often talked of souls and spirits. The two of them were soulmates, they had decided, connected, and throughout their younger years, caught up by the stories of their mother's 'interesting' friends, they were forever dissecting coincidences and strange happenings. Once, Eliza had even wanted to make a Ouija board, but Sarah had vetoed that. Instead, they had decided that when one of them died (imagining this to be far further into the future than in fact was the case), if it was possible to come back, if it was possible to haunt the other, if ghosts were real, then the dead one should knock over a specific blue vase in their mother's study, and then the surviving one would know. A few months after Eliza's accident, Sarah had remembered this, and rushed home to her parents' house, heading straight for the study, but when asked, her mother said that that vase had been broken years ago.

Most likely, the numbers were just the visually pleasing thing. Still, Sarah reasoned, if Eliza was trying to find a way to connect, 5:55 was a good way to do it. Especially in the middle of a storm sent from the beyond. Especially at the moment that Sarah had decided to take action, take revenge, not only for herself and Amelia, but for Eliza too. What was Eliza's message though, blinking through the clock? A blessing, or a warning shot?

5:56.

The alarm would sound in four minutes. For four minutes, Sarah turned her eyes towards her sleeping family – peaceful, entwined, shielded by her and David's force-field of beliefs. For four minutes she watched them this way, and breathed them in; and by 6am she had changed her mind again. Because what on Jupiter was she thinking? What ridiculous notion had made her consider abandoning everything she believed in – honesty, right. In pursuit of what? The winning of a petty, childish game. No, she wouldn't do it, she would 'rise above it', as usual. There were other ways to protect Amelia. Spirits didn't send storms to pleasantly confirm good choices. They were fury-fuelled means of intervention, warnings to decease.

At breakfast, Amelia and Harry were entranced by the goings-on in the garden. Half a month's rain had fallen in an hour and the long summer grass swam beneath a veritable pool on top. The sight of it induced in Sarah's mind visions of her parents' dilapidated swimming pool, but she forced her attention instead to the train timetable on her phone. While she searched for a running line, Harry persuaded David to open the garden door and he dashed outside in his nappy and t-shirt, consenting only later to wellies. Amelia, more restrained in her neat school uniform, stood just inside, pointing out the deepest sections of water for her brother to jump in. Both of them giggled, tickled and surprised by the workings of the world.

"Nothing's on time," Sarah said, glancing up to David. "It's going to take me hours to get in."

"Work from home?" David suggested.

"Can't. Meetings."

He nodded and called the kids back to the table, where he had arranged smiley berry faces on the tops of their porridge. "So, what's on the agenda today?" he asked them all.

"It's drama with Mrs Burke," volunteered Amelia, fastidiously scooping her porridge from the outmost edges, working slowly in on the smile. "And we're finishing our Matisse collages. And it's spellings."

"And Harry has music group," added David. "Followed by a very important nap."

"And I have a closing statement," finished Sarah, allowing herself to shift focus for a moment to the case she should have given far more attention over the past weeks. It was unlike her to be so distracted and she wondered if she'd done enough, or if she'd let Veronica control that too. The case came down to a call of ethics rather than precedent in the end, the spirit rather than the letter of the law. But surely the judge would do the right thing, just as she had that morning conceded to. Surely entrenched values would stand firm, like a protective shield around them.

Later, statement made – in the end rather convincingly – and umbrella in hand, Sarah wondered how she had made it back to Veronica's road. And why.

It was lunchtime and Veronica wouldn't even be there, she would be at school, with Amelia. But something about the pretty, Primrose house had drawn Sarah away from her office in the middle of the pouring day, and back to it, as though it was the scene of something important, or would be. As though it was the ground upon which lightning had struck.

Still raining, few people were about and the emptiness made Sarah feel conspicuous. Wetness had seeped into the soles of her feet, making them slippery inside her heels, and she leaned gently against a railing. Only one other figure was visible. A little way down the road, huddled similarly beneath brolly, stood a large, black woman, vibrant against cloud. Her skirt was bright orange, tipped at the hem by muddied water, her coat a deep red. Sarah would have noticed this woman even amidst a tightly packed crowd. But after first inspection, it was not the brightness of the clothes that kept Sarah's attention, it was the gaze of the woman's eyes. They were focussed in exactly the same direction as Sarah's had been a moment earlier, staring straight at the house across the street.

Immediately, Sarah wondered who this woman was, standing there, watching.

As Sarah stood, watching.

Watching some more.

When suddenly, out of the house next door to Veronica's, stepped a young man. Hooded, he was without an umbrella, but walked with defiance as though he didn't need one, as though the weather didn't apply to him And all of a sudden, the rain began to slow, as if in compliance, and in the distance now the young man seemed to nod, as though satisfied by this thing he had already known. It may be England, but it was summer after all. Damp. Not the time to fantasise about fiery tempests. Rather to calm down. To do the right, measured, expected thing.

Simone

There is no time.

After the social worker left, Simone had done all she could to hide her nerves, to look casual, but she passed by the front window on at least eight occasions, looking for Dominic. He finally materialised just before dinner, but even before they sat down, conversation was commandeered by Terry's recounting of how Simone had given the social worker what for. He'd loved that. He spoke with his hand on her knee, the warmth of it seeping into her skin and sickening her, but she nodded, and smiled, and laughed in all the right places, noticing with a detached interest how in previous days she would have been fooled by these gestures of his, bolstered high enough for him to later knock down. When finally, Terry released first her leg and then Dominic from the table (Jasmine deliberately fed early and deposited in bed), Simone tried to grab a few minutes alone with her son. She needed to explain the happenings of the last week, she needed to explain her plan. But Dominic decisively closed the door to his room, and by the time she managed to casually walk across the living room and reach for the handle, Terry was requesting her presence on the sofa, insisting on a shared spliff to cap off the day.

In the middle of the night, she tried again, attempting to creep from their bed into Dominic's room, but Terry stirred, wrapping himself around her, and the risk was too great. She would get up early, she told herself, catch Dominic before school. She didn't, however, account for the blurring effect of the spliff, and by the time she managed to pull herself from bed the following day, Dominic was gone.

Terry, not gone, was in high spirits. He spent the morning chasing Jasmine around the flat, Simone worrying how she would turn shrieks and giggles into stay-home-sickness. But with a stroke of luck, minutes before they were supposed to leave for the pub, during one last frenzied, hysterical dash beneath the kitchen table, Jasmine cracked her head against it, and amid all the crying, Simone carried her to the bathroom for a plaster, and when she returned, informed Terry that Jasmine had been sick. "I don't think she needs the hospital," she told him. "But we better stay put and watch it for a bit. You go on, don't let us stop you. We'll join you at the pub."

"You sure?" he asked, an arm around her waist, a hand beneath Jasmine's chin, but she kissed him on the cheek, and nodded.

In the end it was easy. He hadn't suspected a thing.

Grabbing the bag from beneath the bed, and adding to it a few extra things of Dominic's that she hasn't been able to pack before, Simone picks up Jasmine and bustles her to the door. The pub is only a few roads away and Terry should be there for at least a couple of hours, but he could always have a change of heart, or, in his new spirit of 'trying harder', he might come back as a surprise, to help. Nevertheless, Simone finds herself pausing at the door, turning back to the room she is leaving, looking one last time. *Move. Move*, her mind tells her as she looks. *Now. Now. Now.* But it has always been more difficult to act than to think of acting.

No, she is going. She has decided. Besides, Polly is waiting, it is no longer her choice.

Just a note though, one last thing…

Tel,
We've gone. You know why. Don't follow. Stay away
or I'll call the police. When we're settled, you can
see Jas. Not me and not Dom. Somebody will be in
touch to arrange it. Don't do anything stupid. Look
after yourself.
Simone

She writes a kiss after her name, and then scribbles it out. Did she ever love him? Fear and need had a way of muddling emotion. She can't tell what she thinks anymore, only that whatever she once felt has vanished – in the tautness of cord around her wrists, and fingers around her throat, and thuds to her son's head. Now all she knows is that she has to get herself and the children away. And that she wants Terry to know she has made this choice, this decision to leave him, that he hasn't stamped her out completely. Simone arranges the note so that it is clearly visible on the kitchen table, picks Jasmine back up, checks once more out of the window, and then hurries down the stairs.

Polly is waiting for her at the school as planned. Walking down the street towards her, Simone's sense of liberation is almost tangible. The rain has stopped and she feels as though she is flying. She practically skips as she pushes the buggy, loaded with both Jasmine and their heavy bag. It doesn't matter that she is leaving the pretty streets of Primrose Hill. Past the old estate she goes, past houses growing increasingly shabby, past the liquor shop, past the Asda and the Poundland and the job centre. None of it matters. Poverty is never what trapped her. And now, they are nearly free. She can't wait to tell Dominic, to see the relief on his face, to watch that heavy, too-adult darkness dissipate from it. To start things fresh.

But as soon as she nears Polly, she knows that something is wrong.

"He's not here," Polly breathes, shaking her head, rushing down the school steps towards her. Not smiling. She places her hand on Simone's arm. "He got in a fight at lunch. Ran off about twenty minutes ago, just before I arrived."

The thing about flying, is there's so much further to fall. Quicker than ever before in her life, fear rips through Simone's skin, burning as it forces its way through clenched pores. Simone flings the buggy into Polly's hands, turns, and runs back towards Primrose Hill, and him.

But there is no time.

Why did she leave that stupid note? A foolish attempt to show Terry that he hadn't beaten her, that, in the end, she didn't need him? Or was it a last wavering, one more desire to connect with him, protect him, explain? Whatever the motivation, it was another poor choice. Another act of senseless, reckless rebellion. Because what if Dominic has gone home already, and Terry is there, and has seen the note? He'll kill him. He will kill him. He'll kill him for sure.

At the top of their road, Simone stops for breath, obscuring herself behind the house on the corner. She takes her mobile phone from her pocket and calls her son, wondering why she hasn't thought of this sooner, but Dominic doesn't answer. It rings through to his voicemail and Simone leaves a garbled message telling him not to go home and to call her straight away. There is a seed of thought that Terry might already have Dominic's phone, so she is wary not to reveal too much about where she and Jasmine will be, or who they are with, or what is happening, but she needs Dominic to stay away from Terry, and also, to know that he hasn't been abandoned to him.

Simone looks at her watch. It has been over an hour since Terry left for the pub. He should still be in the midst of it all, but he might by now be wondering what's keeping them. Tentatively, Simone peers around the wall of the end house and glances down the street, then hurriedly she pulls herself back behind brick.

He is there.

Beer in hand, Terry is strolling merrily towards the flat from the opposite direction. He throws an empty bag of crisps into the gutter and stops to light a cigarette, then reaches into his pocket for his key ring, which he casually spins around his finger. On his face sits an expression of contentment, his world at rights; about to unravel. He is nearer to the house than she is, but if Simone sprints, if she runs with all her might, it might just be possible to get there first, to somehow race up the stairs ahead of him and get rid of the note. But where will she say Jasmine is? And what if he notices their missing things? And if Dominic is there, how will she get him away? Simone hesitates, her feet no longer flying but iron-weighted, sinking into prettily paved stone. Terry reaches the doorstep. He lifts his key. If he sees the note and then she turns up, he will kill her. But if Dominic is there, he will kill him.

Terry opens the door.

There is no time. No time to think or plan. Simone pushes herself around the corner. She forces her feet to move, and they do, they obey, they obey her and nobody else – faster and faster, towards the abyss.

It comes. It happens.

From outside, she hears the sound of Terry exploding, something smashing. In a moment he will be down the stairs again, on the street, looking for her, but still she steels herself towards him. She has to get to Dominic. She has to get to her son. There is no choice, no freedom after all. She moves closer. Closer again, closer to those hands that will grip around her throat. Closer. Closer. Almost there. Until suddenly, just metres away from the door, a face appears in front of her, and a strong, decisive hand pulls her sharply away

"Don't look back," says Lewa.

Veronica

Veronica had only popped home during lunch for some fresh clothes, but there was post waiting for her. A letter from Dr Shirazi detailing in writing the results of her fertility tests that he had already explained to her in person: quite simply, she was fine. There was nothing abnormal, no depletion of eggs, no irregular hormones, no endometriosis or blocking of the fallopian tubes, no anti-sperm antibodies; there was no reason, on her side, that they should not conceive, as he had suspected. He would, however, monitor her next few cycles so that they could pinpoint the optimal time for conception – which according to Monday's appointment would be tomorrow. And they would wait for the results from George.

A week ago, Veronica would have leapt to the conclusion that since it wasn't her, it had to be George, his fertility had to be the problem, because they *had* a problem, and then she would have spent days wondering if and when and how to tell him. Now, instead, Veronica ran lightly up the stairs, confident that Dr Shirazi had been right all along. The obstacles were psychosomatic, there was no issue at all.

Despite the morning's rain, Veronica had cycled to school, enjoying the dodging of puddles and the pattering of heavy drops on her face. She hadn't thought it mattered how wet she became since she kept a spare set of clothes in the classroom, and as she weaved through the bouquet of umbrellas, cycling upright with no hands, she had an urge to laugh at the weather, to congratulate it for its unpredictable wildness, to let it know she understood that spirit, she felt it too. But she had forgotten underwear.

Next door, there was a sudden thumping down the stairs like a bag being pulled, then the slamming of a door, and Veronica moved quickly from her chest of drawers to the bedroom window to look. She hadn't seen Dominic since returning from France, he hadn't knocked all week, and the noise in the meantime had been relatively mild, so the darkness that usually emanated through brick had receded slightly in her mind. Still, she found herself thinking frequently of those children, and listening for signs of life.

On the street, Simone was loading Jasmine into a buggy and arranging a bag on the handles. It was a large bag, a suitcase almost, bulging at the sides and unbalancing the pram so that Simone had to hold it down to stop it from tipping. There was another bag slung across her body. And another stuffed under the pram. Everything she did was rushed and she kept dropping things, glancing twitchily up and down the street. She was leaving! Veronica realised this slowly but with glee. Simone was running, this was it.

Veronica's first instinct was to cheer, to crane her head out of the top floor window and shout after Simone: congratulations, congratulations, you did it – the same praise she had offered the rain. But her second thought, abruptly, was Dominic, He wasn't there. Reasoning in the next moment that he must of course be at school – where she herself should be too – Veronica dashed down the stairs with the intention of grabbing a quick lunch at home before heading back. Stirring soup, the next logical series of thoughts began to surface: did Terry know that Simone had left? How would he react? What would this mean for her and George? Would they have less chance of getting Terry moved on if it was only him living there, or more? What kind of noise would there be when he found Simone gone?

Veronica didn't have to wait long to have this last question answered. Out of the front window, she saw Terry waltzing with his usual arrogance up the steps to his front door, and less than sixty seconds later, there was an almighty roar. Then the sound of something smashing, and something else that could have been wood or may have been flesh thudding against the wall, and then a series of what sounded like chairs being kicked over, and then Terry bounding back onto the street where he span around like a crazed animal, this way and that, into the road and back again, until finally, a visible defeat washed over him and he took a step back towards his open door. A foot before it, he stopped, and suddenly turned his gaze slightly to his left, straight into Veronica's window. Veronica was sitting a few metres back in the kitchen by then, but she was clearly looking at him. Watching.

Look away a voice inside whispered. *Look away*. But she could not, and as soon as their eyes locked, the words Terry had shouted at George echoed around her head, as they had done now so many times before: *I'll have you begging! I'll have you on your knees and broken!*

Look away, the voice of the past year told her again.

And the teacher in Kent.

And the man in Oman.

Veronica put down the spoon and stared straight at him.

"What are you fucking looking at?" Terry snarled from the street.

She wasn't prepared for the volume of the slap as his palm hit reinforced glass.

Simone

Lewa tries her best to calm Simone. Dominic is not at home, she tells her, he has not been there, she promises. She has been watching.

"What do you mean you've been watching? How have you been watching? How long? Where were you?"

Lewa has dragged Simone into the public library a few streets away and they are huddled in a corner by the door. Both of them glance every now and then through the window onto the street, but for now it is quiet. Simone allows the woman to take her face in her strong, firm hands and to stroke hair away from her forehead.

"I've been here a few days, a week maybe. After your email, I had to come. But I didn't want to knock when that man was there."

"Terry. I've left him."

"Good."

"Lewa, I left a note. And Dominic... I don't know where Dominic is. If he goes home... What have I done?"

"What have you done?" Lewa asks, standing back now and broadening her chest. "What you've done, my girl, is you've taken your turn. You're finally taking your turn. About time."

Six years unravel in a minute. With the same ease that Simone remembers, Lewa infuses her with strength and determination, that rare combination that Noah had in such abundance. Despite her fear, Simone feels anchored in a way she hasn't in many, many years, and she is able to gather the presence of mind to call Polly, who is already on the way to the refuge with Jasmine. Simone and Lewa creep out of the library to meet them there, and on the way they attempt to bridge the dark chasm between them, tentatively winding their way back to those awful weeks after Noah died, and that fateful day when they stood either side of a closed door.

"I'm so sorry," Simone says, over and over. "I was so selfish. And such a mess. I should have been there for Noah – I loved him, I did love him, you have to know that. And I should never have lied to you. I should have let you help. I should have let you take Dominic. I've been an awful, awful mother."

But Lewa puts her finger to Simone's lips. "It's okay," she tells her – once, twice. The third time she shakes her head. "Simone, we cannot change what's been. But now, now you are being the mother you need to be. Now we find Dominic."

As soon as they reach Polly, plans begin. She has gathered more information from the school and Simone is shocked to hear that Dominic has hit his best friend Jakub with a rock. Apparently, Dominic had discovered that Jakub had told a teacher about his cut hand, about many bruises before that, about suspicions he had. It was one hit, the teacher on duty had told Polly, one explosive hit, from behind, to the back of Jakub's head, and Jakub had been knocked out by it. But the boy is not badly hurt and thankfully is not seeking to press charges. He has even offered to help search for Dominic. Polly calls the police to enlist their assistance too. "The important thing is that you don't go back," she tells Simone, looking her in the eye. "You must not confront Terry. We'll find Dominic, don't worry about that, we won't let him get as far as the flat."

Simone nods, though she is unconvinced.

Polly is thrilled to discover Lewa, and Jasmine takes to her immediately. As Polly and Simone make calls, Lewa entertains the toddler with the exotic contents of her handbag

– a nail file, a pack of tissues, a rogue coin – none of which contain nutmeg but somehow are still seeped in the smell of it. After a while, Lewa folds Jasmine into her lap, and sings to her. The little girl closes her eyes. Half-remembered gospel-turned-lullaby drifts over the child and around Simone's ears, nutmeg tickling her nostrils, and for a second she closes her own eyes too, wishing more than anything that she could return to Lewa's old, cosy flat, where Noah was wrapped in love and belief, and she was wrapped in him. But of course. she must leave this music, that after all did lead to one good thing: Dominic, who has Noah's sensitivity if not his talent. She must find their son.

It is agreed that Lewa will stay and tend to Jasmine. Polly will return to the office to coordinate efforts between the police, the council and the school. Simone will search the streets. Polly did not want to allow this last part of the plan, but she cannot stop her, and if anybody is going to find Dominic, Simone is convinced it will be her. She starts at the estate. Terry has friends here, one of them is sleeping in their old flat, and Simone feels anxious as soon as she draws near; but she does not think that Terry will have told anybody about her leaving. Not yet. He won't want that humiliation broadcast, he'll need time first to spin it, or to take revenge. Still, Simone holds her breath as she approaches the Concourse.

It is like taking a tour of the past decade. There, hanging off the wall outside the bet shop, sit herself and Noah – his arm draped around her, proud, confident, his friends spellbound by the sparks that fly from his eyes and mingle with their own. There, are herself and Dominic – younger, lighter, fingers entwined as they dash, late, past others who are loitering. There she is again, bottle in hand, half conscious, eyes blurred, on her knees.

Simone shakes her head. Already, the walls have erected themselves inside her, towering around her, it has started to rain again and it is difficult to see. Clenching her fists, she strides purposefully forward.

The boys on the wall haven't seen Dominic, they say, not since the night before. Horror pushes through Simone's chest with the knowledge that he has been here, hanging out, doing goodness knows what, without her knowing a thing, but for now she pushes this concern away. Where next? He is not by their old flat or with any of their old friends on the estate. She looks into a number of stairwells, but he is not there either. She circles back past Jakub's house but Jakub is out, his mother tells her, a scathing look in her eye, Jakub is out looking for Dominic. Simone nods a thanks, an apology, and scuttles away. At first, she does not know where she is heading. She glances into the park, the newsagent, the tube station. She passes deep crowds of people trundling home from work. She walks up and then back down Camden's bridge. It is only once she had gone well past Chalk Farm tube and halfway to Kentish Town that Simone realises where she is going. The same place her son was aiming for days earlier. The iron railings of the steps seem less imposing than she remembers. The deep blue of the door is less shiny. But here is the step she sat on, hollering for the neighbours to hear. Here is the step from which she was turned away, pregnant or not. Here is the step upon which she used to stand listening, hoping to hear music, or TV, or voices that never came.

She rings the bell. Her mother blinks into the dull drizzle, a camera lens opening and shutting, finding focus. Then without saying a word she rushes inside, leaving Simone standing on the doorstep, peering into the corridor where her mother flings open the door to the study that was always so tightly, determinedly shut. A second later, her father appears – older, smaller, but there. Together, Simone's parents return to the door. Together, they hover, unable still to pull Simone towards them, to pull her back, to break their own chains of restraint, though she thinks she sees their desire for this. They hold each other's arms. "Come inside," her father whispers finally.

Come in. Come in. A door open.

But there is no time.

There is no time for the unpicking of a decade. There is no time for recriminations and apologies. The only time is now, and now, she needs only one thing. "Is Dominic with you? Is he here?"

At once, her mother's face changes. "You've lost Dominic?"

At once, Simone feels the accusation, the familiar judgment. She is seventeen again. Buried bitterness stirs inside her. But no, she isn't seventeen, she tells herself, she is no longer an angry, needy child. "I've left Terry," she says, noticing her mother's hands fly to her chest. "Dominic doesn't know. I had to do it quickly – he was at school. And yes, I can't find him. I need to get to him before he goes home. I thought he might be here?"

"We haven't seen Dominic in four years," Simone's father tells her gently, quietly, with what she can see is a great attempt to keep the blame from this truth. Simone waits nevertheless for more – *since you told us to steer clear, since your boyfriend threatened to hurt us, since you let him do that* – but it doesn't come. "Can we help?" he asks.

Can we help?

And *come in.*

Simone's parents stand waiting at the door. They see her, and they see her need, and it is everything she has ever wanted.

Except that Dominic is not there. And the emptiness of that wraps itself around her throat harder than Terry's hands ever did, and turns her away, and pushes her back down the steps towards the street that so many years ago she abandoned in stupid, helpless defiance. Only it is different this time. Because at the last minute, she stops and dashes back up the stairs, past her surprised parents, and past the wide open door of her father's study where she rips a sheet of paper from his ready pad and with scratching nib scrawls her phone number before thrusting it into their hands.

"If he comes here, call me," she tells them.

Her father stays her arm. Ripping a scrap of paper off the sheet, he removes a pen from behind his ear and writes his own number, which he hands to her. "When you find him," he says. "And any time after that too, call us. You can always call us."

A lifeline after all.

He is not down by the canal.

He is not on the bridge.

She checks the estate again and he is still not there.

By the time she returns to the refuge, even the late light of summer has been consumed by rain and night. Lewa beckons her in from the door, whispering so as not to wake Jasmine who is asleep on her lap. Simone notices how content the child seems, oblivious in slumber, and she longs to breathe in her innocence, to take it for herself; but she listens to Lewa's report that there has been no news from Polly. And then she nods. "I'm going out again."

"You need to sleep," says Lewa.

But Simone cannot be persuaded. "I need my son."

Sarah

At 4.44am, Sarah glanced from her clock to David's side of the bed. The storm of the previous day was over and unusually there were no children between them. She should try to go back to sleep, but already she felt she had been laying there fruitlessly for hours. Noiselessly, Sarah crept from the thin summer sheets across the thick shag of white resting on wood. A memory of crunchy grass and night-time adventure slipped between her toes. At the dressing table, she reached for her phone.

There were thirty-four new messages. But nothing from the school. Nothing from Veronica.

Instead, in bold capitals, was a draft judgment from her case the day before, for handing down the following week. Calmly, she clicked it open. In the end, she had felt confident in the weight of her argument in court, and in the certainty of justice ringing through. Perhaps the law was unclear, but the principles weren't; it would have been impossible for the judge not to see that. As Sarah read the opening sentences, however, her brow crumpled inwards. It could not be. She had lost. Lost! She hadn't lost a case in over a year.

Sarah looked over to David, urgently feeling the need for him, but there was no point in robbing his sleep too. In the dark, her legal brain began to kick into action. She would appeal. There were things she could do. But even as she began to compile them, she could see clearly the reasons why she had lost, and would lose again, deluded before. The law was simply not with her, the law was not with Right.

Sarah's heart began to beat rapidly, she felt her palms start to sweat. She was still in the open expanse of the bedroom, but perhaps it was the darkness of the blackout curtains, perhaps that was why all of a sudden she felt confined, and enclosed, and trapped in. Like being on a cattle cart. Or behind barbed wire. Or in a small, locked room of wood. Striding across the floor, Sarah yanked open the curtains, pushing the window open wide and gasping into the storm-cleansed air.

"What's going on?" croaked David from the bed, squinting into the sudden sun.

"Sorry," she turned. "Sorry, go back to sleep."

"What's the matter?" He sat up, shielding his eyes with his palm.

"Just a case I lost," Sarah shrugged. "Sorry. I shouldn't have woken you."

David closed his eyes. "Do you want to talk about it?"

But she shook her head, allowing him to drift back off as she stumbled into the bathroom where she brushed her teeth and wondered how she would justify the loss to her client. As she looked in the mirror, watching her brush move back and forth, she was unable to think of an explanation. Not one she could believe in. And as the morning continued, so did that feeling of disbelief, of spinning, of helplessness.

The people on the street seemed to sleepwalk through the sunlight, as though they had no idea that Right principles had that morning been ripped from beneath them. Most of them, she supposed, would never notice. They might never know that darkness and wrong could be validated, rewarded even, without consequence, and that anything, anything could happen after all.

Simone

Simone's left arm has lost feeling. She's lying on top of it, hidden behind a pair of bins on the other side of the road from the flat, a little way down. Her clothes are soaked through and her toes are crunched from cold. Heaving herself slowly to sitting, she tries to wriggle them, feeling the heavy deadness of her arm pull her sideways. Despite the many transgressions of her years, she does not think she has slept outside before, but she could not leave Terry unwatched. She could not let Dominic near him.

She hadn't meant to fall asleep. For hours she had scrutinised the door, scoured the street, searched for signs of man or boy. But at some point she must have drifted. The last time she looked at her phone it was already gone 3am and now it is only six, so she can only hope – pray – that in the intervening hours, Dominic has not been back.

There is movement on the other side of the road and Simone sees Veronica's husband leaving the house, soft leather briefcase slung across his shoulder, a skip in his step. The feeling is beginning to return to her arm and she arranges herself more carefully behind the bins. For another hour, two, she stares at the building across the street. Simone's eyes are heavy and begin to close. Her stomach hurts with hunger. She is thirsty, and dirty, and she should check in on Jasmine. She wonders about returning to the refuge. But she cannot bring herself to leave. Until finally, the door of the neighbour's house opens again, and this time Veronica emerges from it, merrily perching herself atop of her bike, cycling into the sunshine.

So Dominic is not with Veronica either, thinks Simone. And surely, surely, if Veronica had heard anything happening in the flat, by now there would be police at the door.

Jasmine is awake and bright-eyed when Simone appears at the refuge. She has two plaits in her hair, and she is happily dancing away to a pop song blaring through Lewa's phone. Lewa has done her best to make the room homey. Jasmine's princesses are lined up next to the bed. Simone sits heavily on the chair at the end of it.

"You didn't find him," says Lewa gently, pouring Simone a glass of water.

Simone gulps at the liquid. It is soothing, but not enough. "I'll just sleep for an hour," she tells Lewa. Jasmine's podgy hand has crept onto her leg and with closed eyes, Simone squeezes it. She should pick the girl up, she should reassure her, she should tell Lewa what she did and didn't find, but her eyes are already closed, and the dreams are coming now, the dreams and the nightmares. "Wake me in an hour," she mutters.

Lewa hands her a blanket. "It's okay," she says. "You sleep for a bit. My turn now. My turn."

Veronica

The day took on a surreal quality that Veronica was unable to quite pocket. She kept taking it out and examining it, drawing her focus from the children she was supposed to be instilling with number bonds and capital letters; but even they seemed to sit differently that day, as though the storm earlier in the week had somehow rendered them all in a new, untried state of being.

For Veronica, however, the day's idiosyncrasies weren't weather-made. There were three clearly identifiable sources.

First: the fact that she and George, un-coerced, had been at it like rabbits since their return from France. In bed that morning she had not even had to remind George that it was ovulation day.

Second: although she'd been taken aback by Terry's aggression the day before, it hadn't triggered the old anxiety. If anything, it had bolstered her with indignation, and the very fact of this had strengthened her more. Immediately after he'd slapped her window, she'd called the council, they'd made further assurances, and there hadn't been a sound from Terry for the rest of the day. There was no untended, crying child during the night, she hadn't seen Simone return, and a hopeful, optimistic sense was beginning to creep into Veronica's psyche: the awful man was nearly dealt with; she herself had spoken up; Dominic and his sister were safe; and her and George's haven was almost complete.

Third: Sarah. Out of everything, this had perhaps been the most surprising development, because Sarah had appeared out of the blue at drop-off that morning, with none of the friction of the past couple of weeks. It was as if she'd finally understood that in not following through on the parent-teacher meeting, or Amelia's 'problematic' report, Veronica had retracted her manipulations, and was sorry. Veronica knew she should have found a way to actually vocalise this regret to Sarah – she'd been full of embarrassment about it – but that would have called for explanation, and as far as she'd come, she wasn't yet ready.

Veronica went over to her immediately.

"Sarah."

"It's lovely to see you, Veronica," Sarah smiled, a hand on her shoulder, an openness in her eyes, unguarded, enthusiastic, the image of her daughter. Veronica examined her.

"You too."

"Letter still hasn't arrived," Sarah smiled.

"Oh—" Veronica began, but Sarah interrupted.

"No worries. We should catch up properly sometime, less formally."

Veronica smiled. "We should." She wanted to say: *I'm sorry about Amelia, I'm sorry about Harry, I'm sorry for all the stupid, petty, jealousy-driven things*. But instead, she ushered children through the door.

In the end, it was Sarah who said something. "Well, let me know when you're free, we'll do dinner, just the two of us, no husbands," she suggested. "Lots to say."

"I'd love that," smiled Veronica again.

And the smile that Sarah had returned as she walked away, was warm, and determined, and feisty, just like the girl Veronica remembered from her youth, though laced too with a new, surreal something, fitting of the day, which Veronica pocketed and saved to examine later.

It was George who suggested she invite round a friend. When Veronica arrived home that afternoon, Terry was hanging out of his front door.

"Sent the cops round did you?" he leered as she hastily locked her bike, trying all the time to appear composed and not fearful. Even from a few metres away, it was easy to see that he was intoxicated on something. "Had two of them here this morning," he carried on. "Thanks very much. Nothing to see then though, was there?"

"I don't know what you're talking about," shrugged Veronica.

"Oh no? Not been putting ideas in my girlfriend's silly little head then?" he sneered, taking a step forward from his door.

"Really, I don't know what you're talking about," she repeated, acutely aware of the clipped tones of her voice, and glad of the passers-by as she made her way quickly inside.

Terry, however, wasn't quite done. "You better fuck off!" he shouted after her. "Smug bitch."

Inside, Veronica closed the front door firmly and checked the latch twice. Before anything else, she called their builder who promised to come the following morning. For the first time all day, a creeping anxiety was snaking back inside her. *I'll have you begging! I'll have you begging! I'll have you on your knees and broken.* She couldn't help hearing Terry's refrain, over and again, and with him standing guard at his door, it was no wonder that there was a return also of that foreboding sensation of being watched. Was it him? Had it always been him? What did he want from her? It wasn't her fault that his family had gone. She replayed his words in her mind, wondering what he'd meant by there being nothing for the police to see *then*. Had there been something since then, or before then? Was something coming? Although she knew that Simone and Jasmine were a safe distance away, she realised suddenly that she hadn't actually seen Dominic.

Veronica called the police. As well as fear, Terry had stirred up a deep, dormant anger. Who was *he* to try to intimidate *her*? Who was he to abuse and threaten? Who was any man?

The police dutifully added her complaint to the now open file on Terry.

George couldn't come home. A meeting had run late and there was a conference call with New York, and it would be at least eleven before he made it.

"It's fine," said Veronica. "I'm going to order takeaway and go to bed," then with a seductive smile that rippled through the phone line, added, "you can wake me up though…"

George, however, was concerned. "He's probably in a pretty unhinged state now they've left," he mulled. "I mean, I'm sure there's nothing to worry about, but I'd feel better if there was somebody at the house with you, after that."

"George, I'm fine," smiled Veronica.

"I know, but–"

"What's he going to do?"

"Nothing, I'm sure. But what's the harm of an evening with a friend? Didn't you say something about seeing Sarah?"

Veronica exhaled dramatically. She'd been trying to embrace her new boldness, but he was probably right, and they were both done with hiding their fears – Rosie hadn't itched in over a week. Besides, there was still that niggling scrutinised feeling, an unsheddable shadow. "I suppose I could invite Sarah," she replied finally.

Sarah

Even to Sarah, who had planned it, the laughter felt real and contagious. They sat close on the sofa, clinking glasses of a dry white that Veronica had brought back from a recent holiday, taking turns to pick at the last of the sushi. If she hadn't considered things so carefully in advance, Sarah may even have been lured in by the magic of it, hooked by the old Veronica charm, that intoxicating feeling of being illuminated in her gaze. They had so far stayed away from the topic of Amelia. Instead, Veronica's stories were riddled with humour and scandal, and as they filled each other in on decades missed, Sarah felt in her veins the creeping return of the condition conjured so expertly by the other woman: a treacherous combination of jealousy, and admiration, and love. Veronica was, as always, wonderful company.

Sarah wondered how she did it. Perhaps it was marble-made tenor, or the brightness of blonde, or the easy, flirtatious dance she concocted. The quality was almost palpable, smelling of summer; and yet it was intangible too, not something you could actually hold or feel or copy. When Veronica was looking at you, listening to you, loving you, you felt queen of the world; but you weren't queen, because she was queen. It had always been this way. And despite a new softness, or carefulness maybe, Veronica was largely unchanged from the girl Sarah had known. Feet curled onto the sofa beneath her, hair loose and wet from being washed, Veronica could almost have been wearing a frill-trimmed swimming costume and tugging the ends of her chlorinated locks. She could almost have been devising dares. She could almost have been sidling carelessly across the gulf between Sarah and her sister. Or slamming the door of the pool house and disappearing into thin air.

Sarah had to hurry, before her resolve abandoned her. She had to make Veronica confess: what she had done to Amelia; perhaps, even, what she'd done to Sarah too. At the very least, she had to unravel her somehow, expose the deviousness beneath.

But she didn't seem to be getting drunk. It wasn't working. Handling her alcohol was, apparently, yet another thing at which Veronica excelled. Sarah felt herself growing more and more desperate, laughing too loudly, drinking too much.

When Veronica went to the bathroom, Sarah reached into her handbag for her phone. It was already late. Time was running out. She stuffed the phone angrily back into the folds of leather. And that's when her hand brushed against the small bag of sedatives that she had packed for the MRI scan. An unbidden thought raced through her mind, and almost out of it. But Sarah grabbed on. It was perfect: vindication coated in the consequences of Veronica's own original sin. Quickly, Sarah crushed the pills with the end of her phone, then tipped the lot into Veronica's drink.

"Let's play," Sarah smiled on Veronica's return.

"What?" Flopping down on the sofa next to her, Veronica reached for her contaminated glass and eyed Sarah. "Play?"

"To save your family's life… No, truth or dare. Actually, let's say truth, or drink."

Veronica smiled wistfully. "Okay. But you have to answer honestly."

Sarah grinned. "And the questions have to be hard."

Both women laughed, echoes of childhood stroking their skin. The evening was hot again, and the school term nearly over, the long expanse of summer stretching before them, as ever. Veronica leant forward and abruptly kissed Sarah on the cheek. The surprise of it made Sarah giggle with an unexpected pleasure, but she had a plan, and stuck to it.

"I'll start," said Sarah.

Veronica readied her wine glass defiantly, and waited. "Hard, Sarah," she goaded teasingly.

But this time, Sarah was ready, and her first question came easily. "Okay. Why did you visit David at the museum?"

Immediately, Veronica's face dropped. "I shouldn't have," she said. "I—"

"That's not an answer," Sarah interrupted. "Drink."

Veronica took a deep sip from her glass. As she did so, she kept her eyes firmly on Sarah. "My turn," she said when she came up for air. "Why didn't you want to reconnect?"

"What?" Now it was Sarah who looked flustered.

"Why didn't you want to see me? When we first saw each other at school, I was so happy to find you there. And I know you were avoiding me."

It took Sarah a long, uncomfortable moment to work out how to reply to this without giving away her hidden fury, her deep rooted resentments. But she was determined not to be pushed onto the back foot. "Because I didn't want to be reminded of what used to be," she answered eventually.

At this, Sarah noticed Veronica's eyes cloud in confusion. "You don't have good memories about us?"

"I have all sorts of memories," answered Sarah. "Some good, some not. Some about you. Some about my sister Eliza. You know she died recently?"

"What?"

"She died. In a car crash. Picking me up because I'm too scared to take the tube."

"What? Oh my God, Sarah. That's awful. I'm so sorry. Why didn't you tell me?"

"It didn't seem relevant," Sarah shrugged. "And I didn't want you to pity me."

"I would never pity you," Veronica said meaningfully. "But I am sorry. I know how much you loved Eliza. She was, she was—"

"It's my turn," said Sarah.

Veronica's eyes narrowed now, and without thinking she took another sip from her glass.

Sarah's heart raced. The sedatives should kick in soon. She was doing this. She was actually doing this. She sat up and crossed her legs around themselves. "Okay, next question. Did you actually ever fancy that boy, Adam, at Eliza's party, or were you just doing it to get closer to Eliza, to take her away from me?"

"What? Sarah, that was twenty years ago."

"You did take her away from me, you know. Then. You did it on purpose. And later."

"Are you serious?" Veronica pulled her damp hair off her shoulders and twisted it into a bun.

"Not an answer. Drink," instructed Sarah.

Again Veronica drank, but now Sarah could see her mind working, her guard going up, the open warmth of the previous hour altering.

"For the record, I did fancy him," she said. "I think I did anyway, kind of. I don't really remember. At least I fancied him more than some others, later."

To her irritation, Sarah found herself intrigued by this last reference of unhappy coupling and she wanted to ask more, but she refused to break from her plan, her perimeters, and said nothing. Instead, she watched Veronica take a slow, collecting breath.

"Okay," said Veronica finally. "Here's something I want to know: you said you have some bad memories of us. Why?"

Sarah noticed that Veronica's words were beginning to slur, only slightly but they were definitely loosening a little, losing their pristine marbled sheen. It wouldn't take long now.

"Because of what you did to me," said Sarah. "Obviously."

Veronica shook her head. "What I did to you?"

"Oh no, it's my turn," said Sarah. "If you want to ask more, that'll cost you another drink."

Defiantly, Veronica drank. A deep, bold sip. "What did I do to you?" she repeated. There was an attempt at assertion in the way she said this, but her eyelids closed for a little too long and she had to employ great effort to snap them open again. Half a glass in and at last she was beginning to unravel. Flopping backwards drowsily against the high back of the sofa, she tried again. "What did I do?"

"Do you seriously not remember?"

"What?" slurred Veronica. "Remember what?"

"The pool house?"

"Yes?"

"Locking me in it?"

"What? I mean, what?" It was too late now for a lucid answer. The sedatives had rapidly started their work. Still, Veronica raised her chin towards the ceiling and closed her eyes, either in thought, or sleep, or a pretence of one or the other.

Sarah took out her phone and fondled it in her hand.

"I locked you in?" The words slid heavily from Veronica's lips.

"Yes," declared Sarah. "For hours, Veronica. All night. While you went off to steal Eliza. Come on, you must remember."

Comically, Veronica placed her finger on her face in an exaggerated thinking posture, eyes blinking ever more heavily, sleep flitting back and forth across her brow. But then suddenly, the memory came to her. The arrival of it was almost visible and Sarah shook her head in amazement that it had truly not been present before, that she really had forgotten. "I did," said Veronica. "Shit, I did."

"It's fine," breezed Sarah, lifting Veronica's glass to her mouth and encouraging another sip. Veronica took one, studying Sarah through blurred eyes. "Of course you left me with a debilitating claustrophobia, and that's why Eliza had to drive to get me. That's why she's dead. But I'm fine. Almost."

"What?" mumbled Veronica.

"Nothing."

"What?" Veronica was sinking fast now. Clearly confused, she was trying so hard to make sense of things, but her body wouldn't cooperate, just as Sarah had so many times found that her own body wouldn't cooperate. Sarah watched as slowly, Veronica gave way to it and allowed herself to lean back more fully into the sofa. The folds of the cushions wrapped themselves around her. Her eyes closed and stayed closed. She dropped her glass and it spilled onto her. "Whoops," she half giggled, half cried.

"Let's get you dry," soothed Sarah.

Leaning forwards, she helped Veronica remove her top.

"I wonder if in another twenty years, you'll remember what you've done to Amelia," mused Sarah, spitefully.

"What?"

"Nothing." Sarah lifted her phone. "Why don't you tell me exactly what you have done to Amelia? What you've put in that ridiculous report? And why?"

Veronica was way past explanation now. But the moment had arrived anyway, and Veronica was powerless to resist it. She slumped, eyes half closed, mouth half smiling, body half dressed. Wearing only her bra and a skirt, a wine glass in her lap, she was the perfect picture of irresponsibility. Sarah didn't even need words. She didn't need confession. How easy it had turned out to be. One snap was all it would take. One snap, and a share on social media, or a message to a few parents. Not the ending of a career, not total decimation, but the finale of the façade, the end of perfection. Just a small act to balance the scales of justice. One snap was all it would take.

But into the silence, Veronica suddenly spoke. "I was so jealous," she muttered. "You had everything I wanted."

"What are you talking about?"

"You still do," Veronica muttered again. "Have everything."

"What?" Sarah kept the phone poised, ready.

Veronica's eyes were firmly shut now, but she lifted her hand clumsily, flapping it around for her dropped glass. "Elderflower," she slurred. "It's always elderflower."

"What?"

Sarah wasn't sure she had heard properly and wanted Veronica to finish her sentence, but it was too late, Veronica was gone, finally overwhelmed by the sedatives. Elderflower? What was she talking about? Sarah lifted Veronica's wet top and smelt it. There was a hint of perfume, but the liquid was definitely not wine. No wonder she hadn't got drunk sooner. Immediately, Sarah felt fooled and indignant – manipulated by Veronica again. But it took only another moment for the truth to penetrate. Glancing to the almost finished sushi, she realised that all evening Veronica had stuck to the vegetable options, avoiding raw fish as well as alcohol. Either Veronica was pregnant, or trying to be. Yet this didn't make sense to Sarah. It wouldn't compute. Everything came easily to Veronica. It always had.

Hesitating, thoughts spiralled.

Sarah lowered her phone.

So Veronica's life wasn't as perfect as it appeared. She wanted a baby and didn't have one. If she was jealous, then that was a reasonable, understandable explanation. Sarah felt sympathy begin to rise. But wait, was she really jealous? Had she actually been so when they were young? What would she have been jealous of? Probably, it was rubbish, all of it, just another Veronica drama, another way for her to manipulate, to pull at the heartstrings, to commandeer. Besides, no matter what her own jealousy, it was no excuse for sabotaging Amelia, a child.

Sarah lifted her phone again. Leverage was there for the taking. Power.

Veronica was sleeping soundly now, oblivious and vulnerable. Feet next to faces in a small single bed.

Just one snap.

Three weeks of giggling into the night.

One snap.

Three weeks of living like sisters, in the gap of her own.

One snap, and at last the woman would know consequences, she would know how it felt to not be in control.

Where had Veronica's parents been for three whole weeks of the summer?

Sarah paused. Phone in hand, she paused. And into the pause flooded her own parents, and Eliza, and David, and herself, and the solidity of that circle. Even a member down. Even beset with attacks of panic. Even in the constant flux of unreliable friendships and unjust battles and law that wasn't always Right.

The pause stretched on. For what seemed like many minutes, Sarah stood unmoving, collecting the memories and pieces of thought around her. Collecting them. Weighing them. Sorting them. Unpicking the strands.

If only Eliza had been there to help her as she used to, to be her mirror, to help her know.

Longing breath collected in Sarah's lungs. Desperate, engulfing longing. For her no-more sister. Eliza.

Eliza.

Sarah looked at her phone.

10.10pm.

Something akin to either shame or conspiracy powered Sarah through the next minutes. She couldn't believe what she had done. She pushed her phone hurriedly back into her bag, as though once there she could deny its purpose, and picking up Veronica's top, it was not possible to manoeuvre her arms and head back into it, but she draped it across her chest. Collecting the last remains of sushi, she crossed the room to the kitchen and disposed of it neatly in the bin. She noticed the elderflower on the counter and returned the bottle to the fridge, fighting a quiet but terrifying thought in the back of her mind – what if Veronica was already pregnant, what would the sedatives do to the baby? Sarah shook her head. If Veronica really was jealous, then it was from absence of child, not presence. Everything was fine. Closing the fridge, she wiped spilled drops from the kitchen counter. She corked the wine. She found the remote to the sound system and turned off the soft jazz they'd had playing through the ceiling speakers. Veronica had mentioned that George would be home by 11pm. That was soon. He'd find Veronica and put her to bed. He'd assume she'd been drinking. When Veronica woke, she'd assume their glasses had somehow been mixed up. The colour was the same, the smell not so different. It was feasible. Sarah would see her at school sometime, and either say nothing, or something. Everything was fine.

Taking one last look at the sleeping woman, exquisite despite her ungainly coma, Sarah considered, just for a moment, how beautiful she had always found Veronica. She didn't know why she thought about this, and uncharacteristically, she didn't want to unpack it. Likewise, she didn't know if she truly believed Veronica's supposed jealousies, or if she would ever attempt to discover the reasons for them, or care. In that moment, all she knew, with a certainty that felt like epiphany, was that despite the compelling, wild freedom of Veronica and others like her, Sarah had never been, and wasn't, and didn't actually, in fact, want to be a meanderer.

Veronica slept, and Sarah stood there wondering why it had taken so many years to come to this realisation. Maybe it was the maturity of motherhood, or that oft-touted confidence one was supposed to achieve in one's thirties. Maybe it was 'closure'. Maybe it was seeing Veronica's own struggles. Whatever it was, Sarah was glad she had realised it, glad she had, in the end, remained true to herself. Everything she had so far done was still un-doable, the sedatives would wear off, she hadn't taken a photo, there was no real damage, no real consequence. And if Veronica continued to sabotage Amelia's prospects, Sarah could fight that, she would fight that, she would protect her child. She was the strong one after all.

She let the peacefulness of this new comprehension wash over her. Then steadily, she turned. Quietly, she made her way towards the front door. Serenely, she opened it.

But almost at once, the door to the neighbours' house flew open next to her, shattering the calm, and a man staggered out onto the street. The same man she had seen the day before, hooded in the rain. Wildly, he glanced up and down the road, veering into the way of cars. "Simone!" he yelled. "Simone! Simone!"

Though nothing to do with her, Sarah felt herself tense at this man's madness. He was blocking her path, but she couldn't go back inside, it was nearly eleven and George would be home soon. Besides, she told herself, look: a little way up the road was a woman walking alone; in the other direction a boy, no more than ten. It was perfectly safe. Trouble was behind her only. One last time, Sarah channelled the woman slumped against cushions, gave the man a withering, Veronica-empowered stare, and then left, quickly, decisively, without further collection, letting the front door bang shut.

Veronica

Sirens fought through her grogginess. Then hospital lights and the sound of George at her side.

There were four separate calls, Veronica was told afterwards, as though this would somehow mitigate the fact that they, the police, had still arrived too late. They were understaffed, they'd protested to a vehement George standing soldier in her hospital room, his guard sturdier than theirs, or so he needed to prove. But even when he finally let them through, she couldn't tell them what they wanted to know: how she had come to be so comatose, what he had done. They wanted it first-hand, from her, but it was clear that both of the officers in the room had concluded their truth already – the man tiptoeing around it, the woman's face full of pity. They'd been told in fact four separate times from four individuals who had seen it: Terry entering her house through an open door.

The samples scraped later from her body confirmed his semen. His urine too. Only the scratch to her leg had come after, they thought, in the scuffle when the roofer from the downstairs flat next door had charged in and pulled Terry away.

She had recollections: Terry's face looming over her; a rank smell; hot liquid on her skin; rough grunts. But she wasn't sure if these were real visions, or imagined, or spliced together with teenage rememberings and the sounds she'd heard through walls. Her body didn't hurt, but it felt tired, used up. They said it was the roofer who had saved her. Another witness had confirmed this, a woman, a neighbour. But when she closed her eyes she was sure she could see Dominic – the boy she'd wanted to help, the helpless one – creeping up behind Terry, lifting a steel saucepan to his head. Terry had been standing over her then, she was sure of it – over her, but not on top of her, not actually inside her. And before the roofer she was sure there had been somebody else, too, a woman, a blur of orange and red, smelling of something sweet, pulling Dominic away, lifting him up, allowing him to crumple small into her arms. After that, her ears had filled with soothing melody, church music, or lullaby, and somehow it had swept them all away. She said this once or twice, to the police, to George – the boy, the woman, Terry being by her but not in her. But it didn't make sense, it didn't fit, and in the end she let these visions slacken and slide past her with the rest. In some ways it was reassuring to think of the unthinkable as simply a blurred and distant part of patchwork.

George would not stop apologising. For being late. For being naïve. For not fixing the door. But how had she got like that, he asked, on elderflower? He wanted to call Sarah, but Veronica found that she didn't want Sarah to know. Besides, it was possible, she suggested, that she had simply picked up the wrong glass and not noticed the taste of wine. It was possible. She told herself this too, tried to convince herself of it, but every time she thought of Sarah, something grew just slightly inside her – a sensation of either empathy, or anger, or perhaps both, suppressed for now, for now.

Meanwhile, she held herself together. Humiliation and shame nipped at her heels, but she filled out the necessary forms, and succumbed to the necessary tests, and spoke up. And spoke up. She did not cry. With tears, it seemed to her, the last drops of her power would seep away, and she would not allow Terry, or anybody else, to take this too. So she held herself together, just as her parents would have proscribed, just as her colleagues would have expected. Only George knew different. With George, she held herself together by allowing herself to fall apart, a patchwork unravelling, piecemeal, one square at a time. George collected the cotton gratefully, this something he could do, and he took her lead as much as he was able. It was still difficult for him, trapped not only by his family but the bonds of masculinity – *be a man, be a man*, how damaging those three words – but he bared as much as he could, allowing her to know how angry and devastated and helpless he felt too. Their weaknesses holding them up.

It was with unhidden, tightly entwined hands that they waited for the results of the tests for STDs, preparing themselves for the worst. But in the end, it was the other results that destabilised them: George's tests, for which they were unprepared. These fell casually through the letterbox a few days later and were followed by a much less casual visit to the clinic. He wasn't infertile, Dr Shirazi explained when called upon to do so, not completely, natural conception was still possible even. But it might not be as easy as they'd hoped.

Veronica felt sick about that.

She felt sick and a little dizzy.

Even when she lay down to sleep, the nausea remained with her.

A few weeks later, she didn't even need to take a test to know that of course she was pregnant.

Veronica

George knelt before her, his arms wrapped around her waist. He should already have left for work, but was there in his shirtsleeves, on the floor, bent low.

I'll have you begging! I'll have you on your knees and broken!

The pregnancy test was in his hands. He couldn't stop looking at it. Veronica cupped her own hands around the slightly greying blonde of his head.

"Not broken," she said. "We're not broken."

"What?" George looked up at her. He wouldn't stand, or couldn't. "Veronica, it's fucking his."

There was a trembling to his voice that Veronica had never heard before, unrecognisable from the boy who'd shot bloodied down a rugby pitch, or the man who'd swept into Kenya, or stood just weeks earlier towering over Terry. Veronica was unrecognisable too. She felt her mood swinging violently and bitterness creeping beneath her skin, like all the hands that had ever touched her uninvited. But she fought hard against it. She followed up with all the police inquiries, channelling her rage into action, resisting the temptation to plaster it beneath blankets of muting patchwork. For all their combined pain, George at least was still here, still talking, still talking to her. Veronica found herself musing that this is what it must have felt like to grow up being Sarah.

"It might be yours, George. I think it *is* yours. Don't you? We never even have to find out anyway, if you don't want to. We're going to be okay." She said this to her husband with more confidence than she felt, removing one hand from his head and placing it onto her stomach where despite ambiguous paternity, there once again was a poppy-seed-sized hope. "We are. Going to be okay. All of us. Somehow."

George shook his head, unconvinced, but he rested his lips on top of her hand and kissed it. Veronica leant down and kissed him. And finally, George stood.

They were in the living room, the afternoon glow of summer sun illuminating the smooth wood of the floor. Behind them was the carefully chosen coffee table, and the shelf lined with favourite books they'd once imagined lying entangled on the sofa and reading. Outside the window, somebody glided by on a bicycle. In the distance was the melodious tinkle of an ice cream van. A few minutes later, there was a gentle clipping of passing feet. And then, a soft closing of a nearby door.

A door. Latched and locked. Or not?

Though wrapped still in George's arms, this last sound disturbed Veronica and for a few surreal moments she felt a return of that distinct, unsettling sensation of being watched. It wasn't possible, however, not now. Terry was long gone, refused by three different brothers, apparently, to either pay his bail or have him in their homes. He couldn't come near her from where he was. He couldn't be back. To prove her own silliness, Veronica looked over George's shoulder towards the street, ready for the pretty houses, knitted in such tidy union, to prove her nervousness wrong.

And that was when she saw him – the boy, Dominic.

Dragging a bundle of black bags into a waiting car, he stopped, and looked at her through the window. Again there came that flash in her mind, that vision of him wielding steel, helping her, fixing things. But the memory flickered before her in the sun, and now, he brandished nothing. Instead, without instrument, he nodded. His beady eyes were as unnerving and unreadable as ever, but she imagined an attempt at his conveying something with that nod: apology, thanks, conspiracy, absolution?

With him was a woman she hadn't seen before – much older, black, carrying a laughing Jasmine, something about her intangibly fortifying. Even from the other side of glass, Veronica felt a little fortified. She nodded back to Dominic. But next to him, catching the gesture, appeared Simone.

Simone.

Of course she was there too. Standing face on. Motionless. Looking inside as Veronica looked out.

For a fleeting second, the eyes of the two women locked. Saying nothing, saying everything. Melded that way together. Until abruptly, as though moved by some thought or some new paradigm of life, or simply no longer desirous of looking in, Simone nodded at Veronica, as her son had done, and then turned away from the window, back towards him, back towards her family, and climbed into the car, and was gone.

After that, there was only silence.

Veronica closed her eyes and breathed deeply into George's neck, inhaling his scent. In return, he squeezed her shoulders, and at the solidity of that, she felt tears bubble in her eyes. George lifted his head and saw them. She prepared for him to glance away, steeling herself for it, for a return to this; but instead he looked straight at her, and touched the salty liquid, and wiped the tears. And then the two of them simply stood, holding each other's bodies, holding each other's fears, holding a new life between them, breathing deep into the quiet.

It was, after all, so quiet now.

So quiet.

Others might not notice that.

Epilogue

Sarah watched, from a distance.

The two women leant over the railings of the playground, laughing as they spoke. What were they sharing? A joke? A secret?

The likeness was undeniable. Pale. Thin as a rake. It was her, it had to be.

Sarah had told nobody what she had seen, not even David. But of course she had gone back. Of course she had not left Veronica comatose on her own. Of course she had done the right thing. Or intended to.

Only by the time she returned, the man had been there. She had seen him clearly through the window. Not touching Veronica, but standing over her, touching himself. Sarah had started to run towards the house, but he was mad that man, wild, she had seen it earlier in his eyes. And she had Amelia to think of, and Harry, a responsibility to be responsible, for them. From a safe distance, sensibly, Sarah had called the police.

And watched.

She would intervene, she told herself, if he tried to do anything worse. She looked around even for something to arm herself with – a tree branch, a broken bottle.

But then the boy had turned up with the saucepan, and decked the man from behind, long before he could touch Veronica, or do anything. The woman in red had hurtled into the house after him, and then the neighbour had charged in and gestured for them to go. And the woman had carried the small, panicking child away, down the street, her head bent close into his. And Sarah had stayed watching.

This thin, pale woman had not appeared until much later. But she had seen the man too, slumped over Veronica. She'd taken out her phone, too. She had noticed Sarah, and they had exchanged looks – two concerned passers-by, strangers, calling the police, doing Right.

But why was she there now, here, at Amelia's school? Who was she?

"She's the new Year 2 teaching assistant," Amelia explained later, cartwheeling. "Miss Simone."

In the end, Amelia had gone up to the Junior school with no problem. A letter had never come. A report had never existed. It had all been a game. Just a game. Amelia was in Year 3 now, safe from Veronica's clutches.

Sarah watched.

There was a slight rounding to Veronica's belly. She noticed Veronica occasionally placing her hand upon it. So she and George had managed it. They had what they wanted.

Darkly, Sarah's mind flashed to sushi and sedatives. But surely it would have been too early to affect things. To cause consequence.

Besides, there was light to Veronica's gaze.

There was music to Veronica's laugh.

Sarah couldn't help feeling a ripple of joy for her old, illuminating friend.

Veronica looked up.

Instinctively, Sarah hurried in the opposite direction. It was as if they'd broken up all over again, no longer a two. But Veronica called out.

"Sarah!" she waved. "Sarah!" she beckoned. *Sawah*.

Sarah paused.

The other woman turned, looked. Smiled.

The bell rang.

3.30pm. Pick-up.

There. An easy answer. A reason to avoid her. A reason to move past, move on.

Sarah didn't move.

Seconds ticked by.

Lessons over.

Children released.

Games beginning.

Classroom doors made of wood, opening.

Giggles wafting on the wind.

Acknowledgements

There are many people who have helped me in the creation of this book, and who I would like to thank.

For their insight, wisdom and honesty, and generosity with it: Jane Becker, Jeremy Brier, Naomi Giltelson, Naomi Gryn, Victoria Hayward, Rowan Lawton, Rachel Rushbrook, Anna Seymour, Geraldine Wayne and Sadie Wild.

For their invaluable guidance at every step: my wonderful agent Eve White, and Ludo Cinelli.

For championing my writing from the beginning: the team at Legend Press, in particular Tom Chalmers, Lucy Chamberlain, and my fantastic editor Lauren Parsons.

For their love and support through the whole ride: My husband James. My family – Jeff, Geraldine, Anna-Marie, Zeb, Joab, Damian and Olivia. As well as all the extended Wayne and Kattan clans.

And most especially, my children – Audrey, Alice and Elijah – who inspire me every day.